Title:	This Book Will Bury Me
Author:	Ashley Winstead
Agent:	Melissa Edwards
	Stonesong
Publication date:	March 25, 2025
Category:	Fiction
Format:	Hardcover
ISBN:	978-1-7282-7000-5
Price:	$27.99 U.S.
Pages:	480 pages

This book represents the final manuscript being distributed for prepublication review. Typographical and layout errors are not intended to be present in the final book at release. **It is not intended for sale and should not be purchased from any site or vendor.** If this book did reach you through a vendor or through a purchase, please notify the publisher.

Please send all reviews or mentions of this book
to the Sourcebooks marketing department:
marketing@sourcebooks.com

For sales inquiries, please contact:
sales@sourcebooks.com

For librarian and educator resources,
visit: **sourcebooks.com/library**

PRAISE FOR
MIDNIGHT IS THE DARKEST HOUR

"Ashley Winstead shows her versatility and virtuosity as an author in this dark, eerie, and completely enchanting book about friendship, love and vengeance. *Midnight Is the Darkest Hour* is as creepy as it gets—and a tearjerker to boot! I loved every minute of it."

—Mary Kubica, *New York Times* bestselling
author of *Just the Nicest Couple*

"*Where the Crawdads Sing* meets *Twilight* meets *Thelma and Louise* in this brilliantly realized, totally original thriller. Absolutely sensational—I couldn't put it down."

—Clare Mackintosh, *New York Times* bestselling author

"Dark and lyrical, Ashley Winstead turns her talent toward the Deep South in her latest, *Midnight Is the Darkest Hour*. A compelling story about the occult, evil, and the ways religious fundamentalism can overtake reason, it's also a story about loyalty, friendship, and what connects us all at our deepest roots. Once again, Ashley Winstead spins a tale that is equal parts disturbing and redemptive. (And when you're done reading, please message me so we can talk about that ending!)"

—Julie Clark, *New York Times* bestselling author of
The Last Flight and *The Lies I Tell*

"A gothic tale that blurs the line between good and evil, love and revenge, and the inherent desire to please our parents while simultaneously struggling to find ourselves. *Midnight Is the Darkest Hour* is unique and unnerving from beginning to end."

—Stacy Willingham, *New York Times* bestselling author
of *All the Dangerous Things* and *A Flicker in the Dark*

"Woe unto the preacher's daughter, or at least that's what you might think navigating the dark and broody twists of Ashley Winstead's spellbinding latest, *Midnight Is the Darkest Hour*. Prepare yourself (if you can) for serpents of the Deep South gospel slithering into a beautifully rendered *Twilight* fever dream—like all of Ashley's incredible books, you won't be able to turn the pages fast enough."

—Vanessa Lillie, bestselling author of
Little Voices and *Blood Sisters*

"Ashley Winstead does it again! Making the hairs at the back of your neck prickle while mesmerizing you with prose so rich that you want to dive into this novel with both feet, Winstead delivers another yet multi-layered thriller so nuanced and intricately woven that you absolutely cannot help but race to the end."

—Amanda Jayatissa, author of *You're Invited*

"A dark, sultry fever dream of a novel, *Midnight Is the Darkest Hour* is a powerful examination of love, girlhood, and religion. With lush, gorgeous writing and dynamic characterization, Ashley Winstead carefully dismantles the corrupted hierarchy that has ruled a God-fearing small town, and unleashes the trapped scream of being a young woman in the world. This haunting, twisting story will stay with you long after the last page."

—Laurie Elizabeth Flynn, author of
The Girls Are All So Nice Here

"An utter triumph, *Midnight Is the Darkest Hour* is Ashley Winstead's most dazzling thriller to date. This is a one-sitting binge read, so cancel all plans and prepare to become completely obsessed with Ruth and Everett and the darkly magical world of Bottom Springs, Louisiana. *Twilight* meets *True Blood* meets Colleen Hoover in this completely original, explosive suspense where every line is a poem and every chapter a lyrical symphony. I could not put this book down and haven't been so wholly captured by a story in this way in years."

—May Cobb, author of *A Likeable Woman* and *The Hunting Wives*

"*Midnight Is the Darkest Hour* is a lush, immersive ode to the wildness and violence at the hidden heart of teenage girlhood. The sharp-toothed answer to every fairy tale that warns girls to stay out of the woods... because what if we like what we find? Ashley Winstead has at once crafted an incisive critique of fundamentalism and one of the most unforgettable love stories I've ever read, dressed as a thriller that surprises at every turn."

—Katie Gutierrez, bestselling author
of *More Than You'll Ever Know*

PRAISE FOR
THE LAST HOUSEWIFE

"A dark, twisted tale of feminism and patriarchy, Ashley Winstead has given us a gripping story about a cult and the ways in which women became psychologically bound, while at the same time exploring themes of power and redemption. Timely and terrifying, *The Last Housewife* will haunt your dreams and change the way you view the world."

—Julie Clark, *New York Times* bestselling
author of *The Last Flight* and *The Lies I Tell*

"It's not every day I finish a novel and decide right then and there that the author is now an auto-buy. While I was anticipating a great story from Winstead, I wasn't expecting to inhale her new book in one breathless read. *The Last Housewife* is a propulsive, unputdownable thriller with a dark, beating heart. It chilled me to the bone, and I'm still recovering. Ashley Winstead, I bow down."

—Jennifer Hillier, bestselling author of *Little Secrets*

"A stunning, disturbing thriller that will have your mind and heart racing. *The Last Housewife* is a clever, twisty, unnerving ride through feminism, patriarchy, and power, and it had me gasping for air."

—Samantha Downing, international bestselling author of *For Your Own Good*

"Provocative and downright terrifying, *The Last Housewife* feels ripped from the headlines as it explores the dark world of a violent, misogynist cult in a New York college town. The story unfolds through the eyes of Shay Evans, who returns to avenge the deaths of two college friends and save the women who are still in danger. Winstead deftly tackles the complicated issues of gender, coercion, and agency while crafting an edge-of-your-seat, action-packed thriller!"

—Wendy Walker, international bestselling author of *All Is Not Forgotten* and *Don't Look for Me*

"Ashley Winstead takes her reader into the heart of darkness—and brilliantly reveals the tender, human part hidden in those shadows. Propulsive, smart, and chilling, *The Last Housewife* confirms what *In My Dreams I Hold a Knife* promised: no one writes thrillers like Ashley Winstead."

—Alison Wisdom, author of *The Burning Season*

"The total package—fearless, disruptive, and gripping. Ashley Winstead's talent is astounding. One of the best books I've read this year."

—Eliza Jane Brazier, author of *Good Rich People*

"Only fifty shades of grey? Please. Ashley Winstead's *The Last Housewife* is a technicolor rainbow, provocative and unflinching in its brilliant portrayal of female desire, male violence, and the unsettling link between them. A disturbingly sexy thrill ride that does more than 'twist'—it explodes off the page, confronting dark truths about women in the patriarchy and forging weapons of resistance from the flames. You don't read *The Last Housewife*. You face it down."

—Amy Gentry, bestselling author of *Good as Gone*, *Last Woman Standing*, and *Bad Habits*

"*The Last Housewife* is a seductive, provocative work of literature steeped in a mystery, that kept me turning page after page. The story touches on the loyalty of friendship, the determination to uncover truths no matter how difficult, and the power of a woman in the face of ever-present danger and with all the decks stacked against her. I cannot wait for what Ashley Winstead brings us next."

—Yasmin Angoe, bestselling author of the critically acclaimed *Her Name Is Knight*

PRAISE FOR
IN MY DREAMS I HOLD A KNIFE

"Deeply drawn characters and masterful storytelling come together to create an addictive and riveting psychological thriller. Put this one at the very top of your 2021 reading list."

—Liv Constantine, international bestselling author of *The Last Mrs. Parrish*

"Tense, twisty, and packed with shocks, Ashley Winstead's assured debut dares to ask how much we can trust those we know best—including ourselves. A terrific read!"

—Riley Sager, *New York Times* bestselling author of *Home Before Dark*

"Nostalgic and sinister, *In My Dreams I Hold a Knife* whisks the reader back to college. Glory days, unbreakable friendships, all-night parties, and a belief that the best in life is ahead of you. But ten years after the murder of one of the East House Seven, the unbreakable bonds may be hiding fractured secrets of a group bound not by loyalty but by fear. Twisty and compulsively readable, *In My Dreams I Hold a Knife* will have you turning pages late into the night, not just to figure out who murdered beloved Heather Shelby but to see whether friendships forged under fire can ever be resurrected again."

—Julie Clark, *New York Times* bestselling author of *The Last Flight* and *The Lies I Tell*

"Fans of *The Secret History*, Ruth Ware, and Andrea Bartz will devour this dark academic thriller with an addictive locked-room mystery at its core. Ten years after an unsolved campus murder, the victim's best friends reunite, knowing one might be a monster—but is anyone innocent? Over the course of a single shocking night, Ashely Winstead peels back lie after lie, exposing the poisoned roots of ambition, friendship, and belonging itself. An astonishingly sure-footed debut, *In My Dreams I Hold a Knife* is the definition of compulsive reading. The last page will give you nightmares."

—Amy Gentry, bestselling author of *Good as Gone*, *Last Woman Standing*, and *Bad Habits*

"Beautiful writing, juicy secrets, complex female characters, and drumbeat suspense—what more could you want from a debut thriller?

I'm Ashley Winstead's new biggest fan. If you liked Marisha Pessl's *Neverworld Wake* or Laurie Elizabeth Flynn's *The Girls Are All So Nice Here*, trust me—you will love this."

—Andrea Bartz, bestselling author of *The Lost Night* and *The Herd*

"An unsolved murder, dark secrets, and dysfunctional college days, all wrapped up in a twisty plot that will keep you flipping pages."

—Darby Kane, #1 international bestselling author of *Pretty Little Wife*

"With its compelling puzzlebox structure and delightfully ruthless cast of characters, this twisty dark academia thriller will have you flipping pages like you're pulling an all-nighter to cram for a final. *In My Dreams I Hold a Knife* is required reading for fans of Donna Tartt's *The Secret History* and Amy Gentry's *Bad Habits*."

—Layne Fargo, author of *They Never Learn*

"Looking for an eerie campus setting? This chilling suspense novel has murder, friendship, and defiance when six people return to their college reunion a decade after one of their close friends was murdered."

—*Parade Magazine*

"[A] captivating debut...Winstead does an expert job keeping the reader guessing whodunit. Suspense fans will eagerly await her next."

—*Publishers Weekly*

"A twisty, dark puzzle... Fans of books such as *The Girl on the Train* and *Gone Girl* will find this book captivating, as will anyone who enjoys being led down a winding, frightening path. Highly recommended."

—*New York Journal of Books*

"Packed with intrigue, scandal, and enough twists and turns to match Donna Tartt's *The Secret History*, this is a solid psychological-thriller debut."

—*Booklist*

"Ashley Winstead's mordant debut novel is the latest entry in the budding subgenre of 'dark academia,' where the crime narrative takes place on a college campus... At its heart, Winstead's novel examines what it means to covet the lives of others, no matter the cost."

—*New York Times*

ALSO BY ASHLEY WINSTEAD

Midnight Is the Darkest Hour
In My Dreams I Hold a Knife
The Last Housewife

This Book Will Bury Me

A NOVEL

ASHLEY WINSTEAD

sourcebooks landmark

Published by Sourcebooks Landmark, an imprint of Sourcebooks
P.O. Box 4410, Naperville, Illinois 60567-4410
(630) 961-3900
sourcebooks.com

Cataloging-in-Publication Data is on file with the Library of Congress.

Printed and bound in [Country of Origin—confirm when printer is selected].
XX 10 9 8 7 6 5 4 3 2 1

For my mother, my beloved, who deserves every happiness.

"History is a little man in a brown suit
trying to define a room he is outside of.
I know history. There are many names in history
but none of them are ours."

—Richard Siken, "Little Beast," *Crush* (2005)

Content warnings: grief, loss of a parent, extreme violence, discussions of weight.

PART ONE

—

Here in the Dark,

We're No Longer Strangers

1
—

IF YOU'RE READING THIS, CHANCES are last year you flipped on the news and saw me getting shoved to my knees in the dirt, hands wrested behind my back, gun-toting FBI agents swarming like ants around me into that three-story house. God only knows what the headline below my face must've read. Something about murder, something about shocking twists, underground conspiracies tied to the most famous crime spree in America. It was a provocative introduction, no doubt. It's not surprising you have questions. Especially since the story that's unfolded since that day has been riddled with plot holes, full of inconsistencies and unanswered questions. It's probably driven you more than a little bit mad.

You want me to break my silence and tell you the truth. Trust me, I know—I've gotten your letters, your pleas, and your death threats. Your hunger is legible and familiar. You want what I once wanted: that insatiable longing for answers, the most human of urges. It's what started my journey, too, after all. Our desire to order the unknowable, touch the unreachable, shine a light on what's hidden—it's universal. We're uncomfortable with ambiguity, with living suspended in the mess of the world.

Those people you saw the FBI shove to their knees beside me? They wanted answers as badly as I did. We used to live in the true-crime forums, typing away at our theories, poring through forgotten records, speculating about the angle of a knife strike or a bullet. We were like those Enlightenment scientists of old, pushing knowledge into a new era, so confident in the human mind, our own possibilities. That's why we read and posted and tracked and obsessed. We thought we were edging closer every day to that shining city on the hill where all would be revealed and we would finally be at peace. Call it the City of Heaven, or Justice, or Absolution. Trust me, we really thought we'd get there. All the way up until the bitter end, when our experiment went so darkly south, exploding in our faces.

But I've gotten ahead of myself. A lot of people who weren't close to the story have been getting famous spreading lies, and you deserve the truth. Maybe you're a vulture, reading this simply to pick over my bones. Or maybe you're one of those rare people, curious and open-minded. Either way, I'm going to tell you the whole sordid thing. That's the point of a tell-all, isn't it? Time to let all the skeletons out of the closet.

But I'm going to do it my way. I promise it's for the best. Remember, I used to *be you*. I know you don't just want the cold, dry facts shoveled into your brain. You want to know *why*, how, what the weather was like that day. What kind of mood was in the air. The shoes they were wearing, what they ate for breakfast. Who they hated and who they crushed on. What the first blow must've felt like, the first sting of betrayal. You want to find the causal roots, trace them all the way back and all the way forward, treasure every detail. When it comes to stories like the one I've been holding—when it comes to mysteries like these, the kind they call crimes of the century—you want to savor it. You want as much color as you can get.

Trust me, by the time we're through, you'll bleed color.

Now let's begin.

My story starts with a body, just not the one you might expect.

2

—

ON THURSDAY, AUGUST 31, 2023, at 10:45 p.m., I received a phone call that would change my life. It was a characteristically muggy night in Orlando. The unrelenting heat that had baked into the soil all day wafted out of the dirt, making the night air feel microwaved. The party was at Afton Oaks, a popular apartment complex for University of Central Florida undergrads, of which I was at the time. The crowd was large enough to spill outside, which meant the sliding-glass door that connected the kitchen to the backyard remained half-open all night, turning the inside into a sauna. I remember the sweat that dampened my neck and back, as if some part of me already knew what was coming. We were singing at the top of our lungs to "Gangsta's Paradise" by Coolio, played at an ear-splitting volume, a song choice that now makes me cringe to recall. I was pressed shoulder to shoulder with Gabby Maldonado,* my best friend at the time, having the kind of silly, tipsy night a normal college student might have.

It should be stated that I was never a normal college student. Everyone at that party was a friend of Gabby's, and I was just doing my

---

* Not her real name. I've given "Gabby" a pseudonym to protect her from association with me.

best to fit in. I'd transferred to UCF only the year before from a community college. I'd also started college two years late, making me a geriatric twenty-four to the other college seniors' twenty-two. These two facts together made me kind of a social leper, at least until Gabby took me under her wing. It wasn't that the students at UCF were cruel, only indifferent in the same way we all are—too self-obsessed and unobservant to notice much outside our little bubbles. I've learned that, even in the context of brutal crime, the human capacity for self-preoccupation is staggering, which is why you can get a case like Sarah Atman's, the college student who was murdered in the middle of campus, and yet there were no witnesses.* Anyway, UCF was massive, home to a whopping fifty-eight thousand undergrads. It was a city unto itself.

I'd been so lonely after transferring that I'd contemplated quitting, just packing up my dorm and heading back to my parents' house with my tail between my legs. I even practiced what I'd tell my dad. Then one day a girl who was friendly to me in psych class—we'd roll our eyes together whenever the professor said something cringey—asked if I wanted to grab lunch. Gabby turned out to be one of those rare people born with a tender heart that no amount of life could toughen, the kind of person we introverts thank God for. Soon she was dragging me out on weeknights to off-campus parties; and before I knew it, we had the kind of friendship I'd only witnessed on TV, the kind where two people are so close they're basically codependent. I'd always wanted to be codependent, so I decided to stay. Most of all, I was thrilled I didn't have to disappoint my dad. He never got to go to college, and everything he'd never gotten, he wanted for me.

The night of August 31, the party at Afton Oaks was themed

---

* Or the case of Kitty Genovese, a woman stabbed to death in front of thirty-eight witnesses in Queens in 1964, none of whom called the police.

"Nineties Throwback," hence the Coolio. Gabby looked ridiculous in oversized flannel; I wore a white T-shirt under a spaghetti strap dress like I'd seen on *Clueless*. We kept looking at each other and laughing, partly because of the outfits, partly because of the keg beer. And then my mom called.

Nowadays, I find myself wishing I could travel back to that moment—the second before I pressed Accept. Such a small action with such weighty consequences. Before that, my biggest worry was whether Gabby's friends would accept me like she had. Mark it in my history book, or whatever biographies the true-crime experts write about me. Afton Oaks, Orlando, Florida, August 31: the last time Janeway Sharp was innocent.

My mother was hysterical on the other end of the line. "Your father," she sobbed. "Jane, I think he's had a heart attack. I'm in the car, following the ambulance to the hospital. Please, honey. I need you to pray."

If you've never received a call like this, I'll try to explain. It's like being plunged into an ice bath. Your entire body goes on high alert, every cell awakening, every synapse firing, the same as if someone walked up and pressed a gun to your head. Your mind wipes of everything but the present and how to survive it.

"He's going to be okay," I said, somehow. "Everything is going to be okay. I'll be there in two hours. Hold on."

I believed it. There was no other choice.

Gabby insisted on driving me even though she was in the middle of a party, had never met my parents, and didn't like to drive. That was her soft heart at work. On the road, she stayed silent while I rocked back and forth in the passenger seat, whispering, "You're going to be okay, Daddy. You're going to be okay." I hadn't called my father "Daddy" since I was young, but that was what came out, as if in my fear I'd somehow reverted back to being a little girl.

I must've repeated the phrase several hundred times as we drove.

I was convinced that if I stopped saying it, the worst would happen, as if the mantra was the one thing staving off my father's ruin. I've since learned that in the face of disaster, even the most pragmatic among us often turn to magical thinking. So I rocked and whispered, sending those words out into the universe, into his ear and the ear of whoever was in charge, letting them know my father was loved and should be spared.

Don't you wish it worked like that—that love was any sort of protection?

Forty-five minutes into the drive my mother called again. This time, I saw her name and my chest filled with hope.

"Mom?"

"Jane..." Her voice was ragged. "He didn't wake up. They tried everything—"

"No. That's not true. He's okay."

"Jane—"

"He's going to be okay. He'll wake up."

"Stop it, Jane. I can't take it."

Later I would learn that bald-faced denial is a common response to grief. In fact, everything I did that night and would do and think over the following days and weeks was straight out of a textbook. It's funny—I felt so alone in my pain, felt my grief was so annihilating that I must be experiencing a level of devastation that had never been recorded. But every bit of what I felt had been rehearsed by a billion people over tens of thousands of years of human existence. Death is the one thing we all share. I was just the latest in line.

Even so, the person I was closest to, who'd loved me the deepest, had died, suddenly and unexpectedly, and nothing would ever be the same. It was because of this that the next chapters of my life would unfold in strange and fateful ways.

3

—

WHEN I ENTERED MY PARENTS' squat stucco house, painted
a typical South Florida sunny yellow, I found my mother sitting at the
dining table in the dark, staring at nothing. She wore a cotton pajama
dress; her purse was still slung over her shoulder. The house, normally
tidy, was a wreck—armchairs and consoles pushed to the side, a lamp
tipped over, as if a great force had run roughshod through it. The moment
I turned on the light and saw her, I told Gabby to take my car back to
Orlando. She protested, but I insisted. I was young and unschooled in
death, but I still understood that what would happen next was too intimate for anyone outside our family to witness.

When the door closed, I fell to my knees, hugged my mother's legs,
and sobbed. Being with her was both a relief and the last unraveling of
my restraint. The sounds we made were otherworldly. We cried for so
long I couldn't tell you how much time passed, only that light began to
shine through the dining room windows.

In starts and stops, I got the story. I'll tell it to you the way I eventually learned to do it for witnesses: stripping the pain out, leaving only
the pertinent details.

My parents had an exceedingly ordinary day. They both went to work, heated up leftovers for dinner—lentil soup, since they were on their vegan diet again—and then my father began to complain of stomach pain as they were getting ready for bed. It wasn't gone by the time he'd tucked himself in with his reading glasses and a book, so my mom insisted on running to CVS to pick up some Pepto-Bismol. He told her not to go, but she insisted. She didn't want him to be in pain when a quick trip could solve it.

The closest CVS to their house is 1.9 miles away. She was gone for less than twenty minutes. When she got home, she called to him but received no response. She walked the short distance from the front door to their bedroom and found him lying in bed, his eyes wide open, his book resting on his chest. She didn't understand why he wouldn't talk back when she held up the CVS bag and said help was on the way. I imagine that's the moment she would wish herself back into if she could—those precious few seconds when she beheld my father and didn't yet realize anything was wrong.

But even her desire for everything to be okay couldn't shield her from the sudden realization that there were small bubbles of foam at the corners of my father's mouth. She dropped the plastic bag and rushed to him, crying his name, staring at his unblinking eyes, pressing her hands to his flesh, where no pulse beat. She screamed and called 911, performed CPR with the dispatcher on the line as the ambulance raced to the house. When the EMTs arrived twelve minutes later they burst through the door and swarmed my father, pushing my mother to the periphery, where she was both relieved and terrified to be relegated. Next to her feet lay the medicine for stomach pain, inert and ineffective, much too weak a cure for what had really happened.

They couldn't find a heartbeat or any signs of breathing. My mother thought that meant he would be defibrillated. The EMTs unfolded a gurney and strapped him to it, his weight requiring all three paramedics to shoulder him, and then they hustled the gurney back through the house. Mom thought that must've been when they bulldozed the furniture, but she couldn't be sure. She leapt into her car and raced after the screaming ambulance, calling me and begging me to pray. She wasn't religious, didn't even know if she believed in God, but she thought if anyone could convince the universe to help her husband, it would be me, the accidental baby who'd made Daniel Sharp a father, the person who'd given him his first true taste of purpose.

The truth was, he'd been dead from the moment my mom walked in the house. She'd begged me to pray for him and I'd taken the responsibility seriously, refused to stop chanting, willing him to hold on, but the entire time he was already gone. I don't blame her for making me hope—I understood why she couldn't accept it. But I also couldn't stop thinking that he'd slipped away while I was singing at the top of my lungs at a stupid college party, and I'd felt nothing. When you love someone, you assume their passing from the world will hit you like a disturbance in the Force. My lack of awareness felt like a betrayal, a sign I hadn't loved him well enough.

By the time the first of Mom's friends heard what happened and arrived bearing food, they found her in the same spot at her dining table, and me curled in their bed, in the last place my father had been alive.

What does it feel like to lose a parent? As I stared at his bedroom wall, trying to imagine the last thing he saw in this world, I was overcome with the conviction that he was in fact lost, not dead. My father had grown up in a different era, a shy boy on a small farm in East Tennessee, in a town so rural and struggling most people who were born there never left. He'd been one of the rare ones to get out, reaching escape velocity by doing something nobody in his family had expected: the very hour he turned eighteen, my father marched into a navy recruiter's office and traded six years of his life for passage out. Despite the fact that he wasn't in good shape, known by his siblings as "The Yoo-hoo King," had never traveled outside the state, and had never even seen the ocean, the navy plucked him up. The quiet young man from the landlocked state turned into a sailor.

Two years later, at a naval base in fast-moving, noisy Naples—a very long way from home—jogging up a mountain that faced the Tyrrhenian Sea, only miles from Mount Vesuvius, my father ran into my mother, another navy sailor on her own journey of escape. You couldn't have picked more different people: She was a New York City girl with fiery red hair and the ability to talk to anyone. He was a country boy, tall, dark, and as soft-spoken as she was bold. They fell in love immediately. Less than a year later, I was born. They were twenty-one-year-old kids in a foreign land trying to forge bigger lives, and they were as terrified of being parents as they were determined not to let me down. My dad used to say he experienced love at first sight twice in his life: the moment he saw my mother and, a year later, when I emerged in the hospital. Two lightning strikes of extraordinary luck in an otherwise unremarkable man's life.

For the record, I never thought he was unremarkable.

My mother left the navy to raise me, but my father stayed, and over the years, even as we moved back to America and hopped back and forth from coast to coast, I grew used to the pattern of him: home for six months, then out to sea for six more. When I was young, he brought back foreign coins I'd rub between my fingers. I studied them carefully, as if they would whisper the world's secrets.

That's what it felt like, lying in his bed. Like my dad had gone away on one of his journeys, except this time, he'd gotten lost. That was the only way my brain could process his absence. And I knew that if I went missing, he'd go to the ends of the earth to find me. That's what I needed to do for him. My heart screamed for it.

I rolled off the bed and ran to my mother.

4
—

SHE'D BEEN COAXED OUT OF her chair by a new round of teary-eyed friends bearing casseroles. Rudely, I seized the first pause in their conversation to inject myself:

"Mom, where's Dad?"

I'd startled her. "What do you mean? He's at the hospital."

"Can I see him?"

The two women my mother was talking to exchanged glances. Maybe it was an unusual request.

"No, honey, he's...in the morgue, I think."

The morgue. A cold, sterile place for people who were no longer people. I pictured my father there. How lonely.

"I need to see him with my own eyes." I didn't know how to explain that if I didn't find him and lay my hands on him, I would never truly believe that he was dead and would spend my life searching for where he was hiding.

My mom blinked bloodshot eyes. She was exhausted, and I wasn't making her life easier. "I don't know how to make that happen, honey."

One of the friends who'd been standing there interjected. "After the medical examiner performs the autopsy and they release Dan to a funeral home, you can ask for a visitation. They'll, uh..." She cleared her throat. "Dress him and make him look presentable. There's usually an extra cost."

My head was swimming with thoughts of sharp scalpels and stuffy funeral homes, but I seized on the easiest obstacle. "I'll pay for it, Mom. With my Starbucks money." I'd worked at Starbucks since high school, all the way until I'd left for UCF, and had a tidy savings. "Please. *Please.*"

She winced. "I saw him, Jane. They let me into his room to say goodbye and...he doesn't look like himself anymore. I don't want that to be how you remember him."

"I don't care. I just want to be with him." Nothing would've stopped my father. Even if I'd died a horribly violent death and there was nothing they could do to fix me, he would bear it.

"All right," my mom said wearily. "We can look into a visitation. But it will probably just be you. I don't think I can see him like that again."

You're going to see him, sang the voice in my head, the same one that had chanted to save him. *He's not lost.*

My relief was so intense it was problematic. I can see that now. Knowing I would see him again was enough to calm me so that when the last of the women left and it was just me, my mother, and the lasagnas, I was able to settle down on the couch and flip on the TV, letting the flickering images mesmerize me. For the first time in that relentless day, my pain dulled enough so I could close my eyes.

I'm telling you this so you'll understand why what happened next seized me the way it did. If, like you've claimed, you want to find the causal roots of what unfolded—the first domino that set the rest in motion—it was this: my father's death and my desperation to do something about it. No matter what anyone else claims, no matter what The Person Who

Shall Not Be Named published in That Awful Book* or what Nina Grace and those talking heads say on TV, this was the true beginning.

My focus gradually resharpened. The lights in the house were out and my mother was asleep across the living room in the La-Z-Boy, as unable to confront the death site of her bed as I'd been desperate for it. I don't know what pulled me from sleep, only that I'd become aware of the crisp voice of a newscaster saying, "And now we turn to a horrifying discovery in Lake Okeechobee, where late this afternoon, a man out bass fishing caught something chilling."

I squinted at the TV. The image shifted from a polished newscaster to the reedy shore of Lake Okeechobee, only forty miles away. Police, one of whom held a German shepherd on a leash, formed a ring around something dark on the sand. The midnight-blue water of the massive lake stretched to the horizon behind them.

"Sixty-two-year-old Ray Stevens took his boat out this morning, as he has every Friday since retiring," came the newscaster's voice-over. On-screen, a policeman crouched in front of the dark object. "Except instead of the bass the lake is famous for, Mr. Stevens's fishing hook caught a large black trash bag. When he reeled it in, Stevens says he was immediately alarmed due to the bag's heavy weight and foul odor."

The camera moved closer. The dark object came into focus—it was a trash bag, the same kind my parents used for heavy-duty lawn clippings. I sat up straighter.

"When Mr. Stevens opened the bag, he was met with a grisly sight: the dismembered remains of a human body."

There was a person in the bag. Right there, on the sand.

"He immediately came to shore and called 911," said the newscaster. "Now, police are asking for your help in solving the case."

---

* I've been advised by my lawyers to avoid directly naming this author or book.

The screen shifted to a close-up of a leather-faced man in an officer's uniform. The chyron beneath him read "OPD Detective-Sergeant Clint Abrams." His small blue eyes narrowed against the sun. I leaned all the way to the edge of the couch.

"We have a tragedy on our hands," he said gruffly. "A cruel injustice."

Yes, cried the voice in my head, relieved someone was saying it. *An injustice.* I felt it in my bones.

"A member of our community has been taken from us, coldly and without mercy."

I pictured my father alone in the morgue, in the dark basement of the hospital. Cold and merciless indeed.

"We need answers," growled the detective. "And we need your help. If you or anyone you know has information, no matter how trivial, please call the Criminal Investigations Department tip line at 863-555-0100."

We need answers. For the first time, I had what my father would call a lightning-strike moment. I needed answers. This body didn't belong in the lake, just like my father didn't belong in the morgue. Why did they have to die, out of everyone—suddenly and before they were ready? Could they have been saved?

I couldn't tear my eyes from the screen. A sense of purpose struck me, so intense it caused a searing heat in my chest, as if I were being shocked back to life.

"We can solve this." The detective's piercing eyes stared straight into the camera. "Together, we can bring the perpetrators to justice and grant peace to a grieving family."

There were answers out there, waiting. All I had to do was unravel the mystery.

I pressed Pause on the news and rewound it to the beginning.

5

—

THAT NIGHT I DREAMT MY father was sinking into the sea, his frightened face staring up at me through the dark waters, eyes begging for help. I lunged from the edge of a boat, but I couldn't touch him—all I could feel was the ancient cold of the water that held him trapped. I woke with a start on the couch to an empty living room. Heart pounding and aching with loneliness, I padded into my parents' room and curled up on his side of the bed. At some point, my mom must've finished making the bed, complete with their mountain of throw pillows. The largest read "Our Happy Place" in loopy cursive, a Christmas present from my dad. I pressed my face into the pillow and imagined it was him.

A body in the water, thrown away like garbage. The image of that wet black bag on the shore of Lake Okeechobee came back. I opened my eyes and reached for my phone. ("You kids," my dad had once joked, "must get those things surgically attached while we're not looking.") I googled "person trash bag Lake Okeechobee" and caught my breath when the search turned up dozens of hits.

The body had a name. Indira Babatunde, female, age forty-six, of Indiantown, Florida, according to the first link. I clicked on it, and a small picture—pixelated and grainy—topped a short article. It was a close-up of Indira against a white background. A work headshot, maybe. Her smile didn't reach her eyes. Probably slipped off her face once the flash went off. She had dark skin and small, amber-colored eyes, her hair slicked into a ponytail. She wore a blouse I recognized from Ann Taylor, where my mom shopped. I know you're not supposed to judge a book by its cover, but my first thought was this: Who would viciously dismember a woman who looked like the worst crime she'd ever committed was a typo on her expense report?

According to the article, DNA from the remains confirmed it was Indira, but she hadn't been reported missing. She lived alone in a condo and worked the front desk at the Indiantown arboretum. Her only family was her mother, who lived in a retirement home in Vero Beach. Hungry for more, I swiped down the Google results, clicking every link. The articles mostly repeated the same scant facts, but at least TreasureCoastInfo.com had talked to a neighbor of Indira's, who reported her hobbies were knitting, planting in her small garden, watching "her soaps," and visiting her mother. The neighbor was shocked that anyone would think to harm her.

I felt the same. I sensed a dark story teeming under the void of information. If anything, the vacuum made me more desperate to dig.

It wasn't until page six of the Google results that I hit upon a line from a site called TheRealCrimeNetwork.com. It read, simply, "Indira Babatunde—bet they chopped her to fit in the bag." I clicked, and a forum thread opened titled "Indira Babatunde," subtitled "Lake Okeechobee Trash Bag Woman." I froze for a moment. Imagine losing your life to violence and then getting labeled the "Trash Bag Woman." Insult to injury.

The Real Crime Network appeared to be a true-crime forum, given its tagline: "Where real sleuths solve real crimes in real time." I'd read about the so-called armchair detectives who'd tried to solve the Boston Marathon bombing and Gabby Petito cases—I mean, it was impossible to live in the twenty-first century and not know there was a thriving subpopulation obsessed with true crime. But I'd never hung out in that corner of the internet. I'd pictured it as seedy and a little cheesy, to be honest.

It was more low-tech than I'd imagined. The site was blocky and luridly black and red, consisting of nothing more than a list of old-school message boards, conversation threads dividing into sub-threads and then again into sub-sub-threads, like a million-stringed spiderweb, a million different rabbit holes. Was that really what solved crimes—a hive mind talking? Doubtful, I scanned the Indira thread.

SeattleHawks*: This one's good for us, I think. Case isn't getting much attention outside local media. They need us.

Minacaren: Ignore Seattle's attention-whoring. What do we think, peeps?

Smithsfan: The remains were pulled out of the far eastern part of Lake Okeechobee by a guy out bass fishing. Apparently, the lake is the #1 bass fishing destination in FL, so that checks out.

Mamajama: Floridian here. Locals call the lake the "Big O." Definitely known for bass.

SeattleHawks: Big O's kind of sexual, no? Florida is weird.

Smithsfan: If you check the depth chart I'm attaching, eastern side's one of the deepest parts of the lake. Do we think whoever dumped the body knew where to drop it for maximum sinkage?

Carolrichards68: Interesting theory. The finder was Ray Stevens, 62, a former ad exec who used to live in NJ but retired down in FL.

Minacaren: 62 is early for retiring. Is he loaded?

Carolrichards68: Appears to be doing well for himself. He and his wife bought a $800k house a year ago in Okeechobee, according to property records. Not to mention the boat.

---

* Forum handles used in lieu of names to protect the innocent (assuming those exist).

I blinked at the screen. Property records—anyone could just find those?

> **HiltoftheSword:** No criminal record on Stevens other than a recent
> speeding fine, which he paid on time. His social presence is pretty
> typical. Married once according to Facebook (he doesn't have IG/
> Twitter/TikTok, which tracks for his age). Two kids still living in
> NJ, a few grandkids. Do we like him as an innocent bystander?
> **Minacaren:** That's the sense I'm getting. Just a man in the wrong
> place at the wrong time. Police report describes his behavior as
> what you'd expect: caught the bag, looked inside, rushed to call
> 911. Distraught throughout questioning.

They had access to the police report? I opened a new tab and typed "police report Indira Babatunde," but even after scrolling through every page of results, I got nothing. I returned to the forum. Maybe I was wrong about these true-crime people. There were clearly doors out there that were locked to me but open to them. Hidden worlds, secret hiding places. I wanted and needed to look.

> **SeattleHawks:** What we should do is figure out who Indira was
> dating. It's always the boyfriend.
> **Minacaren:** Seattle, feel free to hop back on the Iris Lapow case.
> We got it from here.
> **GeorgeLightly:** He's got a point, though. Women are much more likely
> to be killed by an intimate partner, especially if that partner is a man.
> **Carolrichards68:** Lightly! It's an honor to have you.

This pandering was interesting. Maybe this Lightly person was a bigshot.

GeorgeLightly: I'm glad this case is getting the Network's attention. Too many dead Black women don't. Especially with Nigerian last names.

SeattleHawks: Preach! We're allies here.

Minacaren: Ugh, Seattle...anyway, I was thinking about the dismembering. That's the striking part, other than no one reporting Indira missing. Do we think it was a pragmatic or emotional choice?

I lowered my phone and imagined someone calmly taking a saw to a woman's body. (Surely it couldn't be done with a kitchen knife?) Joint by joint, starting at the soft, bendy places. Not even breaking a sweat as they tore through flesh, cracked bone. Pure pragmatism.

HiltoftheSword: My guess is the dismemberment was postmortem, done to fit the body into the trash bag. Obvi the autopsy will tell for sure. The lake has one of the highest gator populations in FL. I bet the killer was hoping they'd eat her. No body, no crime, as the great Taylor Swift would say.

GeorgeLightly: Remember, we never make assumptions. We trace threads until a picture begins to form, little by little. From what I can tell from the images—still waiting on OPD to confirm—the trash bag appears to be a Hefty Strong Lawn & Leaf. Same blue drawstrings and sheen on the plastic. Unfortunately, you can find those anywhere, and they've been manufactured for years. So trying to find a purchaser is probably a dead end. Who knows when + where the killer bought it.

Interesting. These people seemed smart. I'd never thought of myself as particularly smart. When I was young, I scored well enough on tests to make me a good student. My teachers seemed excited about me, and I remember school feeling promising. But that was a brief window—as I grew older, my anxiety grew with me, and school turned nerve-racking. I paid less attention to my teachers and textbooks and more to other students. Their wants, needs, fears, and hopes—both petty and profound—were a constant stream in my mind, their concerns crowding mine out. I worried about them, felt it every time another student was on the receiving end of harsh words, a punishment, a teasing. Felt joy over their victories, though those were fewer and further between.

I'd always had this sensitivity about me, if that's even the right word. My mom used to say I was "overly attuned" to people, as if I were a radio receiver stuck on the wrong channel. I knew she meant I spent too much time worrying about other people, got too tangled in their lives. My dad called it "high emotional intelligence," but he was inclined to believe the best about me. Whatever it was—social anxiety, nerves, or empathy dialed up to the pathological—it turned school into a battlefield. By high school, I was too busy dodging social land mines and longing for the bell to ring to concentrate on learning. I envied the kids whose minds were quiet enough that they could focus on test scores and college applications. I wished I could block out the world that well. But I couldn't, and my sinking grades reflected it.

I know what you're thinking—that I'm presenting a veneer of false humility to avoid telling you how I pulled off my investigative feats. You've heard things about me, from the news and The Person Who Shall Not Be Named. But I'm here to set the record straight. And the truth is, no matter how much I wish I could claim I was some sort of Albert Einstein figure, a failure in school because my brain was too advanced, I've never been a savant. Yes, sometimes I can read people well, but what I accomplished, I did through pure luck. Not brilliance and certainly not, as That Awful Book claimed, "a near-sociopathic level of remorseless manipulation."

As you'll come to see, I feel plenty of remorse.

6

MY MOM OPENED THE DOOR to her bedroom and startled me into dropping my phone, halfway through the Indira Babatunde thread. "I found a funeral home. Dad's being transferred there this afternoon."

I scrambled to sit up, feeling awkward lying in her bed when she still wouldn't step inside the room. "You chose a place?"

"The medical examiner called this morning. They finished Dad's autopsy and need somewhere to send him." She swallowed. "I figured it would be better to just choose. Not make it a thing."

"What did the autopsy say?" *What was the cause of death,* said a voice in my head. It sounded like the collective voice of the Real Crime Network.

"A coronary artery occlusion leading to a myocardial infarction."

I blinked.

"A heart attack," she said. "Caused by plaque buildup in his arteries."

Our eyes met, and I knew what she wasn't saying: *caused by his weight.* My dad's weight was the most painful subject in our family. Sometime over the years, the fit navy sailor my mom had met stopped exercising—well, stopped and started, and stopped again—and his weight ballooned. They'd tried everything: couples' exercise, fitness challenges, diets, veganism. Nothing worked for long. No matter how hard he tried—and how hard he tried differed according to who you asked—he remained medically obese.

It was confusing for me. My father was active and strong. He could mow the entire yard in a single burst of strength and sweat. He seemed to eat well, and even when he had the occasional scoop of ice cream or a slice of cake on a neighbor's birthday, that was only human. But even those minor indulgences had become charged in the last months before I'd left for UCF. The tension had come to a head one night when I heard my mom yell that he was throwing his life away, betraying his promise to grow old with her by endangering his health. And now he was dead. What an agony, being right.

I took a deep breath and gripped the duvet. "Did he suffer?"

She paused for too long. "No, honey. I don't think he did."

We were quiet. Maybe she could read the pain on my face and thought she might as well confess it now, because she said, "His doctor begged him to get on blood pressure meds. He said your dad's numbers were dangerous and the medicine could save his life. But your dad refused."

I stared at her, uncomprehending. "Why would he do that?"

My mother's voice was ragged. "I honestly don't know. Your dad was his own person. I couldn't make his decisions for him, no matter how much I wished I could."

I sat there in the after waves of shock. Why would he refuse medicine that could save his life? Were there terrible side effects? Did he not believe his condition was serious enough to warrant it? Another darker thought popped up before I could stop it: Had he not cared whether he lived or died?

My mom finally stepped into the room and held out a pamphlet. Waldorf Funeral and Crematory Services, with a little pineapple logo in the corner. In Florida, even the funeral homes were tropical.

"This is the place I chose," she said. "What do you think?"

What I thought was that I couldn't understand why my father wouldn't have taken the medicine. I couldn't move past it. But she was watching me expectantly, so I took the pamphlet.

"He wanted to be cremated," she added.

I scanned the list of packages until I found *Visitation services: We will provide a private space for you to visit with your loved one. Your loved one will be prepared according to your wishes, in attire you provide. You may choose for your loved one to be presented in a casket or less formally, laid upon a table and covered with a quilt. Visitation times are limited to 90 minutes for sanitation purposes. Cost: $300.*

My head swam. I could barely make sense of it. I felt a sudden longing to go back to the black-and-red world of the true-crime forum.

"It seems like a good place," I said quietly. "And I still want to do the visitation."

"Okay," she said, just as quietly. "In that case, they said they can do it tomorrow. You should go into your dad's closet and pick out what you'd like to see him wear."

———

People underestimate the power of distraction. That night, I fought the words and images swirling in my head—*your loved one, sanitation purposes, but he refused*—by opening my Sudoku app. I played Sudoku on my phone for seven hours, from eight p.m. to three a.m., puzzle after puzzle, addicted to the way it numbed and emptied me. Solving, solving, solving, until I finally fell asleep.

7

—

WALDORF FUNERAL AND CREMATORY SERVICES had a
smell, like too many air fresheners crammed into too small a space. It
was a campus dotted with trees—you could tell whoever built it had tried
to make it nice, but it was only sadder for trying. My mom had invited
my father's family and friends to the visitation, but as she predicted, I
was the only one with the stomach for it. A whole visitation, all the pomp
and circumstance, just for one. At $300, it was the most expensive thing
I'd ever bought for myself, this time alone with my dad.

Before I walked into the room I shook with nerves. The Waldorf
staff member assigned to us said briskly, "Remember, you have ninety
minutes. Please inform whoever else is coming that we can't push the
time. We keep your loved one in the freezer, you understand, and there's
only so long we can guarantee a lack of smell when they're out in room
temperature."

"It's only me."

She waved me toward the door with a sympathetic smile, as if she
hadn't just spoken of my father like meat on the verge of spoiling.

When I entered the room and saw him laid out on the table, wearing
the cargo shorts and maroon polo I'd picked out for him—one of his

outfits for day-to-day errands—I lost control of myself. I cried out, "Oh, Daddy!" and fell to my knees.

His physical presence—the mere fact that he still existed—was so powerful, so deeply reassuring. He looked like he was sleeping. His eyes were shut, hands clasped over his chest, a quilt pulled to his waist. I had never felt such strong, conflicting emotions. Dizzying relief to have found him, to know he was no longer missing, and then dawning horror as I tiptoed closer to the table. This body—it was my father, but it wasn't.

I'd never seen a dead body. I know that's ironic, given what I would later become famous for, but I guess everyone has to start somewhere. Before that day I thought of death as something abstract—a person's time on earth ending, their soul ascending, things like that. For the first time, I confronted the materiality of death. There was something wrong with my dad's face, for one. He had been a handsome man, and he retained that handsomeness even as he aged and filled out—dark, curly hair before he went bald, lively hazel eyes that sparkled, a Roman nose. But now his features were too puffy, his dark eyelashes too spread out, as if they'd been carefully fanned against his cheeks. (I would later learn that the eyes of the dead are often sewn shut to avoid the possibility of springing open.) When I looked closer at his hands, the hands that had held me as a child, I saw his fingertips were blackening at the nails.

This was what my mother hadn't wanted me to see: that for all of our elegant theorems and artistic masterpieces and missions to the moon—for all the complex things we meant to each other—in the end, human beings are bodies that rot. I thought of TheRealCrimeNetwork.com, the way they'd talked about the pragmatics of dismemberment. Those people knew the truth. They dealt in it, no matter how ugly or unsettling. Suddenly, it seemed courageous.

But this was how much I loved my father: I looked at his large hands with the rotting fingertips and remembered how much he loved to be hugged, how he'd grown up in a large family where there was never much physical affection, so he'd made up for it with us. And I pushed my fear aside and held his hands. They were unnaturally cold. Colder than ice, somehow. I squeezed them, my warmth so ineffectual, and told him I loved him, over and over. I told him I was sorry he'd been robbed of his life, all the things he was supposed to do and experience. I asked him why he hadn't just taken the meds, why he hadn't tried everything in his power to stay with me, and my voice nearly broke in half with the weight of it. I poured it all out, and then I released him.

In the end, I spent twenty of my ninety minutes.

8

—

LATER THAT NIGHT, SEEKING DISTRACTION, I returned to the forum, this time on my laptop. There had been developments.

> **Minacaren:** So we've established Indira didn't have a boyfriend? We scoured everything?
>
> **CitizenNight:** We put Goku on it and he found nothing. That's as good as it gets.
>
> **LordGoku:** I swept her socials and was able to log into her arboretum desktop since it's city-funded. Nothing suspicious, but obviously I'm itching to get my hands on her personal computer, assuming she had one.
>
> **SeattleHawks:** I'm guessing we shouldn't ask how you were able to remotely log into a government computer?
>
> **Carolrichards68:** Just say thank you. We're lucky to have Goku and Citizen on this.
>
> **CitizenNight:** Hey, we go where Lightly goes.
>
> **GeorgeLightly:** All right, enough back-patting. We can't totally rule out a boyfriend, or even a first date that turned ugly. Has anyone managed to speak to a friend or neighbor?

I frowned at my screen. Would her friends and neighbors just open up to anyone who approached them? Were people that desperate to unburden themselves, or did they want to be part of the action?

> **HiltoftheSword:** I messaged her next-door neighbor on Facebook. Attached screenshots of the conversation. Indira was *truly* a homebody. The neighbor saw her home most of the time. She'd sit on her front porch knitting. Fed the neighborhood cats. This was not a woman out courting trouble. The only thing the neighbor ever heard Indira complain about was her mom's retirement home. Apparently, a big chunk of her paycheck went to paying for her mom's care, and she wasn't happy with the conditions.
>
> **CitizenNight:** Interesting. I wonder if we should check out the retirement home.
>
> **SeattleHawks:** Theory 1: the disgruntled owner of the retirement home dismembers Indira for threatening to blow the whistle on her secret money-laundering scheme.
>
> **GeorgeLightly:** You jest, Seattle, but I've seen far weirder things in my time.

Curious, I clicked on Lightly's username, which took me to his profile. TheRealCrimeNetwork.com didn't use photos, and the only info was his real name, George Lightly, and a single line of text: Retired detective, Chicago PD.

Wow. Lightly was a former cop. No wonder he commanded respect. What was he doing here?

> **SeattleHawks:** Ha! Looking at the chat transcript. Hilt, you pretended to be a *Palm Beach Post* reporter. Is that legal?
>
> **HiltoftheSword:** Hey, it worked. I also found a woman who worked

with Indira at the arboretum. She said it's a small office and everyone loved Indira. She'd been there for decades.

CitizenNight: Did she say when Indira stopped showing up to work?

HiltoftheSword: Her first absence was the Tuesday before she
was found. She came to work Monday and seemed totally normal,
according to the colleague.

Working on Monday, missing on Tuesday, remains found Friday.

GeorgeLightly: Does her neighbor remember seeing her at
home later in the week? I'm trying to pin down exactly when she
disappeared.

CitizenNight: Why didn't anyone report Indira missing if she stopped
showing up to work?

Suddenly it occurred to me that we would have to tell my dad's
office that he was never coming back. We'd have to tell the people in
his woodworking club, maybe even the people he talked to online in
his *Star Trek* forum. They would all want to know. We would have to
say he was gone so many times, repeating a fact we could barely grasp
ourselves.

HiltoftheSword: I'll go back and ask the colleague why they didn't
report. She made it seem like Indira was the linchpin of the office.
Maybe she was the one who reported absences? It was kind of
like that in my old office. If the responsible person didn't do it, it
didn't get done.

LordGoku: I can scroll her colleagues' email inboxes, see if they
sent any messages remarking on her absence.

GeorgeLightly: Good idea.

SeattleHawks: Lol who are you, Goku? NSA/CIA? Come on, you can tell us.

LordGoku: Remind me what you're contributing to this case, Seattle?

SeattleHawks: Hey, I found Google images of Indira's town house dated only two weeks ago. Attaching here. From what I can tell, she didn't own a ring light or any other video surveillance.

Minacaren: Dammit, that's actually useful.

I clicked on the photos. Indira's condo was a generic cream-colored town house with a small front porch and tall birds-of-paradise in the front yard, the bright, stalky flowers that were practically a requirement here in South Florida. The condo was sandwiched between identical homes.

GeorgeLightly: So we've got a middle-aged woman so quiet she was nearly invisible, except to her colleagues, who universally liked her. And her only beef was that she wanted her mom's retirement home to take better care of her. What in the world was the motive for murder?

HiltoftheSword: I've got nothing.

Minacaren: Sigh. Me neither.

CitizenNight: Guys, Seattle's mention of Google Maps made me realize we could explore the area around Indira's condo. I just found a convenience store at the end of her road. It's the only way in and out of Indira's street. I bet that place has CCTV.

LordGoku: If we could get that footage, we could see if Indira left any time after Monday. Track her Honda Civic.

GeorgeLightly: That's really good, Citizen. Can we call the store for the footage?

CitizenNight: It's so rinky-dink it doesn't have a website. Maybe
Goku could dig through the online Yellow Pages? Don't suppose
there's a chance anyone's nearby and could go in person...

Why did I do it? Go from passive observer, using the Network as
a macabre distraction from my father's death, to active participant,
stepping blindly into my role in history? Why did I feel the need,
drowning in sadness of my own, to take on this other grief, this other
person's death?

The reasons are too complicated to answer cleanly. What I can
tell you is that even though I'd just seen my father, I felt no peace. In
fact, I felt like I understood him less than before. Why hadn't he taken
the blood pressure medication? It was the chink in the armor of my
certainty. Had I actually known my father inside and out? The more I
sat with the question, the more I realized that I'd known certain sides
of him—hugs and comfort and sci-fi movies and the patient voice on
the line when I got a flat tire—but how well did I know the real man,
beyond his role as Dad? And didn't I owe him the dignity and intimacy
of being truly known? Didn't I owe it to myself to unravel the mystery
of who my father had been and how the truth of him might have led
to his death?

Maybe that was the crux of it: Maybe I didn't get involved because
I was trying to be a hero. Maybe I wanted to know my own father but
couldn't figure out how, and some part of me thought that if I helped
decipher other people's mysteries, I could learn for him. Maybe it was
all selfish.*

I navigated to the Set Up Account page. The Network asked for

---

* Can you see I'm trying to view myself through the unbiased lens of history? I hope that
counts for something.

very little personal information. My only hesitation was my username. How did I want to be known? By my real name? By a mask? I thought and thought, and in the end, I decided on something even more honest than my name.

I toggled back to the Indira thread. Everyone had reported that they were nowhere close to Indiantown and couldn't get to the gas station. I took a deep breath and typed my very first post:

Searcher24: I'll do it.

9

I DROVE MY MOM'S HYUNDAI to Indira's condo the very next morning, buoyed by messages of support on the forum. I had a pivotal role to play. The Real Crime Network was counting on me.

As she'd dropped her keys in my hand, my mom had told me to expect my father's ashes to be ready that afternoon, ahead of his memorial tomorrow. Everything was happening too fast. On the drive to Indiantown, I was trying so hard not to picture what it was like to be cremated that by the time I got to the turn for Indira's neighborhood, I nearly missed it.

Righting myself, I crept slowly down her street, taking it all in. Florida is overrun with large, planned neighborhoods, practically plucked from the movie *Pleasantville*. Some of these neighborhoods are sponsored by Disney, some are owned by resort conglomerates, but they're all the same: row after row of identical houses, copy-and-paste communities. Indira's was one of those, with the same birds-of-paradise arrangements in everyone's front lawns. I felt a thrill as I passed the run-down convenience store with its blown-up neon signs advertising "Beer" and "Ice." There was a tell-tale video camera stationed near the door—Citizen was right. They had CCTV.

I drove to Indira's house, feeling nervous, as if I were a stalker, someone who wasn't supposed to be there. There was nothing about the house that marked it as the dwelling of a recently murdered woman—no yellow caution tape or police presence. I swept by, then did a slow loop around the cul-de-sac and headed back the way I'd come. Citizen was right again. There was only one road in and out.

I pulled in front of the convenience store and eyed the camera. There were two lenses: one directed at the door and one at the street. That was good news. I started to get out, then froze. Did I simply walk in there and ask the clerk for the footage? Did I reveal it was for an investigation into Indira Babatunde or keep that a secret?

I sat there for a moment before I realized: I didn't care if I made a fool of myself. My dad had just died. What could happen that was worse than that? I hadn't expected grief to be so strangely freeing.

I marched into the store. The clerk was a teenage boy with aggressive acne, probably not helped by the grease I could feel wafting off the glistening hot dogs that were rolling under the nearby heater.

"Hi, Chris," I said, eyeing his name tag. "This might sound strange, but does your store keep those security cameras outside working?"

He gave me a look of alarm. "You're not thinking of...robbing us... are you?"

"Oh, no—I'm not casing the joint." I laughed nervously, which only made him look more alarmed. "My friend was killed. She lived near here, and the police are asking for help solving her case." Most of that was true, anyway.

His eyes lit with interest. "Do you mean that woman they found in the trash bag?"

Someone sidled into line behind me. "Her name was Indira. But yes. I'm part of a group looking into her death, and we realized your store's footage could be critical to pinpointing what happened." Never had I felt more purposeful. I puffed up my chest.

The clerk narrowed his eyes. "Wait, are you her friend, or are you part of a group investigating her?"

Not even two minutes, and a teenager had called my bluff. James Bond, I was not.

"Um, both?" Behind me, the person waiting let out a sigh. "Could I have the footage? I would only need a few days' worth."

The clerk looked at me like I was crazy. "Just hand it over to you without a warrant?"

So they were still teaching teenagers about constitutional rights. How unfortunate. "Yes—to help Indira."

"Sorry, ma'am. My boss would kill me. Come back with a warrant maybe." He peered around me to the next person in line. "You ready?"

I slunk away, deflated. So much for procuring critical evidence. And I got ma'amed. I could only imagine how disappointed the forum would be.

———

When I returned home, a cardboard box sat on the dining table, stamped with the Waldorf Funeral Services and Crematory logo. I stopped in my tracks and stared.

After a minute, my mom rounded the corner. We faced each other like opposing chess pieces. "I thought you might want to open it together," she said softly.

I didn't. I didn't want to open it or touch it. I didn't want the box to exist.

"I can't," I said. I was failing her, unable to be strong, but she only nodded and got busy pulling it apart. I couldn't look. I felt like I might hyperventilate.

"I asked them to divide the ashes into two." As she slid open the final compartment, I glanced, and there they lay: two plastic bags secured with zip ties, full of light gray dust. What was left of my father. The Man in the Bag.

"We can order urns tonight, if you want." Mom offered me one of the bags. "I was thinking of spreading his ashes at a few of his favorite places. Maybe the beach? And some back in Tennessee?"

I accepted the bag even though every part of me was screaming not to touch it. It was wrong, unnatural, a man burned up and left in heaps. This was so much worse than seeing my dad rotting. Why had no one warned me?

My mom squeezed my shoulder. Her voice was thick. "It's okay, Jane. We're going to figure out how to do this."

———

That night the bag of ashes sat in the farthest corner of my room while I returned to the forum, ready to face my lambasting. Every so often I glanced at the bag out of the corner of my eye, as if I expected it to sprout legs and sneak up on me. What part of my father was in there? His legs, his arms, his skull? How gruesomely intimate, to be able to hold those parts of him in my palms. Finally, I got up and shoved the bag in my dresser, in the drawer that held my pajamas. It was a strange place to put him, but he was better out of sight.

On-screen, the Indira thread was hungry for my report.

Minacaren: Any luck, Searcher?

Carolrichards68: What'd ya find?

SeattleHawks: Yeah, dude, it's been hours—spill!

Searcher24: I have bad news. I drove to the convenience store. Citizen was right—it has two security cameras, and one faces the road.

LordGoku: Wait, that's great news!

Searcher24: Well, I talked to the clerk at the register and asked for the footage, but he said no. So we're back at square one. I'm sorry I botched this. This is the first time I've done any sleuthing.

To my surprise, a flurry of messages popped up.

Minacaren: Aww Searcher! You did great.

LordGoku: You didn't need to actually leave with the tape in your hands, lol! Don't beat yourself up.

SeattleHawks: Searcher, you're adorable. No one expected you to get the tape.

Searcher24: You didn't? I figured one of you would've been a lot smoother in that situation. I didn't know what to say.

CitizenNight: Trust me, we've all been there. The fact that we know there's footage is a great next step.

Searcher24: What do we do now?

GeorgeLightly: We tip off the police, assuming they haven't already gotten a warrant for the footage. And then we use our best police smooth-talker to learn what they know.

Searcher24: So we just give away our clue?

CitizenNight: Aw, kid, you really are new.

CitizenNight: I just realized you might be older than me. Sorry. What I meant was, what we do on this forum is in harmony with the cops.

In harmony? I guess I'd subconsciously assumed it was a competition.[*]

---

[*] See? I swear, we started with good intentions. We wanted to play nice.

LordGoku: Think of it as a symbiotic relationship. Like a shark and one of those teeth-cleaning fishies. We're the shark, obviously.

SeattleHawks: I say FUCK the cops. Right, Lightly?

GeorgeLightly: Not touching that. Don't worry, Searcher, we'll have answers in no time. You did good. Proud of you.

At the time, I couldn't understand why I exited the browser crying or why I fell asleep so soundly for the first time in days. In hindsight, as with most things, I guess it's pretty obvious.

10
—

BEFORE WE GO FURTHER, I think it's important for you to know how badly I messed up my father's funeral. Even though, out of everything, this is the thing I'm most loath to confess. My mom and I weren't religious, so we planned his memorial on a public pavilion overlooking the ocean, which was as close as we could get to the eternal sublime. We invited everyone: our neighbors, all the people in my dad's phone, everyone from his work, even the *Star Trek* forum.

We'd never had money, so it was probably stupid, but we wanted to do something grand, so we spent thousands on a caterer and then hours pulling photographs out of old scrapbooks to make an elaborate display charting Daniel Sharp, from infancy to adulthood. It was the kind of thing you'd see laid out for a historical figure in a museum. We wanted people to understand my dad had been important.

My mom asked me to deliver his eulogy.

You might think I'd balk at that, given how shy I was. But I knew it was my chance to show the world what he'd meant to me, to do it officially, record it in the annals. If you think that sounds dramatic, try being the only child of a man who came from nothing and died before paying off his credit card loans. He had no financial legacy. No cultural legacy. No one to extol his virtues in a *New York Times* obituary or erect statues in his memory. The world would be quick to forget him. All he had was me.

Every moment I wasn't on the Indira thread, I pored over great eulogies from history, trying my hand at drafts. In the end, I wrote a speech I was proud of. When the day came and I strode to the microphone, clutching my printed pages, I took a deep breath and prepared to do something definitive for my father.

Then I looked down at the speech, and the words swam. Instead of what I'd written, I saw stark words from the forum: *Motive? Time of death? I've got nothing.*

I looked up and locked eyes with my mother. The ocean wind was strong that day, battering our photo display and whipping the hair of the crowd. There was pity on my mother's face. Pity for me.

I looked down again at the speech, trying to ignore the throats clearing, people shifting with discomfort. I managed to say, "My father was..."

What? Out of my grasp forever? A man whose decisions I didn't understand? Again, the voice of the forum crept in. *Theory 1: He never took his health seriously and gave himself that heart attack. Theory 2: He wanted to die all along.*

"Jane?" My mother's voice was uncertain.

It felt like the final hole in a sinking boat. "I'm sorry," I mumbled.

I placed the microphone on the ground and walked away, blinking back tears of disbelief that it was happening. A few of my dad's friends stood up to share memories—little moments, stupid things, nothing that captured who he was as a man.

I'm telling you this despite what it costs me because there will come a point in this story when you'll think to yourself, *My God, how could she have done that? Who would ever make that choice?* And I need you to remember who I was at the time: a girl who owed her father a legacy. So when the time comes, please remember—there's no more powerful motive than that.

TWO DAYS AFTER THE FUNERAL, word came back from the Okeechobee police that they'd secured the convenience store's footage and now had a record of everyone who'd driven down Indira's street. It didn't appear she'd left her house after returning from work on Monday. The police were looking into all the license plates caught on the footage, but so far, they hadn't connected any of them to Indira's acquaintances—other than her neighbors, who'd all alibied out.

> **Searcher24:** Sorry I'm a newb, but can someone explain what that means?*
>
> **Carolrichards68:** It's cute to have a baby in our ranks again. It means Indira either left her condo on foot sometime after Monday (weird) or she was somehow smuggled out of her house.
>
> **CitizenNight:** And none of her known acquaintances drove to her house during the critical window when she disappeared

---

* Maybe you were thinking I'd blame the forum for messing with my head, but the truth was, I logged on right after the funeral. It had become my safe space, the obsession that consumed me. And this was even before the case that would come to define my life.

(Monday–Friday). That points to the perp NOT being someone she knew.

Searcher24: You mean a stranger drove to her house and killed her?

GeorgeLightly: It's rare, but it happens. The police ruled out Indira's house as the kill site, though. No evidence of violence. She was transported elsewhere and killed there.

Searcher24: So what happens next?

LordGoku: One of the least glamorous parts of our job. We research the owners of every license plate that drove down Indira's street and try to establish a connection between them and our girl. According to OPD there were 75 unique vehicles that week, right Lightly?

GeorgeLightly: Right.

Searcher24: 75 people to research? That's going to take forever.

CitizenNight: Welcome to the sizzling world of crime investigation.

I looked at my dresser. "Well, if that's what it takes."

I turned back to my screen, then froze.

I'd just talked to my father's ashes. Which couldn't be normal. But I could feel his presence in my pajama drawer. I remembered Poe's story "The Tell-Tale Heart," and the guilty narrator's belief that he could hear his victim's heart beating under the floorboards where he'd buried him. I rose and pulled my father's ashes out, placing him on top of the dresser.

"There," I said. "Now you have air. And you can watch."

My computer chimed with a notification.

SleuthMistress: I come bearing news and an idea.

GeorgeLightly: Whatcha got, Mistress?

SleuthMistress: News first. Sadly, I got my hands on Indira's autopsy. Brace yourselves. Indira was alive when her killer started chopping her.

Carolrichards68: Oh my god. That poor woman.

Minacaren: I feel sick.

Like Mina, I felt my stomach drop. I couldn't imagine dying that way. The sheer pain.

SeattleHawks: When did Mistress get put on this case?

HiltoftheSword: You know Lightly, Goku, Citizen, and Mistress travel as a pack. They can't trust us mere mortals to handle things on our own.

SleuthMistress: Official cause of death was massive blood loss. The medical examiner thinks she was struck on the head with something heavy—she suffered blunt force trauma to the left side of her skull—and then the killer started dismembering her. Wounds are consistent with a large, thick blade. They started with her legs.

I glanced at my dad's ashes. "That's awful, isn't it?"

SleuthMistress: The blow to the head was strong enough to make a large crack in her skull, so there's a good chance it knocked her out.

CitizenNight: Amazing what passes for small mercies around here.

GeorgeLightly: Sorry to make you all queasy, but I have to ask: how clean are the cuts? Are we talking about a killer who was strong enough to wield a blade through bone, or someone sloppy?

SleuthMistress: It was a hack job. Someone put Indira through the ringer.

Carolrichards68: God rest her soul.

I straightened my spine and reentered the fray.

Searcher24: Does that mean whoever killed Indira was inexperi-enced? If they did a bad job?

SleuthMistress: Well, hello, newcomer with the good questions.

GeorgeLightly: Searcher, meet Mistress. Mistress, meet Searcher. Searcher's new to the Network but dedicated and resourceful. Mistress is a legend. She's solved more cases than any of us.

SleuthMistress: Only because I've been here from the beginning. I'm an old-timer.

CitizenNight: No, it's because you can find things nobody else can.

Searcher24: Wow, nice to meet you, Mistress.

GeorgeLightly: To answer your Q, Searcher, it could mean our killer was either A) inexperienced, B) physically weaker, C) in a hurry, D) wanted Indira to feel pain, or E) any combo of the above.

Searcher24: There's never a straight answer, is there?

GeorgeLightly: Now you're getting it.

SeattleHawks: So we have a hasty/inexperienced/weak/vindictive person, who must've made quite a mess killing Indira, if she died by bleeding out.

LordGoku: Good point. The kill site must've been a disaster. Blood everywhere.

CitizenNight: And no one has stumbled on it yet, so it must be somewhere few people have access to. Could it have happened at the lake?

HiltoftheSword: Doubtful. Lake O is pretty busy. Someone would've run into the bloodbath by now.

Searcher24: So that means Indira was taken from her house (or left on foot), moved to a second, private location to be killed, then moved again to the lake to be dumped. That's a lot of effort.

GeorgeLightly: We can't totally rule out the lake as a kill site—we'll know more once the cops finish combing it—but my gut says you're right, Searcher. Someone went to a lot of effort to kill Indira, and yet so far, the evidence suggests that person was a stranger.

SeattleHawks: What the hell...

LordGoku: My sentiments exactly.

CitizenNight: Mistress, didn't you say you had an idea?

SleuthMistress: Yeah. Take this or leave it. But what's the most common motive for murder besides passion?

CitizenNight: Easy. Money.

SleuthMistress: Right. Let's assume our killer wasn't a sadist trying to cause Indira pain, they just wanted to get rid of her. Has anyone looked into her bank records?

Minacaren: No offense, Mistress, but Indira worked the front desk at an arboretum making $25/hr. And all her money went to pay for her mom's retirement home. The woman wasn't a prime financial target.

SleuthMistress: Like I said, take it or leave it.

CitizenNight: I say we look into it. No stone left unturned, right? Goku, want to move to a secure channel to discuss?

LordGoku: On my way.

SeattleHawks: I am genuinely terrified of the two of you.

Could Goku really access Indira's bank records? Wasn't that—

"Jane."

I startled, swiveling in my chair. My mom leaned against the doorframe. She had dark circles under her eyes, limp hair, and there were new wrinkles in her forehead, like she'd aged ten years in a week. "Do you want dinner?"

"Sorry, Mom. Sure. Are you okay?"

"Are *you* okay? It looks like I scared you."

"No, I was just..." I closed the browser. "Killing time."

Her eyes slid to my dresser, where my dad sat in his zip-tied bag. Her expression softened. "I haven't figured out where to put him either. Every place feels either too disrespectful or wildly inappropriate."

I slumped. "I'm doing everything wrong. I'm betraying him." I didn't even have to mention the funeral. That failure was obvious.

She leaned forward and stroked the bag of ashes. "I don't think there is a wrong way to grieve, honey. Come on. We're having fruit for dinner."

I frowned. "Fruit?"

"I threw out everything in the kitchen except for the fruit. It's a bit of a hodgepodge, but it'll work."

"*Everything?* The lasagnas and potpie from Mrs. Cleeves? What about Dad's Cheerios?" He'd loved his Cheerios. Suddenly, it seemed imperative they remained.

As she looked at me, I saw a glimpse of my fierce mother peeking through the sadness. "That garbage is what killed your father. Sugars, oils, processed foods. No more of it in this house. And I bought us a blood pressure cuff. We're going to measure ourselves every day. And we're exercising. I mean, until you go back to school. Then we'll call each other, keep each other accountable."

Back to school. I hadn't even thought of it. It had been nearly two weeks, and as far as UCF was concerned, I was AWOL. My professor's sympathetic emails were increasingly peppered with warnings about missed assignments. Gabby had stopped texting altogether after I'd told her not to come to the funeral, her soft heart finally beaten by my emotional walls. But I didn't feel guilty, because I had the Real Crime Network now. And we were dealing with Indira Babatunde's *life*. School and friendships were trivial compared to that. Gabby and I lived in two separate worlds now. She was still a carefree college student, but I'd been plunged into the cold world of life and death, where anything but the highest of stakes fell by the wayside.

There's no wrong way to grieve, I repeated, following my mom to the kitchen, where a bowl of diced strawberries, blueberries, and browning apples awaited us. I wasn't sure if I believed it.

12

—

IT TOOK ONLY THREE DAYS after Mistress suggested following the money to hit our biggest break in the Babatunde case. I was slouched on my bed, wearing an oversized T-shirt of my father's and a pair of his flannel pajamas. In a fit of grief, I'd torn through his closet and pressed my face into his clothes, longing for a hit of his familiar scent, and now I'd taken to wearing the most deeply scented clothes. I was listening to my one saved voicemail on repeat ("Hey, beautiful. It's your dad. Give me a call back"), when I heard the familiar ding.

I leapt up, bringing my dad's ashes with me. The bag was heavy and unwieldy, but I'd started taking it everywhere. If my mom thought it was strange, she never said. Then again, she was busy with her own strangeness, pulling out her old running gear and aerobics tapes and drawing up exercise schedules, which unfortunately included me.

On-screen, Goku and Citizen had returned triumphant.

LordGoku: You'll never guess what we found.

Minacaren: Good God, what?!

CitizenNight: Seriously. Steel yourselves. This case just started making sense.

HiltoftheSword: My pacemaker can't handle this suspense.

SleuthMistress: Did you find something in Indira's checking account? Credit cards?

LordGoku: No. Those were a complete wash. Nothing out of the ordinary. Actually, pretty depressing. Mina was right, Indira was a lowly government employee, not a secret high roller. She had a balance of $1,200 in her checking account and owed $800 on her credit card. I honestly don't know how she got by.

SeattleHawks: Um, welcome to middle America.

CitizenNight: Goku, you want to do the honors or should I?

LordGoku: So I was feeling bummed that Indira's finances didn't turn up anything. And when I'm bummed, I go into research hyper-drive. I combed back through her email inbox, seeing if I could spot something with fresh eyes. And I did. I'd missed it because it was in her Spam folder.

CitizenNight: Her SPAM FOLDER!

LordGoku: Dated three weeks ago, she got an email from Publishers Clearing House congratulating her on winning a $75k sweepstakes.

SeattleHawks: Oh please. I get bogus emails like that all the time.

Searcher24: Does Publishers Clearing House still exist?

Carolrichards68: You youths. Entering PCH sweepstakes used to be like playing the lotto, but it was free to enter with your little postcards. It was fun.

CitizenNight: It sounded fake to us too, which is why I called Publishers Clearing House and confirmed that Indira Babatunde did indeed win their "75,000 to Clear Your Debt" sweepstakes. A representative delivered the check to her two weeks ago.

GeorgeLightly: Did the rep say whether she'd cashed it?

CitizenNight: He wouldn't confirm.

GeorgeLightly: So our girl came into some money...

Minacaren: Which means she WAS a prime financial target. My bad, Mistress. You were right.

Searcher24: Wait, Goku said Indira only had $1,200 in her bank account.

SleuthMistress: And you checked all of her accounts, Goku? She didn't have any hidden accounts where she squirreled away the check?

LordGoku: I promise, I got it all.

Searcher24: So where's Indira's money?

GeorgeLightly: That, Searcher, is the exact right question.

13

—

INDIRA BABATUNDE'S CASE IS WHERE I cut my teeth, developed the habits I would bring to every subsequent investigation, including the one you're all salivating over. And yes, okay, maybe they weren't all good habits. I will confess I descended into what could be called a light situational madness over the next few days. I stayed mostly in my room, shutting all the blinds. Outside my windows, the Florida sunshine beamed full force; frogs croaked and palm trees swayed, tropical business as usual. But inside my walls, darkness and a near-monastic quiet intensified my focus.

I was learning how to be obsessed. Two obsessions in particular consumed me. One, of course, was the forum. We were waiting for news from the police, who'd gotten a warrant to search Publishers Clearing House's financial records. We couldn't force PCH to tell us whether Indira's check had been cashed, but they could, and it turned out the forum was right: the cops were all too happy to take our tips. In the meantime, we kept ourselves busy reaching out to her friends, neighbors, and colleagues, asking if anyone knew Indira had recently come into money. Either we had some good liars, or the people in Indira's life were uniformly clueless.

Emotionally, the screws tightened when a local news station went to the Sunset Groves Retirement Home, where Indira's mother lived, and interviewed her on live TV. The entire thread watched as the eighty-seven-year-old Rosa Lee Babatunde, hands shaking, voice frail, pleaded with someone to tell her what had happened to her baby girl. She was alone in the world without her daughter. I hugged my father's ashes and vowed to Rosa Lee that I would help find out who killed her daughter.

I gave it everything. Hours went by where I forgot to eat, or go to the bathroom, exchanging theories with the rest of the thread or fact-checking questions. We did deep dives into her neighbors' and colleagues' lives and even tried to guess passwords to Indira's Facebook account based on things we knew were important to her.

In those early days, I knew nothing about the other sleuths. They could've been any age, lived anywhere, in the middle of Siberia or right next door. And yet there was no group more vital to me than those spectral figures. I guess you could say I spent my time talking to ghosts: the ones in my computer and the one in the bag of ashes I carried at my side.

I assumed SeattleHawks lived in Seattle and was a man, given his choice of a football team as a username. His humor was the kind that guys will sometimes deploy when they're desperate for attention but also resentful of everyone for making them work for it. I guessed Mistress was a woman, and since she said she'd been around for a while, I pegged her as older, though how much I wasn't sure. Mina seemed like a younger woman, based on her language choices. Citizen and Goku had a natural leadership quality, and they were obviously talented sleuths, but they also behaved like schoolboys on occasion. I guessed them to be male and on the younger side. The only thing that confused me was this quote on Citizen's profile:

"is it sin

To rush into the secret house of death,

Ere death dare come to us?"

William Shakespeare, Antony and Cleopatra, *Act 4, Scene 15*

I didn't pretend to understand what the passage meant, but quoting deep cuts from the Bard did make Citizen seem a little older, not to mention pretentious.

And then there was Lightly, who I googled.

I did it out of sheer curiosity, not expecting to find much. Imagine my surprise when actual news articles popped up. It turned out George Lightly had retired early, at the age of fifty-two, from the Chicago Police Department following the kidnapping and murder of an eight-year-old girl named Juliana Rubles. The most incendiary headline was from the *Chicago Sun* and read, "CPD detective quits in protest of alleged department failure." The article described the police's inability to find Juliana in time to prevent her murder at the hands of a man named Christopher Pikeson. The picture showed a beautiful young Black girl in a pink-and-purple jumper beaming from a swing set. Pikeson's mug shot was of a sallow-faced white man who stared vacantly.

Lightly was quoted: "It is unconscionable that the CPD has unlimited time and resources to spend when white Chicagoans are in danger, but when a little Black girl goes missing, there's not a tenth of the willingness to spend money or time. We could've saved Juliana Rubles's life—we just needed people to care. I will live for the rest of my life with what I failed to do for her and her family, but I cannot spend one more day as part of an institution that treats people of color like second-class citizens." The article was dated six years ago. I wondered if Lightly had been drawn to the Real Crime Network because even though he'd quit being a cop, he couldn't quit trying to help people.

Besides the forum, my other obsession was the shrine I was building to my father. First, you should know that my dad was a child of the seventies. He saw *Star Wars* in the theater. His brothers and sisters called him "The Yoo-hoo King" because his favorite thing to do when he came home from night shifts slinging pancakes at the Waffle House was to sit with a pack of Yoo-hoo in front of the TV, watching space operas. He loved sci-fi—anything that allowed him to escape. He was a dreamer at his core.

And he passed that love on to me. Since I was little, I'd been his Girl Friday. And there was no series that captured his fascination quite like *Star Trek.* The man was the ultimate Trekkie. He loved every season; loved the characters' fair-handed intellectualism, the Starfleet's altruistic principles, the idea of establishing a democracy with species from far-flung galaxies. Maybe part of him had thought joining the navy would be like joining the Starfleet, sailing to places unknown, and that's why he'd run into that recruiter's office on his eighteenth birthday.

I watched every episode with him, but I preferred magic to sci-fi. I liked movies where people had mystical talents and old objects were imbued with power, rings forged eons ago in the lands of hobbits and magical relics from dying gods. So I knew what I was doing when I asked for the objects my dad had with him the moment he died. I collected the book he was reading—the first in the Wheel of Time series—which he still had in his hand when my mom found him, opened to page 245, as well as his reading glasses, still smudged with his fingerprints. I took the tie he wore to my high school graduation and the cards he'd saved from me over the years, along with a handful of childish Father's Day and birthday messages, printed his best emails, and arranged all of these relics into a circle on my dresser. In the center, I placed his ashes. I knew full well it was a shrine. That was the point. I was trying to make contact.

Right now, you're probably thinking I was more than a little mad if I was building shrines to my dead dad in my bedroom. You're thinking it's no wonder everything came to ruin. Worst of all, you're probably thinking The Person Who Shall Not Be Named was right about every-thing she wrote about me in her slanderous book. "Don't trust her far-ther than you can throw her," she wrote, which is ridiculous.

I have nothing to hide. If I did, I wouldn't offer you any of this, wouldn't rip out my own heart describing my father's death or how I faltered under the weight of it. I could take it to my grave. But this is a trust exercise. I'm trusting you with this knowledge, and I need you to trust me that I'm telling you about it for a reason.

14

—

ON FRIDAY, SEPTEMBER 8, WORD came back from the cops that Indira's $75,000 check from Publishers Clearing House had been cashed at an Indiantown branch of Regions Bank, the day before her remains were pulled out of the lake. The forum exploded.

> **Minacaren:** INDIRA cashed the check? Why cash a check that large rather than deposit it? And why not use her local Chase, where she had an account—why a random Regions?
> **SleuthMistress:** It gets weirder. The cops slipped me the surveillance footage from the bank. Attached here. Take a look.

The cops must've liked Mistress, giving her information like that. I opened the attachment and saw a grainy image of a woman Indira's height and build, with Indira's dark skin and hair slicked back into a ponytail. She wore sensible Ann Taylor–esque slacks and a baseball cap. There were two images: one of her walking in the front door and one of her inside at the teller's counter. Both times she was in profile, so it was hard to make her out, but something seemed off about her energy compared to what I'd seen in the pictures of Indira. It was a tenuous thing to notice, but I voiced it nonetheless.

> **Searcher24:** My gut says this isn't her...
>
> **SleuthMistress:** I'm with you. But whoever this is used Indira's driver's license to cash the $75k check. Her license was missing from the wallet they recovered from her house.
>
> **CitizenNight:** Seriously? Aren't there protections against cashing that much money?
>
> **SleuthMistress:** Not at Regions. They're one of the few banks that don't put holds on large-dollar checks, even for non-members.
>
> **GeorgeLightly:** Wow. Our perp did her research.
>
> **Minacaren:** If we don't think the woman in the surveillance photos is Indira, are we looking at Indira's killer? That would fit with the hack job. She's small. Doesn't look that strong.
>
> **GeorgeLightly:** Maybe she's the killer, or maybe she's just in on it. Mistress, have the cops narrowed down a murder weapon yet, or do we need to start chopping?

I looked at my dad. "Chopping?"

> **CitizenNight:** Beat you to it. Mistress told me the cops were still examining the saw marks in Indira's bones. They know it wasn't a serrated blade, and we can rule out any blades that lack the heft to cut through bone.
>
> **SeattleHawks:** What about a sword?
>
> **CitizenNight:** Unlikely, but I tested for it. And before anyone asks, no, I did not use my ceremonial navy saber. That's mounted on my wall. So no need to get cheeky.

Citizen was in the navy? I felt a sudden rush of affection for him as I typed.

> **Searcher24:** I'm sorry if this is common knowledge, but how do you test weapons?
>
> **LordGoku:** All it requires is disposable income, a lot of time, and a lack of friends to convince you to do more normal activities. Oh, and the ability to handle gore.
>
> **GeorgeLightly:** Careful, Goku, you're going to make Citizen sound like a weirdo;)
>
> **CitizenNight:** Did Lightly just WINK at us? That's a first. Anyway, you're all welcome for doing what no one else wants to do.
>
> **Searcher24:** So you test on...cadavers?
>
> **CitizenNight:** NO! I buy whole pigs from the butcher. Pig and human bodies are very similar. I tested different blades on the pig, then compared them to the marks left in Indira's bones.

"That's disgusting," I said to my dad. "I could've gone my whole life not knowing that."

> **CitizenNight:** I think whoever dismembered Indira did it with a Michigan-style axe. They're mostly used for felling trees. Has this curved shape to the blade that matches the marks on Indira.
>
> **GeorgeLightly:** Where can you buy that sort of axe?
>
> **CitizenNight:** Home Depot. Lowe's. Sadly, most places.
>
> **GeorgeLightly:** You want to tell the cops?
>
> **CitizenNight:** I'll let Mistress do it. They like her best.
>
> **SleuthMistress:** It's because I give grandma vibes.
>
> **CitizenNight:** Work it, Mistress.

Searcher24: Okay, let's assume everything we've guessed so far is right. Someone—maybe this woman from the bank footage—killed Indira with a Michigan axe in order to steal her $75k. But how did she even know about the check?

Minacaren: Maybe she works at Publishers Clearing House. Saw Indira lived alone and figured no one would miss her if she killed her and stole her winnings.

SeattleHawks: Dark. I like it.

GeorgeLightly: I'm not ruling that out, Mina, but in my experience Occam's razor usually applies: the simplest answer is typically the right one. I'm not convinced people in Indira's circle weren't aware she'd won the money. It's easy to lie.

LordGoku: Yeah, I mean, how do you win something like that and NOT tell everyone?

Searcher24: Indira was around my parents' age. When they had news, they always ran to Facebook.

SleuthMistress: Putting aside how old that makes me feel, have we made any progress trying to hack Indira's FB password?

CitizenNight: I know we've focused on her favorite things like knitting and her mom's birthday, but Indira strikes me as a pragmatic woman. She probably used a random password generator.

Searcher24: What about something with "sunflower" in it? When I drove past her condo, her welcome mat and wind chime both had sunflowers.

LordGoku: We need a number, too, per FB requirements. But I'll try some combos. Citizen, if you're right, we're SOL.

One hour later, a notification dinged.

LordGoku: Well, well, well, everyone congratulate Searcher on being a genius. Indira's PW was "Sunflower1977." Sunflower + her birth year.

Minacaren: Way to go, Searcher!!

Alone in my bedroom, I felt heat bloom across my face.

Searcher24: Lucky guess:) But I'm happy it worked. Find anything?

LordGoku: Can you all help me dig? Username is her Gmail.

Feeling a voyeuristic rush, I toggled to Facebook and entered Indira's credentials. I felt like a spy, scrolling through her posts. She'd been fairly active. Unfortunately, I saw nothing that pointed to her sweepstakes win—she hadn't posted any triumphant messages or joined any "PCH Sweepstakes Winner" groups. Then I thought to check her messages.

She had a ton. I was careful not to click on the unread ones; most of what I could see from the preview text were messages of condolence she would never read. I scrolled to the ones dated before her disappearance, the messages Indira had read and responded to. Immediately, a thread caught my eye between Indira and a man named Greg Brownville. The last thing he'd written was "We should go to lunch to celebrate your amazing news!" She'd read it but hadn't responded. I checked the date on his message: the day after Indira was notified she'd won.

I moved at hyperspeed back to the forum, but I was still too late.

LordGoku: Greg Brownville, we have a winner!

Minacaren: Anyone see that message from Greg Brownville? Sounds like he knew!

GeorgeLightly: Greg Brownville indeed. Dates match up.

Searcher24: Well, that was anticlimactic. I thought I was going to get to announce it. Do we know who Greg is?

CitizenNight: Indira's boss. The executive director of the arboretum. Remember, he was on the list of ppl the cops interviewed?

Seattle2: Oh, shit. Plot twist.

GeorgeLightly: I just looked at the list. Greg told the cops he didn't know anything about the sweepstakes.

Searcher24: So either Indira had some other "amazing" news or we have a liar.

CitizenNight: I think it's safe to say we're all on Team Greg. Let's dig up everything we can on this guy.

From the kitchen, I heard the sudden sounds of my mother's weeping, sharp and guttural. I froze halfway out of my chair, unsure whether to go comfort her or let her be. The truth was, her grief made me feel strangely blank, as if her feelings on top of mine were simply too much, and my mind rebelled. For a long time, I stayed crouched. But finally, as her sobs softened, I lowered back down into my chair, opened Indira's Facebook, and returned to digging.

15

—

TWO DAYS LATER, I WAS up to my elbows in photos of Greg Brownville's forty-first birthday party when my mom opened the door and marched into my room. "I got an email from one of your professors. He's worried you're going to fail his class."

"I know," I said, still scanning Greg's Facebook album. It was titled "Getting Frisky for 41." The pictures were from a casino in Tampa. A youthful-looking Greg and his friends double-fisted cocktails and grinned around cigars clamped in their teeth. The women wore short, glittery dresses and the men those Tommy Bahama–style shirts that pass for formalwear in Florida.

"Well," said my mom, walking up behind me, "he says if you don't send in your make-up essays soon, you won't finish the semester."

"It's been hard to think about going back." I clicked through images—looking for what, exactly, I wasn't sure. Some evidence that Greg was capable of cold-blooded murder? I was deep in his profile—he had a lot of photos, spanning years, a devoted Facebook poster—and more than anything, I felt like I was getting to know him. It was strange, the intimacy created by searching through someone's records and social profiles, trying to familiarize yourself with every detail about them. It was like that with Indira too, this uncanny sense that I knew her from poring through her life, learning her speech patterns by reading her posts, even coming to know the people around her, the neighbor who sent her plant pictures, the colleague who religiously marked every birthday. It was my first taste of the phenomenon sleuths call "victim attachment," what others call a parasocial relationship with the dead. (And yes, I know The Person Who Shall Not Be Named calls it a "gruesome obsession," but I disagree.)

To me, Greg seemed like a party boy who'd never grown up, exchanging University of Florida frat houses for casinos and cigar boats. There was no evidence of a love of outdoors, and nothing about the arboretum on his profile.

"I understand it's hard." My mom rested a hand on my shoulder. "I'm in the same boat. I've taken all the bereavement days I'm allowed, and now I have to go back to work. I think you should start getting ready to head back to school." She squinted, noticing my screen. "Who are those people?"

"No one. Just a project I'm working on."

"So many casino photos. You know, I knew someone with a gambling addiction once. My old colleague Mike, remember him?"

I shook my head no.

"Ruined his marriage." She squeezed my shoulder. "Let's talk more about school tonight, okay? I'm going on a run. Want to come?"

"No, thanks," I murmured. Could Greg have a gambling addiction? There *were* an awful lot of photos of him in casinos or with his buddies, playing poker. I kept clicking as my mom shut the door. Maybe he was in debt and desperate for cash, and Indira's sudden windfall had seemed like the perfect opportunity.

I clicked to a new photo and froze. Greg sat at a roulette table next to a petite woman with dark skin and wide, expressive eyes. She was dolled up in a way Indira never would be, but otherwise they could've passed for sisters. I hovered over the photo, and a tag popped up: Sheila Watson. Her profile was restricted, so she and Indira hadn't been friends. Heart thumping, I jumped back into the forum.

> **Searcher24:** Hey guys. I'm attaching a photo from Greg's Facebook account. It was taken years ago, so maybe it's nothing, but does anything jump out at you?

It was the middle of a work day, which I'd learned meant traffic in the forum slowed but didn't stop. Mistress was the first to respond.

> **SleuthMistress:** That woman on Greg's left is a dead ringer for Indira.
> **Searcher24:** That's what I thought. Anyone else?

I nearly rocked out of my chair waiting for someone to weigh in.

> **CitizenNight:** Whoa. Definitely. Could this be the woman who masqueraded as Indira to cash her check?
> **LordGoku:** What's her name? I'll go fishing.
> **Searcher24:** Sheila Watson. But her profile's set to private.
> **LordGoku:** Lol no problem

Who *was* Goku?

> **GeorgeLightly:** Searcher, you're turning into our ringer. What a catch.

In the privacy of my room, I glowed. Maybe I should've confessed to them that while the majority of the sleuths on the thread probably had families and jobs, I had nothing but this. Instead, I remained quiet and soaked up the compliment.

> **GeorgeLightly:** Goku, I think we should give Sheila's name to the police. It's been close to two weeks since they found Indira. I worry they're going to start to deprioritize her case.
>
> **Searcher24:** They do that?
>
> **GeorgeLightly:** You have no idea. Being a cop's as political as any-thing else.
>
> **CitizenNight:** I'm cool with that, Lightly. Mistress, you want to do the honors?
>
> **SleuthMistress:** Official cop whisperer reporting for duty. I'll let them know they need to look at this Sheila Watson character.

Four days later, we received the news that the cops, using our tip, had combed through the convenience store footage and matched one of the cars and license plates—a white 2003 4Runner—to a car owned by Sheila Watson. We had her on tape driving to Indira's house on Monday evening at 8:35 p.m. She drove away only fifteen minutes later at 8:50 p.m.

We had a lead.

16
—

TO UNDERSTAND WHY I DID what I did next, you have to appreciate that I'd never tasted victory like this before, and I was hungry for more. Two days after we tipped the cops to Sheila Watson, I was sitting cross-legged on my bed, scrolling through my father's Facebook profile, when Mistress broke the news: the cops had searched both Greg's and Sheila's houses and cars and found no incriminating evidence. Each of them had recently had their cars detailed, which seemed suspicious enough for me, but Lightly burst my bubble.

> **GeorgeLightly:** Unfortunately, you can't arrest someone for getting their car washed. No matter how suspicious the timing.
>
> **SeattleHawks:** This is bullshit. The cops aren't looking hard enough.
>
> **CitizenNight:** Mistress, the cops found ZERO clues pointing to Indira—no hair or fingerprints? No remnants of blood in their cars or houses? No Michigan axes?
>
> **SleuthMistress:** Not even any Hefty trash bags, or any record that either of them purchased supplies in the last few months. Sorry, kids. I know this one hurts. We felt close.

LordGoku: All those pictures on Sheila's Instagram of her posing with Louis Vuitton bags, praying to "come into some money, hunny." Could've sworn she was our girl.

CitizenNight: Do we want to take a few days off and then regroup?

SeattleHawks: Did you guys hear about the Katie Cassidy murder in Nevada? They found her strangled body on a running trail. It's starting to get buzz.

Minacaren: Ooooh I DID hear about her! I bet she has a Network thread already. Lemme check.

It was like someone had walked up to me and told me my own father's death didn't matter anymore. The betrayal was immediate.

Searcher24: What about Indira? We can't abandon her.

GeorgeLightly: We won't. But Citizen's right that we may need to take a few days to think fresh.

Searcher24: But what about all the other places Greg and Sheila could be hiding things? I mean, Greg works at an arboretum! I'm sure there are axes there.

SeattleHawks: There's no way he'd be dumb enough to keep the murder weapon at his WORKPLACE. Nah, whatever it is, it's at the bottom of the lake.

LordGoku: As much as I'm loath to agree with Seattle, I suspect he's right.

But I couldn't shake the idea. Axes and trash bags—that was lawn equipment. And what was an arboretum if not a big, fancy lawn? Hadn't Lightly said to apply Occam's razor—the simplest solution was usually correct? It made an awful kind of sense to use work equipment to kill Indira and then hide it in plain sight. It would've been convenient for

Greg. And Greg, with his insipid party pics, gave me the impression of a man who valued convenience.

I know the news claimed I did what I did next because I had a savant's hunch. But the truth is, I did it because I was worried the other sleuths were going to give Indira up. And then a quiet woman who'd been overlooked in life—a woman very much like my own father—was going to be overlooked in death. I couldn't let that happen to either of them.

So the next morning, I took my mom's car and drove back to Indiantown. But this time, not to Indira's condo—to the arboretum.

I parked and took a deep breath. The office was a small, nondescript building, but it was wreathed in vines and surrounded by a well-managed forest of tropical trees. Birds and butterflies fluttered in the distance. Inside, I found a strange woman sitting at the front desk, where Indira should've been.

I was the only person in the lobby, but the woman didn't greet me until I'd been standing there for a few awkward minutes. Finally, she pushed her wayward hair out of her face. "Can I help you?"

Indira would've been much more welcoming. "Is Greg Brownville in today?"

The woman blinked. "May I ask what business you have with Greg?"

The lie flowed smoothly. "He's hiring for a part-time position and wanted to interview me in person."

Her entire demeanor changed. "I hope he's hiring to take over this desk. I've got enough on my plate, what with being short-staffed and the budget cuts—" Abruptly, she stopped, maybe realizing she wasn't exactly selling me on the job. "Stay here. I'll go get him."

The moment she disappeared, I riffled through the papers on her desk. They were soil order forms, nothing interesting. When she emerged again, leading Greg, the bottom fell out of my stomach.

17

—

HERE'S THE THING ABOUT MORTALITY: the human brain isn't designed to process it. Think about it. You spend your whole life in active subliminal repression of the fact that one day you will cease to exist. You have to forget this fact in order to get up and eat breakfast and work your menial job and pay the bills. Otherwise, you'd be a sobbing, terrified ball on the floor. The Real Crime Network felt liberating because they trafficked in the truth that death comes for all and, for some of us, in devastating ways.

But until that moment, standing in front of Greg, I hadn't realized how much security there was in confronting hard truths as a faceless person on the internet. I'd felt bold speculating about Greg's motives, imagining the effort required to dismember Indira's body, sneaking into her Facebook profile to spy on him. When you're a nobody hiding behind a screen, you can act without consequences. But I'd emerged. Taken my real body, and put it in a potential murderer's path.

While I'd noticed his height in pictures, in person Greg was strikingly tall, a solid man lumbering over me in khaki slacks and a white button-up. He watched me warily. Something Facebook hadn't conveyed was the calculating intelligence in his eyes.

"Elizabeth says you're here to see me?" His voice was deeper than I'd imagined.

"That's right. About the job opening," I stammered.

He smiled apologetically, but his eyes narrowed. "I'm sorry. I don't remember talking to anyone about an opening. What was your name?"

How dumb was I? I'd wanted so badly to see Greg to get a read, but now I didn't know what to do next. "Are you sure?" I laughed nervously. "We talked via email a little while ago? My name's...Jenny...uh, Smith. Maybe you've been busy?"

He only stared. It was the wrong thing to say. Of course he'd been busy—getting interrogated by the cops thanks to our tip. The air filled with tension.

"Well, we definitely need the help," Elizabeth piped in, shooting Greg a hopeful look. She could probably feel her chances of getting off front-desk duty slipping away.

But Greg was too busy sizing me up. "Are you sure it was the Indiantown arboretum?"

I knew a lifeline when I heard one. "Oh!" I slapped a hand to my forehead. "This is the *Indiantown* arboretum? I meant to go to the *Fort Pierce* arboretum. I'm so sorry to waste your time. So much for attention to detail, right?"

Elizabeth's face fell, but Greg's remained a mask. "Glad we sorted that out." He pointed to the door. "Fort Pierce is about a half hour's drive if you want to get going."

"Oh, you know what?" I pushed my hair out of my face. "Since I'm here, I might as well look around."

Elizabeth grudgingly sold me a ticket, which I paid for in cash. Greg didn't move, his eyes following me through the doors that led out into the beautiful, sun-dappled grounds. I was too afraid to look over my shoulder until I followed the Whispering Willow path around a bend.

Only then did I check to make sure I was out of Greg's line of sight, and I released my breath.

Seeing him had convinced me he'd killed Indira. I can't explain why I was so certain, only that the sensitivity that had plagued me my whole life was firing on overdrive, shouting that Greg was a bad man with secrets.

The darkness emanating from the office was a stark contrast to the mellow, welcoming sunshine of the grounds. As I walked, trying to calm my heart rate, I passed butterfly gardens, ponds where birds shook water out of their feathers, and a patch of tall sunflowers. I could've sworn I felt Indira's presence. That she's the one who guided me around the corner to the shed.

It was a large shed, painted pristine white, with a mural of jewel-toned hummingbirds along the side. As I watched, a man holding a shovel unlocked it and disappeared inside.

I crouched behind a nearby tree and waited for ten minutes until the man emerged again, wearing waders. When he was far enough way, I said a small prayer and dashed forward, catching the door right before it closed. My heart beat so furiously I could almost hear it.

Inside smelled like rich soil and the grassy sweetness of growing things. The shed was relatively well organized—pots, trowels, big bags of earth, hummingbird feed, old lengths of hoses coiled like striped snakes. Trash bags of every size and color—small, white compost bags; large, clear recycling bags; huge black Heftys with blue closures. The Lawn & Leaf line.

Then my eyes fell on the axes.

There were five of them, different shapes and sizes, hanging neatly on the farthest wall. Despite having googled "Michigan axe" after Citizen's gross home test, I couldn't have told you what one looked like. That's not what drew my eyes to the axe in the center.

It was the fact that it was remarkably clean. Not a speck of dirt, while the handles of the other axes were smudged brown from dirty hands, their blades spotted with bits of plant detritus. Either this axe was brand-new, or it had just been cleaned.

Spotlessly, like Greg's and Sheila's cars.

I shoved back and ran to the door, then power-walked back through the office, past Elizabeth at the front desk, who gave a startled yip at my appearance. It wasn't until I'd lit out of the parking lot and sped far enough down the road that I pulled over and opened my phone to the Network, typing with shaking hands.

> **Searcher24:** Guys. I went to the arboretum and found a shed with Hefty bags and a large axe that had just been cleaned. I think it's the murder weapon.

With news that incendiary, it didn't take long to get a response.

> **SleuthMistress:** WHAT DO YOU MEAN YOU WENT TO THE ARBORETUM?!
>
> **LordGoku:** Holy shit, Searcher, you okay? You didn't run into Greg, did you?
>
> **Minacaren:** Are you nuts?! Why would you go there? That's not safe!!!
>
> **Searcher24:** I did run into Greg, but only because I asked for him. He gave me the creeps. You know when you can tell a person's hiding something?
>
> **SleuthMistress:** YOU ASKED FOR GREG?! WHAT WERE YOU THINKING?
>
> **SeattleHawks:** Are you trying to end up in pieces in a lake?
>
> **CitizenNight:** I admire your balls, Searcher, I really do, but what if

you made Greg suspicious and he's following you? Where are you right now?

I glanced in my rearview mirror. My heart leapt into my throat as a car sped toward me, but it kept going. I sank deeper into my seat.

Searcher24: I'm on the side of the road. I know it was dangerous, but I think I found the *murder weapon* in the shed. What do I do? Go back to steal it?

GeorgeLightly: For God's sake, NO! That would make the evidence inadmissible, not to mention it's wildly dangerous. I need you to drive home immediately. Keep your eyes on the road. If you think you're being followed, call 911. Message us once you're home and you've locked your doors. In the meantime, we'll call the tip in to OPD.

SeattleHawks: Searcher, you're crazier than I am. Godspeed, you animal.

Feeling stupid for not grasping the magnitude of the risk I'd taken, I did exactly as Lightly had instructed, making record time back to my house. I startled my mom by bursting through the front door and locking every door behind me.

By the time I reentered the forum to tell them I was safe, Mistress had called in the tip.

SleuthMistress: Not to burst your bubble, Searcher, but they didn't seem particularly excited to hear the arboretum has a clean axe and the right kind of trash bags.

I deflated, despite the heavy dose of adrenaline still coursing through me.

Searcher24: Was I stupid to think I'd found something?

GeorgeLightly: You're not stupid, Searcher, but you were reckless. Promise you won't do anything like this again.

Yes, I know—the *irony*, given what he and I would become famous for.

Searcher24: I'm sorry. I just felt so helpless. I wanted to do something.

Minacaren: We get it, kid. Trust us. Why do you think we're here?

It struck me then, for the first time, that instead of a place where stoic, highly efficient puzzle solvers trafficked in the truth of death, maybe the Network was a place for hopeless, helpless people to raise their tiny swords against the sky. Maybe we were quixotic knights, and these threads were a land of virtual windmills. A place for the desperate to feel like they were doing something noble.

I fell asleep that night without dinner, allowing myself to sink into a dreamless state. It's as if without the possibility of changing something—for Indira or my dad—not even nightmares were worth the effort. I can't tell you when I woke up, because the next few days passed so hopelessly that I don't remember them. Maybe I slept for a week.

People say it gets darkest before dawn. Mostly I think that's bullshit, but in this case, it was true. Because on Monday, October 2, almost five weeks after Indira Babatunde's mutilated remains were pulled out of Lake Okeechobee, Greg Brownville and Sheila Watson were arrested and charged with her kidnapping and murder. We found out, of all people, from Nina Grace.

18

—

IT WAS EARLY EVENING WHEN the Network thread started pinging.

Minacaren: Wtf!!! Is anyone watching CrimeFlash right now?

Searcher24: What's CrimeFlash?

Minacaren: It's Nina Grace's show! How do you not know—nvmd, she's talking about Indira!! Greg and Sheila just got arrested!

LordGoku: WHAT? Why didn't we hear about this first? @SleuthMistress, you there?

GeorgeLightly: Maybe OPD didn't want to spook Greg and Sheila by leaking the news. High probability they're flight risks.

I shot out of bed and ran to the living room.

Searcher24: What channel?

Minacaren: Discovery.

I turned to *CrimeFlash,* where Nina Grace's brusque southern twang narrated a video of four blue-uniformed OPD officers leading Greg

Brownville out of his house in handcuffs. The headline at the bottom read "Co-conspirators arrested in gruesome murder of FL woman for sweepstakes prize."

"What's this?" My mom came up behind me, tossing a kitchen towel over her shoulder.

"Shh," I insisted.

"Can you believe the nerve of these people?" drawled Nina. "We have Greg Brownville and Sheila Watson, two fortysomething lowlifes in Indiantown, Florida, who today confessed to a plan that, I've got to say, brings a whole new meaning to the word 'diabolical.'"

Greg was dressed in his executive director uniform—khakis and a button-down—and he kept his head down, expression blank. The video shifted to Sheila as she was perp-walked toward a Dodge Charger. She was trying to twist in her cuffs to talk to the cop pushing her. When she spotted the news camera, she started thrashing and yelling.

"According to Brownville's confession, he found out one of his employees at the Indiantown arboretum won a seventy-five-thousand-dollar Publishers Clearing House sweepstakes. Apparently, this woman, Indira Babatunde—"

Nina butchered Indira's last name. I winced.

"—had the good sense to keep her winning ticket to herself, probably because she could sense sharks in the water."

I could hear Lightly in my ear: *Never make assumptions.*

"But she made one fatal mistake," said Nina, almost viciously, as a picture of Indira appeared on-screen. It was from her Facebook profile, a nice close-up of Indira with a genuine smile. After all the time I'd spent studying her, seeing her on TV felt like seeing a family member suddenly famous.

"Indira let it slip to her boss, Greg, that she'd won. And little did she know that Greg was tens of thousands of dollars in debt due to an out-of-control gambling problem."

Now a photo of Greg in a casino materialized on-screen.

"Hey," my mom said. "Weren't you looking at that picture the other day?"

"I was. You're actually the one who made me realize his motive."

"Oh, that's nice...wait, *what*?"

"Greg hatched a devious plan with his on-again, off-again girlfriend Sheila," Nina Grace intoned. "He offered a cut of the winnings if she would help him get rid of Indira and access her money. You may be wondering: Why bother roping in Sheila at all? Well, Greg needed someone to pose as Indira to cash her sweepstakes check at the bank, which is exactly what they did."

"I *knew it*," I murmured.

"I'm sorry, what's your relationship to this man?" my mom demanded.

"I found his murder weapon."

"His *what? What?*"

"It's okay, Mom. I locked all the doors. And Greg's right there on-screen, getting arrested."

"And get this, *CrimeFlashers*." The program jumped back to Nina. With her coiffed hair and too-bright suit, she looked like a caricature of a lawyer. "Greg admitted that Sheila drove to Indira's house on the night of Monday, August twenty-eighth, while he hid in the back seat of her car. Once there, they subdued Indira, stuffed her in the trunk, and drove her back to the Indiantown arboretum. They proceeded to strike Ms. Babatunde on the head with the blunt side of an axe, delivering what they believed was a killing blow. Now, any particularly sensitive viewers may want to mute what I'm about to say next. These two geniuses, failing to kill Ms. Babatunde, then proceeded to chop up the poor woman and stuff her into a trash bag. Yes, people, they dismembered a living woman and put her in a bag. They then used a small motorboat owned by the arboretum to travel across channels that led to nearby Lake Okeechobee, where they disposed of Ms. Babatunde's remains."

It had happened just like we thought. Well, there were a few pieces we hadn't imagined yet, like the motorboat. But it had been a puzzle, and we'd solved it. I felt powerful, in direct contrast to the powerlessness of only minutes before.

"It's a good thing Florida isn't afraid to use the death penalty," Nina concluded with a smack of her lips. "Because I think these two greedy scumbags are excellent contenders."

Mom had had enough. "Jane, please explain what's going on before I have a nervous breakdown."

For the first time, I told her everything about the Real Crime Network and Indira's case, fudging only the details about putting myself in danger. She was dumbfounded—all this time she'd thought I'd been sleeping and binging Netflix in a depressive haze. Together, we watched the local news that night, both of us crying as Indira's mom was interviewed.

"I can't tell you how grateful I am to know what happened to my little girl," Rosa Lee said shakily. She sat in a wheelchair, looking even frailer than she had the first time she'd been interviewed. Her voice strained with emotion. "I can go to my grave knowing there will be justice. It's a bittersweet closure, to know."

The most extraordinary melancholy filled me. I'd seen my father in that visitation room, felt his cold flesh, knew what happened to him. But unlike Indira's mother, I felt no sense of closure. It occurred to me: that intimacy I'd created with Indira, tracing the contours of her life—I could do that with him. I could investigate my own father. Comb through every text, email, letter, photo, forum. Contact his old friends. Learn everything there was to know about him, until a picture of the real him emerged, beyond the man who'd been my dad. Maybe then I would crack the mystery of why he didn't fight to live.

My insides twisted with longing. I muted the news and turned to my mother. "I don't want to go back."

She frowned. "Where?"

"I'll get a job, I swear. Help pay the bills. Whatever you need. But I don't want to go back to college."

She was silent. We studied each other, trying to understand the right thing to do in this brave new world where old priorities had shifted. Finally, the skepticism and worry on my mother's face turned into sadness, understanding, and—I think—relief.

"It would be nice to have you here with me," she said softly. "But only if you're sure."

It was settled: I would withdraw from UCF and remain at home. It turned out to be yet another fateful decision. If I'd gone back to college, classes, and parties, would I have eventually forgotten about the Network? Lived a normal, quiet life, the kind that left no legacy, good or bad? It's hard to say.

When I climbed into bed that night and pulled up the forum, the Indira thread was popping. Celebratory GIFs from Seattle, rants from Mistress about the police not tipping her off that the arrests were imminent, mollifying messages from Lightly, back-patting from Goku about the fact that we'd been right about Sheila. After I'd scrolled the whole thread, I noticed something new: a little red flag in my inbox. I had a private message.

It was from Citizen.

CitizenNight: Hey Searcher. You hooked yet? If so, I have a proposition. Mistress, Lightly, Goku, and I have our own private chat. It's where we escape the rookies and kooks to really hash out evidence and theories. We think you have potential. Interested? Fair warning: we take this seriously. It's not for the faint of heart. Prepare yourself to boldly go where no man has gone before.

He'd quoted *Star Trek*. Right there at the end—part of the speech Captain Kirk gave at the beginning of every episode. I'd heard the refrain so many times I could've repeated it in my sleep.

My father was speaking to me.

I can't describe the thrill I felt. I'd begged the universe for a path, and a door had materialized. If my father's death was the beginning of my story, then this invitation was my call to adventure. I didn't even suspect what we all know now—that Indira Babatunde's case would be the one that put us on the map, binding the five of us together, for better and for worse. All I knew was that it felt like fate.

So, look. As important as she was, as fundamental to my hero's journey,* I know you didn't come to read about Indira. Remember, I used to be you. I know you came for the Delphine girls. For *him*. For me and my stubborn secrets.

You came for the next part.

---

* Lest you think I'm calling *myself* a hero—Joseph Campbell, anyone?

19

—

TWO MONTHS AFTER I ACCEPTED Citizen's invitation to join his private group of sleuths, I woke to this email from a *Newsline* producer in my inbox:

Dear Janeway,

Apologies for barging into your life—especially if you were trying to remain anonymous. My name is Randall Mitchell, and I'm a producer for *Newsline* at NBC. We're working on an episode about true crime, with the angle of ordinary citizens who've helped solve major crimes in lieu of cops. There's been a lot of coverage of so-called armchair sleuths and the things they've gotten wrong, how they've inspired doxing, how they're ghouls rabid for voyeuristic details at the expense of victims and families (sorry to get graphic, but you get my point).

We think there's a more balanced story to be told about the ways the true-crime community has helped victims. Indira Babatunde's case came to our attention. Having read through her thread on TheRealCrimeNetwork.com, we know you played a major role in it. Would you be willing to be interviewed? We'd love to hear your perspective.

    Thanks in advance,

    Randall

I flew immediately to our private chat. It wasn't part of the Network—at Goku's insistence, we used the Signal app, which he claimed was encrypted and more secure. Two months in, I'd grown used to chatting with the Network in one tab and with our small group via Signal in another. It was fun, honestly—like being part of the popular clique and talking about everyone else through passed notes. Okay—truthfully, I'd never had that experience before. I was new to feeling wanted.

Searcher24: Check out this email I just got from a producer at Newsline (attached). Anyone else?

We used the same usernames in Signal to keep a smooth flow, though I'd since learned my friends' real names.

SleuthMistress: I got the same email.
GeorgeLightly: Me too.
LordGoku: Me three.
Searcher24: Do we think it's legit?
CitizenNight: Goku checked Randall's background and he's real.
  What do we think, fam? Want to talk to Newsline?

Citizen often referred to us as a family. And as corny as it might sound, we felt like one. But it wasn't that way in the beginning.

TWO MONTHS EARLIER (OCTOBER 4, 2023)—SIGNAL

CitizenNight: Hey, everyone. Say hello to our newest member (trial basis): Jane Sharp, of 235 Hibiscus Dr, Fort Pierce, FL!

I didn't realize they knew my real name and address or that I was invited on a trial basis. Right off the bat, it was an ambush.

Searcher24: Uh, hi. We go by real names in here?
LordGoku: No.
Searcher24: ...okay. Well, happy to be here, I think.
SleuthMistress: Hi, Searcher. We're happy to have you.
GeorgeLightly: Hi, Searcher. Don't let Citizen and Goku scare you. They insist on these initiation theatrics. Blame the navy. Citizen got hazed, so now he insists on doing it here.
CitizenNight: It's an important ritual. How else do you build trust?
SleuthMistress: By being trustworthy?
CitizenNight: Boring. Jane, tell us about yourself.
Searcher24: What do you want to know?
LordGoku: Everything. Who are you? What do you do? What brought you to the Network?

Honestly, I'd come to the Network to escape myself. To become a tabula rasa. Telling them about myself felt counterintuitive.

Searcher24: My full name is Janeway Lynn Sharp.

I didn't get any further before Goku broke in.

LordGoku: And here I thought it was cool you were a Jane, like Jane Doe.

SleuthMistress: Where's Janeway from? I've never heard it before.

LordGoku: Star Trek! Come on, Mistress, you should know that. You're old enough (lol).

SleuthMistress: This granny says FU.

Searcher24: My dad was a big Trekkie. He loved Captain Janeway— she was the captain of the USS Voyager for seven seasons. The first woman. He thought she'd be a good role model.

CitizenNight: Your dad sounds cool. What's he like?

I stared at the screen. I didn't want to write that he was dead. But I also didn't want to lie. In the end, I chose the painful truth, and it was a good thing I did.

Searcher24: He passed away in August, actually. I'm still getting used to it. He was wonderful. (Is wonderful? Using the past tense is still weird.) Funny, kind, smart. He was retired from the navy, working on the civilian side.

CitizenNight: Hear, hear. Good man!

SleuthMistress: I'm sorry for your loss, dear Jane. My husband passed away five years ago. I know what it feels like to live with a hole in your heart.

GeorgeLightly: I lost someone close to me as well—an adopted daughter. We're here for you.

I felt comforted. They understood.

Searcher24: Thank you. I really appreciate it.

LordGoku: Tell us more about you.

Searcher24: I'm pretty average. Average height, average build. White, brown hair, brown eyes. I was a senior at UCF, but I just decided to drop out. I'm going to try to get my old job at Starbucks back to help pay bills. My dad had life insurance, but turns out it takes forever to arrive. Don't get me started on the paperwork.

SleuthMistress: Death is paperwork. It's one of life's nasty little secrets.

LordGoku: A barista in the group. NOICE.

CitizenNight: You forgot to mention you look like a young Winona Ryder circa Beetlejuice.

LordGoku: No way. Young Winona Ryder circa Heathers. Normal with a hint of the subversive.

A chill ran up my spine. I looked around my room, then out the window. I'd recently started opening the blinds again, enjoying the October sunshine. Did they have cameras on me? Were they watching me right now?

CitizenNight: We're looking at your Instagram profile. I particularly like the photo of you dressed as Eleven from Stranger Things a couple Halloweens ago. You can pull off bald.

I relaxed. Of course they weren't watching me. That was crazy. My Instagram was set to Private, but I should've known that wouldn't keep them out.

LordGoku: Quick test: what was the last thing you bought with your debit card ending in 1546?

Now my stomach really dropped.

Searcher24: Wtf? Really, Goku?

SleuthMistress: Come on, boys. Can we skip this part?

LordGoku: Was it $53.46 at the Sunoco on the corner of Highway 1 and Bayview Ave?

Searcher24: I'm guessing you know it was. Is this supposed to be a threat? You know everything about me? I'm confused. I thought you wanted me here.

CitizenNight: We do. But we have to be able to trust each other. It's just a little demonstration.

Searcher24: Did you know about my dad before you asked?

CitizenNight: Daniel Ronald Sharp, deceased August 31 at First Presbyterian Memorial Hospital. Died of myocardial infarction, aka a heart attack. Retired from the navy after twenty years of service, briefly unemployed, then hired as a project manager at NavAir Global. Frequent contributor to the Trek BBS, a Star Trek fan forum. Survived by his wife, Anne Sharp, 45, and daughter, Janeway Sharp, 24, psych major at UCF. Or former psych major. You haven't filled out your withdrawal paperwork yet. Shall I go on?

Searcher24: No.

GeorgeLightly: All right, put down the cloaks and daggers. She gets it: we need to trust each other with sensitive information. If we leak or betray any member of the group, it's mutually assured destruction.

SleuthMistress: Can we get to the video, already?

CitizenNight: Honestly, Mistress and Lightly, it's like you don't believe in security.

A message popped up on-screen: CitizenNight is inviting you to a video chat. Heart pounding, I pressed Accept.

And there they were, for the first time. The people who would change my life.

20

—

LIGHTLY I RECOGNIZED FROM THE newspaper articles. He was a distinguished-looking Black man in his fifties, going silver at the temples. He wore a navy cardigan, and in his background were tall shelves of books. His eyes sparkled with warmth as he regarded me. "Ah, Jane. You're so young."

I blushed. There was something paternal about Lightly. I wanted to make a good impression. "Sorry."

He laughed. "You have nothing to be sorry about. I'm just surprised every year at how much younger people in their twenties get."

"Tell me about it," said the only woman, who I guessed was Mistress. She was older than I'd imagined—in her sixties, at least—with wrinkled white skin, short ash-blond hair, and large, thick bifocals that looked like a holdover from the seventies. She resembled a small owl. She wore a red sweater with a rainbow on it and was knitting so proficiently she didn't bother to glance at her hands as she spoke. If you'd asked me to draw the opposite of a hardened, cop-tipping murder investigator, I would've drawn her. I would later learn that, contrary to my expectations, the vast majority of amateur sleuths are women of a certain age, retirees drawn to investigating as a way to fill their empty hours.

Conversely, if you'd asked me to paint the stereotypical sleuth, I would've given you Goku. He was a large man in his early thirties, larger even than my father, and pale-skinned, a feature emphasized by the fact that he sat in the dark, with only the glow from his computer lighting his face. His eyes were blue, ringed with pronounced blood vessels, the kind you get from staring at a screen for too long. He had longish black hair with sideburns in need of trimming, and he wore a T-shirt with anime characters on it that I would later learn were from *Dragon Ball Z*, his favorite show.

Lastly, there was Citizen. "This is George Lightly," Citizen said. "Tammy Jo Frazier." Mistress waved. "Brian Goddins." Goku saluted me. "And I'm Peter Bishop." Citizen smiled, showing off dazzling teeth. "Figured it was only fair to share our real names since we know yours."

"Hi, everyone," I said shyly.

"So what do you think? Still happy you joined?"

What I thought was that Peter Bishop might be the most beautiful man I'd ever seen. His was not a face meant to be hidden behind a screen. He looked to be in his late twenties—thirty, *maybe*—with short, dark-blond hair, chiseled cheekbones, and big, cherubic blue eyes. His cheeks had a rosy glow most girls my age would've killed for. He was wearing a plain white T-shirt that did nothing to hide his muscular arms, and he sat at a table, a small, warmly lit kitchen behind him. I was suddenly very preoccupied with the fact that he'd called me a young Winona Ryder—who, by any objective standards, could be called pretty. Had he meant to imply he found me pretty?

Since I didn't trust myself to answer Citizen, I pivoted. "Is my initiation over?"

Goku chuckled. "It's over, and you passed with flying colors."

"Then I'm happy to be here."

All four of them beamed at me. "There was one thing you didn't tell us that I was eager to know," Lightly said. "What brought you to the Network?"

"My dad, I guess." Telling them I was on the hunt for answers to who he'd really been felt too complicated, so I only added, "I needed something to distract myself."

Mistress nodded knowingly. "The desire for distraction is a common gateway. But once you figure out what keeps you coming back, we'll know what type of sleuth you are."

Mistress had a theory she'd borrowed from one of her favorite books, *Savage Appetites* by Rachel Monroe, that people who were drawn to true crime could be divided into four main types, in accordance with what drew them. There was the Detective type, a cerebral figure who was motivated by the hunt for answers. The Defender was a hero type who felt a need to protect victims. The Victim identified with those who'd been wronged. And there was the Killer, who felt an affinity—consciously or subconsciously—with the perpetrators.

In the coming months, we would spend a lot of time talking about which types we were. But the most important thing to know at the outset is that each of us was dead wrong about ourselves.

"It's safe to say I'm the Detective type," said Lightly. "Given my former career."

"And I'm a Defender." Mistress pressed a hand to her chest. "It breaks my heart to think about all those poor souls who pass violently, and then they're forgotten."

"If I had to choose," Citizen said, "I guess I'm a Detective, too. Unanswered questions keep me up at night."

"And I'm a Victim," said Goku, then frowned. "That doesn't sound right. I mean, I feel for them. There but for the grace of God go I, you know?"

I wanted to ask them more questions about what had brought them here, and I would in time, but that night I just said, "I guess we'll see where I land."

Two months after solving Indira's case, the five of us had helped solve two more murders—Brittany Clearly, thirty-five, a mom of three in Dayton, Ohio who was shot by her husband, and Selena Rodriguez, a twenty-six-year-old Arizona grad student who was stabbed in a grocery-store parking lot by a serial robber. We'd been stymied by only one case, that of Tatiana Harper, a Russian immigrant who was found strangled in her apartment. And then all of a sudden there was *Newsline*, knocking on our door. And everyone had opinions.

> **GeorgeLightly:** While it would be nice to share Indira's story with a larger audience, I'm not looking for the spotlight.
> **LordGoku:** I'm not too keen on my employer knowing this is what I do in my spare time. Would invite too many questions.

Disappointingly, I'd learned Goku was *not* a CIA operative. He was a high-level technology officer at Amazon Web Services—which, among other things, provides the cloud-based computing platforms for most government systems.*

> **SleuthMistress:** I'm actually warming to the idea. It might be nice to get some recognition. We work pretty hard, and the producer's right—there are mostly negative stories about sleuths out there.

Mistress had given me the opening I was looking for.

---

* If you're thinking that might be how Goku was able to slip into government databases, all I'll say is...you've got a good head on your shoulders. You might want to take up sleuthing yourself.

Searcher24: I love the idea. It would be so cool to be in a Newsline episode.

At that time, I was obsessed with the idea of creating a legacy for my father. Doing something to make people remember him, give him the recognition he deserved. Since I'd failed him at his funeral and didn't have the money to build him a statue, I had to find other ways to get the world's attention.

CitizenNight: Imagine if we became the *good guys* of true crime.

It ended up being me, Mistress, and Citizen in favor of talking to *Newsline*, Goku and Lightly against. So we wrote back to Randall and agreed to be interviewed.

Here's what I'll say about it. By now, you've seen the episode. Everyone has.[*] And true to Randall's word, *Newsline* told a different story than the one the world had heard before. Gone were the Reddit buffoons who'd botched the Boston bomber case, the Cold Cases Inc. forum devotees who'd sent mentally unbalanced people to Christopher Jenkins's door after they wrongly claimed he was Morgan Driver's murderer. In *Newsline*'s narrative, amateur sleuths were unsung heroes, dogged cowboys on the frontiers of justice, with more in common with legends Paul Holes and Michelle McNamara than 4chan trolls.

And we were the face of that new story.

The episode ended up focusing entirely on Indira. Hers was a juicy story, after all: a South Florida woman killed by her boss for prize money and tossed into a lake. The show flew out to interview me, Citizen, Goku, Lightly, and Mistress. The other people on the Indira thread—including

---

[*] Nielsen ratings show ours was the highest-rated episode of *Newsline* in 2023.

SeattleHawks, Minacaren, Carolerichards68, and HiltoftheSword—were interviewed via email, but most of what the producers got from them they tossed. I don't know why *Newsline* chose us to be their stars.

If I had to guess, knowing what I do now about how the media works, it's that the *Newsline* producers simply thought we made the best story. Mistress, the knitting grandma murder-solver. Lightly, the jilted ex-cop on his own mission for justice. Goku, the tech genius using his power for good. Citizen, the handsome hero, helping people in and out of uniform. And as for me? Trust me, I was just as surprised as anyone when they painted me as a savant.

21
—

BY THE TIME THE EPISODE aired, months after our interviews, the entire Network was abuzz. Word had spread to the other forums, too, like Cold Cases Inc. and Websleuths.com, and to Reddit and TikTok. Everyone was eager for some good PR. So when my face filled the screen, and I talked earnestly about why I couldn't let Indira's death go, I represented the whole community's best instincts. When Chris Matthews called me "sharp Jane Sharp," crediting my "uncanny intuition" with tracking down the murder weapon, it wasn't just me he was complimenting; it was all of us.

The episode made a splash. After they watched Citizen sit calmly on camera, explaining how he'd tested a variety of weapons on a pig's corpse, ten new Reddit threads popped up devoted to how beautiful he was, with messages like "this guy could beat my corpse any day of the week." Lightly's authoritative presence won viewers' respect, and then the novelty of Mistress in her magenta tracksuit explaining how she hunted down decades-old property records charmed them. Goku...well, I'm not exactly sure what effect he had, to be honest. Out of all of us, he had the least screen time, and whether that was on account of the news's bias for pretty or his own efforts to avoid the camera, I'm not sure.

Within twenty-four hours of the episode airing,* I got 2 requests for my autograph from Starbucks coworkers and 194 DMs in my Network inbox: 111 fawning messages and 83 hateful ones. The last were all from sleuths who felt it was unfair I'd been plucked for fame after only one case. The most painful came from Mina.

> **Minacaren:** I don't understand why the five of you are content to make it seem like you did all the work on Indira's case, when we all know that's not true. All you have to do is read the thread to see how much work the rest of us did! Those assholes completely cut us out of the story. Yeah, I get it, you went and found the murder weapon. But let's be real: that was stupid of you. And you found it thanks to dumb luck. You felt "bad energy" from Greg? Please. The fact that you're presenting yourself as some sort of, like, intuitive genius is laughable. I expected more.

No matter how many messages I sent apologizing and insisting I had nothing to do with the way the show painted me, Mina never responded. It was my first lesson that notoriety comes with good and bad consequences, and both are equally out of your control.

So it wasn't all roses after the *Newsline* episode. But for the most part, I was on top of the world. I was twenty-four and suddenly famous in the niche world of true crime, which was increasingly coming to feel like the only world that really mattered. Fellow sleuths cheered when the five of us popped up on threads on the Real Crime Network. They took our theories seriously, complimented our ideas even when we didn't deserve

---

* If you're wondering why I haven't mentioned my mom in a while, the truth is, I've decided not to tell her I'm writing this book. I don't think she's going to be happy. Out of respect, it's probably better I keep her out of the story unless absolutely necessary. Mom, if you're reading this...please forgive me.

it. There was a whiff of the big-time about us, as if *Newsline* might circle back for a follow-up any day and those in our favor might borrow some of our shine.

So you can see why, when the Delphine story broke, it had to be us who brought it home. We were the heroes. Everyone expected it. And on top of that, the five of us were wired to *want* to be the ones to crack it. Looking back, I don't think we stood a snowball's chance in hell of resisting the lure of that case. Maybe that's the real definition of fate: when the universe hands you exactly what you want, the one thing you could never turn down, a perfect trap of your own making.

22

—

NEWS OF THE CRIME OF the century broke the morning of March 3, 2024. It was a Sunday, so I was in a Signal video chat with Goku, Citizen, and Mistress, goofing off. Lightly liked to spend time with his wife, Junie, on the weekends, but the rest of us had developed a habit of hanging out. We were lonely, though we wouldn't have admitted it.

On this particular Sunday, Goku was trying to provoke me. "You realize Starbucks is vastly inferior to Peet's, right, Search?" Goku had a lot of opinions, though his strongest were about anime, video games, and politics. He considered himself an anarcho-socialist, which meant he believed in overthrowing oppressive forces like capitalism and the government in favor of individual rule (I think—no matter how many times he explained it, it never really clicked). He assured me that working at Amazon was not reflective of his values, but the money was simply too good. He lived on the basement floor of a house in Los Gatos, California, with his parents occupying the aboveground floors. At first, I thought that was embarrassing—rich, I know, considering I also lived with my mom—until I learned Goku was the owner of the house and let his parents live there for free. Though he made a lot of money, you couldn't tell. He had the habits of a seventeen-year-old computer geek.

I laughed and dug my hands into my dad's hoodie. I remember that clearly because I would end up wearing that sweatshirt for three days straight. "Just because I work at Starbucks doesn't mean I would take a bullet for the place. It doesn't hurt me personally if you don't like it." From the beginning, Goku felt like a brother, and I had no problems giving back as good as I got.

"Has your branch unionized?" Citizen asked. Of all of us, he was the most ambitious, which is probably why he was the de facto leader. He had a chip on his shoulder, the origins of which I hadn't quite figured out yet, which meant he was attracted to anything in which the underdogs took on the establishment. It was an interesting angle for a military man. Citizen was very disciplined in the way he worked out and ate, which I assumed was because of his job. He lived by himself in an apartment in Bremerton, Washington, and liked to say that he got enough people time during the week and preferred to be alone nights and weekends, with the exception of us. Unfortunately, even a few months into our friendship, it still made me nervous to look at him. With his intense eyes, cropped hair, and honed physique, Citizen looked like he belonged on the set of *Top Gun*. I was never my best around him.

"I wouldn't even know how to start something like that," I admitted.

Mistress pointed one of her knitting needles at me. According to Goku and Citizen, I'd get a shipment of hats and gloves from her for Christmas. Mistress lived alone in her house in Des Moines, Iowa. She had two grown kids and one grandchild, all of whom she was enormously proud of. Her daughter, Kristen, who lived in New York City, was a textile artist; her son, Greg, who lived in West Hollywood, was a video game designer, married to a man named Mateo; and Cybil was Greg and Mateo's daughter. At some point, Mistress must've gone into a tourist shop in West Hollywood and bought their entire stock of pride-related merchandise, because her wardrobe consisted of sweaters emblazoned with rainbows, and she had a habit of drinking her coffee out of cups with slogans like "Love is Love" and "I adore my gay sons." I found it endearing.

"You really should unionize," Mistress said. "I belonged to a union at my old library, and they're the only thing that kept me from getting fired the time I accidentally filed a *Hustler* in the children's section."

The three of us started hooting. "We need this story," I insisted. "Who ratted you out?"

"I reported myself," she said. "I wasn't going to let someone else go down for my mistake."

"Libraries carry *Hustler*?" Goku looked intrigued. "Am I about to go for the first time?"

Citizen rolled his eyes. "As if the entirety of the World Wide Web wasn't at your fingertips." He was eating baby carrots and accentuated his point with a loud snap.

I cocked my head. "Do porn magazines still exist after the internet?" And was I actually feeling sorry for *Hustler*?

Mistress sighed. "I regret where I've steered this conversation."

That's when Lightly's video box appeared.

"Lightly!" we all cheered. It was unusual, him popping in during designated wife time. Lightly had no children, though he had a large extended family that lived close to him in Chicago. His wife was the center of his world. Sometimes we could hear her yelling at him while we were chatting, which is how we learned they called each other "bear" and "bunny." Goku made the mistake of calling Lightly "bear" once as a joke and then never again.

Immediately, the look on Lightly's face wiped away our smiles. "Have you heard about Delphine?"

23

—

"WHO'S DELPHINE?" MISTRESS ASKED, PUTTING down her needles.

"Not who," Lightly said. "Where. Delphine, Idaho."

"That's where Northern Idaho University is," said Citizen. "One of my high school friends went there."

I'd never heard Lightly's voice so grim. "There are reports coming out—they're still preliminary, but I'm hearing from some of my old cop channels that there's been a mass killing. Three college girls, all slain in the same house, sometime last night."

Something slippery and cold brushed against the edges of my consciousness.

"Jesus," Goku said. "What do we know?"

Lightly shook his head. "That's all I've got. Nothing on motive—"

"Method?" Citizen asked.

"Haven't heard." The lines in Lightly's face deepened. "I have a feeling this one's going to get big, though. The girls are the right age and demographic."

There was an unspoken understanding that certain kinds of victims elicited more interest than others. The younger, whiter, and more good-looking the victim—especially if they were women—the more likely their deaths would generate attention. Acknowledging this truth makes some people in the true-crime community uncomfortable, but I think the first step in fixing something is to be honest with yourself. There was a reason Lightly was surprised people paid attention to Indira Babatunde and a reason it shocked no one that the Delphine girls became a phenomenon. Racism, classism, pretty bias: they color how we treat the dead as much as the living, no matter how much we swear we're in the justice business. Lightly used to say racism is so pervasive you can't even escape it by dying.

"A thread on Delphine just appeared on the Network." Goku's eyes were focused off-camera. "It doesn't look like anything besides the OP asking if anyone's heard about it yet."

"Nothing on Reddit either," Citizen confirmed. "Searcher, will you scan TikTok?"

"Sure." As the youngest of the group, I was often assigned to search social media. I think everyone assumed I had a native understanding of how it worked, and even though that was far from true, I liked having something to contribute.

It took about thirty minutes of trying increasingly inventive search terms before I hit on something. "Guys," I said, calling their attention. "Check this out."

I sent the link so we could watch together.

"Oh my God, you guys." A beautiful, slender girl in a pink Delta Delta Delta sweatshirt filled the screen. Her handle was @diariesofan-NIUtridelta, and she looked like the kind of girl they'd cast in a movie about a popular clique learning humility, except her eyes were already bloodshot and her voice trembled. "I think something horrible happened last night." She tucked her long, caramel-colored hair behind her ears. "So yesterday was a football Saturday, right? That means tailgating, parties all night. It's a mess, so we're, like, all struggling this morning."

"But my friend Jordan woke up to texts from this girl named Harlow, asking him to come to her house. She lives at this off-campus place that's, like, a really big party spot around here. Four girls live there. They're all KDs. When he got there..." Her voice lowered. "He wouldn't say much over text, other than there was blood everywhere. He's really shaken up. No one knows what happened, but now the place is blocked off by the cops. They haven't said anything, and neither has the university. Whenever there's even, like, a forcible fondling, we get blasted with texts and emails, so I don't understand, and I'm freaking out." She took a deep breath. "If anyone knows anything, please DM me." The video stopped, then started again. I paused it.

"That *is* strange." Mistress frowned. "If there's been a crime, especially a multiple homicide like Lightly heard, why hasn't the university said anything to students? It's part of emergency protocol."

"At UCF they'd text us if anything criminal happened," I agreed.

"What I'm more concerned about is how this friend of hers, Jordan, was able to get into the crime scene before the cops," Citizen said. "Assuming this TikTok girl isn't lying."

"Maybe the Harlow girl called the cops, but Jordan lived closer," Goku suggested. "So he got there first."

"Not to keep bringing up UCF," I said, "but even off-campus, students did tend to live close together." I thought of Afton Oaks. "They'd take over entire apartment complexes."

Lightly frowned. "Either way, it's contamination of the crime scene."

"You guys, this TikTok's blowing up." I squinted at my phone. "The number of viewers is skyrocketing."

"People are flooding into the Delphine thread on the Network, too," Goku said. "This is wild. No one even knows what happened."

"What do you make of the TikTok girl's story?" Citizen asked Lightly.

"If she's got the right information—*if*—then we're dealing with some unusual facts." Lightly rubbed his temples. "Like I said, I heard through my grapevine it's a triple homicide, but it doesn't sound like the students know that. Which means her friend Jordan isn't talking—"

"Weird for a college kid," Goku interjected. "Usually they can't wait to spill."

"Which either means he's under a gag order or he doesn't want to share the details for some reason. Then we've got this Harlow character. The TikTok girl said four girls lived in the house. If Harlow's the fourth roommate, she was spared."

"Maybe she spent the night at someone else's house?" I suggested.

Lightly nodded. "And then you have the cops themselves. Why haven't they released a statement? Controlling the narrative is police comms 101. Otherwise, you get people gossiping and things spin out of your control. Maybe this department is out of its depth."

"Let me see how big they are," Mistress said and started typing.

"Delphine's one of those college towns where the population swells August through May, then empties for the summer," Citizen said. "I wouldn't be surprised if they had a small police force."

"Twenty-nine officers," Mistress reported, and Lightly whistled.

"That's small?" I asked.

"There are over twelve thousand officers in the Chicago Police Department," Lightly said. "For context."

Yeah, okay. That was small.

"Something doesn't feel right," Lightly mused. "We've got intense interest in this case, and weird details leaking out, but no official story."

Citizen steepled his hands. "Do we try to make contact with the cops?"

"Who would reach out?" Goku asked.

We had a protocol. The best scenario for unofficial investigators like us was to have an in with local law enforcement, so we always tried to strike up a friendship, or at least a mutual back-scratching. But the politics of working with cops could be tricky. Indira's case had been the ideal situation because the Okeechobee Police Department was actively looking for tips and willing to work with outsiders. That was rare. Sometimes, cops dismissed people like us or were downright hostile, resenting the implication that we had anything to offer.*

Because Mistress was a unique combination of authoritative, on account of her age, and nonthreatening, on account of being a kindly older woman, she was usually the first delegate. If she struck out, next up was Lightly, who had the cred of being a former cop. However, as a Black man, there were unfortunately some places—the more rural and conservative—where he was distrusted. Third in the hierarchy was Citizen, who as a military man could work the good-ol'-boy angle, and fourth was Goku, as a last resort. I wasn't even on the list. As a young woman, I wielded less than zero authority. To cops my presence was merely an annoyance.

"It *is* Idaho," Citizen said, with a warning glance at Lightly. "Land of proud gun-toting hunters and country music fanatics."

"Mistress, then," said Lightly, with a wry smile.

"On it," she said.

"People on the Network thread have discovered there were multiple killings," Goku announced.

Mistress cocked her head. "*Someone* on the force is leaking. Hopefully they'll leak to us."

I pulled up the Network and started scrolling. Sure enough,

---

* In the case of Tatiana Harper, the Russian immigrant whose murder we failed to solve, we'd actually received a cease-and-desist letter from the Miami Police Department, which Mistress called "unspeakably rude" and Goku claimed was "proof the cops were hiding something."

a picture was starting to form: multiple reports of an off-campus house affiliated with Northern Idaho University, more than one body, weird reticence from the local cops, and an air of mystery that was intoxicating.

"Guys." Citizen's voice was strangely taut. "Look at the last sub-thread."

I raced to the bottom. There, nestled like a Russian doll under the broader "Delphine" thread, was a conversation titled "Where's our *Newsline* celebrities?" The link opened into a litany of messages asking why the five of us hadn't appeared yet.

> **CalamityJane:** Buzzy case like this, I'm surprised we haven't seen the shining stars of true crime pop up and declare this case their territory.
>
> **YoungYung:** Yeah, it seems up their alley. High likelihood of media attention and all.
>
> **SeattleHawks:** We'll probably see them later. I suspect that crew likes cases where everyone else does all the work and they can swoop in at the eleventh hour and take credit. We all know that's what happened with Indira.

Et tu, Seattle?

> **Margarita5:** I'll bet anyone $100 they only pipe up once the rest of us are close to solving. Attention hounds like them give true crime a bad name.

"Citizen," Mistress warned as Citizen started typing. "They're not worth your time."

He replied anyway.

CitizenNight: @Margarita5, I'll take that bet. Feel free to Venmo me at **@citizennight**.

"Well," Goku sighed. "Now we have to solve this case."

To my surprise, a stone-faced Lightly nodded. "No other option."

The five of us looked at each other. And from that moment on, the case belonged to us. Or, more accurately, we belonged to it.

24

—

HOWEVER STRANGE THE DELPHINE CASE seemed during the initial chatter, the real details were even stranger. At seven p.m. that evening, the Delphine Police Department finally announced an imminent press conference "on matters of great concern to the citizens of Delphine." I was grateful I didn't have a Starbucks shift and could stay glued to my laptop, where the five of us watched in rapt attention from our respective corners of the country.

Just as Citizen had said, Delphine, Idaho, was a small, idyllic college town, nestled in the mountains and surrounded by wheat fields. Football was king, skiing was king. Hunting, fishing—"anything outdoors," said the CBS anchor who was reporting from outside the Delphine Police Department, "people here live for it." The flyover shots of the town enraptured me: it looked so small and lovely and completely unlike Florida. Snow on the ground, alpine trees, a water tower painted the green-and-gold colors of the university. It reminded me of an old TV show I'd watched called *Twin Peaks*, though that might just tell you how little exposure I'd gotten to the American Northwest.

The Delphine chief of police was a man named Garrett Reingold. By now, much has been made of Chief Reingold by both his haters and defenders, but in the beginning, what struck me was how emotional he was. I'd seen plenty of police press conferences by that point, but I'd never seen a police chief cry.

Chief Reingold was an average-size white man with a receding hairline, big, bushy eyebrows, and a thick, snow-white goatee. Father Christmas, Idaho style. He wore his well-pressed blue uniform sharply and held himself high over the podium, but from the moment he started speaking, a blotchy redness began to creep across his neck. At first, it was just that—a flush.

I've copied his remarks from the transcript to make sure I've gotten them right:

"I deeply regret to inform the Delphine and Northern Idaho University communities, including any parents, families, and friends watching from home, that we received a report of multiple injuries at 8022 Queen Lace Avenue at approximately eleven fourteen this morning. When officers responded to the call, they found three deceased, all female, all of whom appeared to have been the victim of stab wounds. As is protocol, the official causes of death will be determined after a thorough autopsy, so we ask that you please not speculate in the meantime. We were able to determine the identities of the victims, and they are as follows: Anastasia Flowers, twenty-one years of age; Madeleine Edmonds, twenty-two years of age; and Larissa Weeks, twenty-one years of age. All three were students at Northern Idaho University."

Anastasia, who I would learn went by Stacie. Madeleine, who hated when her name was shortened to "Mad." And Larissa, who would receive the first wave of public frenzy. Three college girls close to my own age. Three girls who could've been me. Each case I'd worked on before Delphine had been personal because I saw my father in the victims, felt their families' desperation because it was my own. But

Delphine was doubly personal, because in the victims I saw both my father and myself. It created a hum of urgency to master the mystery of their deaths.

Chief Reingold was able to keep it together while talking about the boring stuff every officer has to say, about working toward public safety and finding a quick resolution. But then he said, "In light of public safety, and because of certain details I'm not at liberty to reveal, the DPD recommends the citizens of Delphine take extra precautions in the coming days. Please be vigilant as you go about your lives, and report any suspicious behavior to our tip line."

A number flashed on the bottom of the screen. Mistress scribbled it down.

That threw the world for a loop.

"Any NIU students who have not been asked to remain in Delphine by my department may wish to travel home if they feel unsafe. I've spoken with Chancellor Crenshaw, and in light of the circumstances, the university will take every measure to accommodate absences."

"Whoa," Goku whispered. "You ever heard of something like that?"

"They think the perp's still an active threat," Citizen breathed. "They want the kids to clear out."

"So the girls weren't killed in a one-off accident," Lightly said. "This wasn't college students hallucinating on bath salts and going crazy. They think whoever did this could do it again."

25

—

THE CHILL THAT SWEPT OVER the five of us was echoed in the press room as the implications of what the police chief was saying sank in. Someone in the front row called out, "Are the people of Delphine in danger?"

I expected the journalist to get a verbal smackdown like I'd seen at other pressers, but the chief only frowned. "I don't want to cause alarm," he said, measuring his words. "But until we resolve this case, we urge residents to practice extreme vigilance."

"That's code for 'you're in danger, fuckers,'" Goku said.

"Somehow this case got even more interesting," Mistress murmured.

What happened next has been the subject of much debate. And I'm not one for gender binaries—I believe if grown men cried more often, the world would be a better place—but no matter the gender, I have to admit there's something unnerving about watching the person in charge of a triple homicide investigation lose control of himself in front of God and country.

"To the families of the victims," Chief Reingold said. "To the parents of Anastasia, Madeleine, and Larissa, girls close in age to my own two daughters—" His voice broke and his eyes filled with tears. He shook his head firmly, as if to clear the emotion. The press room was deathly silent. Even the officers who stood to the left of the chief subtly turned away.

"That's not good," Citizen said. "He looks weak."

"Give the man a break." Lightly voice was thick. "He's a father."

After another choked-up minute, the chief managed to get a hold of himself. "I promise you, the DPD will do everything in its power to bring the perpetrator to justice. Whoever is responsible for this brutality—" His voice cracked. "We will find you, and we will catch you. In the meantime, we understand this is a matter of public interest even beyond the borders of Delphine, but we ask that the press give us the latitude to do our jobs properly. Thank you."

It was over quickly. When the screen went blank, we looked at each other.

"This is going to get ugly," Lightly said. "I can feel it."

"Do you think we have a serial on our hands?" I could tell Citizen was trying not to sound excited. For many in the true-crime world, nothing was more fascinating than serial killers. I've actually witnessed people in Network threads say they're not interested in a case unless there are multiple bodies and, even better, some sort of sex fetish. But the advantage Citizen had over the average true-crime fanatic was his encyclopedic knowledge of serial killer lore. The man could tell you Dennis Rader's favorite cereal (Post Toasties) and John Wayne Gacy's preferred method of strangulation (sitting on his victim's chest, hands around the throat, or else with a ligature). His interest was near-obsessive.

"Let's hope we never find out," Mistress said. I wondered for a moment at her statement until I realized that in order to find out, there would have to be more bodies.

"Let's see what the peanut gallery's saying about the presser," Goku said, and we all logged into the Network.

That's when we got our first real clue that Delphine was going to be bigger than one single strange and buzzy case. There was no longer only the one familiar thread we'd been tracking. In the span of a few hours, seventy-five new threads on Delphine had cropped up. All of us regulars knew it had to be the result of newbies, because site protocol said you were supposed to create one central thread on a case and branch into sub-threads in order to keep the information easily accessible. The Network had descended into madness. Our orderly home had turned into the Wild West.

"Holy shit," was Citizen's succinct summary.

It wasn't just TheRealCrimeNetwork.com, either. In a matter of hours, Delphine had come to dominate the front page of Reddit, not to mention all the true-crime subreddits. I typed "Delphine murders" into TikTok's search bar, and 102,867 results popped up. There had been *one video* this morning. When I walked into the living room and flipped on the TV, there it was: news of three slain college girls scrolling across CNN. Delphine wasn't a story; in the span of a day, it was *the* story. We didn't know it then, but soon the whole world would be talking about it, from the murder girlies on TikTok to the podcast hipsters to the casual water-cooler corporate slacks. Even my mom would ask if I'd heard about those "poor girls in Idaho." It would trend on every social media app, stream on every news channel. The Delphine girls would travel all over the world.

In other words, soon we'd have a lot of competition.

"Look at this," Goku whistled, throwing a link into our chat. "Pictures of the victims."

I clicked, hungry to see them. Filling the screen was a collection of images that some enterprising sleuth had collated from social media. The girls were beautiful—there was no denying that. It was everyone's first impression, including mine. They were all white. Anastasia and Madeleine were blond and looked like they could be sisters. In many of the photos their sunshine hair fell in tousled waves to their ribs, and they flashed matching toothy grins, the kind you get only after a lifetime of orthodontics. They wore cutoff jean shorts, cowboy boots, and big, oversize NIU sweatshirts, their lashes long and thick with mascara. On that first night, my brain clocked them as a unit, Stacie and Madeleine, and it took a while for me to learn to tell them apart.

Larissa, on the other hand, was shorter, with the kind of stick-straight dark hair that required time with a straight iron. She wore more obvious makeup than the other two—thicker eyeliner, more vibrant lipstick, and showed less skin than her roommates, tending toward jeans instead of cutoffs, sleeves instead of camisoles. While Stacie and Madeleine gave the cameras big smiles, radiating a sense of carefree happiness, Larissa seemed more reserved. But all three shone with that special radiance that comes with being in the prime of your life. They had a glow to them, these girls. A freshness. I looked at them, and even though I was only a few years older, I felt nostalgic, remembering what it felt like to have my whole life ahead of me. In truth, the first time I looked at the Delphine Three, I felt a little jealous.

Fucked up, I know. But I promised to be honest.

"I'm beginning to understand the interest in this case," Lightly said, and I couldn't tell if he was being sarcastic or sincere.

Mistress shook her head. "Three beautiful babies." Then, after a beat, she added, "I'm afraid of what people are going to do with them."

She meant that there are some people in the world who will fixate in unhealthy and even perverse ways on beautiful dead girls. None of us knew how prophetic she'd be, or how that prophecy would include us.

Goku cleared his throat. "Should we do assignments? The clock is ticking."

He was right—the news was out, the sharks were circling, and if we were going to snare this trophy, we would have to move.

"Mistress, you figure out who in the Delphine Police Department is leaking details and see if he'll talk exclusively to us," Citizen said, sliding easily into his role as leader. Mistress nodded. "It would be great if we could have method details beyond stab wounds, and obviously anything they've figured out on the timeline and evidence."

"I'll keep working my cop channels," Lightly volunteered, "and in the meantime I'll focus on getting schematics for the house. Surrounding neighborhood, any surveillance points, the works."

"Great." Citizen turned to Goku. "You comfortable trying to access their accounts?"

In the encrypted privacy of Signal, we could talk freely about the things Goku knew how to do, which included hacking into people's email and social media accounts. He was quite the secret weapon.

"On it," Goku said.

Citizen turned to me.

"I know. Monitor social chatter. Figure out who their friends were and see what they're saying."

"I have a feeling our best source of information is going to come from student speculation," Citizen said, displaying his uncanny ability to read a case. "Think about it. Three NIU students were murdered. And not just any students, but if our TikTok girl was right, sorority girls who lived in a party house. They were socially significant. This is all anyone at that school is going to be talking about."

"Like a popular-girl scandal, but on steroids," I murmured, realizing he was right.

"Which means gossip on steroids. That's why I want to join you on social monitoring, if that's okay."

"Of course." I felt a warm flush at the thought of company.

"Okay, gang." Lightly rubbed his hands together. "Meet back at five p.m. tomorrow to share progress?"

We all agreed. I was supposed to work a double at Starbucks tomorrow but decided I'd cancel. This was far more important.

"Then it's off to the races," he said. "Godspeed. And remember Occam's razor."

"But also think outside the box," Goku added, and we all laughed.

I'm not sure which angle I was applying when I discovered Larissa Weeks's ex-boyfriend.

26

—

IT ALL STARTED WHEN MISTRESS, God bless her, found us a source in the DPD. Cops, I've learned, are like anyone else: some of them feel unappreciated and are willing to boost their egos and incomes by providing insider information for the right price. We always tried to find a cop who just wanted to exchange information, but since Chief Reingold had issued a strict gag order, no cops would cooperate. We were forced to resort to money, which always seemed to find a way to slip through even the tightest of leashes. Thank goodness for Goku and his high-paying tech job.

In the year since Delphine, through countless interviews and under official interrogation, we've never once named our source in the DPD, and I won't start now. Instead, I'll call him Joe.

It was Joe who delivered the first bombshell: the cops had nothing. When Mistress reported this at our 5 p.m. meeting, no one believed her.

"What do you mean, 'nothing'?" Citizen asked. The five of us had worked through the night trying to gather information, and no one had been successful other than Mistress. We were wearing our weariness on our faces, and I, for one, was starting to smell. I'm sure we were a little snappier than usual.

"The DPD has no clue who the suspect could be," she said. "Zero leads. They're still struggling to piece together the timeline of the killings and nail down causes of death."

"It's been over twenty-four hours," Goku protested.

She grimaced. "I know. It isn't good."

"So it *could've* been a college student high on bath salts?" I asked.

"It could be anyone, according to Joe."

"What have they collected in terms of evidence?" Lightly asked.

She hesitated. "Nothing."

"*Nothing?*" This time, Citizen practically shouted it. The four of us stared at Mistress, bleary-eyed and open-mouthed.

"So far, they haven't found any evidence, other than the blood and bodies," she said.

"No footprints, fingerprints, fabric, hair strands, skin cells under the victims' fingernails? Nothing on the bodies themselves?" Lightly looked at her hopefully. "No saliva?"

"I'm starting to sound like a broken record," Mistress sighed.

We sat in shocked silence until Goku broke it. "I'm sorry, but you can't stab three people to death and leave no trace of yourself. It's impossible. It's not like the girls were sniped through the window. The perp was in the house. There has to be something."

"The Carrollton Babysitter Killer left no forensic evidence," Citizen pointed out. "Neither did the Ghost Strangler." He was sitting at his kitchen table with dark circles under his eyes. "But they're considered the elite. For most it's impossible. Even BTK and the Zodiac Killer left evidence."

"So either the DPD is incompetent or whoever killed these girls is a criminal mastermind?" I asked.

"Why not both?" Goku said.

Lightly chewed on his lip. "This does explain the department's delay in holding their presser."

"You were right," Mistress said. "They're out of their depth and scrambling."

And so one of the things that would come to define the Delphine murders in public narrative—the startling lack of evidence—we knew first, thanks to Joe. But no amount of warning could've prepared us for the flurry of vitriolic headlines that would soon come.

"Okay, so we can't count on the cops," I said, rubbing my eyes. My father's ashes sat close by, near my laptop but out of sight of my camera. He'd kept me company all night as I'd searched for friends of the three girls. "That just means our job is even more important, right?"

"This is why we keep you around, Searcher." Goku grinned. "Your youthful optimism."

We ended the meeting to burrow back into our rabbit holes.

"Okay, Dad," I murmured, flipping on my desktop lamp as the sun started to go down. "Let's take a break from social media and see if this school has a forum."

They had two: a public forum where anyone could post, and a private forum where only students and staff with an official @niu.edu email address could enter. I would have to recruit Goku to get me into the private site, which was likely to be the juicier one, where students felt safer to speak their minds. I sighed and entered the public forum.

I'd already scrolled the entirety of Stacie's, Madeleine's, and Larissa's social media accounts. Like typical Gen Zers, they were all open to the public. On each platform, I'd done the exhaustive work of screenshotting each of the girls' following and follower lists, the entire history of their posts, and all the information I could find about what they'd liked and commented on. Goku had taught me to do this mind-numbing work first, as fast as I could, in case the families of victims took down their social accounts or made them private. The total volume of information was staggering, and I knew I needed to start sifting through it. But I figured it wouldn't hurt to do a quick peek at the NIU forum first to see the school scuttlebutt.

As expected, the latest posts were all mournful comments about the murdered girls, RIPs and "may your souls rest in heaven"–type stuff from posters who seemed like NIU parents or even strangers. The most popular post was from a parent asking if others were going to withdraw their kids until the killer was apprehended.

I tried searching "murder," "killing[s]," "Madeleine," "Anastasia," and "Stacie," but it wasn't until I searched for "Larissa" that I got an interesting hit. Curiously, it was connected to a post about Sigma Alpha Epsilon, a popular NIU fraternity. Someone with the username NIUbadger16345 had written: I'm not trying to stir shit, but why is no one talking about the fact that Larissa W just had a bad breakup with an SAE? People saw them screaming at each other a few weeks ago outside Cathy's. It was aggressive.

My heart pounded. I looked at my dad. "And this is why we thank God for gossip."

27

—

I MOVED TO LARISSA'S INSTAGRAM account, which had yet to be locked down. Her most recent posts were flooded with messages from mourners, which made my job of sorting through them harder. Scrolling back into the past, I spotted a tall blond boy with dark-brown eyes in her pictures. They pressed their cheeks together in selfies. In group bar shots, he slung his arm over her shoulders. There was a picture of them at a formal event, all dolled up, Larissa's dark hair in ringlets. Other than his suit for the formal, the guy in question seemed to wear a uniform: North Face jacket, light-wash jeans, cowboy boots, and an NIU baseball cap. Around two months ago, he disappeared from Larissa's grid.

"Gotcha," I said, tapping his photo tag. Chandler Gray. His profile was private, but his bio included the frat letters SAE.

"So this is your guy, huh?" I asked Larissa. I was doing a lot of talking to dead people those days. "What happened to make you fight? Did you get tired of his boots?" Those Idaho kids and their damn cowboy boots. As if they were all ranchers. "Or did he cheat?" I zoomed in on Chandler's face. That patrician nose, those dark eyes. "Was he violent?"

I decided this couldn't wait for our next meeting.

Searcher24: Hey **@SleuthMistress**, any way Joe can tell us what the DPD knows about a guy named Chandler Gray? Senior at NIU, member of the SAE frat, Larissa's ex-boyfriend. Attaching a screenshot claiming the two had a bad breakup and were spotted in a fight.

The whole gang swooped in.

SleuthMistress: On it. What's Cathy's?
GeorgeLightly: It's a bar 2.3 miles from the Queen Lace house, known to serve underage. Popular hangout with the college kids.
LordGoku: Nice job finding an ex, Searcher.
CitizenNight: I can almost hear Lightly whispering "It's always the boyfriend."

The next day, we heard back from Joe: the DPD was already planning to talk to Chandler thanks to Larissa's phone records. The night she died, she'd called him an astonishing twenty-three times, all within thirty minutes.

"That's nuts," Goku said in our video chat, earning a glare from Mistress. "Maybe he dumped her cause she was a Stage 5 Clinger?"

"Don't be sexist," Mistress admonished.

Here's another truth about me: at the time, I'd never had a boyfriend. I was actually still a virgin. It wasn't that I wasn't interested in sex or relationships—the problem was, I knew myself too well. I'd witnessed girls in high school and college turn themselves inside out over relationships, go temporarily mad, temporarily feral. If that was what romantic love did to them, what would it do to me, with all my sensitivity, my limitless ocean of feelings? Annihilate me, I suspected. And when my father, one of the two people I'd allowed myself to love, passed and broke my heart, some subconscious part of me said, *See? Told you love is pain.*

"It's definitely something," I said. "Right? He was the last person she ever called, and she tried him twenty-three times. That signals desperation. What if she was trying to make him jealous and it worked? What if they were in another fight, and he took it too far, came over, and got violent?"

"Feels weak to me," Citizen said. "Why kill the roommates too?"

"Maybe they witnessed him kill Larissa." I was excited. "Should I feed it to the Network, see what they think?"

"We said we were doing this one alone," Citizen insisted.

"The important thing is solving the case," Mistress said. "Not coming in first place. I say post it. It would be good to have the hive mind on it."

So I did. Unfortunately.

Searcher24: Hey, guys. I found a tip that Larissa Weeks had been through a bad breakup with Chandler Gray: 22/senior/SAE. (Screenshot attached.) Verified it against her IG profile—looks like they stopped hanging out around two months ago. And we got word that DPD checked Larissa's phone records, and she called Chandler 23 times before she died. What do we think?

The responses exploded on screen, too fast for my laptop to process.

CuriousGeorgey: It's the glorious return of Sharp Jane Sharp! Where you been, mama?

AndersonBleaks: Whoa, this is disturbing. Did you hear about that case at UVA where the girl's ex-boyfriend got jealous of a new guy, came over late at night and beat her to death? Could be a similar thing.

BorkJamesPhD: Doing us proud, Searcher-Savant.

SloanParks13: I don't trust a frat boy as far as I can throw 'em. I'll look for video footage outside the bar where they were arguing. I think Delphine's Main Street has cameras.

AndersonBleaks: Let's get the hounds to tear through this man's social media. RIP to whatever porn addictions he thought he could keep private.

WigginsSkiShop: Give us 24 hours to know everything about this guy, **@Searcher24**. What he eats for breakfast, where he shits on campus, the books he reads (lol just kidding he's a 22-yr-old frat boy, he doesn't read).

JakesJokes: Let's see if we can access the campus clinic records. I want to know what this guy's been treated for. Chlamydia & gonorrhea are my bets.

I should've known. I can see that now. The forum was a massive pile of kindling, yearning for a spark. Everyone was watching Delphine. They wanted a lead, a clue, somewhere to direct their pent-up energy, and the police weren't giving it to them. But I did.

I set Chandler Gray on fire.

28

—

IT DIDN'T TAKE THE NETWORK long to crack Chandler like a walnut. For the next forty-eight hours, a twenty-two-year-old political science major from Naperville, Illinois, became the most hated man on the internet. Word spread through the true-crime community that he was a person of interest, so soon it wasn't just the Network on him; it was Reddit, TikTok, and all the other forums. I was swept along too. That strange intimacy of sleuthing—studying someone under a microscope, learning everything you could, putting yourself in their head, reenacting their thoughts and feelings as you poured yourself coffee and crunched your cereal—we applied that to Chandler. We snaked ourselves inside him to figure him out.

Here's what we imagined: Chandler was the oldest of three boys, so he'd grown up surrounded by macho energy, used to being in charge. His parents had a decent-size house in a suburban neighborhood outside Chicago; his dad a doctor and his mom a stay-at-homer, so he was used to traditional gender roles, maybe expected them from the girls he dated. He'd done decently well in school, smart but not brilliant, so maybe he had a chip on his shoulder when it came to high achievers like Larissa, who we discovered was premed with incredible grades.

Chandler fancied himself a cowboy despite his suburban upbringing, hence his decision to go to school in Idaho. He attended every country music concert that rolled through town, purchased his cowboy boots, we surmised, his freshman year of college, and was first in line whenever one of his frat brothers asked if anyone wanted to get away for a weekend to go hunting or fishing.

The cowboy and hunting parts were important. They suggested possible delusions of grandeur, an obsession with an antiquated idea of masculinity, the fragile kind that could be challenged, as well as a familiarity with knives, a comfort with using them. The frat thing, too— I'd never realized how much derision the world had for frat boys until Chandler Gray. Don't get me wrong: I'm not here to sing a song of lament for their misunderstood position in the world. I'm simply remarking that if they're into the idea, they could use a PR campaign. To the average sleuth, frats were cesspools of toxic masculinity that existed solely to perpetuate old-money power systems, as well as white supremacy and rape culture. The worst thing Chandler Gray ever did to himself, other than date Larissa Weeks, was join a frat. He was immediately guilty of something.

They had a toxic relationship, Larissa and Chandler, that much was clear. Enterprising sleuths from all corners of the internet stitched together a picture of them woven from their social media comments, photos, and more flagrant and violating sources such as previously private DMs their friends shared and good old-fashioned gossip. Larissa, unlike Chandler, came from a so-called broken home. Her dad had died of a drug overdose when she was twelve, and her mom had rolled in and out of rehab throughout her childhood. She was raised mostly by an aunt, and money was tight.

Unlike Chandler, Larissa seemed to have no delusions about who she was: she had to get good grades because graduating and becoming a doctor were going to be her lifeline out of poverty. According to our sources, she took school seriously. Her involvement in the Kappa Delta sorority was both a social necessity—all the cool kids at NIU were part of Greek life—and a pragmatic one, given the fact that her sorority's multiple charity commitments looked good on her CV. In a sea of wealthy, bubbly, blond KD girls like her two roommates, Larissa was the straight-faced, straight-haired, straight-shooting brunette. The most impractical thing she did was fall under the sway of Chandler.

Word was she loved him and he liked her, an imbalance of affection I was all too familiar with. That was what my friendships usually looked like. According to gossip, Chandler cheated—kept cheating—and the two were known for knock-down, drag-out fights. True to their word, the sleuths had found surveillance footage of the two of them arguing outside Cathy's Bar on two separate occasions. Whether or not Chandler was a murderer, after watching that footage, the entire internet agreed he was a dick. "Larissa, girl," one prominent TikToker said into her camera, "you coulda done *so* much better."

The only person who didn't get swept up in Chandler mania was Citizen. One night, after I came back from a late shift to a dark, empty house—my mom, who still couldn't sleep in her bed, sometimes fell asleep on the lounge chair in the lanai—Citizen was the only one still up and working.

"No offense," he said, his sleepy eyes blinking into the camera. "But I think this is a dead end."

"I'm not offended," I assured him, settling into my desk chair with a cylinder of Pringles. I had to sneak junk food into the house and keep it hidden from my mom, which had the unfortunate effect of making it taste more delicious. I wondered if that's how my father felt about the McDonald's and Dunkin' Donuts I was pretty sure he'd snuck on his way to work. "I'm approaching this scientifically. Chandler as the killer is a hypothesis I'm testing, not a religion I'm committed to." After spending so much time with him since Delphine broke, Citizen's handsomeness had finally stopped being intimidating.

I know it seems like the closest comparison to what we sleuths were doing was guerrilla journalism or amateur detective work, but I liked the scientist analogy better. I'd gotten it from Lightly's repeated reminders about Occam's razor. I liked to think of the five of us as rogue scientists. It reminded me that even though we were operating outside the bounds of the establishment, there were still rules. We needed to stay dispassionate and logical. What we were doing—not just the five of us but the entire true-crime community—was in some ways redefining how to investigate a case. We were using the supercharged method of a hive mind to search and analyze and consider meaning, which allowed us to be in many places at once, think many thoughts at warp speed. To this day, I still believe it's a paradigm shift.

"I've been thinking about the fact that the perp left only a single piece of evidence," Citizen said, leaning over and clasping his hands behind his neck. "How rare that is. What that must mean about him. Killers that good are usually familiar with law enforcement. I think we're looking for a cop or someone with knowledge of the system. Someone really smart and meticulous."

"You sound dangerously close to admiring the guy."

He laughed. "What I mean is, does that sound like a frat boy to you?"

"No," I admitted. "I'm also worried about Chandler's shoe size not matching the footprint."

The footprint. In the last two days while we were looking into Chandler, the DPD had finally done something useful, releasing the homicide timeline. Chief Reingold had remained composed during his second press conference, which probably had a lot to do with the derogatory way the talking heads on Nina Grace and CNBC had discussed his crying.

Here's what the cops now knew: On Saturday, March 2, Stacie Flowers and Madeleine Edmonds drank at their house from 9:00 to 10:35 p.m. (*It's called pregaming*, I'd whispered to the chief). At 10:35, Madeleine called an Uber, which arrived ten minutes later and drove them to Cathy's Bar on Main Street. Surveillance footage showed them exiting the Uber clumsily, laughing, and entering Cathy's, where credit card receipts show they drank vodka sodas and Bud Lights with a group of sorority sisters until 2:00 a.m., when Cathy's closed. Peers who were at the bar reported the girls seemed carefree and happy, which suggested that if they were being stalked or targeted, they were blissfully unaware.

Footage showed them leaving the bar with a group of four friends and walking to a nearby gathering of food trucks, a place popular with NIU students craving late-night munchies. Stacie and Madeleine shared an order of cheese fries and a Coke before the group dispersed. A male friend—Brian Geery—walked Madeline and Stacie the one mile back to Queen Lace, where he said he left them at their house around 3:10 a.m. Footage confirmed Brian walked back along Main Street and entered an Uber at 3:45 a.m.

At 3:52 a.m., a driver from Pizza Hut delivered a large pepperoni pizza to Stacie, which she paid for online, the last thing she would ever purchase. Chief Reingold confirmed the driver continued delivering pizzas until 7:00 a.m., officially ruling him out as a suspect. The girls' fourth roommate, Harlow White, said she woke around 4:00 a.m. to music and sounds of giggling. Her room was on the ground floor next to the living room and kitchen. She yelled to keep it down, which her roommates ignored. Finally, around 4:25 a.m., the music stopped, which Harlow thought meant Stacie and Madeleine had gone upstairs. Due to where their bodies were discovered, DPD believe Madeleine and Stacie fell asleep on either side of Madeleine's queen bed.

The police were vaguer about Larissa's night, which immediately elicited suspicion. At 8:20 p.m., Chief Reingold said, Larissa Weeks drove her 2016 Honda Acura to Savor Wine, an upscale restaurant in downtown Delphine, two streets away from Main. She had dinner with a companion the chief did not name. The forum immediately lit up wondering if it was Chandler. At 9:47 p.m., surveillance footage showed Larissa and her blurry companion leaving Savor and driving separately to a residential neighborhood near the university. Again, the vagueness of this—all the residential neighborhoods were near NIU's campus—made us wonder what the police were shielding. According to the chief, Larissa left her companion's residence at 12:17 a.m. and drove home to Queen Lace, where a neighbor across the street saw her Acura in the driveway while out on a night walk with her dog. The chief didn't mention it in the presser, but the entire internet knew that Larissa then called Chandler Gray twenty-three times between the hours of 1:00 a.m. and 3:00 a.m. He never picked up.

The DPD believed the killer entered 8022 Queen Lace Avenue at 4:55 a.m. through the sliding-glass door in the back of the house, which friends reported the girls frequently kept unlocked. He crept up the staircase to the second floor where Madeleine's, Stacie's, and Larissa's bedrooms were, suggesting a familiarity with the home. The attacks began, police estimated, at 5:01 a.m. and ended at 5:18 a.m., a shockingly short amount of time to end three lives. The killer entered Madeleine's room first, where he proceeded to stab Madeleine and then Stacie with a large knife that cops were still working to identify. The chief didn't tell us how many times those girls were stabbed—we'd find out later on our own—but he did say the pattern of blood spray on the walls, bed, and furniture indicated an attack "of astonishing brutality."

Unlike Madeleine and Stacie, who were killed while sleeping, Larissa might've tried to escape. Her body was found in the open doorway of her bedroom, throat slit, with multiple stab wounds. When I heard the chief lay this out, it didn't matter how matter-of-factly he spoke. There's a thing that happens to me sometimes where I'm pulled against my will into the minds of others. Who knows, maybe it's part of how I'm able to understand other people, what the news called my stupid "savant" ability. It's why I avoid watching sports games and live performances—anything emotionally charged is more likely to trigger me. Since my dad died, I'd been having endless dreams about being trapped in his body, feeling his heart struggle, his brain starve of oxygen, trying to save him as paralysis kicked in. But after that second presser, I started dreaming about being jolted out of sleep by the electric pain of a knife entering my back. Being torn from sleep by my best friend's desperate screams, then feeling the unforgiving blade enter me, over and over—my face, my chest, my arms, nowhere sacred. The gurgle of blood choking my throat, the terror of knowing I'm going to die, that I'll never see the people I love again.

I've always hoped those girls' experiences were nothing like I imagined, but I suspect they were worse.

29
—

THE COPS' TIMELINE DECIMATED MY theory that Madeleine and Stacie were killed after witnessing Chandler murder Larissa, but I still thought he was a viable suspect. Maybe he planned to get Larissa's roommates out of the way before focusing on her.

The only surviving roommate, Harlow, reported she'd woken at 5:04 a.m. to sounds coming from upstairs that her sleep-addled brain interpreted as more late-night revelry. She opened her door and yelled for Madeleine and Stacie to knock it off. After shutting her door and climbing back in bed, Harlow tried to sleep, but when the noises continued, she claimed she opened her door again, this time to find someone walking past her door dressed in all black, face obscured with a ski mask. They were tall but relatively narrow. Harlow thought the person was a friend or late-night paramour of one of her roommates and watched as they left quietly through the sliding-glass door. She then closed her own door, locked it, and fell asleep in the newly peaceful silence. If that weren't strange enough—and trust me, we would have a field day with Harlow's statement—she reported waking at 9:45 a.m. later that morning. Phone records show she called a male friend, also an NIU student, to come over at 10:30. At 11:14, Harlow called 911 to report the bodies.

I don't know if the DPD was prepared for how incendiary the timeline would prove. It contained mysteries that would plague us all the way
until the end. The final pieces of information the chief revealed were
that they'd found remnants of cleaning agents in various places around
the house, ingredients that indicated the killer had used Lysol wipes
to clean up after themselves. Yet there was one piece of evidence they
didn't anticipate: a single footprint outside the sliding-glass door, caught
in slush that hardened thanks to dropping temperatures. The footprint
was from a Vans Ward sneaker, men's size 9.

Of all the things they could've focused on, the media, like Citizen,
were obsessed with the fact that the police had discovered only a single
piece of evidence. The headlines were everywhere: "Three Dead Girls,
No Evidence," "Sorority Killer Leaves No Trace." In the forums, we had
different concerns. Chandler was at least six feet and thus likely to wear
a bigger shoe size than 9. It wasn't out of the question, but the hunt for
his size was on. Several of TikTok's so-called murder girlies—cute young
women, usually nineteen to twenty-five, who seemed to perform true-
crime investigation more than they undertook it—had released videos
begging Chandler's friends to post his shoe size. People were trying to
figure out his size by studying his pictures, while others were seeing
whether he had profiles at retailers like DSW, Macy's, Nordstrom, anywhere that might have a record of his size. Sleuths from r/TrueCrime
had taken a more direct approach, flooding Chandler's social media with
demands he release the information. I'd even seen a Network sub-thread
exploring the theory that Larissa had gone out to dinner with another
man to make Chandler jealous, and in retribution, he and a gang of his
fraternity brothers had descended on 8022 Queen Lace in an act of
vengeance, and it was one of his shorter brothers' footprints captured
in the slush.

Needless to say, even I could feel us stretching.

"Okay," I said to Citizen, crunching on a Pringle. "If not Chandler, who?"

He straightened. "Madeleine and Stacie were killed first, right? I mean, the killer entered the house and went immediately upstairs to kill them. Not only that, but he went to Madeleine's room. Maybe he knew Stacie was sleeping in her bed, or maybe he didn't. For all we know, Madeleine could've been the killer's target, and Stacie and Larissa were just collateral damage."

"I grudgingly admit that Madeleine as the target makes sense," I said.

Citizen grinned. He had a lopsided smile that tugged up more on the left. It was very charming. "Listen to you, Veronica. All reasonable and shit. It's like you don't even belong on the internet."

"Veronica?"

"Winona's character in *Heathers*. Veronica Sawyer." He chuckled, then his gaze focused on something on-screen. "I've been paying closer attention to Madeleine, studying the pictures you pulled from her social, and I noticed something. Here." He dropped four image links in our chat. They were pictures of Madeleine from various parties. In all of them, she was grinning and hugging other girls while rowdy college parties played out in the background. "What do you notice in all four?"

I scanned. Of all the dead girls, Madeleine was the most foreign. Her skin was tan and flawless, her body slender yet curved, her hair the lightest, brightest shade of blond, always curled at the ends. She seemed so perfect. Those kinds of girls were the only people whose brains I could never imagine, project myself into.

It took me five minutes to see it. "The security guard," I finally hissed.

"Exactly," Citizen said. "Name's Kevin Kowalski. Thirty-five, former patrol officer in Twin Falls, fired for a reason I haven't figured out yet. Moved to Delphine two years ago and started working for campus security."

Kevin was a muscular guy, straining the seams of his black security uniform, but not tall. Dark hair, dark eyes, thick mustache. A bruiser's nose. But the most striking thing about him was that in all four pictures, he stood somewhere in the background, eyes fixed on Madeleine. A chill went down my spine.

"You think he was stalking her?"

"I don't know," Citizen admitted. "I need more evidence. But his height fits the profile of someone who might wear a size nine. His law enforcement experience fits. He's someone the kids would trust, not blink an eye if they saw him around. And if he was obsessed with Madeleine, or stalking her, that would explain why the killer beelined to her room."

"You should post this to the Network."

Citizen scrubbed the back of his neck. "You think?"

"Definitely. The way he's looking at her is creepy. And the Network's too tunnel-visioned on Chandler right now. They need something fresh."

"Will you help me search for more pictures? The more we can find with him, the stronger the case."

"Of course," I said, and we were off, searching through hundreds of images of Madeleine in companionable silence, on two sides of the country and yet together, our presences solid comforts on the screen. Madeleine was a Gen Zer who'd documented her whole life on the internet, which was both a blessing and a curse. After a long stretch where the only sound was my mouse clicking, I yawned, rolled my neck, then coughed a laugh at the sight on-screen.

Citizen had fallen asleep with his head against his kitchen table. I stared at him for a moment, his lips parted peacefully in repose, then touched the screen where he lay. My life since my father died had been defined by the very feelings I was experiencing in that moment: deep intimacy and great distance. I'd become an expert at caring for people who existed on other planes. More and more, it was my own small existence—the eight-hour barista shifts I shuffled through, my long vigils at my computer, our small house in a dead-end cul-de-sac, my room with its fever-dream shrine—that felt increasingly unreal. The real world seemed to exist on the other side of the computer screen, or the country. More and more, I felt myself longing to melt into the screen, the barrier, and reappear on the other side.

"Goodnight, Peter," I murmured and switched off the camera.

30

—

CITIZEN POSTED SEVEN PICTURES WE'D collected of Kevin Kowalski watching Madeleine at parties over the course of the last year, along with a point-by-point breakdown of why Kevin fit the killer's profile better than Chandler. And then something unprecedented happened. Kevin wrote back.

> **KevinKowalski99:** Whoa, okay!! Some buddies of mine just showed me this post (I'm a longtime Network lurker but infrequent poster). I need to set the record straight!! I did not kill those girls. I have proof. My wife and I were in Disneyland that weekend! I'm linking to her Facebook album (we made her profile public so you can view it). You can see time-stamped photos from our trip. We were gone from Thursday, February 29th to Sunday, March 3rd. So I wasn't even in the state the night those girls were killed! Here's my boss's number at the campus security department: 208-916-4539. Ask him yourself!!!

The response from the Network was instant and brutal.

Doppleyang04: DAMNNNNNNNN **@CitizenNight** tried to take down an innocent man and Kevin said NOPE I HAVE RECEIPTS.

CalamityJane: I called Kevin's boss and confirmed Kevin was out on PTO Thursday and Friday, back on Monday. And those Facebook photos don't look like deepfakes. How the mighty have fallen. The once-great **@CitizenNight** can't even be bothered to do an alibi check.

Giggitygig: I called his boss too and he said his office is getting flooded with calls! Way to go comrades for checking your sources unlike SOMEONE...

SeattleHawks: **@KevinKowalski99:** How do you explain why you're in such an absurd number of Madeleine's party pics tho? And that look on your face I gotta admit...it's not great.

KevinKowalski99: Look...I'll just say there are perks to my job as a campus security guard, and one of them is getting to attend a lot of parties with college girls!!! You can't fault a man for looking. No one mention that to my wife LOL!!

Soundgardenstan: Sounds like the only things Kevin Kowalski is guilty of are being a perv and flagrant exclamation point abuse. Way to shit the bed, **@CitizenNight**.

Margarita5: I warned y'all the Newsline 5 were going to be tripping over themselves to solve this case for clout. You can't believe anything they say at this point. Making sloppy mistakes in a rush.

On and on it went, a wall of abuse. It was like the Network had been holding its breath, waiting for Citizen to make the slightest slip so they could cut off his head. Goku called an emergency meeting, which I had to take on my phone in the back room of Starbucks.

"Listen," Goku said as soon as we joined. He was sitting in his basement in the dark again. His black hair was messy, like he'd rubbed his hands through it too many times. "This will blow over."

"Fuck those guys." There was so much cold fury packed into Citizen's voice that I shifted uncomfortably against a shelf of artificial flavorings. "They want to try to humiliate *me*? I could run circles around any of them. And fuck Kevin Kowalski, that Disney-loving douchebag. I don't even need his alibi—just reading his messages tells me he's not smart enough to pull off the murders. I hope someone tells his wife he's ogling little girls at work all day."

"It's my fault," I said. "I'm the one who told you to post it."

"It's not your fault." Mistress stood in her kitchen, sprinkling salt over a casserole. "Unfortunately, we all know our community can be juvenile and cutthroat, willing to eat their own. But I agree with Goku— soon they'll be onto something else. You've been around almost as long as I have, Citizen. You know how this works."

Lightly crossed his arms in his leather armchair. "Listen, son. There's an ugly instinct in some people where they start to shrivel when someone else succeeds. There's a famous experiment that shows if you offer a pig more food when it's full, it won't eat it. But if you offer that same food to another pig right in front of them, it doesn't matter how full the first pig is, it will fight to the death to make sure no other pig gets it but them. Humans are the same way. As soon as someone starts to fly a little too high, everyone wants to take them down. You've done too good a job over the years, and now you're suffering."

His words instantly relaxed us. Lightly was something of a father figure to us all, but especially me and Citizen. It turned out Citizen had lost his dad, too, at the tragically young age of seventeen. Cirrhosis of the liver, a result of too much drinking. When I'd asked why he hadn't mentioned it the night I first joined, when the group was going around sharing people they'd lost so I'd feel less alone, he said he'd felt strange mentioning his dad in the same company. Lightly, Mistress, and I had loved the people we'd lost, and he wasn't sure what he felt about his father. He'd been a hard, exacting man, a navy vet who treated Citizen like he was in boot camp his whole life, like he could never do anything right. After he'd died, Citizen's mom ended up sending him to military school in Montana, a banishment he'd always understood as an unspoken punishment for his father's death. Their relationship had been complicated.

In contrast, Lightly was the ideal father: calm, patient, and measured, with a quiet, unshakable authority and a warmth you could always feel under the surface. You wanted him to be proud of you. His compliments were worth their weight in gold, and on the flip side, when he urged you to do better, you were anxious to accommodate. It was a shame he never had any children. He would've made an excellent parent.

"I was just floating a theory," Citizen agreed, picking up Lightly's thread. "I could care less if Kevin isn't the killer—great, that's one more person off our list. The fact that the forum's using this as some sort of proof that I can't hack it anymore is bullshit. The whole point of the Network is to brainstorm. Fuck them for turning their backs on me."

I kept quiet about how eager all of us had been to "win" the case before the rest of the Network as Lightly nodded. "Your only crime was trusting the hive mind to be reasonable." The hive mind was a mixed bag, we all knew: the most incredible investigative tool of the twenty-first century, the innovation that allowed us to explore new frontiers, but also a hydra, a many-headed serpent that was difficult to wrangle, capable of exceeding your grasp and turning its fangs on you in an instant.

"I'm busy, Mom!" Goku suddenly bellowed into the background. "Can it wait?"

The door to the back room swung open, and my manager Fred burst in. "Jane, what are you doing back here? Are you on your phone?"

"Sorry," I yelped, immediately clicking my phone dark. "I was just taking a short bre—"

"You left Kandi all alone to handle the post-work rush." He gestured for me to get my ass out there.

"Sorry," I repeated, ducking around him. "Won't happen again."

But I was a liar. Not even an hour later, my phone lit up with Google alerts. Someone was talking about the Delphine girls, and it was getting major attention. I darted a glance at Kandi. She was a high schooler and easily overwhelmed, but there was only one person in line. She could surely handle that. I ducked into the bathroom, ignoring the fact that it was a disaster, toilet paper everywhere, and locked the door.

31

THE SOURCE OF THE COMMOTION was immediately traceable to a TikTok video someone named @TiffyTracksKillers had just uploaded. I clicked Play. A girl with her hair in two long braids, wearing a short, pleated skirt and a white collared shirt tied at her waist, sat at a desk. The shot was from far away so you could see her coltish legs and knee-high socks. I grimaced. She looked to be in her early twenties, wearing the schoolgirl ensemble as a kind of shtick. You'd see that sometimes, the costumes. Social media allowed people to be whoever they wanted, and it often rewarded people who chose an extreme persona. Some of the murder girlies pretended they were young schoolgirls on the hunt for serial killers, a kind of Britney Spears–meets–Veronica Mars cosplay, or else students in a dark academic mystery, large bows in their hair, parsing out clues by candlelight, or edgy Nordic goths like Lisbeth Salander. Mostly I left these corners of true crime alone because the staggering force field of need that emanated from these people—to be seen, liked, fawned over—was so raw it made me uncomfortable.

TiffyTracksKillers tapped a pen against her desk. "I have a *huge* bombshell to drop in the Delphine case. My day ones know I've been obsessed with this story from the moment I heard of it. But something wasn't sitting right about the police not disclosing who Larissa Weeks went to dinner with the night she died. I mean, *hello*? The girl goes to a nice steak restaurant with someone and then goes back to their house for a few hours? Anyone under the age of thirty can tell you that's a date."

She twirled one of her braids around her finger, and I willed myself not to roll my eyes. "Not to be, like, invasive or whatever, but the cops said there was no evidence of *nonconsensual* sex. That still leaves room for consensual sex. So I got to thinking, could Larissa have hooked up with someone that night? Could it have been Chandler? Maybe she thought they were getting back together and then they had another blow-out fight. She could've left his place and gone home, then called him twenty-three times to argue. But instead of talking it out, he decides he's going to be done with her forever and comes over and kills her and her friends. *Or,* maybe Larissa wasn't with Chandler at all. It would also make sense if Larissa went on a date with someone new and Chandler caught wind of it and that's why he killed her. I knew I had to find out who Larissa was with, and you aren't going to fucking believe it."

She leaned closer to the camera. "I had a hunch there might be cameras outside the restaurant since there's cameras on Main Street. Turns out there *are*—and don't ask me how, but my crew and I got a hold of the footage. Look at this." She pointed into empty air, and grainy video footage appeared there. I squinted at it. You could make out Larissa leaving the restaurant with a man who leaned over and kissed her cheek before they broke for separate cars. Try as I might, I couldn't identify him. But he was older than Larissa. Definitely not Chandler.

"Do you see that?" Tiffy crowed. "That man *clearly on a date* with our twenty-one-year-old Larissa is none other than forty-three-year-old Northern Idaho University biology professor Patrick Cook. Married father of two, might I add. And guess whose wife and kids were away at their grandparents' house that weekend? You guessed it. Professor Cook is our mystery man. I *told* you this was a bombshell."

A Signal message dropped down while Tiffy's video played.

LordGoku: You guys watching this TikTok?

Tiffy rose out of her desk chair and pointed into the air again. "One." The number one materialized. "Patrick Cook has to be a suspect. Maybe Madeleine or Stacie threatened to reveal he was sleeping with a student, so he killed them. He would want to protect his job and marriage, right? That's a powerful motive."

CitizenNight: This girl has done the bare minimum research and the Network's acting like she's the second coming of Hercule Poirot. Where's *their* research into Patrick Cook's alibi? Hypocrites.
SleuthMistress: Putting our animosity aside, this is a bombshell. Digging into this professor. Bear with me.

"And two," Tiffy said, pointing to where the number two materialized. "What if Chandler Gray found out his ex-girlfriend was sleeping with a professor and he was humiliated? Like, maybe he's one of those guys where if he cheats, it's fine, but if the girl steps out, he goes ballistic."

The Signal messages continued to roll in.

SleuthMistress: Did you guys see that two of Chandler's frat brothers just posted on Reddit? Linking here. They're saying the true-crime community is ruining Chandler's life.
LordGoku: Bet that accusation's going to go over well.
SleuthMistress: It's a bloodbath.

"Y'all know that in addition to being an investigator, I'm kind of a psychic," Tiffy said. "Like, I'm so weirdly right about things all the time. And my gut is telling me one of these two men killed our girls. So I need your help. We've got to get Chandler and the professor to talk. We need the police to get off their asses and pay attention."

> **CitizenNight:** I'm stuck on how ridiculous this TikTok girl is. What an airhead. And that outfit? She belongs in the trash.

I frowned, leaning against the bathroom sink.

"Join me in campaigning for #JusticefortheDeplhineThree," Tiffy said as the hashtag appeared above her head. "We can't be afraid to cross lines in service of justice."

The video ended.

> **GeorgeLightly:** I just watched it. That woman is going to get Chandler Gray killed.
>
> **Searcher24:** The cops are going to have to address it, right? It's too incendiary. Mistress, I'll help you dig on the professor. And maybe we can get Chandler's friends to talk to us if the Reddit goons haven't run them off. I think—

"Jane," boomed Fred, pounding on the bathroom door. I jumped and almost slipped on a paper towel. "You in there?"

"Shoot," I muttered to myself, then yelled, "Be right out!" and began washing my hands for authenticity.

A lot can happen when you look away from your phone for a night. As I pocketed it and finished my shift, running around filling customers' orders and ignoring death glares from Kandi, reporters from all over the country, sniffing the blood Tiffy the TikTok vixen had spilled, began to descend on Delphine. Later, the townspeople would call it "The Great Bombardment," though the more cynical among them would name it "The Dead Girl Gold Rush." Journalists had been watching us sleuths, it turned out, lurking in our forums and subscribing to our YouTube channels, and the story had finally gotten too delicious to resist. They could no longer sit idly by in their big-city studios, commenting via satellite footage, when the eyes of the country were fixed on Delphine.

While I untied my apron and apologized again to Fred, while I drove home wearily to the soggy baked potato my mom had left saran-wrapped for dinner, they were already boarding their flights, instructing their ground teams to roll giant RVs onto Queen Lace Avenue, getting their producers to reach out for the twentieth time to the families of the slain girls for comment. They were settling into their new homes at the center of Delphine's nightmare, a nightmare none of us realized was only beginning.

32

—

TWO WEEKS AFTER THE MURDERS, Chandler Gray finally broke his silence. I'd known it was coming because I'd done what no other sleuth could manage and made friends with his frat brothers. At first, I didn't know their real names—the two boys had created Reddit throwaway accounts called u/SAEGentleman1 and u/SAEGentleman2—but Goku tracked them and verified they were Chandler's pledge brothers Mike Downey and Xander Williams. Even though both Mike's and Xander's parents had insisted they decamp back to their homes in California and Arizona while the killer was on the loose, they'd stayed in contact with Chandler. They described him as tortured, both by Larissa's death and what they called "the witch hunt" against him.

All the other sleuths had come in guns blazing, bludgeoning Mike and Xander with questions about Chandler's shoe size and alibi, but I knew the real trick would be to get them to trust me. So I sent DMs on Reddit commiserating with what the sleuths and media were doing to Chandler, how he was being unfairly tried in the court of public opinion, and after a few hours of non-response I even threw in a line about how of course this was happening because Chandler was a straight white guy in a frat, so the world had it out for him. That last part worked like a charm. Soon

I had them venting in my inbox about the death threats Chandler was receiving, how his poor mom was so worried about him she'd started abusing benzos, how everyone at NIU had decided the SAEs weren't to be touched with a ten-foot pole, and now school would never be the same. I had a hard time restraining myself when Xander wrote that he didn't even know if anyone would show up to their parties anymore.

Was it duplicitous of me to commiserate with them, since I was the one who'd brought Chandler to the Network and thrown him to the wolves? Maybe.* But I told myself a few white lies were worth the truth, and with Lightly coaching me, I finally got the golden egg out of Mike and Xander. Apparently, Chandler had a solid alibi for the night the girls were killed but hadn't wanted to reveal it publicly out of respect for Larissa. He was dating one of the girls he'd cheated on Larissa with, a girl Larissa was wildly jealous of. That's why she'd called him twenty-three times the night she died—apparently, in the two months since they'd broken up, she'd swung between trying to shove her new relationship with an older man in Chandler's face and telling him nasty things about his new girlfriend. Chandler had decided to take the high road by not answering Larissa's calls, so the idea that *he'd* been the jealous one, jealous enough to kill her, was laughable to his bros.

Mike and Xander's story, if true, would invalidate the very theory I'd proposed, and yet I believed them. Why? Because as soon as I heard it, it clicked. I'd spent weeks poring through Larissa Weeks's life. Finding pictures of her as a five-year-old that family friends posted on Facebook, combing internet chatter for people's stories of how they'd known her and what she was like. I felt I knew her well. Larissa was an ambitious

---

* To The Person Who Shall Not Be Named: Once again, we need to distinguish between using small white lies and "having complete disregard for the truth whenever it serves her," as you claimed about me. I understand why you're hurt. I would be too. But I don't know how many more times I can apologize. Your exaggeration has gotten out of control.

girl who'd been born to troubled parents. While her friends ate lovingly prepared bag lunches in elementary school, she'd had to beg the lunch ladies to let her eat without paying again. Her friends had new boxes of crayons and Barbies; she had whatever the Salvation Army angels deigned to give her in their yearly Christmas drives. She had to work harder for everything, for even the hope of a middle-class life. Pragmatism ruled her life: she chose NIU because it was a state school that gave her a scholarship. She roomed with Madeleine, Stacie, and Harlow at Queen Lace Avenue because the rent was cheap split four ways. Everything in her life she'd earned or willed into being through sheer grit and determination.

And then along came Chandler, the handsome SAE. And no matter what she did, Larissa couldn't make him want her like she wanted him. He was the first thing she couldn't get through effort, but that old, reflexive determination must've been hard to shut off, because she couldn't stop trying. It probably drove her a little mad. The kind of mad she would've looked back on in ten years, if she'd been allowed to live, and thought to herself, *My God, I went a little crazy over that boy, didn't I? Thank God I grew up.*

I believed Chandler's alibi because my gut told me it fit Larissa's character.

So I urged Mike and Xander to convince Chandler to go public, citing my concern that things would only get worse for him if he didn't. Truthfully, Lightly had told me it would be important for us to see Chandler's proof laid out.

So when Chandler suddenly appeared on the news, standing on the steps leading up to the Northern Idaho University chancellor's office, flanked by his parents, his lawyer, and Chancellor Crenshaw, wearing a somber navy suit, his blond hair carefully brushed to the side, the Network blew up with expletive-filled messages like HOLY SHIT ARE

YOU SEEING THIS???? THAT SCUMBAG CHANDLER GRAY IS ON TV!!!!!! But the five of us knew it was coming and were already seated. Goku had even popped a bowl of popcorn for the occasion, which he tossed and caught in his mouth while cameras panned over the crowd that had gathered to hear Chandler speak.

"Look at all the reporters," Mistress murmured. "It's a mob scene."

"I heard all the major studios have someone living in Delphine now, covering it twenty-four seven," Lightly said. "I saw that anchor from *Newsmax* camped outside the Queen Lace house, trying to get in their families' faces while they cleared out their things."*

"I've been forced into an untenable position," Chandler began, his voice cracking. He stood tall and his suit fit him sharply, but his face was pale and gaunt. He looked ten years younger than the boy in the cowboy boots and North Face from Larissa's pictures.

"Untenable," Goku repeated, crunching a kernel. "His lawyer definitely wrote this script."

"I wanted to keep this matter between me and the Delphine Police Department," Chandler continued. "But due to the extreme harassment I've experienced, I feel I must go public." He glanced at his lawyer, a stern-faced man, who nodded. "On the evening of March second, from approximately eleven p.m. to noon the next day, I was with Sarah Benningfield at her home, where I was also witnessed by her roommate. Both Sarah and her roommate have confirmed my alibi with the DPD, and I've been cleared as a suspect in the murders of—" Here, he choked. "Larissa Weeks, Madeleine Edmonds, and Stacie Flowers."

---

* Since I've gotten so many messages about it: yes, I support the lawsuits being filed against the major networks by the victims' families. They were clearly interfering in the investigation. I don't, however, support including amateur sleuths in those lawsuits, as has recently been threatened in the wake of public outcry over That Awful Book. If you want to quibble with how we handled the case, take it up with the FBI. You'll learn why soon enough.

"Well, folks," Lightly said, dropping his feet off his desk. "That's a wrap on Chandler. Who's next?"

"The professor?" I asked, glancing at Mistress. I'd already made peace with Chandler's innocence. I was ready to move on.

She shook her head. "Joe says the cops have cleared him. The professor's wife FaceTimed him while she was on her morning jog at her parents' house. Seven a.m. New Jersey time, four a.m. in Delphine. The call lasted twenty-five minutes, and she says he was in bed the whole time."

"She called him at four a.m. to talk?" Goku shook his head. "No wonder he's cheating."

"She could've suspected him," I said, thinking of the extreme lengths I'd witnessed girls go to in order to catch their boyfriends in the act. "Maybe she was trying to surprise him. Catch him out."

Citizen whistled. "Well, she definitely knows he was cheating now. Poor woman had to be an alibi in the murder case of the girl he was nailing."

"I've received disturbing things in the mail," Chandler continued on the computer screen. His mother, who until then had remained stoically still, gripped his shoulder. "Including detailed death threats and a dead rat with a noose around its neck. I've had people email my professors saying I'm a killer who should be kicked out of school, and if I'm not, the school will be sorry. Chancellor Crenshaw says alumni are threatening to pull their donations. Strangers on the internet are threatening to follow me for the rest of my life to make sure no one ever hires me. I've stopped going outside out of fear."

"Oh, no," Mistress murmured. "He's crying."

"Wah, wah." Citizen rolled his eyes. "I dated a dead girl and now I have to prove I didn't kill her instead of everyone just believing me. Only a white boy in America."

We all side-eyed Citizen—a white boy in America—but still. He wasn't wrong.

Tears glistened in Chandler's eyes. "I've very sorry for what happened to Larissa, Madeleine, and Stacie, but I need my life to return to normal. That's why I've decided to withdraw from NIU and my fraternity. I hope this prevents anyone from targeting either of those institutions."

Chandler was quitting college? My mouth must've dropped open, because Lightly said, "You can't be that surprised, Searcher. Look what's happened to him."

I knew pointing your finger at someone had consequences, but I'd never imagined this. A whole life reshaped.

"Oh, shit, guys." Goku's attention had been snagged by his phone, his voice almost gleeful. "*Fox News* has the professor coming out of his house."

Chandler was still mid-sentence, but we muted him and pulled up Fox News, where an intrepid reporter was hustling after Patrick Cook as he made his way to his car. It was strange to see him in broad daylight after witnessing him in the grainy surveillance footage. Chandler had looked younger in his fear, but Patrick looked old and bedraggled.

"Professor Cook!" the reporter shouted. "Patrick! Did you kill those girls?"

Patrick shielded his face and tried to dart for his car, but the cameraman was in the way.

"Were you sleeping with Larissa Weeks?" continued the reporter. "Do your wife and kids know?"

"Leave my kids out of it," Patrick growled. I felt a knee-jerk flash of sympathy. He was a father.

"What do your colleagues have to say about you sleeping with a student?" the reporter persisted. "Did you follow Larissa back to her house that night—"

"Would you people leave me alone?" Patrick roared, his unshaven face bright red. "I've resigned from my job. I'm losing my family. What more do you want?" Spittle flew from his mouth. "I made a mistake. I know I did. But I didn't kill those girls. I didn't!"

"He's cracking," Lightly said. "And it's only been a few days. Even if he didn't have an alibi, I don't think he has the disposition of a cold-blooded killer."

We all muttered our agreements and clicked out of both Patrick's and Chandler's news stories.

"Well," Goku yawned. "Back to the drawing board."

Citizen was on his phone at work, hiding out in his office at the naval base. "I still think we should focus on Madeleine. Figure out if she had any beefs with anyone or if there was a guy who was paying her too much attention. Someone she dismissed who she should've taken more seriously."

"Was there anything interesting in her email?" Mistress asked Goku.

He shook his head and wiped his popcorn hands on a paper towel. "Nah. Mostly homework assignments and sorority event reminders. She must've kept the juicy stuff elsewhere. I'm working on getting into her social accounts."

I perked up. "Prioritize Instagram. She was really active." Out of all the girls, Madeleine was the Instagram super-poster. I'd bet money her DMs were chock full of good stuff.

"Today was underwhelming," Lightly said with a sigh. "But let's keep our spirits high. Sometimes crossing people off the list is nearly as important as a lead heating up."

"Just another day in sleuth land," Mistress agreed. "At least we live to fight another day."

The next morning, we woke to news that Chandler Gray had been jumped outside a gas station and beaten within an inch of his life. He was on life support at the Mountain Medical Center, where the bodies of the Delphine Three had been rushed only two weeks before.

33

—

THE BACKLASH AGAINST THE TRUE-CRIME community was swift and brutal, led by Chief Reingold. In all the accounts I've read about what happened in Delphine—even the recent Awful Book that's gotten so much acclaim—everyone agrees that Chandler's beating was a turning point. Before, the police and we sleuths kept each other at a distance, regarding each other with wary distaste. If anything, we shared a healthy condescension toward the journalists, with how little they seemed to care about the case getting solved so long as there was a circus to film. But when Chandler Gray landed in the hospital, assaulted by three men who'd read the subreddits and became convinced Chandler was getting away with murder—that was when Chief Reingold decided America's armchair detectives were public enemy number one. At times it felt like he was angrier at us than the killer.

And who was the face of true crime? Whose stories had been shared on *Newsline*, their names, faces, and handles plastered everywhere? Of course the five of us became the scapegoats. Looking back, I understand why the chief chose us. We'd made ourselves too convenient.

At first, we weren't even going to watch the presser. That's how little we thought of it. We already knew the facts—Chandler was in the hospital with a brain bleed, the three men who'd driven in from Grangeville were in custody—and we didn't think Chief Reingold had anything to add. It was more habit than anything that made us tune in. So to see Citizen's face appear on the projector behind the wall of officers caused the bottom to drop out of my stomach.

"What the fuck?" Goku hissed, but Citizen shushed him, waving to listen.

"As you've likely heard," the chief began, his face already red with emotion, "late last night Chandler Gray was assaulted outside a Love's Travel Stop by three men. He was rushed to Mountain Medical Center, where he remains in critical condition. The perpetrators have been arrested and will be prosecuted to the fullest extent of the law."

Chief Reingold took a preparatory breath. "But I'm not here to talk about the men who jumped an innocent university student and left him with life-changing injuries. I'm here to talk about the insidious force that convinced those men to get in a truck and drive close to two hours to commit assault, believing they were on the right side of history. The true-crime community, also known as the amateur sleuth community, is the invisible but no less culpable perpetrator in this crime."

"You're kidding me," Lightly breathed, his eyes wide with alarm. "That's where he's going with this?"

"Since news of the murders at Queen Lace Avenue broke, my department has been battling the true-crime community every step of the way. These are people with minimal or no law enforcement training who feel entitled to speculate on this horrible tragedy. What's worse than their invasiveness is that they are believed by so many. They're able to put targets on people's backs."

"He can't blame Chandler's attack on us," I cried. "That's absurd."

"Consider the man whose picture is over my shoulder," said the

Chief, turning to point at Citizen. The picture had to be several years old, because Citizen looked younger and slightly feral, his head buzzed, his eyes so bright they seemed a tad mad. "This man, Peter Bishop, is currently known by the handle Citizen Night. Three years ago, while he went by the alias Citizen of the Underbelly, he led an online campaign that wrongfully targeted a forty-eight-year-old father of four as the Cuyahoga Cutter serial killer. DNA evidence eventually cleared him, but not before he lost his job and family home in Ohio."

"That was *one* mistake!" Citizen shouted at the screen. "Tell them about all the guilty people I've helped put away. Tell them about the lives I've saved! Jesus, I wasn't even one of the people who thought it was Chandler."

"While he was known as Citizen of the Underbelly, Peter Bishop's manifesto, as stated in his profile, read 'Most people like to pretend the world is a happy place and people are inherently good. But those of us who are awake understand it's a hellscape. We crawl the dark underbelly of human life looking for glimpses of the truth, rare visions of the monsters we all are under our masks, driven by compulsions to hurt and destroy that burn like secret bonfires in our hearts.' That's the kind of person you have leading the internet's search for the killer. And take his companion."

Citizen's photo was replaced by a picture of Goku. Like Citizen's, the picture was old. Goku had a thick beard in it, unkempt hair, bloodshot eyes. I would've walked to the other side of the street if I'd seen him.

"Oh, Goku," Mistress said softly. "I'm sorry."

"Brian Goddins. Up until a few years ago, this man was a member of DieHardTrooper.net, an online community known for its violent and misogynistic rhetoric, and more recently as the hangout of several incel-related killers."

"What?" I gasped. I would've been less surprised if the chief told us

Goku was an alien from another planet. My friend was gentle and kind behind his wall of sarcasm. Right?

Goku shook his head. "I can explain." He pressed his hand over his mouth. "If my mom sees this…"

"Leaders in the true-crime community *working* on the Delphine case"—the chief stressed "working" so we knew he hardly considered it work—"also include George Lightly, a failed detective with a history of assaulting law enforcement." A mug shot of Lightly replaced Goku's bloodshot eyes. In it, Lightly had a shiner and he looked utterly resigned. I hadn't seen the mug shot in my research.

"How *dare* they represent you that way?" Mistress cried. "The cop you hit was a racist asshole!"

Lightly only shook his head. "Wouldn't be the first time they told the story backwards. Won't be the last."

I hadn't known any of these things. Clearly, I didn't know the people I called family as well as I'd thought.

Chief Reingold cleared his throat. "We have a retired children's librarian who insists people call her Mistress. Real name Tammy Jo Frazier." An old employment headshot of Mistress flashed on the projector. She beamed at the camera, wearing blue corduroy overalls with ABC stitched into the front in primary colors. There was no one in the history of the world who had ever looked less likely to solve brutal murders than the woman in that photo. "And a twenty-four-year-old college dropout who claims she's an investigation savant, real name Janeway Sharp." My high school yearbook photo appeared behind Chief Reingold, and my soul departed my body. I had so much acne in that picture.

"I never claimed I was savant!" I screeched. "That was *Newsline*."

"No one goes after Searcher," Goku vowed. "That's crossing the line."

"Yeah, not Veronica," Citizen agreed.

"You guys. I'm not a child in need of protection."

155

Mistress frowned. "I don't understand why he didn't go after the people in the forum who were actually out for Chandler's blood. Why us?"

"Or TikTok Tiffy," Citizen said. "The girl who said any action was justified in the pursuit of justice."

"I bet whoever wrote this speech for the chief needed targets fast and just copied and pasted from the *Newsline* website," Goku said. "Did some quick digging to turn us into villains. Lazy fucks."

"The true-crime community is a menace," Chief Reingold insisted, his face now tomato red. "They're keeping my officers from carrying out justice. They're condemning people to punishment before a fair trial. Inciting violence against the innocent." He lifted a meaty finger and pointed at the seated press. "If you want a story, stop hounding my department. These people are changing the way justice unfolds in America. Playing judge, jury, and executioner. *They're* your story."

"You should see the Network right now." Goku's eyes were on his other screen. "They're terrified. People are posting that they're going to delete their accounts."

"The chief's trying to deflect from all the negative attention he's gotten for not having any leads," I said.

"I think you're right." Lightly rubbed his jaw. "The whole world's watching, and the DPD has nothing. And now a boy is in the hospital, all on the chief's watch. He's not in control, and he knows it. He's cornered, so he's puffing up and lashing out."

"I don't care why he's doing it." Citizen's voice was steely. In his face, I saw it all come together: The chip on his shoulder. His distaste for authority. The battle the navy had been training him for since he enlisted. All of it wove together until there was only one possible response. "The chief just fired a missile. Now it's war."

Like I said: I've come to think fate is a trap we set for ourselves.

34
—

GOKU AND CITIZEN DIDN'T LIKE to talk about it, but each of them did have a checkered past. After Chief Reingold splashed us all over his press conference, I learned the story from Goku himself. Years ago, before Goku became involved with TheRealCrimeNetwork.com, and before he got onto the executive track at Amazon, he struggled with anger. He used to be a low-level coder who lived with his parents, two middle-school teachers who were on the verge of being priced out of their home in California. He had a hard time making friends—he either came on too strong or kept quiet and was labeled a boring nerd. And forget about women. As Goku told it, being overweight made him invisible to girls. By his early twenties, he'd resigned himself to dying alone.

It started with 4chan. One day he was looking for people to talk about *Fullmetal Alchemist* with, his latest anime obsession, and found the website. There, he discovered a bustling community discussing anime and manga, video games, how to build your own computer, Python versus Java. These were his people, and they'd been waiting for him on the internet. Goku spent more and more time on 4chan, where he could be himself—if anything, the other posters were more acerbic, made more biting jokes, held more outrageous opinions. And as is typical of spaces where men gather to talk anonymously—so Goku told me—talk often turned to women.

At first it was jokes, then grosser jokes, then diatribes. And there, too, Goku found he wasn't alone in feeling unlovable. When some of his favorite 4chan posters started raving about a new site, DieHardTroopers. net, he was curious. They said there were fewer rules on Die Hard—no mods sweeping the boards and deleting inappropriate comments or banning posters—and because it was a little more "Wild West," people were willing to talk about more interesting topics; rawer, more cowboy things. It's probably human nature to get desensitized to whatever you're addicted to and go in search of a stronger hit, and that's what Goku did with Die Hard.

Conversations *were* rawer there. There was less discussion of video games and more talk of politics. Goku had always liked politics, and a lot of what these guys were posting sounded philosophical, with their talk of rights and what human beings were owed. Yes, some of the debates seemed like dick-measuring contests, and some of the posters could be nasty about women, but that was simply the internet, and Goku just steered clear.

It wasn't until he met a user called @CitizenSerial that he got introduced to the really edgy stuff. Like his handle suggested, Citizen was obsessed with serial killer lore. He told Goku that at any given time, the FBI estimates there are between twenty-five to fifty active serial killers in the U.S. who haven't been caught. Citizen wanted to catch them. Goku had never really been into true crime, but serial killers *were* fascinating in the same way great white shark documentaries were: thrilling to witness such cold, lethal power. What's more, he liked Citizen—the guy was smart, funny, never punched down. If it was possible to be a decent person on the internet, Citizen was it.

But Citizen's sleuth's curiosity, maybe even his hero complex, had led him into the heart of Die Hard, where he'd made friends with some of the site's founders and received invites to private threads where they were planning...well, something. At first Citizen wanted Goku to join him in these threads as a witness to help him figure out what they were up to. But when Goku advertised his skills as a hacker, honed during his many lonely afternoons in high school with nothing but his computer, and the Die Hard founders started salivating, Citizen got spooked.

"He told me we needed to get out of there," Goku said, the night we had our private chat. For once, Goku wasn't in his basement, instead talking to me from his living room couch. I was amazed at all the light up there and couldn't stop blinking at the new, warmly lit Goku. "It wasn't that I agreed with anything those guys were saying—I just liked having friends. Having something to do with my time that was useful and appreciated. Citizen said we could do even more helpful shit if we dropped *Die Hard* and joined the Network."

"So that's how you got into true crime?" It was my one night off, and I was supposed to be using it to read Madeleine's Instagram posts from 2018–2020 or read through my dad's Gmail since I'd just figured out his password. But Goku had asked me to talk, and I was too curious to decline.

He nodded. "We dropped Die Hard before those fuckers started hurting people.* If Citizen and I had still been active users, we might've gone to jail. Citizen saw the danger before I did. He's why I figured out I liked sleuthing, and he's who convinced me I was good enough at what I did to talk to my bosses about the path to CTO. Now I make good money

---

* For those unfamiliar, DieHardTrooper.net co-founders Levi Jameson and Keith Hartley were arrested in 2020 for mowing down three women in south Michigan in Hartley's car. Cops found what the media termed "incel manifestos" in both of their apartments, thought to be their motive for the attack. They're currently serving life sentences in state prison.

and my parents and I can afford to stay in California. He saved me and made me better. I owe him everything."

It occurred to me then that even though Goku had said he was drawn to investigating because he empathized with the victims, that might've been guilt talking. It sounded to me like he was a Detective, drawn to true crime for the cerebral challenge, the ability to use his hacking skills in order to be widely admired in a community that appreciated him.

"That's why you're so willing to go out on a limb for him?" In the days since the presser, Citizen and Goku had squirreled themselves away to plan something they were keeping from the rest of us. I knew why—Lightly had warned Citizen to drop the issue with the DPD, put his head down, and get back to investigating. The best revenge, he said, would be solving the case. But I could tell that didn't satisfy Citizen—I'd learned to read the determined set of his jaw, the glint in his eyes. And I knew where Citizen went, Goku followed.

"Look, Searcher, the reason I wanted to talk to you alone—obviously, besides explaining myself, because I didn't want you to think I'm some incel creep—was we found something on the DPD. A lot, actually. And I want to know if you're okay with us going public with it."

I glanced at my father's ashes, as if he'd share my look of surprise. Combing through his Gmail, I'd been reminded of how often he said "Wowza!" whenever I surprised him. Peak dorky dad. I imagined him saying it now. "What'd you do?"

Citizen leaned closer and glanced in either direction, though he'd told me his parents were out for the day. "I hacked the DPD."

Maybe he was expecting me to be shocked—the look on his face certainly said he was bracing for it—but back then I was naive. "Okay. Is this the first time you've done that?"

He laughed. "Searcher, do you know anything about cybercrime? Technically, all black-hat hacking's illegal, but what the Feds actually care about prosecuting is a small slice of the pie. Hacking a police department definitely falls into that slice. This is the shit you can really get in trouble for."

"Okay," I said slowly. "So you risked your neck."

"Citizen figured there had to be a reason the chief went nuclear on us. I only downloaded the Queen Lace file—didn't touch any other case—and he and I have been reading through it these last few days. I actually took time off."

"That explains your pajamas."

He grinned. "At least I'm not wearing a University of Tennessee hoodie. The Vols? Come on, Search. That's weak sauce."

I glanced down at my dad's sweatshirt and decided I didn't feel like explaining his wistful love for the home-state college he could never afford. Unlike Goku, I hadn't had the luxury of taking time off since Chief Reingold blasted us at the presser. Not when my manager was irritated at me and my mom and I needed the money. I'd been lucky none of the customers recognized me from the news. Even still, I was tired.

"Anyway." Goku lifted a coffee mug and took a sip. "We found a pattern of neglect."

"What does that mean? Shoddy policing?"

His ceramic mug hit the coffee table with a clatter. "Basically. Listen to this. You know the roommate, Harlow White? She and that guy she called, Jordan Beckett, walked all through the crime scene. Apparently, they even moved the bodies. It's right there in the police report, even though it's never been released publicly. That's contamination number one. And when Harlow called 911, she didn't say her roommates had been murdered. She said they were hurt. So EMTs came, and only two cops, and they walked through the house for such a long time without any precautionary measures that the chief formally reprimanded them. Contamination number two."

"Sorry, but what does that mean?"

"It means the integrity of the murder scene was compromised. Fingerprints, footprints, the positions of the bodies. Who knows what else. The evidence could've existed, but the scene wasn't properly handled by Harlow or the cops. A savvy lawyer could argue that any evidence they pull from the scene should be thrown out in court. If people knew that, there'd be an uproar. But that's not the only strange thing."

I waited. What else was the chief hiding?

"DPD detectives dismissed Harlow as a suspect, even though they have emails from her to her friends complaining about her roommates. She *hated* them. Hated their partying, hated how loud they were, was barely talking to them before they died. Harlow was so miserable in that house she tried to get out of the lease, but Madeleine and the other girls wouldn't let her. In one of the emails, Harlow said she wished they'd drop dead."

"None of that was released."

"I know. And they're not questioning her. I don't know why."

"Her story was already weird," I said, remembering. "I mean, she straight up saw someone in a black ski mask in her house and did nothing? And when she found her roommates murdered, she called a friend instead of the cops? How does any of that make sense?"

"Exactly. But no one's talking about her because the cops aren't." Goku's cheeks were rosy, which meant he was nervous.

I narrowed my eyes. "Why are you telling me this?"

"Because Citizen and I know that Lightly doesn't want us to release this. And Mistress will side with him because she always does. You're the deciding vote."

"I don't want to go against Lightly," I said automatically.

"Yeah, I get it. But Search, you know what's happening to us out there. Don't you want it to stop?"

Of course I did. More than anything. They were eating us alive.

35

—

THE FIRST OF THE ARTICLES about us had hit the web even before Chief Reingold was finished with his press conference, sensationalist pieces that called us everything from the worst thing that had ever happened to criminal justice to internet trolls trumped up on ill-gotten power. The best of the coverage from thoughtful journalists like Rachel Maddow didn't focus on us personally, but rather the question the chief had raised about whether true crime had grown out of control. "Are we witnessing an unprecedented moment in the history of investigation?" Maddow had asked on her show. "Police departments have largely treated internet sleuths as nuisances, streaming companies and podcasts have milked their obsessions for profit, but are fans of true crime now insisting on being key players in criminal investigations? One police chief in Idaho thinks so..."

Rags like *Daily Mail* and *New York Post* raked the five of us across the coals. I read one quote from a girl I went to high school with who called me a weird loner who never talked, and then said, "I'm not surprised Jane is into dark stuff on the internet—I guess we're lucky she, like, never brought a gun to school and pulled a Parkland."* That's when I decided not to read any more stories.

To be fair, none of us got it worse than Citizen and Goku.** By the time Goku and I had our private meeting, you couldn't scroll X without reading someone's opinion of them. It was brutal. I'd experienced exposure with the *Newsline* special, but that was net positive, nothing like being thrust into the receiving end of mass public vitriol. Looking back, I think the only things that kept me sane in those days were my dad-investigation, which gave me something to disappear into, and my grief. Again, when the worst thing has already happened to you, you go a little numb.

The only places that didn't tear us apart were the forums and Reddit. The initial terror that had led roughly a thousand people to delete their accounts from TheRealCrimeNetwork.com had passed, replaced by a fomenting anger. Citizen was right that the chief had started a war—but not just with us. Sleuths across the internet were foaming at the mouth.

"Don't you think this information about Harlow deserves to be out there instead of buried?" Goku asked softly. "It belongs to the people."

His words hit home. Internet folk tended to believe that knowledge should be democratically accessible. It was one of the key philosophies that united people across all corners of the web. In my months of sleuthing, it had sunk in.

"Okay," I said. "I'm on your side. Let's release it."

---

* In another article I was described as "the hot co-ed crime-solver," which captures the general media confusion over how to depict me once we were labeled villains—was I a weird goth girl audiences should be scared of or a salacious college-aged sleuth they could lust over? The tabloids never quite figured me out.

** A small selection of article titles from this time: "Who's Watching the Watchers? Do These Two Cretins Have Access to Your Private Info?"; "So-Called 'Murder Trolls' Descend on Idaho Investigation"; "How Is Jeff Bezos Connected to the Delphine Massacre? (Click to Find Out)"; "Internet Thirsting Over Dead-Eyed Officer-Turned-Vigilante."

His eyes lit up. "Thank you, Searcher. That means a lot."

So on Thursday, March 20, the five of us gathered in the Signal chat. It was after my shift. I'd taken a shower to look and smell more presentable, even though they couldn't smell the coffee on me through their screens. I was nervous.

Goku and Citizen presented what they'd learned about the DPD to Lightly and Mistress, along with their plan to release the information—and, as expected, Lightly was horrified.

"Absolutely not." He surged higher behind the desk in his library. "You release this information, you could jeopardize justice ever being served in this case. Think about it. If the cops catch the killer—if *we* catch the killer—and then his case gets thrown out because the judge decides the evidence is inadmissible, what then?"

"You're talking about helping to cover the DPD's mistakes," Citizen argued. He was in rare form that night. Passionate and articulate, eyes bright and hungry. "Burying the things they've done wrong because we're afraid of possible repercussions. That doesn't sound like the Lightly I know. The Lightly *I* know would stand up to the cops."

Lightly's nostrils flared. "Don't compare Chicago to this, I warn you. And don't pretend you want to go public because you think it's the right thing to do. You're smarting because the chief insulted you and now you want to strike back."

"Everyone wants to strike back," Goku insisted. "The entire Network."

"We've got to be the bigger people. It's not about you and me. It's about those girls and what they deserve."

"What if we released the parts about Harlow, but not proof of the contaminated crime scene?" I asked. "That way we don't jeopardize anything; we just steer the sleuths."

Citizen shook his head, gripping the edge of his kitchen table so the muscles in his forearms flexed. "The chief abused his role going after us, and he's leading a second-rate investigation. Maybe he deserves to get this case taken away."

"That's not the—" Lightly began, but Citizen cut him off.

"Why can't I be on the side of the girls *and* want to hold the cops accountable? You're too old-school sometimes, Lightly. Even after everything, you're conditioned to protect your boys in blue."

"They're not my boys," Lightly snarled, and we all froze. We'd had countless debates before, but never a real argument. It was the first time I'd seen Lightly angry.

"Searcher." Mistress must've figured out I'd given Goku and Citizen my vote to release the files, so she implored me directly. "Sometimes ideological purity comes at too steep a cost."

"I think we can have it both ways," I insisted weakly.

Lightly shook his head. "I can't talk about this. I'm too disappointed." The look he gave us made me rear back and reach for my father's ashes. "I just pray I've gotten through to you."

36

—

AT PRECISELY 9:00 A.M. EASTERN the next day, more than a dozen news sites across the country received the confidential Delphine Police Department file on the triple homicide at 8022 Queen Lace Avenue through their SecureDrop tip systems. Goku and Citizen swore they'd done it in a way that would ensure their fingerprints weren't on it. And they held nothing back. The reporters got everything.

By 9:00 p.m. that night, the tenor of the media firestorm had changed. It was like we sleuths had never been the enemy, as if the last few days had been wiped from collective memory. The headlines were so perfect I don't think Citizen and Goku could've written them in their wildest dreams. CNN ran with "Breaking: Leaked Files Show Delphine Police Bungling Massacre." The *New York Times*: "Idaho Police Chief, True-Crime Naysayer, Now Under Fire." Fox News took an unsurprisingly chauvinistic route: "Crying Chief Reingold Unfit to Lead Homicide Investigation." Maddow, once again with the most nuanced take, devoted a whole show to the war of words between Delphine police and the true-crime community. She was the only one who speculated that the leaked files might've come from sleuths looking for revenge. Every other news site ignored that angle in favor of the sexier question: Should the chief in charge of America's most famous murder case be fired?

Oh, how the forums crowed.

TimoSmith76: THIS IS THE BEST THING THAT'S EVER HAPPENED TO US! That dumbass Reingold was out there slinging rocks while living in a glass house.

RussiaMotherland: Are you guys getting in the weeds of these files like I am? The DPD might as well have invited the whole town to tour the crime scene. And they had the balls to accuse us of being sloppy.

EdgarAllenPoot: No wonder Reingold was crying. He knew he had no chance of solving this.

Margarita5: The audacity of the DPD coming after us. Amateur sleuths make no money doing this. We do it purely because we care. And Reingold tried to tell the world we're trolls, or worse, murder-voyeurs. Whoever leaked those files and called the DPD on their shit is a hero.

SeattleHawks: Anyone else think this has LordGoku and CitizenNight's fingerprints all over it? I mean, come on. A hack?

Margarita5: There's no way. If it was them, they'd be racing through the forum taking victory laps. We'd never hear the end of it.

CitizenNight: For once I have to agree with **@Margarita5**. Too bad, though. Whoever did it must be brilliant.

It was clear the journalists were in our forums, watching us again—not to catch and vilify us this time but to print what we were posting. Shortly after a Network user theorized that the DPD was purposefully bungling the case because the killer was a cop and they were protecting their own, a *Daily Mail* headline screamed "Delphine Cops Protecting One of Their Own in Sorority Massacre Case?"

But the turn of events that really shocked us—the thing no one could've predicted—was Madeleine Edmonds's parents appearing on the *Today* show.

37

—

IT WAS EASY TO TELL Mr. and Mrs. Edmonds were Madeleine's parents if you'd spent as much time staring at Madeleine's pictures as I had. Her dad, the owner of a hardware-store franchise, was tall and lean like her; her mom, a dental hygienist, had the same heart-shaped face and white-blond hair. They sat side by side in plush chairs on the brightly lit *Today* show set and discussed the nightmare of losing a daughter to violence. Mr. Edmonds talked about the person Madeleine had been, Mrs. Edmonds the way she used to make Valentine's cards every year for her granny. But no one remembered much of that, because the thing they said that reverberated around every newspaper and corner of the internet was this:

Mr. Edmonds sat up tall, folded his hands together, and looked the anchor in the eye. "Given the length of time that's passed without any leads, and the files that were recently leaked showing the Delphine police have mismanaged the crime scene, my wife and I no longer have confidence that Chief Reingold can solve our daughter's case."

Mrs. Edmonds turned away from the anchor and addressed the camera directly. "Chief Reingold, if you feel differently, please consider returning our calls. To the true-crime community: we need your help.

Please use everything in your considerable arsenal to find our daughter's killer. He's out there, free to hunt and kill more people. We don't have anyone else to turn to. You're our last, best hope."

You couldn't have devised a more perfect entreaty to hook us. We were sleuths, yes, but first and foremost, we were nerds. In that moment, Mrs. Edmonds rearranged the galactic battle raging between law enforcement, the media, and the internet. She became our Princess Leia, and we her Luke Skywalker. We would've promised her anything. The Network's web of Delphine threads was alight with vows, exclamation points, *Star Wars* GIFs. Historians of the case have widely criticized the Edmondses for their appearance, which "incited the mobs and inspired the second wave of the Great Bombardment,"* but they seem to forget that they were desperate, grieving parents. You don't know what you'll do until you've been there.

After the Edmondses humiliated the police, Goku, Mistress, Citizen, and I gathered in Signal to celebrate, toasting how quickly the tables had turned. Mistress had a bottle of white wine—Riesling was all she could stomach—Goku had a rare sake, Citizen had a glass of Kentucky bourbon, and I'd raided my parents' dusty liquor cabinet for a small glass of something called Amaretto.

"It's incredible," Citizen said, looking every inch the triumphant captain. "I'm still reeling at how fast the leak spread. And to have Madeleine's parents on our side."

"Barely any media stories about us today," Goku reported.

"Thank God." Mistress exhaled. "I don't think my sons could've handled any more. They were already threatening to sue everyone from NBC to Nina Grace."

---

* *Hunting the Idaho Butcher: The Case That Transformed American Investigation*, Karen Calloway, page 209.

"Here's to an end to Greg and Mateo's high blood pressure," Citizen said, raising his glass.

We all toasted, then took big sips. I almost spit out my booze. The Amaretto was sickly sweet and tasted like almonds.

Goku burst out laughing. "Look at Searcher's face! You lightweight, Search?"

Though it did nothing to convince them I was worldly and experienced, I stuck out my tongue before adding, "It's nice to be the good guys again. But everyone's talking about the chief. No one's talking about Harlow White."

"Give them time," Citizen urged.

Suddenly the Signal frame wavered and Lightly's face appeared on-screen. The chat fell silent. We hadn't seen or heard from him since the leak hit the news. We'd all assumed he needed time to cool down. We looked at each other for a long, fraught moment, and then Citizen said, "Hey, Lightly."

"How dare you?" Cold fury was packed into his voice. Sweat pricked my armpits.

Citizen tried to keep a calm tone. "I had to—"

"You did not!" Lightly yelled.

Citizen's chest heaved. "When someone hits you, you hit back!"

"Wrong. Sometimes you turn your cheek and take the beating."

Citizen's face shuttered. "You sound just like my dad."

Lightly raised a finger. "I told you that your ego was going to be your downfall. I *warned* you. Do you understand these are the actions of an unhinged narcissist?"

"Hey—" Citizen started.

"Hey, *you!*" Lightly boomed, and I gasped. I was wide-eyed, heart pounding. "None of you have ever been cops. You don't understand that it's not enough to solve a crime. You have to solve it the *right* way, crossing your t's and dotting your i's, or it's all for nothing. When it comes to the law, the ends don't justify the means. Say we catch this killer and he hires some fancy-pants lawyer who gets all the evidence against him deemed inadmissible because *your* leak undermines all confidence in what the DPD has done. All because you just had to go and one-up a man who slighted you. It's not about what's best for you—it's about those three girls!"

"Lightly," Mistress pleaded.

"Wait," I whispered. "Please—"

"No. Whatever happens from now on, I want no part of it." Lightly sucked in a breath. "I quit."

38

—

CHIEF REINGOLD HAD BEEN LEVELED. In his next press conference, there was a grayness to his skin, like he hadn't been sleeping
properly. In a quiet voice, he announced that the FBI would be taking
over the investigation. Everyone knew it was a punishment. Rumors
swirled that the governor of Idaho had called Chief Reingold himself and
demanded he bring in the Feds. You could practically see the chief's tail
between his legs that day.

We were humbled too, after losing Lightly. For days after he quit, the
four of us didn't talk. It was painful. Our family of sleuths had become
the center of my life after my dad died, and for the second time in less
than a year, my center had unraveled. I started having my stress dreams
again, the ones where my dad sank into a cold black sea and there was
nothing I could do to reach him. I regretted voting to release the files and
reached out to Mistress to say so.

"You know, the more I think about it, the more I understand why
Lightly quit," Mistress said, her knitting needles moving rhythmically.
It was an hour before I was due at Starbucks to start my shift, and even
earlier for Mistress in Des Moines. Luckily for me, she liked to watch
the sunrise. That morning, warm reddish-gold light glowed through my

bedroom window, promising a fresh start. It wasn't only the sky that was comforting—being in Mistress's presence had a soothing effect. She was a gentle person, and as someone who's waded deep in the muck of humanity, I think gentle people are vastly underrated.

"What do you mean?"

She worked the yarn. "Do you know why he quit the force?"

"Because he thought the Chicago PD didn't respond properly to a little girl's kidnapping, and it resulted in her death."

Mistress nodded. "Lightly and his wife can't have children." Off my surprised look, she clucked. "A medical reality, I'm afraid. But their best friends, people they grew up with, had a little girl. Juliana. And to Lightly, Juliana might as well have been his biological child. That's how close they were."

"Oh no," I murmured, because I knew that name from the news.

"One day, Juliana didn't come home on the school bus, and the Rubleses panicked. Lightly assumed the Chicago PD would be all over helping him locate her, but they slow-rolled him, told him to check her friends' houses and the like before assigning police resources. Except, only two months earlier, an eight-year-old white girl had gone missing, and a massive search sprang up immediately. That case was all over the news, even in Des Moines."

"What did Lightly do?"

"He played ball. He checked every known acquaintance of Juliana's, but she was nowhere. By then, her parents were having a meltdown. And Lightly had a feeling in his gut that something terrible had happened. He managed to convince his boss to let him organize a search party with K-9s, but it was one-third the size of the group that came out for the little white girl. I mean, cops were volunteering their time off to search for her, but not Juliana. They didn't find any trace of her, but they found a witness who said they saw Juliana get in a blue Volvo with a white man outside her school."

I sat in front of my computer, mesmerized and sickened.

"Then the Rubleses got a ransom letter, asking for a million dollars to be dropped off at an abandoned warehouse on the outskirts of Chicago. They were both doctors, so they had money. They were willing to pay the ransom, but Lightly did his detective thing with the note, figured out via surveillance cameras how it had been dropped off at the house, traced the Volvo back to an address, and figured out that the nephew of the woman who lived there had a record of sexual assault, even though he hadn't reported himself as a sex offender living in the area. He asked for a team to bust down the doors and search for Juliana, but the neighborhood was a well-to-do place, and his superiors were skittish about conducting a raid. They told Lightly to drop the ransom money instead."

Mistress's knitting needles stopped. "Unfortunately, it turned out the man who took Juliana had no intention of giving her back. When he didn't show up at the drop site, Lightly ignored commands and raided the house anyway, just him and his partner. They found Juliana's body in a pool house in the backyard. She'd been dead less than eight hours. If Lightly had been able to go in when he asked, he could've saved her."

"That's horrible."

"Not only did Lightly lose his surrogate daughter, but the Rubleses blamed him for her death."

"What? Why?"

She sighed. "Grieving people don't always think logically. All they knew was they were hurting, and Lightly was the detective who should've been able to protect her. They needed somewhere to direct their pain. He says he understands, even if it breaks his heart."

"Were there consequences for the Chicago PD?"

Mistress resumed knitting. "There were some protests outside department headquarters. Lightly attended as a civilian and ended up getting in a fistfight with an officer who came to shut it down."

"I guess that explains the arrest and mug shot."

Mistress chuckled. "Lightly is a principled man who became disillusioned with the institution of policing. It didn't sit well on his conscience to participate in an organization that turned its back on Juliana. So he quit. But he couldn't stay away from cases for too long. The need to help burns bright in him."

"I think he was wrong about his true-crime archetype," I said. "You know your thing from *Savage Appetites*? He said he was a Detective, but the work isn't cerebral for him. It's about standing up for people. He's a Defender."

"Huh." Mistress cocked her head. "You might be right."

"But why did he quit over the leak? Wasn't the Delphine PD messing up like the cops in Chicago?"

Mistress got a faraway look in her eyes. "He believes we weren't putting the victims' needs first. And he knows firsthand what can happen when politics get in the way of solving crimes."

39

—

IT WAS A GRIM TIME in the wake of Lightly leaving, but there were two silver linings. The first I stumbled into after I decided I needed an escape from the Delphine case and put all my effort into my dad-investigation. By then, I'd read all of his texts and emails, and it had occurred to me that another way to hear his voice would be to read his posts on the *Star Trek* forum. Like me, he'd spent a lot of time online, so there were pieces of him digitally archived, artifacts I could trace his presence in.

The only time I'd been on his *Star Trek* forum was when I signed in under his name to tell his friends he'd passed. We'd been flooded with messages of sympathy that I couldn't bear to read at the time. Now I read them all. Then I registered my own account. I figured I'd come as myself, Janeway Sharp, but for the first time in my life, there was an overabundance of Janeways—the website suggested I try Janeway239586647, which was staggering. So I went back to my standby, @Searcher24, and jumped into the boards.

Searcher24: Hey, all. My name's Janeway Sharp. I'm Daniel Sharp's
daughter (**@commanderdanielsharp**). I was the one who posted

to invite you to his funeral. I'm missing my dad and wondered if anyone has anything about him you could share? I'll take it all, no matter how small.

After about thirty minutes—clearly, Trekkie forums weren't as lightning-fast as true crime—someone answered.

BillDonohue: Hi, Janeway (excellent name, by the way, but I wouldn't expect anything less from Dan). I was friends with your father and would be happy to tell you anything you want. Off the top of my head, I remember a few years back when @AnnikaHansen joined the group and started getting harassed by this guy, but people wouldn't say anything because he was a bigwig in the fandom and she was new and young (and a woman). But Dan chewed that guy a new one and took the fandom to task for allowing the harassment.

AnnikaHansen: Yeah, Dan was the best. Funny as hell, too. Hi, Janeway. Was sorry to hear what happened.

MikeCarpenter: Dan was a model Trekkie: he believed in reason, progress, and a humanitarian spirit.

BillDonohue: Have you read his fanfiction?

My brain short-circuited.

Searcher24: His...what?

BillDonohue: Ha! Dan loved writing. Said if he hadn't gone into the navy, he would've liked to have been a screenwriter.

Searcher24: I honestly didn't know that. My brain is kind of exploding.

BillDonohue: Your dad had this longer fic that got pretty popular. Want me to find it for you?

Back then I had a very particular idea of what fanfiction involved. I gulped.

> **Searcher24:** I'm kind of scared to ask, but is it...sexy?
> **BillDonohue:** Oh, NO. Not that kind of fan fiction. Your dad loved exploring the mythology of the *Star Trek* universe. And writing cool battle scenes.
> **Searcher24:** In that case, I would love to read it.
> **BillDonohue:** Give me a few days. Pretty sure I saved it somewhere.

Reading a story my dad had written, no matter how nerdy, was an even better gift than I'd imagined. I felt almost giddy with anticipation.

The second good thing that happened was that people finally starting talking about Harlow White. Because the Network reminded me painfully of Lightly, I'd temporarily abandoned it for r/TrueCrime, and Harlow was the talk of the subreddit.

> **lunalove:** Okay, in breaking down what Ms. Harlow told the cops, 4 things strike me as red flags. #1: She claims she mistook the sounds of Mad, Stace, and Lar screaming as them partying. In what world do the screams of people dying sound like partying?
> > **tornadowatch:** Yeah, it's not like those sorority girls listened to death metal. Don't know how she confused it.
> > **ursulareid:** I actually think this is believable. Think about it— she was sleeping and her sleep-addled brain just interpreted it as partying.
> **lunalove:** #2: SHE SAW THE GUY IN THE SKI MASK and just let him go!!! I'm sorry, do college students hang out in ski masks these days?
> > **redwhiteandcool:** No way. I live in freaking Alaska and no one wears a ski mask INDOORS unless they're committing a crime.

idahoobsessed: I can't believe she full-on admitted she saw the murderer walk by and everyone's just like, ok cool. Why didn't she call the cops?

thankyounext: And why did the murderer just walk past her and let her go?

redwhiteandcool: Nothing about this case makes sense.

lunalove: #3: She admitted she locked her door after seeing the guy in the mask. To me that's a sign she knew he was up to no good.

mightymouse5: Good point. She was scared enough to lock her door, so she knew something was up.

lunalove: #4: Harlow wakes up, sees what must've been the most horrific crime scene you can imagine—the police report said there was blood all over the walls, even on the ceiling—and then her next move is to call her friend Jordan? FIRST MOVE IS THE COPS!

billandsookie2: Has anyone dug into who this Jordan guy is?

moonlightxx: His name's Jordan Beckett, he's a senior at NIU, and he's from Burlington, Vermont. A forensic science major. Not in a frat.

lunalove: He's a forensic science major?! Do you think Harlow called him to ask a forensics question? Didn't the police file say they touched the bodies?

Searcher24: I'm also wondering what made the cops dismiss Harlow as a suspect so quickly. Why are they treating her like she's just an innocent victim when there are so many red flags in her story?

electricboogaloo: Are you saying you think she could've been the killer?

Searcher24: Let's not make Harlow the next Chandler. I'm just saying it's weird.

goodtimesroll: Maybe they ruled her out because she doesn't fit the size 9 footprint outside the sliding-glass door. That would be a women's size 11. That's really big for a girl.

Searcher24: I've been reading a bunch of serial killer lore. Did you know the Shoe Fetish Killer and the Phoenix Grim Reaper purposefully wore the wrong-sized shoes to throw off detectives?

goodtimesroll: Do you really think Harlow is that smart?

Searcher24: Why not?

goodtimesroll: She's a 22-year-old girl. She dressed up like the sexy Easter bunny for Halloween, lol. Not exactly a criminal mastermind.

Searcher24: See, I'm worried this attitude is exactly why the cops dismissed her.

I *had* studied pictures of Harlow. I'd started combing through her social media, thinking about the circumstances of that night, drawing my own timelines. And something wasn't sitting right about the picture she'd painted of herself as the traumatized victim, arbitrarily spared.

Call it a savant's intuition.

40

—

"THE KILLER COULDN'T HAVE BEEN a woman." Goku leaned back in his desk chair and chewed on a stick of licorice. "A woman wouldn't have the upper-body strength to strike the victims with that much force."

"That's plain sexist," Mistress countered. "A woman could be strong enough. Especially with adrenaline."

"Did you see the Network's calling Harlow 'The Girl Who Lived'?" Citizen shook his head. "What nerds."

The chatter around Harlow had gotten loud enough that we'd decided to have our first Signal chat without Lightly to discuss it. We were doing our best to soldier on, but the whole tenor of the meeting felt wrong. The magic was gone.

"I think it's sexist to dismiss her, too," I said. "I mean, the stab wounds were made by a fixed-blade weapon, right?" I had the autopsy results open on my computer, the little sketches the medical examiner had made to mark where the wounds had fallen on each body. "Everyone immediately assumed it was a hunting knife."

"Because there are a million hunting knives matching the stab wounds, and hunting is big in Idaho," Goku said. "Occam's razor, remember?"

"Yeah, well, the problem with Occam's razor is that it's still subjective. Sometimes what you think is the simplest explanation is colored by your experience. Or your gender." Regrettably, I felt like my gender studies professor, but I pushed on anyway. "Because what are kitchen knives if not fixed-blade knives?"

Goku burst out laughing, rubbing his bloodshot eyes. I wondered if he was getting as little sleep as I was since Lightly left. "Come on, Searcher. Next you're going to tell me the footprint wasn't a Vans sneaker, it was a ballet slipper. And the killer murdered on behalf of feminism."

"Rude."

"You know the percentage of murderers who are women is ten percent, right?" Citizen was bouncing around his kitchen as he listened. He seemed keyed up, and I wondered if he was feeling even more pressure to lead now that Lightly was gone. "Largely speaking, women kill children, or domestic partners in retaliation for abuse. And they don't stab people. They poison, drown, or asphyxiate. There are hardly any women serial killers, and the ones who do qualify tend to be nurses—caretakers who get a God complex or have a mental breakdown."

"Just because the odds are slim doesn't mean we can rule it out," I insisted.

Silence stretched.

Mistress smiled sadly. "This is usually where Lightly would offer some peace-making statement."

I sighed. "It's not the same without him."

Citizen frowned. "We're a family with or without Lightly."

I stared at my screen. All the little marks on the body-shaped drawings from the autopsy report swam into a blur of black ink, a sea of slashes. I frowned at one of the bodies, denser than the others. "Guys?"

Mistress looked up. "What's wrong, Searcher?"

"Do you have the DPD files open? I'm looking at page seven of the autopsy report."

"Give me a sec," Mistress said. I could hear Citizen and Goku clicking. "Got it."

"Look at the drawing of Madeleine's wounds. Compared to the other girls."

"Holy shit," Goku said. "Why didn't we notice this before?"

"She was stabbed so many more times." Citizen's eyes scanned the screen. "Did they give numbers?"

"Thirty-seven times," Mistress murmured. "Stacie was stabbed ten times. Larissa six, including the throat slash."

"Overkill," Citizen said abruptly.

I squinted at him. "What?"

"Overkill is when a killer injures their victim above and beyond what's necessary to kill them. Excessive trauma. It can indicate strong emotions like rage or helplessness."

"I can't believe I didn't notice," Goku murmured again.

"So the killer went straight to Madeleine's room and stabbed her almost four times as many times as the other girls," I said. "It looks like you were right to focus on her, Citizen."

"I guess it's a good thing I finally hacked her—"

An ear-splitting howl came from Goku's screen, making all of us startle back.

"Jesus!" I gasped as he scrambled to stop the noise. "What is that?"

"Police scanner website!" he shouted. "I've been listening to the DPD's radio!"

Citizen jammed his hands over his ears. "Good God, man."

Finally, Goku muted it. "Sorry. I wrote a program to issue a loud alarm in case I was playing video games. But it's only supposed to go off for certain codes..." His face paled.

"What?" Mistress demanded.

"Hold on," he said and raised the volume on the audio. A staticky voice cut through. "Officers, we have a 187 at 1756 Collegiate Parkway. Multiple DBs. All vehicles requested."

"What's—" I started.

"Homicide," Goku said, eyes wide. "Multiple dead bodies."

41
—

ON SUNDAY, MARCH 31, A bewildered Chief Reingold stood behind the podium bearing the Delphine Police Department seal, flanked by stern-faced members of the Federal Bureau of Investigation, and announced what we already knew: a serial murderer was stalking the streets of Delphine. We listened in somber silence as he relayed the latest horror, struggling to keep his words clinical.

Sometime the previous night—technically, between 2:00 and 4:00 a.m. that morning—someone had entered 1756 Collegiate Parkway, a residence close to campus, where three Northern Idaho University juniors lived, all members of the women's track team. The house was an unassuming, two-story wooden box painted royal blue, not a show-piece but a solid rental for less-than-discerning college students. It was located less than half a mile from NIU's track field and only one mile from 8022 Queen Lace Avenue. Just like before, upon entering the house the killer swiftly ascended the stairs to the second-floor bedrooms, demonstrating familiarity with the house's layout. He murdered twenty-year-old Greta Danvers first, stabbing her with what preliminary reports suggested was another fixed-blade knife. She was sleeping when he attacked, so defensive wounds were minimal. The majority of her injuries were sustained in her back, the back of her neck, and her skull.

He then moved to twenty-one-year-old Katya Novik's bedroom, where, from the position of her body, it looked like he caught her as she was climbing out of bed. After stabbing her multiple times in the face, chest, neck, and arms, he left her to bleed out on the floor. So much blood pooled around Katya that it leaked through the wooden floorboards to stain the first-floor carpet. It temporarily confused the first officers on the scene, who searched the first floor for the source of the blood.

Detectives speculated the killer left Katya suddenly because he heard Greta and Katya's third roommate, Shuri Washington, rush out of her bedroom and down the stairs. Shuri's mangled body was found splayed at the bottom of the staircase, blood from the numerous wounds in her back staining the off-white carpet. The killer then left the house, most likely the same way he came in, which detectives speculated was, again, the sliding-glass doors at the back of the unit. Almost move for move, he'd repeated his actions from 8022 Queen Lace. In a show of staggeringly brutal violence that spanned less than twenty minutes, the Delphine Three had become the Delphine Six.

I remember feeling numb as I absorbed the details. Goku's police scanner had alerted us to the fact of the slayings, but the press conference, conducted only hours later, with the FBI by Chief Reingold's side, confirmed the cases were connected.

"It can't be Harlow," Goku said. I could tell my friends were as shell-shocked as I was. Even Citizen, the serial killer enthusiast, looked distraught. "What motive would Harlow have to kill three members of the women's track team?"

"We shouldn't assume anything," I said, trying to channel Lightly. "We should check to see if she knew them. And we should still talk to

Jordan Beckett. See why she brought him over that morning. That part of the story still bugs me."

"The killer is watching these girls," Mistress said suddenly. Her gaze was searing. "Whoever's doing this knows when they're home in bed. They know the interior of the houses. They're stalking them."

"That's good for us," Citizen said, and before I could protest, he raised a hand. "It increases the likelihood that there will be evidence. The more time this guy spent following them, the more opportunities there were for him to be caught on camera or video, or for a witness to remember one of the girls having a tail."

"Hey." Goku looked at his second screen. "Did you know SeattleHawks and some of his cronies are in Delphine?"

"What?" I frowned. "Right now?"

"Look at his latest posts on the thread. He said he and a few others rented an RV and road-tripped from Washington to Delphine. He's outside the second murder house describing the scene. Says there's a ton of people gathered behind the crime tape snapping pictures and filming for their MurderTubes."

"Like it's a concert." I was filled with a conflicting mix of envy and secondhand shame. Seattle was on the ground, looking at the house in real life. He was clearly being exploitative, but still—he could smell the pine trees, feel the mountain chill, be in the thick of things.

"The sleuths are flooding in while students are flooding out," Mistress said. "I don't know if you've been following student TikToks, but they're saying campus is a ghost town. The minute the news of the second murder hit, everyone packed up and left."

"I've seen a few people from Reddit—" Citizen stopped midsentence, eyes widening.

A ringing sound like a doorbell came from the Signal interface. A message popped up: GeorgeLightly requests entrance.

42

—

SHOCKED SILENCE HUNG OVER THE group. "Is it real?" I asked.

"I...think so," Goku said, though he sounded just as unsure.

Lightly, our lost father, was knocking on our door.

Mistress snapped. "Citizen, you going to get that?"

He cleared his throat. "I should, right?"

"*Yes*," we all shouted.

He scrambled to click Accept. Lightly's face filled the screen. "Hi," he said in his sonorous voice. "You've seen the news?"

"We watched the presser." Goku coughed to clear the thickness in his throat. "You?"

"Same." Lightly leaned back and kicked one leg over the other, resting his hands on a chino-clad knee. "Look, this second slaying changes things. Shuri Washington was a Black girl. I'm not saying I don't care about solving the murders of the white women, because I do. But he murdered a woman of color. I can't pretend that doesn't gut me in a whole new way." He frowned. "I also can't pretend I'm not still angry at you all for leaking confidential police files for your own vendetta."

Thankfully, Citizen remained silent.

Lightly sighed, and some of his bravado fell. "But I'm sorry we fought. And I miss your friendship." He shifted. "Mistress, it's especially strange not having your voice in my ear all day. Junie says she misses you."

"Tell her I miss her too," Mistress said softly.

"I would like to come back," he said. "I think you four are the best out there, and we can catch this son of a bitch if we work together. If you'll have me back, I have some thoughts about the second killings." He said it all in classic Lightly style—matter-of-fact but with sincere emotion.

I cleared my throat. "I don't know if we're supposed to take a vote or something, but I want Lightly back."

Citizen looked at me and started laughing. "Of course we want you back," he crowed. "Nothing's the same without you, Light. We're a family. We belong together."

"And I'm sorry," Goku said. "We should've had more discussions before we leaked the file. I was out of my mind with all the journalists crawling up my ass. I wasn't thinking clearly, and I've felt sick about it."

"I prayed you'd come back," Mistress said, wiping her eyes. "I didn't know if I had it in me to do this without you."

"Thanks, guys." Lightly's eyes were warm. "One more thing, and then I'll stop with all the mushy stuff." He looked away from the computer. "I think I'm quick to distrust people, after Chicago. My colleagues let me down, and now it's easy for me to assume the worst in people. Junie's been on me to—" he lifted his fingers to make air quotes—"'unpack it.'"

"We all have our things," I said simply. When Lightly smiled at me, I felt some part of my heart weld back together. He clapped his hands. "All right, enough with that. Back to the case."

A buzz filled the air. Lightly was back, and so was the magic.

"As soon as the news broke this morning, I started thinking," he said. "All this time, we've been focused on the girls, their relationships to boyfriends and roommates, and so on. But this second slaying—it suggests the murders may not be personal."

"That's what we were saying." Goku straightened in his chair. "That the killer's a stalker. Choosing his victims because they're in the right place at the right time. We should find out if the track girls also went out partying the night they were killed. Some serials look for vulnerability, and being drunk's a big one."

"Random predator theory," Citizen said softly. "The wolf in the night."

"This flies in the face of what they usually tell you to do, which is figure out your victims." Lightly steepled his fingers. "But if it's not about the girls, we have to figure out the killer. What do we know about him? I was thinking about the part of the case you were so focused on, Citizen—his ability to kill three people and leave virtually no evidence."

Citizen looked flattered.

"I looked into which FBI agents had been assigned to Delphine," Lightly continued. "And lo and behold, I found my old buddy Lawrence Hale on the task force. We went through the Academy together. Funny thing about Lawrence is, he told me he'd make a statement supporting me back when everything went down in Chicago, but he pulled out at the last minute, saying it was too risky for his career. The man owes me a favor."

"Are you saying we have a new in?" Mistress asked. "I don't have to go back to Joe and beg?"

"Fuck Joe," Goku said. Joe had ghosted us after the leak.

Lightly nodded. "I reached out to him, and he said the FBI is eager to steer clear of the high-profile wars Chief Reingold waged. They want to avoid mass hysteria now that they've got a serial killer. I asked if the second crime scene matched the first, nearly clean of evidence. He said yes."

"From what I can tell," Citizen said, "the second crime scene is even cleaner than the first. Practically perfect. Like the killer's getting better."

"Ah, but," Lightly said, raising a finger, "no one's perfect. To pull off violence like this, a person would have to undertake a massive amount of planning. With that much blood flying around and soaking the floor, the killer's bound to step in it. Which means, if they didn't track bloody footprints, they either wore booties they discarded or they brought something like a cloth to clean their shoes. They wore gloves and a mask, but those things don't prevent every hair and eyelash you discard from dropping to the floor. They knew that, so they brought Lysol wipes, maybe tucked into their jacket. Even in the throes of violence, this person had the wherewithal to clean. And quickly, too."

"They're meticulous." I'd been listening intently to Lightly's thoughts, trying to envision the kind of person he was describing. "They know enough about crime scenes and forensics to know what to avoid. Like you said, Citizen." I nodded at him. "Maybe law enforcement or security experience. Maybe even medical?"

"They know the girls' routines on Saturday nights," Mistress added. "So they're conducting either physical or digital stalking. They knew to go through the sliding-glass doors. Maybe they'd been to the houses before and noticed the girls kept them unlocked?"

"Sliding-glass doors are notorious for being the easiest to break into, anyway," Citizen said.

"I asked Lawrence for the crime scene photos of the second house," Lightly said.

"Whoa." Goku raised his eyebrows. "And he sent them?"

Citizen whistled. "The detective comes bearing gifts."

"I'm throwing the link in the chat now," Lightly said, double-tapping at his computer. "Take a look."

43

—

BLOOD-SOAKED IMAGES FILLED MY SCREEN. Women's bodies contorted in painful, alien ways. My stomach seized as if I'd been punched, but I enlarged the first in the series anyway. A strawberry-blond girl lay on her stomach in bed, her head turned to the side, eyes wide and unseeing. I think her sheets might've been blue before the blood. Her back was gouged, the strikes so deep you could see inside her body to her sinewy muscles and the white glimmer of her rib cage. Her hair was matted with blood. It sprayed up the white walls of her bedroom like a demented Jackson Pollock.

"This is Greta," Lightly said. "The first kill. This is where the killer was most in control, had the greatest element of surprise. You can see she barely even got the chance to move."

My stomach lurched in warning.

"Go to the next," he instructed, and I obeyed. A raven-haired girl lay hunched over near a bed, on all fours but slumped over, her forehead resting on the floor. I couldn't see her face, and I was grateful for that. Wicked cuts had torn apart the flesh of her arms, which were splayed around her. I'd never seen such a wide, dark lake of blood in any crime scene photo.

"Katya Novik," Lightly said. "She made it out of her bed."

"How sad," Mistress whispered. "Look at her all hunched up trying to protect herself. Little baby."

I bit the inside of my lip.

"And next, Shuri Washington," Lightly said. I took a deep breath and clicked to the next photo. And before I could get control of myself, my stomach heaved, bile racing up my throat. I lunged to the side and threw up all over the tiles.

"Searcher?" I heard Citizen call. "What's happening?"

"She threw up," Goku said.

"Jane, honey, are you all right?" Mistress asked.

I straightened, hand hovering over my mouth. It was humiliating. "Give me a second." I turned off my camera and rushed to the bathroom.

As I spit the minty toothpaste into the sink, then scrubbed the tile with lemony cleaner, I thought: *What's wrong with you? These aren't your first crime photos.* Not by a long shot.

When I turned my camera back on, everyone was looking back at me with eyes full of compassion. "I don't know why I threw up," I said. "Sorry. I can be professional."

"Don't be embarrassed," Mistress insisted. "It doesn't make you weak. It shows your humanity. Frankly, it's worrisome the four of us are so desensitized."

I nodded quickly.

"You ready to continue?" Lightly asked, and I nodded again. I forced myself to confront the picture as Lightly talked. Shuri lay on the carpet at the bottom of the stairs. The shot was taken from above by someone standing on the stairs. Each of her limbs was twisted in a different direction. Most disturbing was her head, twisted so far on her neck that she faced us with unblinking eyes. It reminded me of the moment in *The Exorcist* when the demon twists the little girl's head 180 degrees, except this was real. Shuri was wearing a pajama set I'd recognized immediately, the familiarity a shock: it was from Aerie, plaid pajama shorts and a hot-pink T-shirt with small hearts stitched across the back. I knew the front side, which we couldn't see, said "Daddy's Favorite." I'd gotten it for Christmas four years ago.

"It was a fast, brutal affair," Lightly said. "Nearly perfect in execution."

"Nearly?" Citizen raised an eyebrow.

"No matter how well a person plans something, life is never fully within our control. We need to look at what exceeded the killer's planning that night. Maybe that's where we'll find our clues."

"Shuri," I said weakly, swallowing down more bile. "Shuri running down the stairs surprised the killer. He abandoned Katya to run after her. And Shuri was a track star. She must've been fast. The killer's lucky he caught her before she escaped. The big knife wound in her back is long but shallow, so he must've lunged for her and barely caught her. He was lucky."

Lightly looked at me like I was an A student. "Exactly. Those few minutes almost exceeded his control. I was hoping you'd help me analyze the photos of the staircase. But Searcher, if you're not up for it—"

"No," I said quickly. "This is what I'm here for." I would not look away from the brutal truth of Shuri's death. I would not betray her.

We spent the next hour moving methodically through the thirty-seven pictures crime scene investigators had taken of Shuri's room, her doorway, the staircase, her body, and its surroundings at the base of the stairs. We talked through every inch of the images, calling out everything that could be a bloody fingerprint—no, a shadow on the wall; a fingernail fragment; no, a piece of lint—or a footprint (inconclusive).

As we came to the last picture, Citizen shook his head. "He left nothing."

I stared at the picture. It was a close-up of Shuri's back. I'd zoomed in, hoping the magnified view would help me repress the fact that I was looking at a mutilated body. But against my will, it came to me:

I was full of a fear so intense I'd never felt its like before, mixed with lingering disbelief that this nightmare was real and not a dream or horror movie. But the screams of my friends, those guttural, primal noises, had ignited an instinct in me, and I knew I needed to get outside to freedom. I lunged out of bed, swung open my door and tore out the doorway, my socked feet slipping as I turned for the stairs. I could hear the heavy thud of footsteps behind me, and the panic was nearly paralyzing. But I pushed myself forward, those well-honed muscles in my legs, the ones I'd cultivated, reacting with muscle memory. I was making it, I was flying down the stairs, I would see my mother again, my father, all was not lost—

And then that first strike, the blade of the knife parting the skin and muscle of my shoulder, agony lighting up my body. But I kept moving, and maybe I heard a grunt, a sound of exertion, my end not coming easily like my roommates'. My feet hit the bottom of my stairs, so close to freedom, and then he lunged again. The knife found me and I went down, hitting the floor hard, rough carpet tearing my face as I turned it, struggling to breathe. And then he was on top of me, striking as I writhed, brain screaming at me to stop him, find some way to save myself, find some way to tell my parents I loved them across a thousand miles. I needed them to know the pain was extreme but my life with them was nothing short of perfect.

I choked back a sob and ducked my head so no one could see my face. "Shuri made it to the bottom of the stairs." I forced the words out. "He must've been panicking. He had to leap, strike her multiple times before she fell, and then he kept stabbing her, wanting to guarantee she died."

"What do you think that means?" Mistress asked softly. Citizen was looking at me like I was an alien, Goku with pity, but Lightly was nodding.

"She frightened him," Lightly said. "Which means he was the least calm in that moment. Searcher, I think you're earning that savant title after all. Let's zoom as close as we can around Shuri's back. Steel yourselves. This won't be pretty."

I held my breath and zoomed in all the way, pulling the cursor across the picture millimeter by millimeter, searching the floor, her outstretched arms, the gruesome wounds that had killed her.

"There," Mistress said suddenly. "On the carpet next to her right hand. Near her pointer finger. Is that an eyelash?"

We raced to examine it, stretching across her right side to her hand. And there, tiny but promising, was the slenderest black hair.

"Holy shit. I think so," Goku said.

"I don't know." Citizen squinted. "Even if it is, it could be Shuri's."

"Only one way to find out," Lightly said gamely. "I'll shoot this over to Lawrence. Let him know we found a possible DNA source."

"Can you imagine if it *is* the killer's?" Mistress said. "Then no one could say we didn't add value to this case."

"Good work, Mistress and Searcher," Lightly said.

I felt proud then—weak and nauseous, but proud. We had our old fire back, and I was doing something that made a difference. I had no way of knowing then that our big break would only make the Delphine murders a thousand times stranger, raise a thousand more questions. Twist the case into a place no one—not us, not the FBI, not the world watching—could've imagined.

44

IN THE FIVE DAYS IT took to get word back from the FBI on our potential DNA source, I decided to keep pushing on my pet project, which was Harlow. The true-crime community had abandoned her as a suspect after news of the second slayings. But I couldn't shake my suspicion. I especially wanted to talk to the mysterious Jordan Beckett, the forensic science major who'd deleted his social media in the wake of the murders. No one had been able to make contact with him. He seemed to have disappeared, which was kind of impressive.

I tried his school email—NIU students' emails all followed the same first name–last name formula, so it was easy to figure out—but predictably got no response. Finally, in my desperation, I paid a sketchy guy on Reddit fifty of my hard-earned dollars to track down Jordan's cell phone number. While I was 90 percent certain I'd essentially lit my money on fire, lo and behold, a day later the guy dropped a number into my inbox. It started with a Vermont area code, which was promising, so I tried it.

Jane Sharp: Hi, Jordan. I know it's weird that I have your private
    number, and I apologize. But my name is Jane Sharp, and I'm one

of the amateur detectives working on the Delphine cases. I was wondering if you could answer a few brief questions?

To my surprise, he wrote back immediately.

Jordan Beckett: How did you get this number? I scrubbed it.

Damn. The Reddit guy was good.

Jane Sharp: I'm a detective. Figuring stuff out is what I do.
Jordan Beckett: I don't want to talk. How do I know you're not a journalist? Delphine is crawling with them. They're waiting outside our classrooms, following us home. It's sick.
Jane Sharp: Go ahead and google me. Trust me, I know a thing or two about unwanted media attention. I promise I'm just a regular person trying to find answers.

About twenty minutes later, when I thought I'd surely lost him, he responded.

Jordan Beckett: Wow, people like you even less than they like me.
Jane Sharp: Yep. Want to help out a fellow pariah with a few harmless questions?
Jordan Beckett: I'm not saying I'll answer. But what do you want to know?

This was my chance. I tamped down my giddiness and composed a response.

Jane Sharp: How do you know Harlow White? You're not in Greek

life. She's an English major and you're forensic science. Just curious how your paths crossed.

Jordan Beckett: I figured this was about her. Harlow dated one of
my friends last year. She seemed like a cool person, so we stayed
in touch after they broke up.

I made note of the past tense—"seemed."

Jordan Beckett: You want to know why she called me to come over
that morning, don't you? That's what everyone wants.

Jane Sharp: Well, yes. I won't lie to you. But I also want to know
why you haven't talked to anyone about it, when it seems like
everyone else at your school is on TikTok every day making
videos with the latest gossip. You're holding a trump card and
you're not using it.

Jordan Beckett: None of those idiots saw what I saw. Those girls
were people, turned into...things. Mutilated objects. They didn't
smell the blood in the air. It was so thick I could taste it. I brushed
my teeth so many times that night I made my gums bleed.

So Jordan had disappeared because he was traumatized. I started to
type, but another message appeared.

Jordan Beckett: It's a game to them. You know, a puzzle. A whodunit
starring girls they know. Is that what this is for you?

Jane Sharp: Of course not. It's an injustice. Especially the fact that
there's been no leads. That's why I was drawn to true crime in the
first place—people deserve better.

It wasn't untrue—I didn't lie to Jordan like I'd lied to Chandler Gray's

fraternity brothers. It was just that the truth was more fulsome, complicated. A minute went by, and then he wrote back.

> **Jordan Beckett:** Harlow called me that morning sounding upset. It
> was weird enough of her to call out of the blue on a Sunday morn-
> ing, and then when I answered and she sounded like she'd been
> crying, I thought...maybe something had happened to her the night
> before, like sexual assault. She asked me if I was still a forensic
> science major, and when I said yes, she asked if I could come over
> right away. I figured she thought I could help with whatever had
> happened to her, I don't know, advise her how best to report it to
> the cops. So I speedwalked over to her house.
>
> **Jane Sharp:** Did you know right away something else was wrong?
>
> **Jordan Beckett:** You couldn't smell the blood on the first floor,
> where Harlow's room was. It looked normal. Nothing out of
> place. I asked her when she'd been assaulted, but she took me
> upstairs and said she'd woken up to find her roommates like
> that. The instant I saw the first one—Larissa—I freaked out
> and started yelling at her to call 911. I couldn't believe what I
> was seeing.

Harlow had ambushed Jordan with her roommates' dead bodies.
The whole thing was so strange.

> **Jane Sharp:** What did she want from you?
>
> **Jordan Beckett:** She asked if I could tell anything about the person
> who'd killed them. She seemed to think being a forensic science
> major meant I could pick up on clues from the scene, like a detec-
> tive in a TV show. She seemed pretty desperate.

Had Harlow been so in shock that her first instinct was to try to identify her friends' killer? Or—my God—did she have a suspect in mind?

> **Jane Sharp:** Did you get the impression she was trying to figure out if the killer was someone in particular?
>
> **Jordan Beckett:** I've thought about it, but I don't know. She asked if I could tell the height of the assailant, whether they were right- or left-handed, if they'd left any clues that I could interpret. I was so shocked I just kept telling her that we needed to call the cops. At one point she reached down and rolled Stacie over in her bed, and that's when I screamed at her not to touch anything. Around then it dawned on me that our DNA was now part of the crime scene. I told her we could get in big trouble, and if she didn't call 911 right away, I would. That finally convinced her.
>
> **Jane Sharp:** Did you tell the police what you told me?
>
> **Jordan Beckett:** Every word. I'm not trying to hide anything. I just don't want to feed the vultures.

If that was true, why wasn't Jordan's interview included in the police report?

> **Jane Sharp:** Thank you. This is really helpful.
>
> **Jordan Beckett:** Do you want to know why I think Harlow called me over? The honest truth?

My heart pounded.

> **Jane Sharp:** Absolutely.
>
> **Jordan Beckett:** I read later that she saw the killer in the middle of the night when she opened her door. She told the cops she thought

it was one of Madeleine's and Stacie's friends or fly-by-nights. I think that morning she realized the person she'd witnessed was the killer, and she was desperate to know if the evidence backed that up. If she'd truly let her roommates' murderer walk by unscathed, or if there was some clue that could've absolved her, pointed in a different direction. I didn't tell the cops this, obviously, but I got this sense of guilt from her. Guilt and maybe... self-preservation.

I started to type, then heard a crash outside my room. I leapt to my feet and flew out into the hallway, calling, "Mom! Are you okay?" Losing someone out of the blue can turn you paranoid. In an instant, I pictured my mom sprawled out on the floor.

But she was up in the attic, peering down the wooden ladder. "Sorry, hon. I dropped a box."

It took me a second for my heart to calm. I used the time to reach for the dropped blue bin in question, its contents spilling over the floor. "What's this?" I asked, holding up an old black sweater that smelled of mothballs.

"Part of your father's winter wardrobe. We were saving it in case we ever moved back to somewhere with seasons." Mom started climbing down the ladder. As I watched her descend, all bony legs and loose skin, it hit me how much weight she'd lost since August. She was tiny.

I sniffed the sweater, hoping for a scent of my father, but there was nothing but must.

"Do me a favor?"

I looked up at her.

"I'm bringing all of your dad's stuff down out of the attic, and pulling it out of the closets and dressers. Will you go through and pull anything you want to keep?"

I frowned, slow to comprehend. "To keep?" We would keep everything, wouldn't we? These were the only pieces of him we had left. For the rest of my life, clutching his sweater was as close as I would get to hugging him. I'd already added his *Legends of the Fall* CD, high school diploma, a half-finished book of crossword puzzles, and the mug I'd gotten him for Christmas in second grade to my shrine.

"I'm going to sort through it and do a yard sale," she said briskly. "Whatever doesn't sell we can donate."

"You can't." My words lashed like a whip, making her flinch. "They're his things."

"Honey, every time I walk through this house and see pictures of him, or walk into my closet and see his clothes, I feel like I'm about to lose it. I won't survive. Can you understand?"

I didn't. "So you're going to erase him? This house is going to look like he was never here?" It was so antithetical to what I'd been doing—saving his messages, reading through his emails, his Trekkie forum. Collecting every bit of him to wrap around myself, build into a fortress of solitude that I could hide in, a monument I could feel proud of. She wanted to shed him like she was shedding her weight, get rid of everything heavy.

The ugliest thought struck me: Was I alone in caring for my father for who he truly was?

"Of course I'm not trying to erase him." My mom was the opposite of my dad. When my dad punished me, he always came back to apologize. But she turned hard, not soft, when she was hurt. "That's a shitty thing to say."

"Just don't get rid of anything. *Anything.*" I turned and fled back to my room.

I was curled on my bed with my door locked, reading through my dad's texts, pausing over each time I told him I loved him and he replied *Love you too, honey,* when the Signal chat chimed.

GeorgeLightly: Lawrence just called. He has news on the DNA and wants to speak to all of us. Possible to drop whatever you're doing and join the chat? **@CitizenNight**, I'll DM you his email.

Distantly I remembered I was due to work soon, but there was no universe in which I was going to miss an honest-to-God FBI agent.

Minutes later the five of us were gathered in the chat, smiling at each other nervously, too keyed up to make small talk. Mistress, Goku, and I were in our usual spots at home, but Citizen was talking from an empty office on base, and Lightly was taking the meeting from the law firm where he ran security. Our interface lagged, freezing everyone in place for a second. And when it unfroze, Hale was with us.

45

—

FBI AGENT LAWRENCE HALE WAS a handsome Black man roughly the same age as Lightly. But while Lightly looked like a kindly professor, there was a sharpness to Hale, in his features and the canny glint in his eyes. He was dressed in a staid navy suit with a tiny American flag pin on the lapel, sitting in an office. I glanced down at my oversized gray hoodie and tried to fold in on myself.

"Howdy, folks." Agent Hale spoke brusquely but with a southern accent. Let me tell you, the two were in tension. "I know this is highly unusual and you must be wondering why the heck I wanted to meet. To get straight to the point, I have confidential news I'd like to share with you. I also wanted to introduce myself to the folks my old friend George is working with. The ones who caught the eyelash."

"So it *was* the killer's?" Citizen's wide blue eyes were locked on him.

"Pardon our manners," Mistress said, shooting Citizen a look. "I'm Tammy Jo Frazier. It's a pleasure to meet you."

One by one, we went around and introduced ourselves, using our real names, and Hale greeted us each of us, taking time to study our faces. I sensed he'd come to take our measure.

When introductions were done, Hale said, "What I'm about to share with you is known only to the FBI and DPD. At this point, we have no plans to make it public. If that changes, I'll let you know. In the meantime, please don't share what I'm about to tell you with anyone, including family members." He cracked a smile at Lightly. "Not even Junie."

"Ten-four," said Lightly.

"Good man. You were the folks who identified the DNA source, so I figured you deserved to know. And I trust George immensely, so hopefully that means I can trust the rest of you as well." Agent Hale picked up a stack of papers. "I also wouldn't mind a fresh set of eyes on this case, as long as we're in agreement that you won't discuss anything I tell you in any public forum."

"We're agreed," Citizen said, and the rest of us nodded.

"All right." Hale glanced down at his papers. "Then strap in, because we're about to go on a ride."

A frisson of thrill raced through me. My phone rang, but I quickly silenced it. A voicemail popped up—my boss.

"We conducted DNA analysis on the eyelash and can conclude it belongs to a male," said Hale.

"There goes the Harlow White theory," Goku murmured.

"It obviously doesn't belong to any of the victims, and Greta, Katya, and Shuri had no other roommates, no boyfriends. From the position the eyelash was discovered in, resting near the tip of Shuri Washington's finger, we believe she may have struck her assailant before her death. We're reasonably confident the eyelash belongs to our perp."

The magnitude of the news washed over us. Mistress said simply, "My God."

Hale smiled wryly. "You don't know the half of it. As I'm sure you're aware, these killings in Delphine have been remarkable for the lack of forensic evidence. It has been incredibly frustrating and, if you'll allow me some candor, quite a struggle for the DPD. They're used to dealing with stolen bicycles and college student DUIs. Not homicides at this level of sophistication."

"Did you run the DNA through CODIS?" Lightly's voice was so fraught it nearly trembled.

"We did. And this is where I tell you we have more questions than answers. The sample pulled from the perp's eyelash didn't match any known offender records—but it did match DNA pulled from a previous crime scene."

Goku blinked rapidly. "What?"

"Exactly," Hale said. He was personable. I could see how he'd risen through the force and into the FBI. I wondered how this smart, urbane Black man with a southern accent was gelling with the nearly all-white, country-boy DPD. "It matches DNA recovered from a twelve-year-old cold case out in Carraway, Oregon. The strangulation murder of a seventeen-year-old girl named Bridget Howell."

"Holy shit," I said, then blushed.

"Indeed, Ms. Sharp."

"So, let me get this straight." Lightly crossed his arms. "We think our killer got his start in Oregon?"

"It's possible," Hale said. "DNA from the eyelash matches the only unknown DNA pulled from Howell's crime scene, which investigators have assumed belongs to her killer."

"How did they get that DNA evidence?" Citizen asked. He looked slack-jawed. "The investigators in the cold case, I mean?"

"It's fortuitous, actually. The chief of police in Carraway, who used to be the detective on the case, read about advancements in DNA technology that allowed trace amounts of DNA that were formerly thought to be too corrupted to be tested. They went back through the evidence in the locker room, tested what they had, and sure enough, were able to pull the killer's DNA twelve years after the crime. They just uploaded it to CODIS a few months ago. That's all I know about the Howell case, though I'm hoping you'll help me figure out more."

The five of us looked at each other. I could practically feel their thoughts buzzing through the screen. "You want our help?" Lightly asked in a measured tone. Thank God one of us could play it cool.

"Yes. I'd like to commission you as consultants on the case," Agent Hale said.

"We'd be official?" Goku blurted.

"Official *consultants*," he stressed. "You wouldn't be deputized. Or paid. But yes, officially sanctioned and given a higher clearance level." He paused. "Look, I don't know what went down between Reingold and you sleuths. And I'm not going to ask questions, even about how that file got leaked. Consider this a truce. But before we make it official, I'd like to ask you to do me a…small, unofficial favor."

He could not have piqued my curiosity more. "What kind of favor?"

"You might know that the majority of genealogy websites bar law enforcement from using them for investigation purposes."

Mistress nodded. "That's why, in the case of the Golden State Killer, Barbara Rae-Venter didn't advertise her affiliation with the police.* She was a civilian genealogy researcher who passed along her results to law enforcement, and that's how they narrowed down suspects to Joseph DeAngelo. All technically legal."

"Exactly," Hale said. "Technically legal."

Lightly laughed his big, booming laugh. "Let me guess. You want us to pull a Barbara Rae-Venter?"

Hale smiled. "Always the sharp one, George." His face straightened.

---

* The woman who nailed the Golden State Killer is a legend among sleuths, to the point that sometimes on the forum we'd just call her BRV, and everyone knew who you were talking about. For more, see her book, *I Know Who You Are: How an Amateur DNA Sleuth Unmasked the Golden State Killer and Changed Crime Fighting Forever* (Ballantine Books: 2023).

"It would be a big help. If there's any way to identify this guy on Ancestry. com or any of the other ones, I don't mind playing a little fast and loose with the rules. Worth it to get him off the streets."

"I have experience with those sites," Mistress said. "I used to work with the Doe Network, trying to match unidentified remains.* You'd give us the DNA files to upload?"

"Absolutely. Anything you need. Listen, folks." Hale leaned forward and tightened his jaw. His dark eyes scanned the screen, as if he could look into our souls. "Bridget Howell makes seven bodies. Seven young women slain by one man. And what we know about serial murderers suggests he's not going to stop. Our profilers speculate he's remained in the area. Probably watching every move in the investigation, following it online if not in person. We have to come correct on this. An advantage to the five of you is that he might not see you coming. But still, I have to caution you before you decide: helping the FBI is not without risk."

I pictured my father, the boy who couldn't swim, boarding his first navy cruiser to sail across the Atlantic. Jogging up that Neapolitan mountain, neighbor to the lethal Mount Vesuvius, only to run into my mom. Discovering he would be a father at the age of twenty-one and deciding to invest his heart in me, sight unseen. Like him, I was entering an unknown world filled with risks, with no guarantees. This was a chance to be my father's daughter. To be brave like him.

I took a deep breath. "Nothing worth doing ever is."

---

* Did you know, according to the Bureau of Justice Assistance, that roughly 4,400 unidentified bodies are discovered in the U.S. every year, with 40,000 Jane and John Does waiting to be given their identities back at any given time? These nameless people are the opposite of the Delphine Six, whose faces the whole world knows. They disappeared into death as if they'd never existed, their deaths making no ripple. I can't imagine anything sadder.

46

—

IT WAS A HUGE TURNING point in our investigation. We'd gone from nuisances to public enemies to investigators sanctioned by the damn FBI. It was probably a good thing Agent Hale instructed us not to tell anyone, because I fear Goku's and Citizen's crowing on the Network would've been so severe none of us could've come back from it. I'm certain it took all of Goku's willpower not to message SeattleHawks the news specifically.

There was something about our new assignment, about Bridget Howell's death, that really stuck with me. Maybe it was because she was the youngest victim, or the first, the person whose death had triggered our killer's dark hunger. Or maybe it was because I found out she'd died alone in her living room, an hour before her parents came home, strangled to death on the couch while she was doing her homework. Whatever it was, I couldn't shake her.

Per usual, once Agent Hale logged off and we'd stopped seeing stars over our promotion, we'd divvied up assignments and gotten to work. I was grateful for the routine, which helped combat some of the overwhelmingness of what we now faced: a spider web with seven murders and three separate kill sites, spread across twelve years and two states.

We decided Mistress and Goku would work the killer's DNA through the genealogy sites, Lightly would make contact with Carraway's police chief and procure Bridget's file, Citizen would see if he could connect anyone in the Delphine Six's orbits to Carraway, and—as always—I was in charge of assembling information about Bridget from the internet.

She was my most elusive ghost to date. Bridget had been dead twelve years, and she'd died before social media was as pervasive as it was now. If she ever had any accounts, they were long since deleted, probably by heartbroken parents unable to stomach her smiling face popping up in their friend lists. There were only three articles about her still available on the web: "High School Senior Slain in Her Home," "Murder of Carraway Teen Rocks Quiet Town," and "Tenth Anniversary of Teen's Death: Still No Answers," all from the *Portland Press Herald*. Carraway didn't have its own newspaper.

Here's what I learned. On Thursday, September 6, 2012, Bridget's parents came home from work together—they worked two blocks away from each other in downtown Carraway and often carpooled—entering the home through the front door, which they found locked. They spotted Bridget immediately, slumped over on the couch, but assumed she was taking a nap and called to her to wake her up. Bridget had suffered a bout of mono several weeks prior, so it wasn't strange to catch her napping. When she didn't rouse, her father bent to shake her, and that's when he realized she wasn't sleeping. The Howells called 911 right away.

Because of the temperature of the body—she was found still warm—the medical examiner put her death at roughly an hour before her parent's arrival, or around 4:45 p.m. Marks on her neck indicated she'd been strangled with fabric, likely a dish towel from the Howells' kitchen, as they later reported one missing. She had not been sexually assaulted, thank God, but for years investigators had been flummoxed by the lack of forensic evidence. Authorities were torn between two theories: The first was the random predator theory, a phrase I mentally circled, since it matched the thinking in Delphine. The police chief at the time, long since retired, believed Bridget's killer was most likely someone passing through town, either a vagrant or someone with a transitory job, like a trucker. Her death was Carraway's only homicide in 2012, which supported the idea that the killer had been passing through, spotted Bridget—maybe walking around the neighborhood, headphones in, oblivious to danger—and followed her. A chance encounter with fatal consequences.

The second theory, favored by the lead detective on the case—the man who'd risen into the chief's job—was that Bridget had known her attacker. The main evidence for this was that all the doors and windows in the home were found locked, including both the front door, which required a key, and the back door, which required a code. Mr. and Mrs. Howell swore Bridget was a cautious young woman who always locked the doors behind her when she came home. The officer theorized someone Bridget knew may have come to the door, causing her to let her guard down.

It wasn't until a year ago that the now-chief read that fateful article about advancements that allowed scientists to pull DNA from seemingly corrupted cells. He remembered there'd been skin cells under Bridget's fingernails—likely from her attacker—but at the time they'd been deemed unusable. The chief wrote to the lab quoted in the article and was able to convince them to run their test on the skin cells the medical examiner had saved from Bridget's case (the new evidence had thus not come from the "evidence locker room" like Hale said but, rather, a refrigerator in the ME's office).

The chief's persistence was rewarded when the scientists successfully pulled DNA from the degraded skin cells. Unfortunately, there was no match to a prior offender in CODIS. The chief had dutifully logged the new evidence and crossed his fingers for a break.

And here we were: his break.

In the newspaper photo, which looked like her high school yearbook picture, Bridget was a mousy-white brunette with limp hair, chocolate eyes, an obligatory pearl necklace, and a shy smile. But I was proud of myself for uncovering more candid photos in her family's Facebook albums. After some digging, I discovered she'd been close with a cousin named Farrah, who'd dedicated a whole album to Bridget, titled *~*tHe bEsT gIrl iN tHe wOrLd*~*. In these pictures, Bridget's personality shone. She looked like a happy kid playing with her cousin on wooden playground sets, dangling a fishing pole into the Pacific with her dad, making kissy faces with friends in prom dresses. And boy, did she love animals. There was photo after photo of her snuggling kittens and walking dogs at the animal shelter where she worked as a teen. In one photo, Bridget clutched a black-and-white puppy to her chest. Farrah had captioned that picture "Bridget and Gatsby: soulmates 4 lyfe! Uncle Brad, THANK YOU for finally getting her a dog!!!"

I was so invested that I actually gasped when I got near the end of the album and found a picture of Bridget stapling a "Missing Dog" flyer to an electrical pole. Gatsby's face was enshrined in the center. Bridget looked back over her shoulder at the camera with grief in her eyes, but the optimistic Farrah had written, "Missing her soulmate but DETERMINED to get him back!!" I wondered if she ever had.

Obviously, none of these details about Bridget were necessarily relevant. They certainly wouldn't have impressed the FBI. But I was beginning to develop my own method of investigating, separate from my mentors', and it helped me to get a thorough sense for who a victim had been.

So that's how it was for a while: the five of us worked in

round-the-clock shifts, trying every angle we could think of. The unspoken tension underlying our work was our desire to show the FBI that it was worth pulling us into the big leagues. In the days following Hale's news, I missed another shift at Starbucks and got Kandi to—grudgingly—cover another, so I knew my next paycheck was going to be light. But my obsessive instincts were running wild. Maybe other twenty-four-year-olds would've gone off the deep end after losing someone they loved in cooler and more romantic ways: by having sex with nameless people, snorting drugs off counters in club bathrooms, rolling out of strangers' beds in the weakly lit sunrise hours, empty and aching. Or slashing paint across a canvas, screaming catharsis into a microphone. Quitting their jobs and sailing across the world. Squeezing someone's neck until they stopped breathing. But I suspect I was born to fall into rabbit holes. My brain produced a natural Ritalin, allowing me to stick like glue to a question for hours. So I spiraled by sinking deeper and deeper into the screen, forgetting about life outside it, convinced I was chasing seven women, a killer, and my missing dad across the universe.

47

—

ONE NIGHT, I WAS ON shift with Mistress and Goku, working side by side on video, when I saw my boss calling and remembered I was technically supposed to be at work. Feeling knee-jerk guilt, I told Mistress and Goku to hold on and switched off my video and audio.

"Fred, I'm sorry. I know I'm supposed to be there. If you'll just give me—"

"You're fired," he said.

"What?" It was the most obvious causal reaction in the world—mess up too many times, get fired—and yet I couldn't track it. "But I've worked for you since I was sixteen."

"Listen, Jane, I don't know what's going on with you—" He cleared his throat. "I mean, I guess I do, and again, I'm sorry about your dad. But missing so many shifts is unacceptable. As is coming to work and being on your phone the whole time. Kandi showed me the *Daily Mail* article, by the way. The one about you getting mixed up in online murders. If that's what's causing you to flounder, you should think long and hard about where your life is headed."

"I…" I lowered my voice. "Fred, I need the money."

"I'm sorry, Jane." His voice was firm. "You should've thought about that before donning the green apron and disrespecting Starbucks."

And just like that, a switch flipped and I no longer cared. Mistress and Goku were searching their last genealogy website, 23andMe, and all I wanted was get back to that. "Okay, then. Sounds good. Have a nice life."

He hung up on me, which I might've deserved. I took a deep breath and went to flip on my video and audio, only to realize that, in my haste, I'd left my audio on. Mistress's and Goku's faces appeared on screen, their expressions dire.

"Did you just get fired?" Goku asked. Subtly was not his strong suit.

"Yeah, but it doesn't matter." I looked down at my keyboard. I'd nearly worn off the letter A.

"You just said you need the money," he pressed, and I felt myself blushing.

"I'll be fine."

"Jane, honey." Mistress drew close to her camera, peering at me. "Are you sleeping? You look exhausted."

"I'm sleeping," I lied. "Besides, this is crunch time."

"What are you eating these days?" Goku asked. "Vegetables? Protein? Are you drinking water?"

"Okay, Mr. Taco Bell." I swept the Flamin' Hot Cheetos crumbs off my desk.

"Do as I say, not as I do," Goku said sagely.

"Honey, I'm worried about you." Mistress frowned. "I recognize obsession when I see it."

"I just want to solve these murders. That's all I care about. My stupid job doesn't matter."

"Starbucks really is stupid," Goku agreed. "Especially now that they let you go."

Mistress ignored Goku. "Trust me, I've been there. You feel like the only real things are the cases. The life-and-death stakes. But you need boundaries, and you need to stay healthy. Otherwise, you're going to burn out."

"I burned out once," Goku said cheerfully. "In my early days. Got so sick of dead ends and so paranoid around other people that I couldn't get out of bed for a month."

"Okay, I hear you." I was being a little childish. "Back to 23andMe. Still not close to the killer?"

Goku snorted. "We've narrowed it down to 1.5 million people who could be related to him across North America. Whoever this guy is, his family doesn't believe in testing their DNA for shits and giggles."

But Mistress wasn't done. "Jane, I'd like to tell you about something that happened to me when I was young."

"Oh boy," Goku mumbled. "Citizen's favorite story."

Curious, I said, "I'm listening."

She settled back in her chair. "Back in 1980, when I was twenty, I worked as a clerk at a gas station off I–80. I was doing it part-time while I was in college, just for a little extra spending money. A lot of long-haul truckers on their way out to Chicago used to come through. One night I was on the schedule to close alone, which meant I was there by myself until three a.m. It was slow that night, very few people. Around midnight, this man pulled his truck in and came inside. Went straight to the pop aisle. He was tall and lean and dressed a little better than the average trucker—a button-up instead of a T-shirt. That was the most I noticed about him, because I really needed to pee. We weren't supposed to go to the bathroom when there were customers in the store, but I was desperate, so I told myself I'd be fast."

Mistress took a deep breath. "I was in one of the stalls when I heard the door open. I figured a woman had come in after I'd stepped away, and that's who was in there. But then I caught sight of the person's shoes under the stall. Brown leather boots. Men's boots. I realized it was the trucker. He'd followed me in."

"What did you do?"

"At first, I was so scared I couldn't move. Just sat there with my heart going a mile a minute and no thoughts in my head besides fear. And then he talked to me. He said, 'You in there, little girl?' He had the most distinctive voice. So deep. There was something about him speaking that unfroze me. I'd chosen the big handicapped stall and there was a window that unlatched in one wall. I opened it as quietly as I could, stood on the toilet, and climbed out."

"Oh my God," I whispered, trying to picture it.

"Fell clean on my ass on the ground outside, but you should've seen me run. All the way down the highway until I got to a diner, then called the cops. By the time they got to the gas station, he was long gone, of course. And there weren't security cameras everywhere like there are now." She smiled faintly. "He didn't steal anything, but I still got fired for leaving the cash register unattended."

"That's bullshit."

She shrugged. "I wouldn't have gone back anyway. I was too scared. After that, I used to avoid even being in the library alone. Ten years later, I'm watching TV and I see a report on a serial killer who'd been apprehended in Arizona with a naked woman chained in the cab of his truck. His name was Robert Ben Rhoades, but they were calling him the Truck Stop Killer. Apparently, he'd murdered a string of women across the country, mostly off highways. He was a sexual sadist who used to chain up women and torture them for weeks—raping them, sticking fish hooks through their breasts—before finally killing them. All young women, like I'd been, though mostly prostitutes and hitchhikers. He was from near me in Iowa, Council Bluffs. They showed him in the courtroom, I didn't recognize him until they played a clip of him entering his plea. It was the same voice from the bathroom, I swear it. Immediately, I was right back there."

"Jesus Christ, Mistress. I'm so glad you're okay."

"Thanks, honey. You know, it was another ten years before I saw the Doe Network crop up. I'd read everything I could about the Truck Stop Killer by then, and one of his victims was still unidentified. I had this feeling, like it was my responsibility to help her. I'd almost *been* her."

"Did you ever find out who she was?"

Mistress shook her head sadly. "No. She's still a Doe. But I do hope I find her before I die."

I wanted so badly in that moment to tell her she'd been wrong about being a Defender—Mistress was clearly a Victim, drawn to true crime because she was haunted by her brush with violence. She saw herself in the dead women, saw the fate she could've met if one little thing had gone differently. But I held my tongue. It wasn't the right moment to correct her, challenge how she wanted to see herself.

"The reason I bring this up," she said, "is because for a few years when I'd just started working for the Doe Network, I lost my mind."

Goku started to snicker, but I shushed him with a look.

"I had a full-time job, a husband, and two young kids to take care of. And yet I spent every waking hour on the internet, reading about unidentified bodies and trying to match them to missing persons reports. I'm ashamed to say I forgot to pick up my kids from school on more than one occasion. Forgot to make dinner when it was my turn, stopped wanting to go on Friday movie dates with my husband. I fell so deeply into the work that my husband finally intervened and told me I needed to get a grip or start seeing a therapist. I did both, and I'm glad." Her expression turned wistful. "Now that he's gone, I regret every moment I spent by myself in front of a screen when I could've spent it with him. Hindsight can be a bitter medicine."

The three of us were silent. It was getting dark, and the only sound was the crickets outside my window.

She sighed. "Just take this old woman's advice and be careful, Jane. The path you're racing down is dangerous. Ruinous, even, if you don't know how to stop and catch your breath. It's a long, dark night out there. Horrors around every turn. Protect yourself."

I know what you're thinking, and I agree. I damn well should've listened.

48

—

IN THE WEE HOURS OF the morning, long after Mistress and Goku had retired, with my head slumped against my desk, cheek pressed into the keyboard, finger rotely pressing through photos of Bridget Howell's crime scene—that's when I found it. I snapped from near-sleeping to vibrating alertness, grabbing my laptop and yanking the screen so close my nose brushed it.

To anyone else in the world except for lock connoisseurs and those of us who'd been teenagers from 2012 to 2017, the picture would've looked innocuous. It was a photo of the outside of the Howells' back-yard, facing the exterior of the house and zoomed in on their back entrance. But I recognized that shiny silver lock with the black keypad. It was a distinctive shape—a long, skinny oval—and back in my day, in the first wave of the keyless entry craze, everyone seemed to have one on their doors. The thing about this lock that made it unique was that there was a hack: press zero seven times in a row and it locked or unlocked, regardless of its owner's unique entry code. Maybe it was meant to be a loophole for forgetful homeowners or emergency services—who knows. Somewhere along the way, some enterprising teenager figured it out and word spread like wildfire. High school kids used the hack to sneak into people's houses and raid their liquor cabinets. Eventually they started stealing bigger stuff—I remember hearing about a ring of boys who got arrested for breaking in and stealing jewelry from some of the big houses down on Indian River Drive.

We'd had one on our house. When the company eventually recalled it under threat of lawsuits—obviously, the security risk was massive—we'd had to hire someone to come out and reinstall a new lock, all on our own dime. My dad was so annoyed, grumbling about the unfairness of having to pay for the company's mistake: "They should be paying *us* to say they're sorry for making us robber bait."

My heart raced as I googled "keyless lock recalls," just in case I'd remembered wrong. But there it was, at the top of a homeowners' forum: "The Infamous Kwikset Powerbolt-9200 Recall." The most expensive recall in Kwikset's history, apparently. And it was the same lock we'd had, the same lock on the Howells' door in the photo, the same lock every teenager worth their salt knew could be opened with enough zeros. Triumph flooded me.

Had they known about the hack in Carraway, Oregon? I remembered the articles I'd read about Bridget's case, the cops divided over the profile of the person who'd killed her. The only piece of evidence undermining the random predator theory was that all the doors to the house had been locked, suggesting Bridget would've known the person who killed her because she'd let him inside. But if her back door could be opened with a numerical trick, then it opened up the possibilities of who could've killed her. It *could've* been a random predator. Who was most likely to know about a malfunctioning keypad? Locksmiths, construction workers, real estate agents. That could give us a place to start looking.

Had I discovered how Bridget's killer entered her house?

I rushed to the Signal chat, hands shaking with exhaustion and excitement.

Searcher24: Guys. I think I found something.

49

THE FIVE OF US MADE the decision on a stormy Tuesday night, drunk on power and possibility. Outside my window, lightning lashed in a jagged spike, wind whipping rain against the glass. It wasn't hurricane season yet—that didn't start until June—but down in my part of Florida we held the title of "the lightning capital of the world," so we were used to these kinds of displays of fire and brimstone.

"We can't know for sure this lock is the same one Jane remembers," Lightly cautioned. "Or that anyone in Bridget's community knew it had a hack, particularly Bridget's killer. It wasn't recalled until a few years later, and that's when it hit the news."

For the first time, I felt like rolling my eyes at him, frustrated by his restraint. "Of course we can't know for sure. But it's a lead. It gives us a theory."

We'd convened a tribunal to dissect my discovery. I could tell word had spread that I'd lost my job, because even though Citizen and Lightly had startled upon seeing me—I was still wearing the same oversized hoodie from days ago, except now it featured more Cheetos dust, and who knew what kind of rat nest my hair had morphed into—no one made fun of me. That was highly unusual, given that our group love language was casual ribbing. Clearly, they thought my situation was too dire to poke fun of.

"I think it's promising," Mistress said loyally. "A heck of a lot more than the genealogy websites turned out to be."

"And my emails to the chief in Carraway have gone unanswered." Lightly's voice was bone-tired. "You'd think he'd be grateful someone's finally paying attention to his case."

"What about the ME?" Citizen's cheeks had a ruddy flush that told me he'd just come back from working out.

"He said he wasn't able to divulge any case information over email or phone without the FBI's order. And anyway, Carraway's so small they haven't updated from paper to digital case files yet. If we want to look at the originals, we need to take a road trip to the Carraway Police Department."

Citizen's eyes were unnervingly blue. "Why don't we?"

A few of us scoffed good-naturedly.

"Back to the lock," Goku said. "Surely we can call the manufacturer—"

"I'm serious," Citizen interrupted. "Why don't we go to Delphine? Investigate in person. It's only a four-hour drive to Carraway from there. Easy to get to."

Lightly laughed. "I think you're forgetting some of us work for a living. Yourself included."

"Not all of us," I said, in an attempt at a joke. But the four of them only looked at me pityingly.

Lightly cleared his throat. "Hang in there, Searcher."

"I've got some leave saved up," Citizen pressed. "Don't tell me you couldn't get the time off, Lightly. You run your firm. And Goku, your job is remote. Come on. Imagine actually being there. Feeling that cold mountain air. Seeing what the killer saw. Tracing our girls' steps."

A thoughtful look had stolen over Goku's face. "Seattle and his goons are boots on the ground. Hardly seems fair they get to be and not us."

"Exactly." Citizen lunged from his kitchen table and started to pace. His eyes were fever bright. "This is what we're missing. Hands-on access." He splayed his hands on the table. "No matter how good we are, there's only so much we can do from our kitchens. Sometimes you've got to be there in person to take control. Don't the girls deserve that?"

"It *would* be nice to get the files from Carraway PD," Mistress said. "Otherwise, it's submitting FOIA requests and waiting weeks for them to come through. We could also take a look at the Howells' old house. Maybe the lock's still on it and we can verify the hack."

"You know what I want to do?" Goku asked. "Walk the neighborhoods around Queen Lace and Collegiate Parkway. Get a feel for how the perp might've stalked the girls. Really slide into his skin, you know?"

"We could make the same walk Madeleine and Stacie made their last night," Mistress sounded excited. "From Cathy's Bar back home."

To my surprise, Lightly cupped his chin. "Lawrence is making us consultants." He tapped a finger. "It's not unheard of for consultants to be on-site. Internet sleuths, sure—that's inappropriate. But consultants..."

"Wasn't Junie just saying she wanted to spend time at her sister's?" Mistress prompted. "On account of her arthritis flaring up?"

"That's right," Lightly said, wearing the light-dawning expression of person sliding a piece into a puzzle.

The four of them were humming along so perfectly in sync that it was jarring when they stopped talking and peered into their cameras.

"Well, Searcher?" Goku raised his eyebrows. "What do you think?"

Even after months of friendship, of getting to know each other's daily routines and inside jokes and thought patterns, weathering obstacles and victories together, it still surprised me when they did this. Forced me to stop being the girl on the sidelines, watching and nodding along, and treated me like someone with opinions equal to theirs.

"Me?" The doubt was still a reflex.

Citizen raised his chin impatiently. "You in? What are your savant senses telling you—should we do something kind of nuts?"

Thunder crashed outside my window.

It's unusual, I know, to finally come into yourself—to grow into a full human being, vivid and Technicolor-real—while on a mission hunting ghosts. But that's exactly what happened to me.

I smiled. "Let's go to Idaho."

50

—

THE NIGHT BEFORE I BROKE the news to my mom that I'd been
fired and wanted to use the last of my savings to fly to Idaho to hunt a
serial killer, Bill Donohue from the *Star Trek* forum messaged me links
to my dad's fan fiction.

"Sorry it took a while," he wrote. "Forgot we archived a bunch of
our old stuff and threw it up on AO3 for safekeeping. Anyway, your dad
was a solid writer, and he knew his *Trek* lore inside and out. Feel free
to message me anytime, by the way. I'm happy to talk. Loved your old
man, and if you don't mind me saying, you seem like Dan's girl, through
and through."

If only he could've known how much that single sentence meant
to me.

Curious, I clicked on the link to "Two Wolves in the Night." It took
me to a no-frills fan fiction website. Sure enough, there was my father's
name on the author byline. How strange to discover this new side to him;
how precious the opportunity to hear his voice. His story was set during
the *Voyager* years, with Captain Kathryn Janeway commanding the USS
Voyager starship against its greatest threat yet—simultaneous siege by
not one but two of the series' most formidable villains, the Vidiians and

the Borg. The Vidiians were a disgusting species afflicted with a tissue-melting disease called the Phage, and were obsessed with harvesting organs to try to heal themselves. The Borg was a hive mind of cyborgs bent on assimilating the *Voyager* into its Collective, led by the cunning Borg Queen. As I read, memories of watching the show with my dad came back until I could picture each of the characters.

Bill was right: my dad was a good writer. His style mimicked the tone of the show, a little stiff and grandiose, but his command of pacing was excellent, his premise intriguing. What would the heroic Captain Janeway do if faced with annihilation from two sides and no one to turn to for help? Her ship, *Voyager,* was famously lost in the Delta Quadrant seventy thousand light-years from Federation territory—that was the premise of the series. It meant that, more than any other captain, Janeway truly was venturing where no man had gone before.

As I curled up in bed reading about the darkest night of Janeway's soul, I wondered if my dad had ever imagined I would read these words. I hoped he had. I even fantasized about him hiding some message in the story just for me. But I knew that was magical thinking. Like my name-sake, I was probably on my own.

Cleverly, since *Star Trek* was famous for alluding to classic literature, my dad wrote that Janeway's reread of *The Count of Monte Cristo* inspired her with a brilliant but risky plan, which she called "Two Wolves in the Night." The *Voyager* wasn't capable of defending itself against two foes simultaneously—and if the *Voyager* perished, there would be no stopping the Vidiian and Borg. They'd be free to continue killing across the universe unchecked.

So Janeway dreamed up a way to pit the Borg Queen against the leader of the Vidiian, convincing the Vidiians they needed the Borg's cybernetic organs to heal themselves and convincing the Borg the Vidiians were bent on destroying them. As the two species turned their warships on each other and traded explosive detonations, the *Voyager* raced away to freedom. Janeway, the self-described "rabbit," had outwitted the two wolves.

My favorite part of the story came at the end, during a quiet moment between Captain Janeway and her crewmember Seven of Nine. Seven had been rescued years earlier from Borg assimilation and was still learning, painstakingly, how to be human. As the two stared out a window into deep space, Janeway asked Seven what was troubling her.

"I had a feeling," Seven said, "when the first of the Vidiian phasers hit the Borg Cube..."

"What kind of feeling?" Janeway asked.

Seven stared at the stars. "That's the problem. I can't find the right words to describe it."

"Ah." Janeway smiled knowingly. "Welcome to humanity, my friend. We are a species that feels deeply and yet often lacks the tools to convey it. There are some experiences that simply exceed language."

Seven arched a cybernetic brow. "How inefficient and unsatisfying."

Janeway laughed the droll laugh she often used in Seven's company. "I've developed a trick I use whenever language fails me. Would you like to hear it?"

"Of course."

Janeway held her hands behind her back, the portrait of a captain at ease. "I try to describe what the thing isn't, rather than what it is. Little by little, I circle closer. And although I rarely arrive at the thing itself, the circling is satisfying. Almost like composing a still-life by sketching around an object until its form emerges. Would you like to try?"

For a long moment, Seven was quiet. Then she said, with a

tentative glance, "What I felt when the Borg Cube was attacked wasn't relief, but it was like it."

"Good," said the captain. "Go on."

"It wasn't fear, like when I came out of assimilation. Not anticipation, like when Neelix cooks something good for dinner. It wasn't joy, or winning, or sadness for all those creatures still stuck on the ship. It was bigger than that." She turned to Janeway. "You truly find this satisfying?"

The captain gave another laugh and patted Seven's shoulder. "Sit with it for a while. Sometimes the joy of being human lies in the things we cannot describe." With that, she left Seven behind, still whispering "Not missing. Not mourning. Not feeling small."

The story ended.

I rested my laptop on my legs. A warm tear rolled down my cheek. I'd never known my dad had ideas like this. Thoughts about what it meant to be human, the limitations of language. He'd never gone to college. Did he really get all of this from reading and watching TV? It was like he'd predicted that the enormity of missing him would feel impossible to explain.

Reading his story, I realized that he was not quite the man I remembered. Not quite the eighteen-year-old farm boy or the sailor or the middle-aged sci-fi fan or the too-young victim of a failing heart. He'd been someone different, and more complex. Harder to define. I wondered if, despite my investigation, I would ever truly reach him.

51

—

AS IT HAPPENED, THE NEXT morning my mom walked in on me packing my largest suitcase with my warmest clothes—sneakers and hoodies, God help me—thus saving me from having to figure out how to broach the subject of leaving for Idaho.

"What's this?" Her hands found her hips.

Ever since I'd found her cleaning out Dad's stuff, we'd been on shaky ground. Maybe that's why I chose to bulldoze in. "You know how I research crime on the internet?"

"Uh-huh," she said warily. She'd gotten a thorough education on true crime ahead of the *Newsline* interview, but since then she mostly chose to stay out of it. She thought it was morbid.

I tossed a pair of jeans into the suitcase. "Well, I need to go to Idaho for my latest case. It won't be for long. Maybe a few weeks." The truth was, I had no idea how long it would take. We'd all purchased one-way tickets except Citizen, who was close enough to drive.

People in the next state probably heard my mom scoff. "Oh yeah? And is Starbucks allowing remote latte-making these days?"

I cleared my throat. "Actually, I quit." Even to my own mother, I couldn't admit to getting fired.

"What?" she screeched, moving into the center of my room so I couldn't avoid her. "Since when? What are you doing for work?"

"I need a short break." I bent down to roll a stack of T-shirts. "Actually, this case is work."

"That you don't get paid for."

"Doesn't mean it isn't important."

"Jane." My mother knelt on the other side of the suitcase and placed her hand on my stack of T-shirts so I had to pause. "What's going on? This isn't like you."

I met her eyes. "Just give me a few weeks, and then I'll come back and get a job and pay you everything I owe for rent and bills. Right now, they need me there." It was true, and I was proud of it. "Goku's paying for our Airbnb, anyway, so all I have to do is fly there and chip in for groceries. It won't be that expensive. I'll eat ramen."

She waved a hand. "This isn't about money. What case has got you so worked up? Idaho…" Her eyes went wide. "Wait, the massacres? Those sorority girls?"

She always talked like that, like what happened on the news occurred on an entirely separate planet. "Only three of them were sorority girls, Mom."

"I—Jane! This man's a serial killer. He's like—he's a new Ted Bundy."

"I know. That's why we have to catch him as quickly as possible." I wasn't trying to sound brave. I was blunt with her because deep down I was angry that now, when I needed her to let me go, she'd finally decided to pay attention to me.

"I'm sorry." She shook her head. "I'm not letting my daughter traipse off to the middle of nowhere to join a group of strangers she met on the internet so they can track a serial killer with a penchant for murdering twentysomethings. What part of that sounds reasonable to you?"

I started back on the T-shirts. "It doesn't have to be reasonable. I'm twenty-four, remember? You can't lock me in my room."

The fiery New Yorker in her flashed. "Watch me."

"Come on. Like you'll even notice I'm gone."

"What's that supposed to mean?"

"You're too busy doing step aerobics and reading vegan recipes and throwing out everything of Dad's."

She blinked. "What are you saying?"

"Never mind. I need to pack my toiletries."

"You know all I've tried to do since your dad died is what's best for us, right? I'm trying to navigate an impossible reality, while keeping us safe and healthy."

"Safe and healthy?" I rose to my feet, towering over her. "Mom, look at you. You're skin and bones. You eat like a bird."

"I do not." She pulled herself up, too. "I'm healthier than I was months ago, which is more than I can say for you. When was the last time you measured your blood pressure, Jane? You stopped doing aerobics. And I can tell you're sneaking processed foods. You've gained weight."

I looked down at myself, at the fullness of my thighs, my soft stomach, trying to process both her accusation and the complicated whirlwind of shame and defiance it provoked.

"You know that's what he used to do, right?" My mom's voice was weary. "He snuck around, like I was some shrew wife nagging him about what he ate and how often he exercised because it was fun for me. For the record, I can't imagine anything I wanted *less* than to turn into my own husband's mother. But I was trying to save his life!"

"God, Mom." Nonsensically, I kicked the suitcase. "Can you stop? All you do is talk about his weight. He was more than that."

"It's what killed him! It's what took him from us."

"We don't know that."

She laughed incredulously. "Jane, what kind of fantasy world are you living in?"

I meant to say something like, *Give me time—I'm still searching for answers,* but I couldn't. She didn't give me a chance, anyway.

"Is that what Idaho is—a fantasy where you get to play at being a detective instead of a twenty-four-year-old college dropout who lost her father?"

I could feel my face turn red. Maybe she'd stumbled too close to the truth, or maybe I'd been bottling up my secret anger for months. Whatever it was, I exploded. "It feels like you're waging war against him ever since he died. Like all this dieting and exercise is some long, extended critique. So what if Dad was overweight? That was one part of him. Stop diminishing him. *He was my father.*"

I'd stunned her into silence.

They say if you don't have certain key experiences early in your life, you're doomed to seek them later. I'd never stood up for myself, never braved it against a bully, so as I stood there in my bedroom shivering with anger, that's what it felt like I was doing. Never mind that I was yelling at a woman who loved me, who was trying to protect me in her own imperfect way.

A year later, I can remember nothing about the ten-hour slog from Florida to Delphine except for a single image: the clouds outside my window. I remember staring at them midflight, buoyed by the bitter-sweet certainty that when I'd left home, telling my mom that my dad and I didn't need her, and I would take care of his memory now, I'd been his protector. Like my dad at eighteen, I was setting off into an unknown adventure. I was his girl, through and through.

And so we broke out of Florida and turned our attention to the monster in the West.

PART TWO

———

So Step into the Light,

And Let Me Look at You

52

THEY WERE STANDING ON THE steps of the rental house when my Uber pulled up, like they were posing for a family portrait. Ever since I'd landed, it was as if I'd stepped through my laptop screen. Delphine was just like it appeared in pictures: nestled in a valley between snow-topped mountains, ringed by bushy firs and tall pines, the downtown a collection of small, quaint brick buildings, green-and-gold NIU signs in all the windows. It was April 17, sunny but still chilly to a Florida girl, the temperature hovering in the fifties. There was so much space everywhere. It took me a while to figure out that's what I was reacting to on the drive in from the airport. South Florida used to have that same kind of openness, buildings cropping up next to empty fields, long stretches of highway without construction, uninterrupted views of the sky. But more and more people had moved in, and it was getting cramped. Delphine still had a kind of Wild West sense about it that struck me as both freeing and desolate. It was so unlike anywhere I'd been that it made me wonder at the vastness of America, to contain such different geographies.

But my friends—my online family. That was the truly surreal part. I was so nervous pulling up that my stomach dropped like I was on a roller coaster.

"Looks like your friends are waiting on ya," my Uber driver said cheerfully, throwing the car into park. "You guys having a reunion?"

"It's the first time we've met," I said and opened the door.

"Searcher!" Mistress rushed off the porch. She was barely over five feet—so small it was a shock—but her energy made her seem larger. Her short-cropped hair feathered against my cheek as we hugged, and I breathed in the scent of her, vanilla and something comforting, like dough. Smell was something you didn't get online. "It's so good to see you."

"It's great to see you." My voice was muffled, face pressed against her sweater vest.

"Come on, Mistress, don't suffocate the girl" came a voice that had to be Goku's. When I pulled back, there he was, ambling down the driveway, a big smile on his face.

"It's really you," I said and threw open my arms. He squeezed me, lifting me off my feet and making me laugh.

"What, you thought I was a simulation?"

"No." I laughed again. Real-life Goku was warm and soft. "It's just..." I looked around. Lightly and Citizen were pulling my suitcase and backpack out of the trunk and waving goodbye to the Uber driver. I stared. I'd never noticed Lightly had a light dusting of freckles over his nose, or that there was hazel in his eyes. When he smiled at me, his skin crinkled into fine lines. And Citizen. He was taller than I'd guessed, over six feet, and while his face was the same one I'd grown used to seeing on-screen— wide blue eyes, long lashes, sculpted cheekbones—his sheer physical presence took me by surprise. His dark-blond buzz was growing out at the bottom, hairs starting to curl around the nape of his neck. When we locked eyes, a corner of his mouth lifted in that lopsided smile.

Whatever it is that attracts one human to another, that turns on our biological radar, gives us goose bumps, makes us sit up and pay attention—whatever chemicals our bodies exchange, speaking in a language we're not consciously aware of—Citizen did that for me. It was the sort of thing I never would've discovered sitting behind my computer.

"What?" he asked, slinging my backpack over one shoulder. They were all watching me.

"All of you. You were flat and now you're three-dimensional," I blurted, and they laughed. But it was true. The computer had flattened them. Here in person, I could hear the fullness of their accents, Mistress with her slight Midwest elongation, Goku the upturned, airy end to his sentences. I caught the idiosyncrasies of their movements, the restless ropiness of Citizen as he cracked his knuckles, the slight hitch to Lightly's step. They were real, honest-to-God people. For the first time, what my mom had called them—*strangers you met on the internet*—seemed true. I'd felt close to them, and yet I'd known only a fraction of who they were.

"This is weird, right?" Goku shook his head, dark hair tumbling. It was longer than I remembered, brushing over his ears.

"Some people call this old-fashioned friendship, you know," said Lightly, dragging my suitcase toward the house. "Seeing each other in person. Enjoying meals together. Making small talk that doesn't involve evidence or affidavits."

"Are we supposed to call each other by our names?" I asked.

The five of us stopped and looked at each other. Citizen started laughing.

"Too weird," Goku insisted.

"It's normal to feel awkward," Mistress said, toddling after Lightly toward the house. "I'm sure it'll go away. Hey, you want a tour? Goku chose a real nice place."

"It's less than a mile from the second murder," he said, wiggling his brows.

I looked up at the house. It was a white, three-story building, with a canary-yellow front door. Like all the other houses I'd seen while I was driving in, it was built like a square box and surrounded by trees. "It doesn't have a sliding-glass door in the back, does it?"

Goku grinned. "I made sure to find a rental without one."

Thank God.

I stepped inside. I was used to Florida interiors—lots of light, liberal use of seashells, ceramic tile floors. Inside this house it was much darker. Everything was the same color wood, a sort of caramel oak—the floors, the walls, the fireplace in the living room. Even the leather furniture was caramel colored. A buck's head was mounted above the flat-screen TV.

"It's...cozy."

"I know, right?" Goku put his hands on his hips and surveyed. "Got it for a steal, too. The description said it had 'hunting lodge vibes,' but I don't really get that. Do you?"

I looked at the old-timey shotguns mounted above the dining room table. "Uh, kind of..."

"Up here, Search." Lightly wrestled my bag up the stairs, and I dutifully followed. Citizen trailed behind me with my backpack.

"Are you sure I can't—"

He gave me one of those half smiles. "Nah, I got it."

"We put you beside Mistress in case that made you more comfortable," Lightly said. Each stair creaked. "Us boys will stay on the second floor. This can be girl territory."

"That's really nice," I said, gripping the wooden banister.

"And here you are." Lightly opened the room at the end of the third-floor hall. It was tiny and the ceiling was low—I almost had to crouch to enter the bathroom. A small window overlooked the front yard. "Is this okay? I know it's small."

"It's perfect. Thank you." I was really here, in Idaho. It was dizzying.

"Oh no," Lightly said as Citizen put down my backpack, revealing an orange stain down his white T-shirt. "Something's leaking in your backpack."

"My Gatorade." I rushed to the bag and pulled out the offending bottle—sure enough, the cap was loose and the bottom of my backpack had turned into Gatorade soup. "Shit. I'm sorry, Citizen. Can I get you a washcloth? I'll buy you a new shirt if it doesn't come out."

"Relax," he said and tugged his shirt over his head in one swift movement. It was impossible not to stare at the muscles in his shoulders, the indentations of his abs above his jeans. How much working out did you do in the military? "I'll just toss it in the wash." He turned to leave, and that's when I saw the snake coiling up his back in glossy black ink, curving in and out of the knobs of his spine, intricate scales gleaming. The tail flicked toward the small of his back, and the snake's mouth, wicked fangs out, reached for his neck.

Talk about unexpected. I was still staring after Citizen when Lightly said, "I have something for you. Hold on a minute—I'll be right back."

By the time I'd emptied the Gatorade and started mopping out my backpack, Lightly had returned holding a beautiful wooden vase. Well, no, it had a lid on top, which made it—

"An urn."

"I hope you don't mind that I took the liberty." Lightly held it out. The wood was smooth as silk as I turned it slowly in my hands. "I noticed the ashes you kept next to your computer. Figured they might be your dad's and you might appreciate having a dignified place to put him. Sorry if I've overstepped."

"You saw them?" I thought I'd hidden them from view.

"A few times, on video calls. It's nothing to be ashamed of. Look here. I made this myself. Do a bit of wood carving as stress relief. This is Swiss pine—real strong and durable, but still pretty. I thought it would look nice."

Near the bottom, an inscription was painted on the wood in a shaky hand: *It's what we will never know about the ones we love that binds us to them.* I stared at the words.

"I know the inscription's not as neat as it could be." Lightly scratched the back of his neck. "I tried to keep my hand steady, but sometimes these fingers shake—" He grunted as I threw my arms around him.

"You like it?"

"I love it. Thank you." And I did. I didn't yet understand the meaning of what Lightly had painted, but it made me think of my dad's story, the scene between Janeway and Seven of Nine, and Seven's unknowable words. Plus, the fact that Lightly had done something nice for me and my dad felt like an almost overwhelming gesture of kindness.

"All right, then," Lightly said, patting my back. "Just wanted you to know you're not alone."

53

—

THAT NIGHT WE DECIDED TO go to Cathy's. We loaded ourselves up in Citizen's Suburban, me wearing one of Mistress's warm parkas, and made our way through downtown.

It was buzzing. People pushed past each other in both directions, crowding Delphine's brick-laid streets. Downtown was dotted with old-fashioned wrought-iron lampposts and four-faced clocks. We drove past a group posing for pictures in front of the clocks. It had the strange energy of Disney World. "I thought more than a quarter of NIU students went home," I said.

"They did." Lightly was squished in the middle row beside me. He followed my gaze out the window. "As far as we can tell, these people are sleuths."

I knew our idea to come to Delphine hadn't been original—for God's sake, even SeattleHawks was here—but I hadn't realized exactly how many people had flooded in.

"They're murder-tourists," Goku said from the back seat. "Don't give them the dignity of calling them sleuths."

When we got to Cathy's, a harried-looking hostess told us there was a fifty-minute wait for a table. "I wasn't under the impression Cathy's had waits," Citizen said under his breath. "Thought it was a dollar-beer-dive kind of place."

The place *was* a dive, all beat-up wooden walls with dingy dartboards and limp posters peeling off. The main theme was NIU football—there were green-and-gold pennants everywhere in support of the Badgers. A row of booths lined a wall of windows, and tables had been crammed into the center of the room, but the majority of seats were at the long, packed bar, behind which scowling bartenders zipped around assembling ingredients.

"Maybe the hostesses are new." Mistress swept her hand around the bar. "On account of all this." "All this" was the wall-to-wall people. Most, I could tell, were sleuths trying to play at being ordinary, but some couldn't help themselves. A squirrelly-looking woman I could've sworn I recognized from YouTube snapped pictures of the inside of the bar. She wove around tables with her iPhone before being rounded up and put back in line by an annoyed server. Another couple waiting to be seated wore matching CrimeCon sweatshirts, with those ubiquitous neon-yellow fingerprint logos.

"Am I crazy," Citizen murmured, brushing his arm against mine, "or has Cathy's turned into a theme park?"

"It's grim," I agreed.

"Keep your eyes peeled for Seattle," Goku said.

"Do you know what he looks like?"

"No." Goku's eyes trailed around the room. "But I suspect he'll give off a douchey energy that's impossible to miss."

It wasn't even five minutes after we were seated in a booth, the five of us getting comfortable being squashed together—I was smushed between Goku and Citizen, facing Lightly and Mistress—when a glass slammed so hard against the bar the entire place went silent.

"I'm so sick of you ghouls coming in here, asking questions about those girls," raged a bartender with a handlebar mustache.

Citizen leaned in and whispered, "George Dabrowski."

Everyone familiar with the case knew George. He was the bartender who'd served Madeleine and Stacie the night they died. He was also Cathy's manager.

"Don't you have any shame?" George yelled. Another bartender, a smaller man, was tugging on his arm, but George didn't budge. The object of his ire was a middle-aged man with a beer belly and a backwards baseball cap who'd been leaning over the bar. "Asking me how much I served them. You're not the cops, man! Go home to your pathetic life and find some other horror to fixate on!"

A red flush spread over the back of the middle-aged man's neck, but when he didn't budge, George lunged toward him. "Leave! Now!"

The man scrambled, almost knocking over his barstool, and beelined for the exit. I caught a glimpse of his humiliated expression as he rushed past.

George swung out from around the bar. "That goes for everyone. If you're here because of the murders, you need to get the fuck out of my bar! We're tired of you." He pointed to the couple in their matching CrimeCon sweaters. "That means you." When they didn't move, he took a menacing step in their direction. "I'm not joking! Forget about your bill. Just go!" The couple pushed out of their chairs, incredulous looks on their faces, and stormed out. George power-walked to the double doors leading to the kitchen and shoved inside.

"Sorry about that." Our server, a woman wearing pigtails and heavy makeup, appeared, plunking waters on the table. Around us, people starting talking in hushed whispers. "We're usually a lot nicer to visitors, but these last few weeks have been a nightmare."

"No problem," Lightly said smoothly. "I take it you're seeing a spike in tourism?"

She laughed wearily. "I guess you could call it that. These media folks and amateur detectives, or whatever they call themselves, are everywhere. I can't tell you how many people have asked me for an interview for their little podcasts or video shows. And I wasn't even here the night those girls…" Her voice trailed off. Then she cleared her throat and looked cheerily around the table. "But what brings you here?" Her eyes fixed on me. "You go to NIU?"

Everyone turned to me. I opened my mouth. "Uh…yeah." I nodded. "I'm a student. And this is my family. They're visiting."

The lie just rolled out, but no one, not even Mistress or Lightly, corrected me. We all just turned to the server to see how she'd take it.

She looked around the table. Her gaze snagged on Mistress's sweater. It was part of her Pride collection, with a large rainbow heart over her breast and the words "Love is Love is Love" below it. "Well," said the waitress, "good for you. I know not everyone around here would say the same, but I think God made us all equal, and families come in all shapes." She pulled out a notepad. "What can I get you to drink besides water?"

"Cathy's Famous Iced Tea," Citizen said, grinning up at her. I almost winced. According to the kids who were out with them, that's what Madeleine and Stacie drank all night. They were rumored to be stiff drinks, Cathy's version of Long Island Iced Teas. Some redditors had theorized that maybe the girls had been followed home by the killer but they were too tipsy to notice.

"All right," said our server brusquely. If the drink was overly popular at the moment, she didn't remark on it.

"Me too," said Goku, handing her his drink menu.

"A pale ale, if you have it," said Lightly.

"Bourbon on the rocks," Mistress said. "Kentucky is best."

"And you?" The server turned to me. "You want what your brothers are having?"

It took me a second to process she meant Goku and Citizen, who'd both turned their faces, presumably to hide their laughter.

"Uh, yes, please," I said meekly. "I'll have the tea."

As soon as she walked away, Goku and Citizen exploded with laughter.

Lightly shook his head. "I don't even want to know how she thinks this family is related."

I pressed my palms on the table. "I'm so sorry for lying. I didn't know what else to do."

"No, that was a good choice." Citizen, still catching his breath, nodded at the bar, where the manager, George, had finally returned. "Imagine if you'd said 'No, actually, we're more ghouls here to investigate the murders.' We would've gotten booted."

"This is certainly not the atmosphere I was expecting," Mistress admitted, looking around. "I knew Delphine had a large media presence, but I didn't realize there'd be so much..."

"Competition?" Goku suggested.

"We could say we're FBI consultants," I said. "No one else can claim that."

"Yeah, but ninety percent of the value of being here is talking to people with their guards down." Citizen leaned back in the booth and crossed his arms. I'd taken off Mistress's parka since the heater was on full blast, and now it lay half across my legs, half across Citizen's, but he didn't seem to mind. "If we tell them we're working with the cops, they'll clam up. Didn't Hale say the advantage to us is that no one would see us coming?"

"So what, then?" I asked. We all fell silent as our server returned to dole out drinks. I took a sip of mine and—holy *shit*. Four different kinds of booze battled it out in my mouth.

Goku laughed. "Look at Searcher's face!"

"They weren't kidding," I sputtered. "This stuff's lethal."

Citizen tapped my head. "Let's keep our eyes on Searcher tonight, yeah?" He took a sip of his tea and didn't even flinch.

"On the issue of how to present ourselves," Lightly said as soon as the waitress took our food orders and was off. He leaned in close, so we all followed suit. "Normally I'd say no to lying, but this is a unique situation. There's a lot of vitriol between the townspeople and everyone involved in the case."

"We could go undercover." Goku slurped his tea. "Keep our identities a secret."

I almost rolled my eyes but stopped when Lightly looked thoughtful.

"Not for the purposes of exploiting anyone," Mistress said quickly. "Just so we can go about our business without attracting unnecessary attention."

"What do we do if someone recognizes us from *Newsline* or any of the tabloids?" Citizen asked.

"I think the odds are pretty low," Lightly said dryly. "Though maybe higher for you, pretty boy."

"You just had to be a heartthrob," Goku said.

"We can deal with that on a case-by-case basis," Lightly said. "Though it might make sense for us to use fake names, to prevent people from googling us." Lightly's eyes roamed the table, trying to get a read on us. It was a familiar gesture from our video chats, but more effective in person. "How do we feel about that?"

"I'm for anything that keeps me from getting kicked out of restaurants when I'm hungry," Goku said.

"As usual, Goku with the important ethical insights." The tea was already at work in me.

"I think any strategy that gets us closer to the answer is fair game," said Citizen.

I shrugged. "So are we going with the story that I'm a college student and you're visiting me?"

Lightly and Mistress looked at each other.

"If we're your brothers," Goku said, "does that make them your parents or your grandparents?"

"Watch it, punk." Lightly winked. "I'm not that old."

"Food!" our server sang, and we got busy distributing—burgers for Lightly and Goku; chicken fingers for Mistress, who said they'd been her guilty pleasure since her kids were young; a chicken Caesar for Citizen, who got booed by Goku; and something called a Badger Brat for me, which turned out to be a fat bratwurst stuffed into a hotdog bun. Cheesy fries for everyone.

As we ate and drank, smushed in our warm booth overlooking the cold outside, I felt unexpectedly happy. Maybe it was the second Cathy's Tea I ordered, but when I looked around, I saw a real family—not a lie to avoid being outed but an emotional truth: No matter what anyone has claimed about us, we didn't set out to deceive. We just wanted to exist in Delphine without trouble, solve the crimes, and catch the killer. We didn't get off on hoodwinking people, and anyone who claims otherwise is gravely mistaken, especially She Who Must Not Be Named in That Awful Book.

At some point, the tea overtook my reason. At a natural lull in the conversation, I found myself blurting: "None of you were right about what sleuth types you are."

Four sets of confused eyes blinked back at me. I hiccuped. "From Mistress's book. Remember? There are four reasons why people are drawn to true crime. The Detective, the Defender, the Victim, and the Killer. Everyone said who they were, but you were all wrong."

"Don't say killer so loudly," Goku whispered, eyes darting around.

"Lord, are we talking about this book again?" Lightly sighed.

"It's a good book," Mistress said indignantly. "What were you saying, Searcher?"

"This ought to be good," Citizen muttered, but there was a smile in his eyes.

I took another sip of tea. "The night I joined, Lightly told us he was a Detective. But Detective types are drawn to true crime because they have an innate desire to solve puzzles. It's a cerebral challenge. Lightly's smart, of course, but he's all heart. He does it because every victim is another Juliana."

The table went quiet, stricken, but I rambled on. "He's a Defender. And Goku." I turned to him. "You're not a Victim. You might feel sympathy for victims, but you *do* like the puzzle. You like the excuse cases give you to go on the dark web and talk to people on the fringe."

"Can you also not mention the dark web so loudly?" Goku hissed. Citizen laughed.

"What about me?" asked Mistress. "I'm not a Defender?"

"No." I shook my head, like a doctor delivering bad news. "You're a Victim. It could've been you at the truck stop, and now you want to help everyone who wasn't as lucky."

"Hmm." Mistress looked across the bar. "I guess that's true to some extent..."

Citizen leaned in. "What about me?"

I met his eyes. The crystal blue was hard to make heads or tails of. "I still haven't figured you out," I admitted. "You're tricky." He invested too much emotion to be a Detective; he wasn't really a crusader, like Lightly, so he wasn't a Defender. Could he be a Victim? There were hints he'd given me about his past, little clues about his father, that could point in that direction. But I needed to know more.

"What about you?" Goku stole one of my fries. He sounded a little resentful that I thought of him as a puzzle master. "What's your type?"

"I don't know that either."

"Maybe you're a Killer," said Citizen, "but you don't want to admit it."

"Guys." Goku stopped mid-chew. "The killer could be in this bar. Right now."

"Do I have to take those teas away from all three of you?" Mistress made a show of grabbing for them, but Citizen batted her away.

"Agent Hale said they think he stayed in the area," Goku said. "And he's watching the investigation. So it's not out of the realm of possibility that he's here."

"Bundy would return to the scene of his crimes to sexualize the corpses." Citizen swiped another of my cheese fries. I pushed the basket out so he and Goku could reach them more easily. "BTK followed the police investigation for decades and finally got so frustrated he handed cops the evidence to find him."

"Can we institute a 'no necrophilia' rule during meal times?" Mistress shot Citizen a look. "Otherwise, I fear we won't last long as roommates."

"Maybe I'm none of the types," I said. "Maybe my reasons don't fit any of the boxes."

"Or maybe they fit every box," Lightly said. We all stopped. Lightly rarely engaged in our games. "Maybe you're a little bit of every type, and that's why it's hard to pick."

"I—"

"Maybe everyone is." He wiped his hands on a napkin. "Maybe the five of us are sitting here in the middle of Bumblefuck, Idaho, because we're all a little bit Victim, Defender, Detective, and Killer. We can see it from all angles, and that's why the pull's so strong." He rose and shook out his coat. "And before you tell me that's not what Rachel Monroe meant when she wrote *Savage Appetites*—" Mistress opened her mouth, then bit back the words—"I'm going to say you were right about those teas. I think we should head home."

255

"My head doesn't feel so great," I agreed. The floor of the bar had begun to tilt.

"Come on, Searcher," Citizen said, tugging me out of the booth. "One step at a time. Lean on me if you need to."

"Now we know how Search would fare if a night predator were after her," Goku said as we stumbled out of the bar. "Goner for sure."

54

—

THE NEXT MORNING MISTRESS KNOCKED on my door at six a.m., singing, "Wake up, sunshine! Coffee's on in the kitchen. Grab some before you get in the car!" And that's when I remembered, through a head full of Cathy's Famous Tea, that we'd agreed to get an early start on our road trip to Oregon. I groaned deep into my pillow.

Twenty minutes later the five of us were bundled up and backing out of the driveway, a hodgepodge of coffee tumblers in the cup holders. Citizen was driving, Lightly beside him playing navigator, Goku and Mistress in the middle seats, and I was stretched out pathetically in the last row.

"I'm never drinking again," I moaned, feeling every bump.

Goku turned around and patted me on the head. "Of course not. A lifetime of abstinence for you."

"Should we listen to some music?" Mistress asked. "Perhaps some ABBA or Patti LuPone?"

"Sorry, Mistress." Citizen pressed a button, and heavy rock assaulted us. "Driver's choice."

"Oh, God," I whimpered, covering my ears.

After a few minutes of driving, the car slowed unexpectedly and the music stopped.

"The second murder site," Goku said, awe in his voice.

"Figured we could drive by both houses on our way out of town," Citizen said.

Headache be damned, I shot up. 1756 Collegiate Parkway was bigger than it looked on the news, and somehow uglier, its boxy shape more pronounced. Yellow caution tape was staked around the perimeter, and a cop in a DPD uniform stood at one corner, watching the small crowd of people outside the tape. A short distance away, a reporter spoke into a microphone, his cameraman's lens trained on him. The street was congested with cars and a large RV. A clothesline hung outside, draped with clothes.

"Is that reporter *living* here?" Mistress asked.

"I heard that was happening," said Lightly. "That way they make sure they capture every development."

I scanned the house, looking for...something. A malevolent presence, a sign that something extraordinarily evil had taken place here. But it was ordinary. Worse—it was dull. An uninspired place to die.

"The killer was smart to choose this house," Lightly said. "It's on a through street, plenty of retail on either side of the neighborhood. That makes it easily accessible and gives anyone caught by security cameras driving past an excuse for why they're there."

"And the neighbors' windows don't face it," Citizen pointed out. "That's unusual."

Lightly nodded. "I'll have to ask Lawrence if they've had any luck with surveillance footage."

"It feels desolate," Mistress said quietly, and I murmured my agreement.

"I'm sure the track girls figured it was just a year of their life, and then they'd be on to bigger and better places," Goku said as we pulled away from the curb. "Anyone can put up with anything for a year."

It took only five minutes down suburban roads to get to the first murder site, where there was an even bigger crowd outside the crime tape, and a larger police force.

"So this is where the party is," Goku joked.

There was a note of resentment in Citizen's voice. "Bullshit to give some of the killings more attention than others."

"I think it might have something to do with that hullabaloo," Mistress said, pointing.

Next to the crime tape, a small group of women waved posters that read "Tear This Place Down" and "No More Spectacle." The other people gave them a wide berth. I recognized the woman in the center from funeral photos. Natalie Flowers, Stacie's older sister. Unlike Stacie, Natalie had dark hair. Otherwise, they were carbon copies.

"Roll down the window," I said, and Citizen obliged.

Natalie and her friends' voices carried. "Tear down this house," they chanted. "No more trauma porn!"

"This is where my sister died," Natalie shouted. "It's not your entertainment!"

Ironically, some of the people filmed the protestors on their iPhones, as if they were part of the murder-house package. Others with more self-awareness watched them out of the corner of their eyes or ignored them completely.

"She's brave," Mistress said, eyes on Natalie.

"But calling for the house to be torn down?" Goku turned to Mistress. "The cops don't even have a lead yet. Doesn't she know they need it for evidence?"

"I don't think she's operating on logic right now," Lightly said. "And that's okay. We're the ones who need to be logical and dispassionate so she doesn't have to be. Let her yell. She deserves it. And while she does, let's catch her sister's killer."

"Oh, shit," Citizen said as a cop ran up to us.

"You can't park here," the cop yelled. "Residential parking only. Turn around and leave, or find somewhere else to park, and be prepared to show your IDs."

"Our time is up," Citizen muttered as he waved at the cop and rolled up the windows. "Asshole."

"Why do they even let people come see the houses?" I wondered. "If it's pissing off the families and neighbors?"

Mistress twisted to face me. "I expect they want to see who shows up. If serial killers are likely to return to the scene of their crimes, the cops want to let them."

"So he could be here right now?"

"Could be."

"Next stop, Oregon," Citizen called as he drove away. "Settle in and get comfortable. We're not stopping for at least an hour." The rock music started up again.

I searched the crowd for suspicious faces until the house was nothing but a speck in the distance. And yet, for all that effort, I still missed the clues.

55

—

THE CARRAWAY POLICE HEADQUARTERS WAS a sleepy three-room brick building—well, four rooms, if you counted the bathroom—on a small plot of green land. Everything in Oregon was green, even more than Idaho. We checked in at the front desk, where a woman in spectacles on a chain made a lot of appreciative noises as she reviewed our paperwork from the FBI. Hale had promised us we had official FBI consultant badges on the way, but in the meantime, he'd written a letter explaining that we were working with the agency and should be granted similar rights of access. Standing in front of the desk waiting as the receptionist called the chief and asked him what to do ("He's away all weekend on a fishing trip," she'd explained) felt a little like a being a kid in the principal's office holding a permission slip.

Finally, we got clearance to view the case files.

"The chief hasn't even returned my emails," Lightly grumbled as the receptionist led us to smaller building in the back, which served as the CPD Evidence and Records Room. "And yet he has time to go fishing."

After we signed our names in the log, the receptionist unlocked one of the lockers and pulled out a single cardboard box.

"That's it?" Goku asked.

"That's it," she said and left us.

"This place makes Delphine look like a bustling metropolis," I said, and Citizen snickered. He wore what I was starting to realize was his uniform: a plain white T-shirt and jeans. Maybe he'd gotten so used to wearing uniforms in the military that it had become second nature, or maybe he just didn't care much about fashion. The T-shirt covered the snake tattoo. Unless you'd seen him undressed, you wouldn't even know it was there. I was fascinated by that—the hidden layers to people, the things you could only discover by peeling away.

"All right, well. Let's dig in." Mistress opened the box and started pulling out folders. "We've got Autopsy, Crime Scene, Suspects, Evidence, Community Statements. Let's divide and conquer." She passed out the folders.

"Community Statements, please," Citizen said, and Mistress tossed the folder to him.

I looked at my folder—Autopsy—and my stomach lurched. I almost asked for a different one, but I took a deep breath and opened it up.

There she was: Bridget Howell, naked on an examining table, her skin the pale, waxy texture I'd come to recognize as the signature of dead flesh. It was hard to see the contrast between the vibrant girl in her cousin's Facebook album and this one, almost alien. Unlike the Delphine girls, whose bodies were horrifying maps of deeply gouged valleys, Bridget was largely untouched except for her neck. It was a vivid canvas of color—dark purple, almost black, faded blue, greenish yellow. The bruises formed a thick, uniform band around her throat.

"Ligature marks begin on the neck below the mandible," read the report. "The widest is dark purple and encircles the neck, crossing the midline. The width of the mark varies between 0.8 and 1cm and is horizontal in orientation. The skin above and below the mark shows petechial hemorrhaging. The absence of abrasions, along with the variations in the width of the mark, is consistent with a soft ligature, such as a length of fabric."

The report continued that way, coldly discussing Bridget as "the victim" or "the body," whose cause of death was asphyxia due to ligature strangulation. Someone had wrapped a kitchen towel so tightly around Bridget's neck they'd cut off her blood flow and air supply, first knocking her unconscious and then killing her. I supposed being unconscious was a small mercy. I studied the close-up photos of her hands. Her nails were painted baby blue. They were chipped, either because she'd struggled or because she'd been due for a fresh coat. Under her nails, reddish material lined her fingertips that the report confirmed were blood and skin cells "not matching the victim."

"She got you, sucker," I whispered, then blushed when everyone looked at me. "Sorry."

"Well, what have we got so far?" Lightly asked. There was only one chair in the utilitarian Evidence and Records Room, and we'd given it to Mistress without hesitation. The rest of us had folded ourselves against the walls. I was sitting on the floor, legs crossed, back against one of the evidence lockers.

"Nothing new here," I said. "Just what we already know. She was strangled to death with fabric, assumed to be the kitchen towel missing from her parents' kitchen. Was found in the outfit she'd worn to school. No signs of sexual assault. Blood and skin cells under her fingernails believed to be the attacker's, so he would've had scratch marks. But no record of him in the system."

"Mine's interesting," Mistress said. "It looks like the police had three main suspects, but they were all ruled out when they compared DNA. The first was a neighbor down the street, a married guy. An anonymous caller reported she saw scratch marks all over his arms. He was home sick at the time of the attack, so he didn't have an alibi, and the theory was that Bridget would've let him in. The police were pretty sweet on him until his DNA wasn't a match. Then there was a service technician who'd installed the Howells' cable upgrade the week before. He had a record of home invasions his employer didn't know about, and the cops figured he could've memorized the back door code or made a copy of the key. But of course, no match. And then a year after Bridget died, a man was arrested up in northern Oregon, a door-to-door salesman who'd broken into a few women's houses and raped them, killing one. They found out he was in Carraway around the time Bridget died and got excited, but again, no dice."

"That's a pretty small pool of suspects," Lightly said. He turned to Citizen. "Anyone say anything in the Community Statements you think warranted a closer look?"

Citizen was resting against the table in the center of the room, one ankle crossed over the other, looking strangely comfortable. "Not really. Most of the stuff in here's about how Bridget was an angel. You know, not involved in anything like drugs or hooking that could invite an unsavory element." He nodded at Mistress. "And there's a few statements from other neighbors pointing to the neighbor Mistress mentioned, a Mr. Leopold. But nothing juicy."

"Crime Scene's more or less what we already know," Lightly confirmed. "And they seemed to have done a thorough sweep, as far as I can tell. They ran the whole house dusting for fingerprints, shoe prints, anything out of order. But nothing. Locked house, clean scene except for the body."

"Our stealth killer was good even twelve years ago," I sighed. "Unfortunately."

"Here's something, maybe." Goku shifted his weight against the door. "There was one thing cops couldn't explain. They found a small piece of a sticker stuck on Bridget's couch that her parents didn't recognize." Goku flipped the file around so we could see the pictures.

"We can do better than that," Lightly said and rooted around in the cardboard box. He pulled out a small, transparent bag, tightly sealed. Inside was the scrap of sticker. It was bright orange and clearly torn off a larger sticker. All that remained were three letters: LAK.

"CPD figured out it was torn off a Lake Ridge High School parking permit," Goku said. "That was the name of her school. Except, the catch is, Bridget didn't own a car."

"Huh," I said, staring at the scrap. "And this didn't make the cops suspect any of her classmates or teachers?"

"The sticker could've gotten stuck to Bridget's pant legs at any point at school," Citizen pointed out. "Or transferred to her a million different ways."

"True. But you have that school sticker and then the keyless lock on her back door." I could feel myself starting to get excited. "Back when I went to school, every kid knew how to hack those locks."

"Didn't you go to high school four years after Bridget?" Lightly asked. "Not to rain on your parade."

I fought the urge to snap at him that four years wasn't that long in the scheme of things. That was happening more often as I grew surer of myself. Anytime someone tried to poke holes, I got defensive. *Be a scientist,* I chanted to myself. *Logical and detached.* "True," I managed to say. "But that's hardly a generational difference."

"I'm sensing it's time to take a look at her house." Mistress slapped her hands on her knees. "Why don't we copy these files and snap pics of the evidence bags, then hit the road?"

"Sure." Goku rolled himself off the door. "This place was kind of bust anyway."

Of course, as you and I now know, that was far from true. The answers we were looking for were at our fingertips, hidden in the pages we pressed against the glass. Right there, but we couldn't yet see them.

56

—

THE "FOR SALE" SIGN HAD been staked into the front yard of the Howells' home for years. Carraway was small enough that it didn't get many new people, and all the locals knew 110 Green Hollow Lane as the murder house. Offers to buy it hadn't poured in.

The house did feel haunted as we pulled up to the curb and swept slowly around the perimeter. Or maybe it was just so different from the murder sites at Queen Lace and Collegiate Parkway, with their spectators, smartphone flashes, and wary, watching cops. By comparison, Bridget Howell's former home was unnervingly still, a grand Victorian with stained-glass windows on the second floor.

"Bridget's parents were project managers and data analysts?" Goku asked as we clomped through the overgrown grass. "Amazing what you can afford if you're willing to live in the middle of nowhere."

"I'm not sure house envy is the emotion you're supposed to be feeling," Mistress said. The five of us came to the tall wooden fence guarding the backyard.

"Well." Citizen turned to me and made a basket of his hands. "You ready?"

"As I'll ever be." I seized his shoulders—I'd never been very athletic—and placed my foot in his hands. Immediately, he launched me up, and once I regained my balance, I swung my free leg over the fence.

"Now just hop onto the other side," Goku instructed.

"Easy for you to say," I grumbled. "It's, like, seven feet."

My leap was not graceful, but I made it with only slightly muddy knees, and unlocked the gate for everyone else.

"Pretty backyard." Mistress pointed to the far corner. "You can tell they used to have a flower garden. I bet Bridget tended that with her mom."

That was one of Mistress's quirks—she often daydreamed about victims, making up stories. It was her wishful thinking talking, her desire for them to have led good lives.

I beelined to the back door.

"Moment of truth!" Goku called.

Just as I'd suspected, the keyless lock was a Kwikset Powerbolt-9200—it said so right at the bottom of the oval. "Watch this," I said, though I was less confident than I sounded. Imagine if, after all this, I was wrong.

I pressed zero seven times, heart pounding—and sure enough, the lock whirred and the deadbolt slid away. Triumphantly, I swung open the door and turned to my friends with a curtsy.

Lightly whistled. "Look at that. Now we know how our killer got in and locked the door behind him."

We fell quiet as we entered the house. The silence lingered as we moved through the empty rooms, as if we were at a memorial. It smelled musty, likely because the place hadn't been aired out in a while. I didn't spend long in the living room, where Bridget died, even though Lightly and Citizen did. I climbed the stairs to the second floor and wandered from room to room. From the police report, I knew the middle bedroom overlooking the backyard had been Bridget's, so I walked the edges, observing the small nail holes drilled into the walls where she'd undoubt-edly hung pictures or posters. I stopped in front of her window and gazed out. The Howells' house was on a slight hill, so you could see far.

"A pretty place," Mistress murmured, coming up beside me. "I bet she had a happy life."

"I think she did," I said, "as far as I could tell. Her cousin came over to play a lot."

"Look," Mistress said suddenly. "Is that her high school?"

I looked where she was pointing. It *was* Bridget's school. I'd known it was close—that was why she hadn't needed a car—but I hadn't realized how close.

"Must've taken her five minutes or less to walk," I said. "I bet she got to sleep in later than all her friends."

"They renamed it. Look at that sign up front."

She was right—the marquee no longer read Lake Ridge High School in blocky letters but Bridget Howell High.

"That's lovely they named it for her," Mistress said. "What a nice legacy."

An acute guilt stabbed me. What had I done for my father to ensure anyone would remember his name? Nothing. I was still searching and had no answers to why he'd been taken so abruptly. I wasn't giving him what he deserved.

"Are you okay?" Mistress turned. "What's wrong?"

"Nothing. I just think I'd like to go now, if that's okay."

"Of course." She rubbed my shoulders. "Let's get the others."

On the drive out of town, as I sat stiffly in the back seat, my earlier headache returning, I turned to look out the window right before we got on the highway and saw the most peculiar sign: Fort Jones Naval Base.

"Hey." My voice was sharp. "What's a naval base doing out here? We're completely landlocked."

Everyone turned in their seats. "Citizen?" Lightly asked. "Any clue why your people would put a base out here?"

He shrugged. "I don't know. Ballistic testing? I'm not familiar with anything in the area."

But I knew what it was, this improbable navy base. It was my father trying to tell me something.

57

—

TWO DAYS AFTER WE RETURNED from Oregon, we accepted an invitation to appear on the *Murder Junkies* podcast. I remember it clearly, because it was the day after the Delphine killer got his official nickname—the Barbie Butcher—and it was all anyone could talk about. Veejay and Byron, the podcast hosts, must've dropped the name a hundred times during our interview.

It was Mistress's idea to reach out for help. We'd finally gotten our badges naming us as FBI consultants, and Hale had given us the all-clear to talk publicly about our involvement—and, more importantly, about the killer's DNA connection to Bridget Howell.

We got in an argument about it over lunch. Citizen had set up an old-fashioned murder board on a giant corkboard he'd lugged all the way from home. It was divided into three sections: Queen Lace Murders, Collegiate Parkway Murders, and Bridget Howell. The rental house had a printer that he and Goku had used liberally, printing out victim photos, pieces of evidence, and key questions and pinning them to the board. Citizen had wheeled it into the dining room while we ate PB&Js.

Our visit to Carraway had been less fruitful than we'd hoped. All we'd pinned in Bridget's section was "Killer accessed house via back door," "High school parking permit—relevant?", "Strangled—different MO," "Clean crime scene—similar MO," "Motive: pleasure killing? Sadism? No sex assault," and "No apparent connections to Delphine/ Delphine girls." In other words, we didn't have much.

Mistress set down her sandwich. "If we put out a call to the community to help us figure out connections between Bridget and the Delphine victims, it would extend our reach. We're racing against the clock, right? The killer could strike again any moment. We have this incredible resource at our fingertips—"

"Resource?" Citizen scoffed. "Ninety percent of the sleuths on the Network or Reddit couldn't find their assholes if given a map." There was no doubt he'd soured on them since they'd hung him out to dry.

"Look what they did to Chandler Gray," Goku added, and privately I winced. Everyone else seemed to forget that the Chandler theory had originated with me, but I would never. At least by then, Chandler had woken out of his coma.

"Our whole value-add is our connection to the community," Lightly countered, unsurprisingly taking Mistress's side. "That's why the FBI's interested in working with us. Because we have an in to the hive mind."

"That's presumptuous," Citizen said, wiping his mouth with a paper towel. "I'd say we're pretty damn good at what we do."

"Let's not make this an ego thing, like with the DPD leak," I said. Citizen visibly bristled. "There's no shame in asking for help. There could be people out there who know things about Bridget Howell, or the Delphine girls."

"Yeah, but Search," Goku said through a mouthful of peanut butter, "telling people our insider information destroys our competitive advantage."

"You know, for an anarcho-socialist, you're very concerned with winning," I pointed out.

Even Citizen's mouth twisted into a smile before he righted himself and scowled. "All right then, Searcher. What do you recommend? Dumping everything we know on the Network and letting the jackals have at it? Because that worked so well the last time."

Of course he was bringing up Kevin Kowalski. I still felt guilty for telling him to broadcast that on the Network.

Mistress snapped her fingers. "*Murder Junkies.*"

Collectively, we stopped chewing to squint at her. "The podcast?" Citizen asked. "What about it?"

In the years following the *Serial* podcast phenomenon, *Murder Junkies* had risen to become one of the top true-crime podcasts in the country. The angle of the show was that, rather than dissect cold cases, its two hosts, Veejay Singh and Byron Cohen, tried to solve murders in real time. Like the women of *My Favorite Murders,* they approached the serious subject matter with a jocular, irreverent tone. To be honest, I'd always found them kind of grating.

"They've been asking for one of us to come on to talk about the Delphine murders," Mistress said.

"Since when?" Goku sputtered. I was glad I wasn't the only one surprised by the news.

Mistress picked up her sandwich. "For a few weeks now. I helped Veejay with one of his cases a few years ago. We've stayed in touch, and I guess he and Byron know we're the ones at the heart of Delphine."

"So you want to go on their podcast and what, drop the bomb about Bridget?" Lightly asked. "I'm not critiquing; I'm just trying to wrap my head around it."

"Imagine this," she said. "We break the Bridget news on the podcast, thereby giving the boys an exclusive, which means they'll promote the heck out of the show—"

"And they already have incredible reach," I piped in. "I heard over a hundred million people subscribe to their show. That's way more than the Network."

"Exactly." Mistress straightened in her chair. "It's a bigger audience, and it's a female-skewing audience, as opposed to the Network, which we all know skews male—certainly in its energy. If we're going to reach people with connections to our girls, I think it makes sense to target women. We can offer a tip line for listeners who know something—"

"Not my number," Goku said quickly. "I don't want to field crazies for months."

"It isn't really something the DPD or the FBI would do," Lightly said thoughtfully. "Again, not a critique. We can do things they can't."

"What do you think, Goku? Citizen?" Mistress watched them. "Want to take a swing? Oh," she added, before they could answer. "And I think Searcher should be the one to give the interview."

"Me?" I twisted in my chair. "Why?"

"Because the eyelash DNA was your find," Goku answered for her. "And so was the lock. You're the reason we have Bridget, if you think about it."

"That's right. Plus, you're roughly the same age as the victims," Mistress said. "You speak their language. Friends of theirs might be more willing to approach you."

In other words, I was the least intimidating. I didn't know what to say. I couldn't deny the that idea of being on a famous podcast was exciting, but I was also overwhelmed.

"Last hole I'll try to punch in the idea," Goku swore. "Aren't we supposed to be undercover?"

Mistress waved her hand. "It's a podcast. No one will see her face."

"Fine," Citizen sighed, picking up his plate and heading for the kitchen. "Let's see what fishing with dynamite gets us."

58

—

"YOU CAN HEAR US OKAY?" On-screen, Veejay leaned back in his armchair. The *Murder Junkies* studio was really just Veejay's spare bedroom, which he and Byron had filled with oversized leather recliners and posters of their favorite noir movies. From there, they'd launched an empire.

"I think so." I adjusted my headphones. "Can you hear me?"

Goku, Citizen, and Lightly had gone out to give me privacy, but Mistress had stayed for moral support. We'd set up my laptop in the attic, where the house's router was. She gave me a thumbs-up from the other side of the screen.

"Loud and clear," Byron confirmed. Both he and Veejay wore flannel shirts, sneakers, and beards. Their brand was "just two crime-obsessed guys shooting the shit about murder and solving crimes along the way." Byron nodded. "Let's dive in, okay? I'm going to hit record. Technically, since this isn't live, we can stop and edit if you really need to, but we try to keep these episodes free-flowing, so let's avoid that if we can."

"Right." I nodded. No mistakes.

"And here we go," Veejay said. A tinny voice announced, "Now recording."

Immediately, as if they'd been pulled by a string, Byron and Veejay straightened. "Welcome to another episode of *Murder Junkies*," Byron said, his voice animated, nearly singsong. "I'm Byron Cohen."

"And I'm Veejay Singh."

"And we're here with a special guest today, who's going to speak about the case it feels like the whole country's talking about—"

"The whole world," Veejay corrected. "I was on Indian TikTok yesterday and saw a ton of theory vids."

"The whole world," Byron modified. "Which is obviously the Delphine, Idaho, massacres. We've got a young woman here by the name of Janeway Sharp—is that your real name, Janeway?"

"It's real," I said. "But you can call me Jane."

"Right, Jane Sharp, who—get this—is one of a select few amateur sleuths anointed by the FBI as a consultant on the case. Is that true, Jane? I was shocked when Tammy Jo told me."

Veejay whistled. "How'd you manage that?"

"Well—"

"And we'll get to that," Byron interrupted. "Jane's going to share everything she knows about the case for our Delphine-obsessed listeners. But first, we have to get to the news of the moment."

I glanced up at Mistress, who shrugged.

"Which is of course the fact that the Delphine murderer has gotten an official nickname," Veejay said. "My sources say it was the *Daily Mail* who coined the term, which was quickly picked up by news sources everywhere, and now the whole internet is abuzz with the controversy. Have you heard this, Jane?"

"Uh, no," I admitted. Great. Two minutes into the podcast as a supposed expert, and I was already behind.

"The 'Barbie Butcher,'" Veejay said.

I frowned. "The what?"

"Let's break this down." Byron crossed his legs. "The idea is that they're calling him this because all six of the girls he's killed have been attractive coeds, is that right?"

"Exactly," Veejay said. "He started with three steamy sorority girls and moved on to three hot track stars. The man has a type, clearly, like most serial killers, but unlike most, he's not going for sex workers or runaways. Oh no, he's killing girls who have everything going for them. So-called Barbies. Jane, what do you think about the name?"

I had no talking points for this. Mistress's eyes were wide. I was on my own. "Knee-jerk? I think it's demeaning to the victims, calling them Barbies. As if the most important thing about them is what they looked like."*

"Ah," Veejay said triumphantly. "Sounds like Jane's siding with online critics who are bashing the nickname for its alleged sexism. *Teen Vogue* tweeted, and I quote, 'Female murder victims are already so dehumanized. #BarbieButcher adds to this fetishizing tradition.'"

"Amazing that we're talking about *Teen Vogue* as an important cultural critic," Byron quipped.

"Hey, don't participate in the sexism yourself," I warned, and Veejay hooted.

"You have to admit that the Barbie Butcher is catchy, though," Byron insisted. "I think that's the number one requirement for serial killer nicknames. You want something sticky people will remember."

"And here's Byron analyzing the killer's marketing campaign," Veejay joked. "All right, listeners, sound off on social about what you think: 'Barbie Butcher,' sticky or sexist?" He turned to Byron. "Should we start asking Jane some more serious questions?"

---

* Though she is likely loath to admit this, this is one point on which She Who Shall Not Be Named and I agree.

"Let's do it." Byron pulled up his phone. "So, Jane, give us the inside scoop. What do our listeners need to know about the Butcher?"

This was my moment. "They might be interested to know he's killed seven people, not six."

Veejay and Byron stared. I'd actually managed to shock them into silence. "Whoa," Veejay said, recovering first. "Are you serious?" He leaned forward. "Is this a scoop?"

"This is a scoop," I confirmed. "The FBI found a stray eyelash at the Collegiate Parkway house, near Shuri Washington. They tested it, and the DNA is a match to an unsolved murder from twelve years ago. Seventeen-year-old Bridget Howell, who was strangled in her living room using a kitchen towel."

"Holy...I mean, my jaw has dropped," Byron said. "Listeners, you can't see it, but I'm in full Kevin McAllister *Home Alone* mode right now. Jane is breaking news here. We've got a seventh victim—"

"No, a first," Veejay corrected.

"Right, the first victim. Or, who knows, right? Maybe not even the first. But we have another girl slaughtered by our perp." Byron addressed someone off-camera. "Can we get some research on Bridget Howell?" He turned back. "While our producers google, tell us more."

"Well, the reason I'm talking to you, really—" Over the laptop, Mistress nodded. "Is because we need listener's help crowdsourcing information about Bridget and how she might be connected to the Delphine victims. If you have any information for us, please call our tip line." Mistress held up a sheet of paper with the number of the burner we'd bought. "208-969-7430."

"Jane, how did you and your friends—'cause I understand there's five of you—how'd you manage to get a consulting gig with the FBI?" Veejay asked.

"We're the ones who identified the eyelash in the crime scene."

Byron chuckled. "That'll do it. Hot damn. Jane, since you're obviously an expert—I mean, we've been dissecting this case for months and haven't gotten nearly as far as you—what do you know so far about the Barbie Butcher?"

I squirmed. Once again, the veneer of expertise was uncomfortable. I took a deep breath and told myself I wasn't an impostor. I'd been living and breathing this case for as long as anyone else.

"Well," I said slowly, "as the DPD has said, because of the multiple attacks, we believe he's still in the area and likely watching the investigation. He's probably dialed in online. He might even be listening to this podcast right now. Carraway, Oregon, where Bridget was killed, is only a few hours' drive from Delphine, so it's safe to assume the killer has lived in this general area for a while, maybe even born and raised here.

"From the fact that there's so little evidence pointing to him at the crime scenes, and that our killer cleans up after himself with bleach wipes, we know he's a highly organized killer. He thinks ahead and plots. Even if his choice of victims is arbitrary and comes down to who he senses is vulnerable—young women after nights out or, in the case of Bridget, alone in their homes—he's planning meticulously. He values order and control. In fact, that might be a primary motive—killing to exert control over the victims, which is how he feels powerful. He might even kill after experiences with powerlessness as a way to regain control. He knows how a crime scene is investigated, which points to someone with insight into law enforcement, maybe someone with a cop or security background."

"So many serial killers have cop backgrounds," Byron added. "Think of the Golden State Killer."

"Right. And even though, as you pointed out, he's choosing attractive victims, he doesn't seem motivated by sex. There's no evidence of sexual assault."

"Could he be getting off on the murders themselves?" Veejay asked. "Lots of serials are sexual sadists, right?"

"Maybe. But power is the big thing, I think. This will be someone with a big ego, an easily wounded ego, someone who doesn't like to be put down." I glanced up at Mistress and hesitated, fumbling for a moment because of the way she was looking at me.

"This is really great stuff, Jane," Veejay said. "Thank you."

"Yeah, man, this girl knows her stuff," Byron quipped. "I hate to say we have to turn to commercial, but it's time for ads from our amazing sponsors." He nodded to someone off-screen, and a prerecorded ad started.

"Whoa," Veejay said, the minute we stopped recording. "You didn't warn us you were dropping a bomb!"

"Sorry."

"No, this is amazing. Our listeners are going to lose their minds. Is she hot?" He turned abruptly to Byron, who'd been handed some papers by a ghostly producer's arm.

Byron scanned what I presumed was the producer's research on Bridget. "I mean, she's young, obviously, only seventeen, so we'll want to avoid sounding like pedos, but yeah, man, she's attractive."

"Oh, this is gold." Veejay turned back to me. "You have no idea how viral this is going to go. Sit tight, Jane. You're about to be real fucking famous."

59

—

VEEJAY AND BYRON WERE RIGHT about the episode going viral. Within two days of airing, it was their most downloaded show. Luckily for me, due to the nature of podcasts and the fact that I was just a disembodied voice in people's ears, listeners largely ignored the messenger in favor of the message, aka me in favor of Bridget. Hashtags like #BridgetBarbie and #BarbieButchersFirstKill were everywhere. All the true-crime forums launched in on her, trying to dredge up everything they could, which of course we'd wanted. Bridget had gone from an obscure cold case to the talk of the town overnight. Calls came in to our tip line round the clock, but so far nothing had been useful.

That second day after the episode aired, it was my night to cook dinner, so I borrowed Citizen's car and drove to the nearest Safeway. I had neither money nor culinary skills, so I was planning to buy as much spaghetti and tomato sauce as I could for ten dollars, throw it in some pots, and hope for the best. I was standing in the middle of the discount Easter candy aisle, debating whether ten dollars could stretch to include a few half-price Cadbury eggs, when a voice said, "My daughter loved those things. They were her favorite candy."

I turned, ready to make small talk, then froze. I recognized the woman standing a foot away, even though she wore a sweatshirt and holey jeans, so different from the staid black dress she'd worn to the funeral. It was Stacie Flowers' mom.

"I—uh." I glanced around, as if expecting to find a hidden camera. Was this really happening? I knew the Flowers were the only family out of the victims who lived in Delphine, but the idea that Mrs. Flowers was just going about her life, going to the grocery store, while her daughter was the subject of a hundred thousand discussions every day…well, I guess they still needed to eat. But it was surreal.

"Uh, Mrs. Flowers." Guilt coursed through me. "I hope this isn't weird, but I know who you are. I know your daughter."

Suddenly, I realized my mistake. Of course the mother of one of the victims hadn't just walked up to me in a supermarket out of coincidence. She must've heard the podcast and looked me up, maybe followed me here. She was going to read me the riot act about using her daughter's case to launch my own fame. A litany of explanations sat poised on my tongue, but before I could speak, Mrs. Flowers's eyes softened.

"Oh my goodness. You knew Stacie? You must've gone to school with her."

I looked down at my NIU Badgers sweatshirt. We'd all bought merch from the college bookstore to help us fit in. "Well, I—"

"Were you a KD too?"

"No, not in a sorority." What could I say at that point?

"Classmates?"

My mouth hung open until I remembered to close it. "Um…yes. And I'm so sorry for your loss, Mrs. Flowers. Truly. My father—" I cleared my throat. "My father died in August. I miss him every day."

Her eyes filled with tears. "You can call me Laura. What's your name?"

I panicked—it was knee-jerk. "Veronica." Damn Citizen and his teasing about *Heathers*.

She leaned forward and snagged a bag of Cadbury eggs. "Veronica, I would really like to spend the evening with someone who knew my daughter. Would you consider coming to eat dinner with me and my family?"

She must've seen my surprise, because she quickly added, "It would mean a lot to me. I'm sure you know how unpredictable grief is. I've learned to just follow my instincts."

I was having an out-of-body experience. How could I say no to this grieving mother, staring at me with wounded eyes? Of course I knew how unpredictable grief was. It was the entire reason I was standing in the middle of a grocery store in Idaho, considering her bizarre request.

"Okay," I said finally and followed her to the register.

———

Stacie Flowers's family lived about twenty minutes outside downtown Delphine, in a sprawling lodge-style home with showy stone walls, on acres of land lined with pine trees. I'd known Madeleine and Stacie both came from well-to-do families, but the sheer size of the house and the fact that it looked like a fancy ski resort took me by surprise. The spaghetti and tomato sauce sat in a brown bag on my passenger seat as I pulled into the driveway. I knew I should text someone to tell them where I was, but truthfully, I didn't want Mistress or anyone to talk me out of it.

I followed Mrs. Flowers into her home and to her large kitchen, where she put away her groceries and opened the bag of Cadbury eggs, shyly offering me one.

"Your house is beautiful," I said, looking around at the timber-and-stone interior, mouth full of chocolate.

She leaned against her kitchen island. "I guess Stacie never brought you home. She loved bringing her friends here. Natalie went away to college, to California, but it was so fun to have Stacie close by. It let us keep an eye on her..." Her voice trailed, and then she cut her head away. I got the uncomfortable impression she was holding back tears.

"Mrs. Flowers, do you want me to—"

"Laura," she insisted, wiping her eyes. "Do you want to see her bedroom?"

"Oh." She would not stop surprising me. "Of course."

Stacie's room was on the third floor, just like it had been in the Queen Lace house, though the size of this bedroom was about three times bigger. I entered the space, eyes roaming, trying to memorize the details, while Mrs. Flowers leaned against the doorframe.

"We haven't changed anything," she said softly.

It was a princess's room. A queen-size bed in the center, with a soft-pink canopy, tied off with pink bows. Stacie's love of pink wasn't a sorority thing, then. I examined a velvet bulletin board plastered with pictures of Stacie and her friends.

"She and Madeleine were attached at the hip," Mrs. Flowers said. "Which I'm sure you remember. Stacie just worshipped her."

"They were friends for years, before college," I murmured, studying a picture of the two of them from middle school. Stacie wore braces.

"Madeleine used to live here before her family moved away. Then Stacie followed her to NIU." She smiled. "Joined KD because Madeleine did. Lived at that house because Madeleine did." She walked to Stacie's bed and adjusted the pillows. "The one part that didn't shock me was hearing they'd been killed side by side."

I turned to her. Her fingers trailed over the books and alarm clock on Stacie's bedside table. "I'm grateful they had each other, at least. She wasn't alone."

I watched Mrs. Flowers's fingers brush over the novel that lay open, forever resting where Stacie had left it. My mind flashed to my own bedroom, my father's copy of *The Wheel of Time,* turned to page 245. I knew what this room was. I was standing inside a shrine.

I walked across the room and threw my arms around Stacie's mother. She gave a small, startled "Hmmph," then squeezed back.

"Mom!" a voice called, at the sound of the door cracking open. "We're home!"

"Oh." Mrs. Flowers pulled away and wiped her eyes. "Natalie and Rod are back. Excuse me. I'd better start dinner."

60

THE FOUR OF US SAT awkwardly around the Flowerses' kitchen table, watching each other over plates of Stouffer's lasagna Mrs. Flowers had burned in the oven. My appearance on the staircase had caused a small scandal. Even though I'd retreated to the bathroom, I'd been able to hear the three of them arguing.

"*Again?*" Mr. Flowers had hissed. "Laura, I thought we talked about this. You can't just bring people off the street into our house. I know how much you miss Stacie, trust me, but it isn't safe."

"Veronica knew Stacie," Mrs. Flowers had protested. "They were friends."

"Mom, it's twisted," Natalie had said. "You're springing strangers on us."

"She wanted to see Stacie's room."

"Are you kidding?" Natalie barked, and from the hallway, I winced. "That's so creepy."

Now the four of us sat in tense silence, chewing and watching each other.

"So, Veronica," Mr. Flowers said, with a strained smile, "how exactly did you know Stacie?"

"Um, from class."

Natalie gave me a skeptical look, so I kept going. "I mean, I didn't know her well. Only enough to know she was a great person."

"Did you party at Queen Lace?" Natalie asked. "I know their house was a big party spot."

I hedged my bets. "No. I'm not the biggest drinker."

She snorted. "No wonder you didn't know Stacie well."

"Natalie," her mom admonished.

"What?" Her expression was fierce. "Stacie liked to have a good time. There's nothing wrong with that. It's not like it meant she was asking for what happened."

"Of course not," I said quickly. "She was just cooler than me, that's all."

The ghost of a smile tugged at Natalie's mouth. "She was cooler than me, too."

After that, things got more relaxed. It felt sacred, being at that table with them. It seemed family dinner every night was a ritual for the Flowers family, and what was more, they talked about Stacie lovingly and without reservation. It was a far cry from the two-ships-in-the-night relationship I'd had with my mom since my dad's death. I wanted to tell the three of them that they were lucky, but of course I couldn't. What grieving family wants to hear that?

After dinner, Mrs. Flowers excused herself with a headache, and I didn't miss the way Natalie's worried eyes followed her out of the dining room. When she got up to wash the dishes, I went with her. I'm not sure why—I was drawn to the pain I could feel slipping out from under her tough mask, maybe.

It was just the two of us alone in the kitchen. Through the window above the sink, I could see the stars. There were a lot more visible in Idaho than in Florida.

I picked up a towel and started drying. "My mom had migraines too, right after my dad passed." Carefully, I stacked the finished dishes on the counter. "Eventually they went away."

Natalie eyed me as she scrubbed the lasagna dish. "I'm sorry, by the way. For the icy welcome. It's just, you wouldn't believe how many vultures are out there who want a piece of our family since Stacie died. It's hard to trust anyone."

I flushed hot with guilt and turned my gaze away. "I saw you one day. At the crime scene, protesting."

She raised her brows. "You went to the house?"

"Only to pay my respects," I lied.

She nodded and turned the water hotter. "All those people who go there to gawk. It's like the worst thing that ever happened to us is their entertainment. That's why I want the house torn down."

"It's like a tourist destination," I agreed. "My friend called Delphine 'Crime Disney' the other night."

"Yeah." Natalie handed me the dripping lasagna pan. "The true-crime people descended like locusts. No one's worse than them."

"You really think so?" I knew I was walking on treacherous ground, but I couldn't help myself.

"The gawkers—they're like rubberneckers on a highway. The sleuths are like idiots pulling over on the side of the road and walking up to an accident in fake cop uniforms, pretending to be in charge. Every one of them thinks they're entitled to private details about Stacie because they're convinced they're the shining knight who's going to swoop in and solve the case. You should see some of the emails we've gotten. Not to mention the phone calls, asking who Stacie was sleeping with and whether she did drugs." She nodded toward the dining room. "It upsets her most of all." Her voice softened. "She's sensitive, if you haven't noticed."

I hoped fervently that none of the five of us had ever called the Flowerses.

"Anyway, thanks for being normal," Natalie said, her gaze still on the dining room. "Most of all, thanks for being Stacie's friend. She deserved all the love in the world."

It was reprehensible, what I did to them. Pretending to be someone I wasn't, lying about being a sleuth. I admit it, and I've said a million times, in public statements and via my lawyers, how much I regret it. But I didn't secretly record the Flowerses, as has been suggested. I didn't sneak back into Stacie's room and take covert pictures to upload to the forum. (To this day, I have no idea how those pictures got there.)* I didn't run to Reddit and brag that I'd sat at Stacie's spot at her family table, or use anything the Flowers family told me for my own gain. When Natalie and I were done washing dishes, I simply left, calling Mistress on the way home when I saw my friends had dialed my phone eighteen times.

Everything Natalie Flowers would go on to claim about me—everything she wrote in That Awful Book—is a lie. I want to say this for the record, lawyers' advice be damned. I know it looks bad, everything that happens next. But I went home with Mrs. Flowers because one grieving woman recognized another. The title of Natalie's book—*Angels of Death: The Shocking Villains at the Heart of the Delphine Massacres*—the fact that it's become a *New York Times* bestseller, that suddenly Natalie's famous, all for painting a false portrait of us. It's unconscionable. She was barely part of the case—she knows so little of the truth. The fact that everyone has turned on us, that they're calling us villains—well, I had no choice but to write this book.

Read the rest, and then tell me who's the villain.

---

* My only theory is that Mrs. Flowers was apparently in the habit of bringing stray college students home, according to her own family's admissions. So it could've been any one of them. If you're the jerk who uploaded the pictures, confess and let me off the hook.

61

THE NEXT NIGHT, A KNOCK sounded at my door while I was playing sudoku.

"Come in," I called. After they'd gotten over their worry, everyone had been annoyed at me for making contact with a victim's family ("Very unwise," Lightly had said, "not to mention potentially unethical"). I'd followed it up by cooking them a late—and underwhelming—spaghetti dinner. So I figured it was probably Lightly or Mistress at my door with another lecture.

But it was Citizen. He ambled in and stopped in front of my bed. A few tiny beads of water clung to the hairs at the back of his neck, so he'd just gotten out of the shower. I fought the urge to wrap my arms over my chest. I wasn't wearing a bra under my sweatshirt, and there was something about the way he could look at me that made me feel exposed.

"What?" I asked finally.

"Get changed," he said. "We're going out."

—

We took an Uber outside downtown to a dive bar called the Alpine

Lounge. It was packed with NIU kids, the same ones who'd been missing from Cathy's since the influx of journalists and sleuths. I looked around, amazed. "How'd you find this place?"

Citizen raised an eyebrow. "Come on, Search. You know I'm good at what I do." He nodded toward the bar. "Let's get a drink."

It made sense the students had found a new place. I wondered if Citizen had caught mentions of it on social media—maybe some of the kids he'd been keeping an eye on had geotagged their posts. As we wound past the kids standing in tightly clustered groups, I remembered with a jolt that they were my age. Investigating them had created a sense of distance that made me feel older. But that night, in the middle of them, with a sped-up remix of a Taylor Swift song playing over the speakers, listening to fragments of their conversations—"No way, dude, that's sick," "She did *not*," "He's such a skeeze"—I was pulled back to UCF. Girls thronged together, laughing and eyeing guys across the room. The requisite too-drunk kids stumbled on the dance floor. Guys in cowboy boots knocked back longnecks, trying to look cool. Couples made out in corners. This was where I'd belonged not long ago.

"What do you want?" Citizen asked, when we bumped against the bar.

I looked around. Everyone was drinking beer. "Just a Coors."

He nodded and got two, then clinked his bottle against mine. He turned to rest against the bar and I followed suit, swallowing a mouthful of the yeasty beverage.

"What are we doing here?" It was unusual to be out just the two of us. I surveyed him. That straight nose, those full lips resting against his beer, a furrowed brow as he watched the crowd. Not that I was complaining.

"Come here," he said, crooking his finger. I followed him to one of the bar's dark corners, my curiosity spiking. "I have an idea for you."

I took another swig of beer. Being this close to him made me nervous. "Okay."

"Kappa Delta is holding a recruitment event this weekend. Some fashion show thing for upperclassmen who might want to rush next year." His voice dipped sarcastically. "Apparently they need to beef up their numbers."

"And?"

"I think you should go. Pretend to be a recruit and make friends. Those girls were the Queen Lace victims' closest confidants, and they're the only ones who aren't talking. They might know something."

This was a more elaborate deception than lying to the Cathy's waitress or even the Flowers family. It would mean taking a real risk of getting caught. I frowned. "Why KD? Why not try out for the track team?"

He arched an eyebrow. "And how fast do you run a four hundred meter?"

I almost spit out my beer.

A smile tugged at the corner of his mouth. "That's what I thought. Hate to break it to you, Veronica, but you're more sorority girl than athlete."

No one had ever suggested I had anything in common with a sorority girl. Maybe a dropout who'd quit to go goth, but not one of the blond-and-sparkles ilk. I tucked a piece of hair behind my ear. Citizen tracked it.

"You look even more like Veronica these days." He nodded at my hair.

The heat in my cheeks was instant. I'd been waiting for someone to notice. "I actually cut it myself, right before I came." It had been after the argument with my mom, when I was feeling angry and nihilistic, eager to be a different person. I'd stood in front of my mirror with a pair of kitchen shears and chopped my dark hair above my shoulders with a few rough cuts, then a straight line of bangs. Against all odds, I actually liked it. But I couldn't look at Citizen while I admitted this, so I dropped my eyes. "Figured I'd lean all the way in."

"It looks good," he said. "Suits you."

"So this undercover thing. You really think it's okay? I won't get in trouble?"

"Listen." He leaned back, shoulder blades hitting the wall. I leaned too, without thinking. He had that effect. "First of all, it's barely a lie. You were a college student not even a year ago. We'll say you transferred from UCF. The smallest fib. And this is how we're going to solve the case. By immersing ourselves. People don't realize it's not about having all the data. It's about getting as close as possible."

I pressed my fingertips to the wall to keep myself from leaning too far into him. "But where's the line?" I bit my lip. "Do you think I crossed it talking to Stacie's family?" Citizen was the only one who hadn't read me the riot act.

He snorted. "Searcher, there is no line. That's what people like Lightly and Mistress don't understand, no matter how much I love 'em. Crime is interactive these days. It isn't some drama playing out on TV, some *48 Hours* bullshit. This is our world, our stories to enter. The idea that there are boundaries—it's an illusion. Solving the case is just a matter of who's most willing to go the extra mile. That's who wins."

"Tell me the truth." I couldn't help it. My eyes drifted to the collar of his T-shirt, where it brushed the tan skin of his spine. I wanted to see a hint of the snake. Just a tip of the ink, so I knew I hadn't imagined it. "Is there anything you wouldn't do to win?"

It was almost like he knew what I wanted. He shifted against the wall, the wood paneling tugging his shirt. The tiniest flicker of the snake's tongue appeared. "Is there anything *you* wouldn't do?"

My gaze jumped back to his eyes. His expression wasn't accusatory. He simply watched.

We stood there for a long time, until Citizen bumped my hip and peeled off the wall. "Come on, Search. Let's have some fun. Make some new friends." He looked back at me and winked. "You're only in college once."

62

—

EVERYTHING I LACKED THAT NORMALLY made going out and talking to people intimidating, Citizen had in spades. He was confident and charismatic, unafraid to talk to strangers, capable of making them laugh. We switched from longnecks to Jack and Cokes, served in little plastic cups with lime slices and red straws. He grinned at me, then sidled up to a group, bumping one of the guys with his elbow.

"Anyone drop this?" Citizen held up an ID.

"Oh, shit," said another guy. "That's my fake. Must've dropped it."

"Here you go." Citizen tossed it at him.

"Thanks." He shoved it in his pocket. "Would've been SOL without that."

Citizen took a casual sip of his drink. "You guys NIU students?"

"Of course." One of the girls smiled widely at him. I didn't blame her. "Are you a grad student or something?"

"No." Citizen laughed, then turned to me. "But my friend just transferred, so we're checking out the scene."

Like he'd spoken some kind of magic words, the circle opened for me. I stepped beside him.

"Really?" another girl asked. "You transferred at the end of a semester?"

"Hell of a time to do it," the guy Citizen had elbowed laughed. "Shit's been crazy."

Come on, Jane. Make or break. I forced a laugh. "It's been so weird." I could feel Citizen smiling at me. "I thought this place was supposed to be a party school, but obviously not lately..." I let my voice trail off, raising my eyebrows in mock disappointment, just another college student determined to drink and hook up, the real world a distant second thought.

"No way," protested one of the guys. I'd wounded his school pride. "It's still fun. You just have to know where to go."

"Speaking of," Citizen said, "anyone want to do a round of car bombs? On me."

And with that, we were in. The hours tumbled forward in an increasingly hazy procession of Jäger-spiked beers, shouting, laughing, listening to gossip, and meeting everyone who slid into the group, our network of friends growing wider until it felt like the whole bar was just one big circle. I was Veronica again, and Citizen was JD. He was the perfect social lubricant, handsome enough to make everyone welcoming. A country song came on when I was in conversation with two ADPis, listening to them break down NIU's Greek system, and out of nowhere Citizen appeared. "Veronica!"

"Yeah?" I didn't miss the girls' envious glances.

To my surprise, he took my hand and pulled me onto the dance floor. No amount of alcohol could've prepared me for it. I dug in my heels.

"Come on," he coaxed, laughing as I shook my head. "It's a line dance. It'll be easy. Follow me."

Students in cowboy boots lined up on the dance floor, swinging their legs in rhythm. I took a deep breath and let Citizen lead.

We danced through that song and then the next, Citizen trying to demonstrate, me fumbling and turning in the exact wrong directions, no matter what. But the entire time, he held my hand. Secretly, I knew that's why I was flustered. I could pay attention to nothing beyond the feel of his skin.

When the songs were over and we were trying to catch our breath, he pulled me outside to the deck, where students in thick coats stood smoking. I'd had enough to drink that I barely felt the cold.

He bummed a cig off a guy, then turned. "Want one?"

I shook my head, rubbing my hands together for friction.

"Smart. Bad habit." He stuck it in his mouth and lit it, then wandered over to an empty patch of deck.

"That was really fun in there." I shoved my hands in my pockets and leaned forward.

He blew out a puff of smoke. "You're a natural."

"At dancing?" For some reason, probably because I was drunk, I found this to be the funniest thing I'd ever heard. I couldn't stop laughing.

"No, smart-ass. At making friends." He smiled. "Getting people to trust you."

"Yeah, well. I think everyone mostly liked you, to be honest."

He looked at me for a long time as he took another drag. I was drunk enough to simply look back. The corners of his eyes crinkled.

"I like when you smile like that," I said. "It's nice."

"Nice?" He dropped the cigarette, grinding it with his heel.

"Nice is a compliment."

He laughed. "A weak one."

We stood facing each other. The booze warmed me from the inside.

"Hey, Search," he said suddenly. His expression was serious. "Would it make it weird if I told you I have a crush on you?"

In a million years, I never would've guessed. Boys didn't like me. Never boys who looked like him. I completely froze.

He took a half step back. "Oh, shit. It did make things weird. Sorry. Forget I said anything."

"Okay," I said, then turned robotically. "I should probably call an Uber."

"Yeah, of course." He pulled up his phone. "Let me get it."

"You don't have to come."

"Pssh." He frowned like I'd said something ridiculous. "I'm not letting you go home alone. There's a killer on the loose."

In awkward silence, I followed Citizen as he closed out his tab and said goodbye to our new friends. Everyone was drunk enough that I wondered if they'd even remember me if I ran into them again.

We walked out into the parking lot, still uncomfortably quiet. My mind was racing. I couldn't get past the shock of what he'd said, or the little voice in the back of my head that whispered that this didn't happen to girls like me, so there had to be some catch. But there was another part of me—a bigger part—that thought…maybe. Maybe this time, I could reach for what I wanted.

I looked at him. He was facing the street, waiting on our car.

"Citizen?"

My heart pounded.

He turned. I could see the question on his face. But before he could form the words, I pressed one cold hand to the side of his face and kissed him.

His mouth was warm and tasted faintly of cigarettes and sweet Coca-Cola. After a heartbeat of surprise, he placed both hands on either side of my jaw and leaned in, kissing me in return, his enthusiasm so strong I had to take a step back. The kiss grew more intense, the two of us adjusting to each other, our bodies pressing together until we swayed.

He wrenched away, still cupping my face.

"What?" I said breathlessly. "Did I—"

"No." His eyes scanned me. "It's just, you've been drinking. I've been drinking. Let's save this for another time, okay?"

I blinked at him until he kissed me on the nose. "Okay?"

"Okay."

He wrapped his arms around me. "Hey, look." A pair of headlights swept into the parking lot. "Our ride."

63

THE CALL CAME INTO OUR tip line the following Monday, when Mistress and I were in the attic poring through thousands of unsolved murder cases in the states of Oregon, Idaho, and Washington. We were looking for similarities to Bridget Howell or the Delphine girls. It was my day to man the burner, and I'd been counting myself lucky it had stayed silent—so when it finally rang around three in the afternoon, I groaned.

"The glamorous life of a detective," Mistress murmured, scanning her laptop. "Say hi to the crazy for me."

I answered with a sigh. "Bridget Howell tip line."

The voice on the other end hesitated, then spoke in a breathy voice, "Hi—can I—report something anonymously?"

"Sure," I said, eyes still on my screen. "Just know we'll have to verify whatever you tell us before moving forward."

"Oh—right. Of course. I just—a friend of mine heard the podcast and was telling me about it. She knows I grew up in Carraway."

Interesting. I sat back in my chair. "During what time?"

"Well—I." The caller was so nervous. It leaked from her voice. "I was Bridget's best friend. Other than her cousin."

"And what was her cousin's name?"

"Farrah Howell."

I sat up and waved at Mistress. She put down her laptop.

"Do you mind if I put you on speakerphone?" I asked. "Just so my colleague can hear."

"Okay," she said shakily. "But do you mind not recording?"

"Sure." I raised my eyebrows at Mistress and threw the call on speaker. "I will take notes, though. So, uh, caller, you were Bridget's best friend?" I nodded at Mistress, and she started typing. "For how long?"

"From when we were kids. We grew up together, kindergarten through high school. It was a small town, except when you added the base kids."

"The navy base?"

"Right."

Mistress held up her laptop. There was a picture of Bridget and another girl from Facebook. I squinted at the name. Susan Ramsey.

"The thing is, I'm a mom now," the caller said. "And I know this person...this man who killed Bridget and the other girls, in Delphine... I'm afraid of him coming after me and my kids."

"It's okay." I used my most soothing voice. "We'll keep you anonymous as long as you want. It's brave that you're coming forward."

"This is Tammy Jo," Mistress said. "Anything you can tell us makes a big difference. Bridget was her parents' only child, as you know."

The combination of Mistress's words and her gentle voice seemed to put some steel in the caller's spine. "What happened to her was a tragedy, and she deserves justice." She took a deep breath. "Back when Bridget died and the police interviewed me, I told them that there was a creepy boy at school who Bridget didn't like."

Mistress and I frowned at each other. "Interesting," I said as Mistress grabbed a notepad and scribbled. She turned it to face me. *Nothing in B's case file about a creepy boy.*

"You're sure you told the police?" I asked. "I know things can get confusing after traumatic events."

"I absolutely told them," she insisted. "But the police were dismissive. The officer I talked to said they didn't have time to get involved in high school drama."

That might explain why it wasn't in the Community Statements—the cops might've thought so little of the tip they hadn't included it, just like we didn't record the crazies who dialed the tip line.

"Why didn't Bridget like this boy?" I asked.

"It might've been a few things," Susan said slowly. "But mainly it had to do with her dog."

"Gatsby?" I frowned at Mistress. "The one who went missing?"

"Yes, but..." She hesitated. "The thing is, I think Bridget stopped thinking Gatsby went missing. I might've read too much into it, but I got the feeling she thought this boy had done something to her dog."

Whoa. Mistress and I locked eyes for a millisecond before she bent over the phone. "What was his name? Age?"

"Michael, maybe? Or Simon? I'm so sorry I don't remember more clearly. It was twelve years ago. I remember talking to the police about him, though. I'm pretty sure he was our year."

"Do you have a yearbook?"

"Not anymore. I moved far away from Carraway and started over. I wanted to forget." Susan's voice was steeped in regret. "But if I saw his picture, I might know him."

"That's okay," Mistress said encouragingly, though I could feel her disappointment. "Would it be all right if we took down your number in case we need to ask you a question?"

The line went silent.

"Please," I begged. "Bridget's parents have spent the last twelve years not knowing who killed their daughter. And now that man is

301

out there hurting other people's daughters. We have the chance to stop him."

"Okay." Her voice was small. "I'll give you my number. And I might as well give you my name. I'm Susan Greenberg. My maiden name was Susan Ramsey."

Mistress and I gave each other silent thumbs-ups.

"Thank you so much, Susan," we gushed, after she'd given us her cell. "You're a hero."

When we hung up, Mistress whooped and launched out of her seat. "This is big. I can feel it."

"Really?"

"If Bridget's suspicion that this boy harmed her dog was right, that's a powerful clue. Animal cruelty is part of the MacDonald triad."

"The what?"

She paced. "A psychiatric theory first proposed by J.M. MacDonald in the sixties that says you can predict future violent behavior by the presence of three traits in youth: persistent bedwetting, fire-setting, and cruelty to animals. The theory's been born out in an astonishing number of serial murder cases."

"Okay, but—not to be a party pooper—we're still looking at a large number of ifs. *If* Susan's memory is right, and *if* Bridget's speculations about this boy were right. There's a chance she was just torn up over losing her dog and anxious to blame someone."

"All true." Mistress stopped pacing. "But it's a lead. Which means I need to get my hands on that yearbook."

64

TECHNICALLY, THE NORTHERN IDAHO UNIVERSITY Kappa Delta fashion show was a charity fundraiser. Getting a ticket cost me twenty of my dwindling dollars, a sum I was loath to part with. Mistress had offered to help me get ready—without even discussing it, it seemed the whole group understood I'd require a makeover to pose as a convincing sorority hopeful—but I'd bypassed her help as tactfully as possible in favor of sitting on my bed, applying makeup alongside a YouTube tutorial.

I'd spent hours on the chapter's Instagram trying to get a feel for what the girls looked like, as nervous as I would've been if I were really rushing. I'd MacGyvered haphazard curls out of pencils and rubber bands and had even gone so far as to slice suggestive tears into my favorite jeans to give them the slightly grunge look I saw all over the sorority's grid. The end result was as close as I'd probably ever come to Madeleine and Stacie's version of glossy, coquettish girlhood. When I walked downstairs, Goku whistled. Citizen looked at me with a private smile that made my chest burn. Since the night of our kiss, I'd been trying hard to appear nonchalant, but I was anxiously awaiting his next move.

Walking up to the KD house, I swallowed quiet shock over the size and beauty of it—a massive white colonial-style mansion with a circular balcony out front and gold letters spelling Kappa Delta above imposing columns. It was a warm day in early May, a day that felt like spring, and the lawn was jam-packed. With the stage, lights, and crowd, it looked more like a concert than a charity event.

When I signed in, the girls at the table asked whether I was a "potential new recruit" or just a friend of the sorority. I said recruit, which meant I got a giant shamrock with my name on it pinned to the front of my shirt. They explained this would make it easy for the actives to find me. It was much easier than I'd imagined to get in—not only had I simply walked on campus to their house, but I'd told the girls my fake name and they'd just believed me, no ID necessary. Apparently not even six murdered girls and a serial killer warranted tighter security. Everywhere I looked, KD sisters in name tags shaped like teddy bears laughed and tossed their hair.* You never would've known three sisters had just been brutally slaughtered. College students' capacity for resilience was either inspiring or psychopathic.

At first, I was too shy to talk to anyone. Luckily, the fashion show—a thinly veiled excuse for the KDs to dress up in designer clothes—took up the first forty-five minutes, giving me time to relax. But then it ended and the volume of the party dialed up, and I twisted my fingers anxiously, casting my eyes around for anyone I recognized off the dead girls' Instagram.

"Hi. You're Veronica Sawyer?"

I turned. Three nearly identical blond girls, all wearing fashion show outfits, approached. I was elated and terrified. My world was one of

---

* Don't ask me how teddy bears and shamrocks make sense as part of the KD sorority symbology. I suspect whoever dreamed it up might've been under the influence of LSD.

flat, 2D text, where people wearing anime avatar masks ruled comment threads with pithy quips and takedowns, and you weren't forced to be... present, three-dimensional, accountable to the face and body to which you'd been born. Mine was the brave new frontier, and this world, where people were beautiful and charming and it still mattered, was the old and antiquated. I'd never fit in here. Long live the internet, the revenge of the nerds.

"That's me." I tried to think of how Citizen had played it at the Alpine Lodge. Cool but complimentary. "You guys looked amazing up there. I love your outfits."

"Thanks!" The three of them gave me toothy grins. "Tell us about yourself," said one, whose name tag said Brooke. "You're thinking of rushing next year?"

"Oh, definitely." I resisted the urge to pat my curls. "I'm just torn between options." That was good. Make them feel competitive. "I'm a transfer student from UCF, so I'm still getting to know the campus."

"Ooh, Florida," squealed a second girl, whose skin was very tan. Her name tag said River. "My family has a house on Marco Island. Is that near you?"

"Oh...no, not really." Marco Island was a fabulously wealthy island. Nowhere near Orlando in any sense of the word.

"So what do you like to do, Veronica?" The third girl, named Olivia, was businesslike. "For fun, I mean."

"Well, I'm a psychology girl. Psych major. And a total Swiftie, obviously."

"Obviously," echoed River.

"I guess I love, like, the normal things? Tailgating with my girls, quiet nights in my comfies watching *The Office* reruns—"

"Oh my God, *same*," Brooke gushed. I was ventriloquizing the captions from their sorority Instagram posts, regurgitating their own language back at them. It was surprisingly easy. But I needed to turn to what I really wanted to talk about, lest I get trapped in a two-hour conversation about the Eras tour or Pam and Jim.

"And I'm a *huge* true-crime girlie."

"Me too!" River nearly jumped with glee. "That *SNL* skit where, like, the girls watch murder documentaries on Netflix to relax? That's so me."

"Oh my God, yes." I widened my eyes and lowered my voice. *Play it soft, Jane.* "I had no idea I'd be walking into, like, a real-life true-crime show by transferring here."

There it was—my gamble. How would they react?

Olivia stiffened. Brooke gave me an uneasy smile. But River—bless her—widened her eyes to mirror mine. "I know, right? It's been insane. I never expected to, like, actually know someone who got murdered or, like, be questioned by the police. Wild."

"It's so sad," Brooke said quickly.

"So sad," River echoed, nodding vigorously.

"Tragic," I agreed. "The girls seemed so cute. I mean, it's hard not to look at their Insta, you know? And, like, wonder why them? They seemed so sweet."

Olivia snorted.

"What?" I prayed her derision wasn't aimed at me.

"I wouldn't exactly call them sweet. But yeah, it's fucked up."

"What do you mean?"

"They were big party girls," River said, in a confidential voice, as if relaying classified information. "Like, everyone used to go to Queen Lace to pregame."

"And postgame," added Brooke, studying her cuticles.

"The parties, like, never stopped there. It was fun for us—I mean, we have a rep as kind of a wild house, so it was fitting." River's smile dimmed. "But I actually felt bad for Harlow."

"Oh yeah," I said, playing dumb. "She was their other roommate, right?" I looked around. "Is she here?"

It was Brooke's turn to scoff. "Yeah, right. She hates us. She never comes to things anymore."

Olivia shot her a dirty look. "She *withdrew*, Brooke. Duh." Olivia glanced around. "Anyway, this conversation is ghoulish. We should probably make the rounds."

The other girls straightened on cue, as if someone had pushed a button. They gave me those wide, toothy smiles again.

"It was so nice to meet you, Veronica!" River said.

"So nice," Brooke repeated, winking. "We'll see you around."

And just as fast as they'd shown up, the blonds left, migrating to a group of girls with bigger curls than mine and shamrocks pinned to their day dresses. I spent the next forty minutes wandering the lawn, smiling at actives in the hope that they'd talk to me, but it was like Olivia, Brooke, and River had issued some secret warning. The other girls avoided eye contact and walked in the opposite direction. Had my talk of murder put me on some sort of no-fly list? Oh, God—maybe one of the girls had recognized me from the news and the actives were deciding how to kick me out.

Eventually, the crowd thinned to a handful of actives and recruits mingling around the stage. I edged closer, biting my lip—and after being on my own for so long, almost jumped when someone stepped next to me.

"Hey," said the brown-haired girl. She wore a midriff-baring top she tugged in a fruitless effort to pull it down. "Having fun?"

"Oh, for sure," I said brightly.

She snorted. "You don't have to lie. Recruitment events suck. I hate them."

I let out a breath. "Yeah. It's pretty awkward."

She gave a bigger snort. I looked at her teddy bear nametag. *Rylee.*

"So." Her tone was skeptical. "You really want to join KD after everything?"

I blinked, taken aback by her frankness. "You mean the murders?"

"Obviously." She looked around the lawn. Green and white trash was strewn everywhere. "I didn't expect so many people to show up. Maybe they wanted to see the famous dead girls' sorority."

"Could be," I agreed, grateful she didn't seem to be lumping me in with the gawkers. "People can get weird about that kind of stuff."

"Story of my life."

A towering woman flew out of the KD house, holding a platter of cookies in one hand and a pitcher of what looked like lemonade in the other. "Refreshments!" she sang. She was older than the actives and wore a strange sack dress that even I knew wasn't fashionable—a house-dress, I think they call them. Like the trash, it was also green and white, sorority colors, which struck me as sad for some reason.

She rushed to the largest group of girls and extended the platter of cookies. "Here you go, girls. Fresh out of the oven." Only a few recruits reached for one. "Anyone for lemonade?"

"I'll have some," said one of the girls, and the woman beamed at her, then froze. She had brown hair so long it brushed the small of her back, a length I'd only ever seen on women being pulled out of religious cults in Netflix documentaries. She was bony and nearly translucently pale. She did not, to put it lightly, seem like KD material. "Oh my goodness, I forgot the cups," she cried, so loudly that everyone turned. "I'll be right back."

As she scampered back toward the house, the girls started tittering. "Oh my God," one of the actives groaned. "She is *so* cringe."

I turned to Rylee. "Who was that?" They were reacting like she was some freak monster they kept chained in their basement.

"Our house mom. Lizzie."

"I didn't know sororities had those. That's cool."

"I guess." She crossed her arms. Rylee wore a lot of dark, smudged eyeliner. If Citizen and Goku could see her, they'd crown her the new *Heathers* Veronica. "Unless they're Lizzie. Though I guess her job has gotten a lot easier recently."

"What do you mean?"

"Well, obviously, none of us have been going out as much as we used to. Because of, you know—"

I nodded. *The murders.*

"Less partying, less vomiting, less fights in the bathroom. Less drama and running boys out of the house in the middle of the night."

"Is it really like that?" I don't know what I'd thought sorority life was like. Tea parties and pillow fights? It occurred to me my references were dated.

"Honestly?" Rylee looked me in the eyes. "It's a horror show."

"Wow." Rylee was the anti-recruitment chair.

She chewed a piece of hair. "Though I guess her life would've gotten better no matter what, with Madeleine and Stacie gone."

That threw me until I connected the dots. "I did hear they were pretty wild."

"You have no idea. They were constantly on probation. Madeleine the ringleader and Stacie the sycophant. Rooming with them was the worst decision Harlow ever made." She glanced at me. "She was on scholarship, you know."

I hadn't, so I didn't need to fake my surprise. Unlike Larissa, with her obvious knockoffs and ever-present air of insecurity, Harlow had hidden her background well. From the research I'd done, she'd seemed like every other privileged girl here.

"Her staying in school literally depended on her grades." Rylee nodded at the house. "She was always sleeping here to get away from them. Which of course, Lizzie loved."

As if summoned, Lizzie burst back out of the house, this time with the lemonade and a stack of plastic cups she balanced against the tip of her chin. It was bizarre how she was acting, like an overblown caricature of a maid. By the time she returned to the group of girls, social pressure had worked its magic. All of them declined the lemonade, even the girl who'd asked for it in the first place. Lizzie's large shoulders sank.

"What do you mean, she loved it?" I asked, but Rylee's face suddenly turned blank.

"Lemonade?" Lizzie stood in front of us, dangling the pitcher. Up close, her elongated nose and prominent brow made her resemble a horse.

"I would love some," I said automatically, feeling wicked for the unkind thought.

"Good," she said, then thrust the stack of cups at me. "Hold this." She plucked one from the top, filled it to the brim with lemonade, then traded me back.

Lizzie turned her eyes on Rylee. They were gray eyes, the color of a winter sky. The intensity of her looking reminded me of Citizen, except where Citizen's stare made you want him to keep looking, Lizzie's was uncomfortable, a thing to escape. "Ms. Lopez?"

"No. Thanks." Rylee backed up. "I've got somewhere to be." She turned and beelined across the lawn without even a goodbye.

Lizzie watched her go. "They're always in such a hurry," she murmured. But before I could respond, she'd swept away to the next group of girls, leaving me standing alone on the lawn with an unsettled feeling and a watery glass of lemonade.

65

—

WHENEVER I FELT OUT OF sorts in Delphine—when I felt lost or lonely or far from solving anything—I turned to my dad-investigation. I'd taken a page out of HiltoftheSword's book and was reaching out to his Facebook friends in batches of twenty at a time, letting them know he'd passed and asking for their remembrances, any stories they could share, since that had worked so well on the *Star Trek* forum. So far, I'd had about a 60 percent response rate, though a lot of people only shared vague platitudes, like "Your father was a great guy, very kind and honorable," which didn't tell me anything new.

I was hungriest for details of my dad's life from his formative years in Tennessee that remained more or less a mystery. I knew, from his rare stories, that he'd grown up working on the farm with his five siblings (only two of whom were still alive) and that money had been nonexistent—a good Christmas meant an orange in your stocking, and a birthday to remember was a trip to McDonald's. When he was in high school, he'd been so good at basketball the coach implored him to join the team, but his parents hadn't allowed it. They needed him to work and bring money into the household. That was the full sum of what I knew. My dad, who could talk for five hours about Picard versus Janeway, rarely talked about his childhood.

But an hour before I was due at our investigation update meeting, I struck gold. I logged into his Facebook account, doing my daily rounds, and saw a new message from Darrel Woodruffe, one of my dad's acquaintances who had the same high school listed in his Education section and still lived in Morristown, Tennessee.

Darrel Woodruffe: Hi Jane, my condolences. Dan and I knew each other since first grade but lost touch after he left town. It made me happy when we connected on Facebook and I saw he had a good life and a loving family. I used to wonder where he'd gone off to. What kind of stories are you looking for? I'm sure I have them.

Jane Sharp: Thank you, Darrel. I'm looking for anything, really. I just want to get a sense of who my dad was before me, you know? I'm trying to understand him better.

Darrel Woodruffe: Oh man, your dad was such a clown! In middle school he was the guy who'd pull pranks as soon as the teacher's back was turned. And he always had gum on him. That was currency back then. I don't know where he used to get it, but he'd pay people in gum to do something silly. A lot of girls in school called him "Crazy Dan."

Jane Sharp: I cannot stress enough how weird that is to hear. Very unlike the man I knew.

Darrel Woodruffe: Ha! In high school we both got jobs as line cooks at Waffle House.

Jane Sharp: He worked there instead of joining the basketball team, right?

Darrel Woodruffe: I don't remember anything about basketball. Maybe? It was a wild era. We were always pulling late nights. I don't know if you've ever worked in a restaurant, but the people who do are some of the craziest mofos you'll ever meet. We had some mighty benders.

Jane Sharp: I can barely remember my dad drinking. Maybe one or two beers max, on a holiday.

Darrel Woodruffe: Probably because he got his fill in high school. It was nothing too crazy, in case you're worried. Just drinking a bunch after our shifts, playing pool, shooting shotguns, dancing. Your dad, for all his goofiness, was pretty shy around women. I was always trying to convince him to talk to them.

That sounded more like him.

Jane Sharp: Do you remember him being obsessed with Yoo-hoo? One of the only things his siblings told me was they remembered him parking in front of the TV and drinking Yoo-hoo for hours. They called him the Yoo-hoo King.

I'll be honest: the nickname had always bothered me. It took a few minutes for Darrel to write back.

Darrel Woodruffe: Sorry, I had to think about that one. I remember Dan started getting really serious about losing weight later in high school—I don't know if you knew this, but he was husky growing up. He started buying fitness magazines and running. Looking back, I guess he knew he was going to sign up for the navy, though it came as a shock to me when he said he was going to boot camp. I think he read somewhere that drinking chocolate milk was good for recovering after runs. It helped build muscle or something.

313

I felt a swell of triumph. His siblings had painted my dad like a lazy glutton, and all along the Yoo-hoo had been a running aid.

Darrel Woodruffe: Jane, I don't know if this is appropriate to tell you, and if it's not, I'm sorry. But your dad told me something in confidence when we were young and I've regretted keeping the secret ever since. Maybe I would've been a better friend if I'd betrayed his confidence and told someone. And now he's gone before I could work up the courage to bring it up. But if you don't want to hear, I understand and will keep this to myself.

My stomach dropped. What had my father been hiding?

Jane Sharp: Of course I want to know.
Darrel Woodruffe: All right. When we were twelve, your dad confided that he had an uncle who used to abuse him. He didn't give a whole lot of details other than the abuse happened to his older brothers, too, but they refused to talk about it. He felt pretty ashamed, but I think he needed to get it off his chest. He made me swear not to tell anyone. The uncle had just passed away, I think. That's what made him bring it up.

I stared at the screen, shell-shocked. My dad had never even hinted at something like this. When I was young, he'd talked to me about stranger danger, how to tell adults if something was wrong. When I was older, we'd watched molestation plotlines on *SVU*. One year I'd even written a report on child abuse for an assignment in high school. He'd never breathed a word.

My father had carried this inside himself? He'd lived with it? I tried to square the information with the man I remembered, but couldn't.

Darrel Woodruffe: I'm sorry for unloading on you, but I haven't known what to do with this all these years. It feels good to tell someone, like I'm finally doing the right thing.

I stared blankly at the wall. This critical information about my own father, this formative wound. Had my mom known?

Was this the essential piece of information I'd been missing?

66

"SEARCHER!" LIGHTLY'S VOICE RANG UP the stairs. "Dinner's ready!"

Numbly, I closed my laptop and walked downstairs, where an aproned Lightly was dishing out pieces of a thick, cheese-crusted lasagna that smelled like basil, garlic, and tomatoes. He'd showed up my spaghetti rather embarrassingly.

"Here you go," he said, placing a warm bowl in my hands. Then he cocked his head. "Everything okay?"

"Yeah." I didn't know how to begin describing what I was thinking. The existence of the new knowledge was like a parasite, worming through my memories, making me wonder.

We draped ourselves around the living room: Goku stretched across the couch, Citizen sideways in an armchair. Mistress propped herself up with pillows that helped her sciatica, and Lightly sat straight-backed in a dining chair he'd pulled into the room. They'd left me the plushest armchair, a simple kindness that suddenly made my throat feel thick. I pushed the emotion away and forced myself to sit. Despite the glassy-eyed mounted buck and overabundance of leather, the living room was actually cozy.

"All right," Lightly boomed, eyeing the murder board, which he'd wheeled in. "I'm calling this meeting to order."

"First order of business: your lasagna is heavenly." Mistress's fork poised over her bowl. "Truly."

"I hope there's enough for thirds," Goku said, shoveling pasta. "You are a meat-and-sauce artist, my friend."

Lightly brushed his shoulder. "Oh, you know, I've got a few tricks up my sleeve. Family recipes and all." He caught my eye across the room, and his smile dimmed. "You really okay?"

I nodded quickly and dropped my eyes. I could feel everyone's attention turn to me, and that was the last thing I wanted. I was still stuck in the quicksand of shock that my father had been hurt as a little boy. I wanted to go back in time to save him.

"All right, then. I'll get started." Lightly slapped his knee. "No real updates from the FBI, but it sounds like Lawrence is going to let me do a walk-through of the two murder sites."

Citizen sat up. "Can I—"

He shook his head. "Just me. You know the DPD's still dealing with blowback over crime scene contamination. Lawrence trusts me not to disturb the sites."

Blowback thanks to our leak. It was enough to quiet Citizen.

"So I'm planning that for tomorrow. I'll take pictures, of course, and note anything unusual. Hoping to have more for you tomorrow night." Lightly scanned the circle. "Searcher, you want to fill us in on the KD event?"

I could do this. The investigation was my safe place, the one thing I knew how to talk about. I set down my bowl of pasta. "It ended up being a mixed bag. On the one hand, everyone bought me as a KD hopeful, so I don't think I'll have trouble going back. But I didn't learn anything we didn't already know. Queen Lace was a well-known party house.

Madeleine and Stacie especially were wild. Heavy drinkers. They had a reputation for it among their sisters. They were a pain in the ass for the house mom."

I thought back to Rylee's face before we were interrupted by Lizzie. "I did meet a girl who seemed more willing to talk than the others. I think she might've been close to Harlow, because she knew things about her that Harlow wasn't advertising. Like that she was a scholarship student who needed to keep her grades up."

"Not a good fit for a party house," Goku observed.

"Yeah. This girl I was talking to…she seemed bitter, or scared. I don't know. I got the impression she had more to say."

"It's hard to go deep with someone when you're in a big group," Mistress said. "You might have more luck if you meet her privately."

"Get her drunk," Citizen suggested and then, off our looks, shrugged. "What? It works."

"I'll go next," Mistress said, still rolling her eyes. "Searcher's update is actually a good segue. Remember how we talked about the impossibility of the killer being a woman?"

"Because the eyelash DNA proves it's a man?" Goku asked, over a forkful of lasagna.

"We're not one hundred percent sure that DNA is from the killer. It could be from anyone."

"Mistress," Lightly said disapprovingly. "That's our best lead so far."

She put up her hands in a mea culpa gesture. "I'm just saying. I've been doing some research on female serial killers. And I think you should hear what I found."

"All right." Citizen crossed his arms, amused. "Let's hear it."

Mistress adjusted her glasses. "Remember how we were saying we couldn't think of any examples of real-life women serial killers? Scientists think there are actually a lot more than we know of, maybe even an equal number to men. But female serial killers don't tend to get caught."

Goku snorted, but Mistress pressed on. "Part of the reason is because their profile is so different from male serial killers. Think about this: everyone in the world who's watched an episode of *Criminal Minds* could tell you the basics of a serial killer's profile. Loner, typically suffering psychosexual issues, often abuses animals while young, maybe demonstrates bedwetting. Usually abused by their parents, made to feel small. Killing is about exerting power and dominance, so they tend to circle back to their crime scenes, keep trophies, and taunt the police—all ways of exerting power and being noticed."

It was similar to the profile of our killer I'd given Veejay and Byron on *Murder Junkies*. Lightly frowned. "But female serial killers are different?"

"Exactly," Mistress said. "Our entire concept of what a serial killer looks like is modeled on the male serial killer. But from what researchers have seen, female serial killers don't often kill to exert power. Typically, they kill because of a distorted savior complex, or in defense of themselves or others—or, at least, they convince themselves that's why they're killing. That's why, when female serial killers *do* get caught, they're often nurses who've lethally injected their patients, thinking they're 'saving' them, or other kinds of caretaker-gone-wrong situations. And because it's not about ego, female serial killers don't display the post-kill behaviors we've come to associate with male serial killers. Preliminary studies show they aren't likely to revisit their crime scenes, keep trophies, or taunt authorities. That's part of why it's so hard to catch them, because they give cops fewer opportunities."

I'd become engrossed in what Mistress was saying. "Would that mean that female serial killers are more likely to know their victims, or have interacted with them in some way, if they're working off an emotional connection? Wanting to defend or save them, I mean?"

Lightly finished my thought. "So the opposite of the random predator theory—the victims aren't simply chosen for convenience."

"I don't know," Mistress admitted. "Honestly, the body of research is still growing, trying to catch up with everything that's been produced about men. I recapped most of what's out there on JSTOR. But if you ask me, that sounds right, that female serial killers would be less likely to be random predators."

"This is all very interesting, don't get me wrong," said Citizen, turning in his chair to face us straight on. "But we're dealing with a highly sophisticated, highly intelligent killer capable of leaving no trace—"

"And you're saying that couldn't be a woman?" I asked.

"You didn't let me finish. Who kills by stabbing, which isn't a common method for women, and who we've already deduced chooses his victims randomly."

"And the DNA," Goku said. "Why are we even debating this? The eyelash DNA points to a man. Besides, didn't you tell us Bridget Howell's friend remembered some possible animal abuser guy from high school? What happened to that?"

"Bridget Howell High doesn't have a digital archive of their yearbooks," Mistress said with a sigh. "I have to track down someone who went to school with Bridget and has a copy. And anyway, I was just sharing information I thought you'd find interesting."

"Well." Citizen eyed Goku, who leaned forward and brushed off his shirt. The two of them were buzzing with a secret. "If everyone else is done, we actually have something to share."

67

—

"GOKU AND I HAVE BEEN working the random predator angle," Citizen said, "using the profile our dear Mistress maligned only moments ago."

Mistress arched her eyebrows but said nothing.

"We know serial killers often kill after a triggering event," Goku said, taking over. "And we figured that even if our killer is picking targets he has no relationship with, there has to be some way he's coming into contact with them. So I hacked NIU records and searched for students and professors who'd received bad grades, or disciplinary actions, or tenure rejections in the last year."

Despite myself, I nodded. It was a smart idea.

Citizen and Goku exchanged glances. "We found someone," Citizen said. "His name is Odell Rhodes. He's twenty-eight years old and a first-year criminology grad student. Within the last six months, he's received two complaints against him by students he TA'ed for and two disciplinary actions following altercations with a professor—the last of which is looking like it might cost him his fellowship. If he loses that, he'll be dropped from the program."

"So he's facing an extinction event," Lightly mused. "The end of a way of life. That's a powerful trigger."

"And get this," said Goku. "The complaints filed against Odell were both from female students complaining about creepy behavior."

Mistress perked up. "That's interesting. Whoever our killer is, the people in that person's orbit are definitely noticing their strange behavior. They just haven't imagined the depths of what it could mean yet."

I turned the information over in my mind. Odell Rhodes, twenty-eight, criminology student. A lightbulb flashed. "The killer's familiarity with crime scenes—could that be explained if he's a criminology student?"

Citizen's smile was triumphant. "I was hoping you'd notice."

"And for the coup de grâce..." Goku drummed on the couch. "I hacked his Instagram. Not only does he follow Madeleine and Larissa, but five months ago, he sent Madeleine a DM that said, 'Hey, how's it going?' We didn't find it when we checked Madeleine's inbox because she must've deleted it without responding."

Odell Rhodes had known our victims. *And* tried to make contact—in a desperate, creepy way. The girl who'd ended up stabbed thirty-seven times was the one who'd dismissed him. "Whoa," I said. "That's huge."

Lightly jumped up and scribbled *Odell Rhodes* on an index card, then pinned it to the board. "This is really promising, guys. Excellent work."

Citizen and Goku glowed.

He turned from the board. "We should put him on Lawrence's radar. Get the FBI to start digging, maybe put a tail on him if they like what they see."

"No," Citizen said quickly. "We need to keep vetting him. We've made too many false accusations. I don't want another Chandler Gray or Kevin Kowalski. Goku and I want to make first contact ourselves."

"Guys." Lightly frowned. "If Odell's the Butcher, he's dangerous."

"We'll be careful," Citizen promised. "Besides, the Butcher likes women."

"Pretty sure he hates women," I said, but no one paid attention.

"What will he do if he thinks you and Goku are on to him, though? He could hurt you." Mistress's voice was thick. "You should let the FBI handle it."

"We won't give anything away." Citizen turned to me. "We were actually hoping you could ask your new sorority friends if they'd ever heard of Odell. We know no KDs were enrolled in any of his classes, so we're looking for another connection."

"I can do that." I dropped my fork in my now-empty bowl. "I'll ask that girl Rylee to coffee."

"Thanks, Search." Goku rolled to his feet and grabbed his bowl. "Now, is anyone else having more lasagna, or can I go to town? All this Butcher talk is making me hungry."

68

SINCE LIZZIE THE HOUSE MOM had mentioned Rylee's last name—Lopez—I used it to send her an email from a burner Gmail account. I kept my wording casual and employed Citizen's trick of compliments, telling her she seemed like exactly the kind of girl I could imagine being sorority sisters with and would she have thirty minutes between class to grab coffee? My treat, of course.

It worked. Within a day she wrote me back and suggested we meet at the Badger Den, NIU's on-campus coffeehouse. By that point, lying about being an NIU student had become second nature. I no longer got nervous—on some level, I think I actually believed I was a student. When Rylee appeared at the coffeehouse five minutes late, in a huff because her professor was being "a total bitch about accepting late work," I'd smoothly lied and said I had a TA like that too. Did she know Odell Rhodes?

Rylee's face had scrunched up. "Odell who?"

"Rhodes. He's my criminology TA. Super hard on us and kind of a creep to girls, if I'm being honest. Do any of the KDs ever hang out with grad students?"

"Ew, no," Rylee said, then ordered a mocha frappuccino. She turned back to me. "I honestly didn't even know NIU had that major. What, you study criminals? Morbid."

"Mostly forensics," I said, after placing my order for a plain coffee, the cheapest item on the menu. "So you've really never heard of Odell or seen him around?"

She frowned. I could tell I was throwing her by harping on the subject. "No...should I?"

"Never mind." That was a dead end. The cashier asked for my Badger card to pay for the coffees, and I said I'd left it at home and handed over my debit, asking Rylee to grab a table so she wouldn't read my real name on the card. Faking it as a student had gotten so comfortable that I felt genuine empathy whenever someone complained about the "fucking vampires" who'd infiltrated campus, otherwise known as the amateur sleuths—as Rylee did the moment I sat down.

"Those fucking vampires, I swear." She took a sip of her frappuccino. The whipped cream left a sticky mustache above her lip. "Ever since the girls died, they've been following us everywhere, trying to get us to talk. Literally ambushing us outside the bathroom. They think we have insider information just because we were in the same sorority."

"That's awful," I said, the world's biggest hypocrite. "As if you haven't suffered enough."

"Exactly. This whole place is a joke."

I looked around the busy coffee shop. "The whole...college?"

"The college, the entire town of Delphine. I can't wait to graduate. I have no idea why I thought going to school in Idaho would be charming."

I knew she was from Los Angeles from her Instagram, but I asked anyway. "Where's home?"

"LA." She rolled her eyes. Like the first time I'd met her, she wore heavy black eyeliner. Today, she was dressed in her own clothes, not a fashion show outfit, so it was matching head-to-toe black. She looked like she was aiming for goth or punk, but she was too pretty and clean to be convincing. Overall, she read like a girl going through a phase. "Not that I'm rushing to get back to California, either. Maybe I'll go to Seattle. It rains a lot there. That would suit my mood."

"I heard Forks, Washington, is the rainiest place in America," I volunteered, and it didn't occur to me until days later that I'd "heard" that factoid from a little book called *Twilight*. So maybe I wasn't the smoothest liar after all.

Luckily, it didn't ring a bell. Rylee took another sip of coffee. "Sorry. I guess I'm not doing a very good job of selling you on KD. But to be honest, you probably want to steer clear of those bitches anyway."

"Really?" I leaned in. "How come?"

"I mean, does three of us being stabbed to death not deter you?"

"That could've happened to anyone, right? What about the track girls who were killed?"

Rylee sat back. "I don't know anything about the track girls. Never met them. But all the girls in my sorority had one very clear enemy."

What—why had I never heard anything about this? "Who?"

"Lizzie."

It took me a second. "Your house mom?"

Rylee's expression was grave. "No one on the outside can see it because of that show she's always putting on. Tripping over herself to get us snacks and clean up after us. And when she tries to reprimand us, it comes off as pathetic. So she seems like this defanged dog. But the truth is, she hates us. And she hated the Queen Lace girls most of all."

"Just because they were partiers?" My voice was too loud, and Rylee flinched. I lowered it. "Because they were wild?"

"I mean, they also shit on her more than anyone." Rylee tapped the lip of her cup. "They were constantly making fun of her so she could hear. Madeleine was the worst. I mean, it's not like Mad or any of those girls were *wrong*. Lizzie's so hateable. But that's not even the reason she did it."

"The reason she did what?"

Rylee's dark eyes stayed locked on mine. "Killed them."

My mouth actually dropped. "You think *Lizzie is* the killer?"

"Keep your voice down," she hissed. "I'm trying to do you a public service by warning you, but I'd prefer not to get outed and, like, targeted in the process. Lizzie is already suspicious of me because I was Harlow's friend."

"I'm sorry," I said, "but what does Harlow have to do with any of this?"

"Harlow was the only one Lizzie liked. Or—'liked' isn't the right word. She *loved* her. Whenever Harlow was in the house, Lizzie wouldn't let her out of her sight. She followed her like a puppy. She even tried to follow her into the bathroom once. And she'd bake Harlow cookies before tests. She hung a banner when Harlow got an internship. All these weird things she didn't do for anyone else. It was like Lizzie was obsessed with her."

"What did Harlow think about it?" My mind was spinning around these new facts.

"She was totally freaked out. It was super uncomfortable. But Harlow had no choice. She had to stay at the KD house all the time because her roommates were fucking degenerates and there was nowhere else for her to go."

"And Lizzie knew Harlow hated living with them?"

Rylee rolled her eyes. "Everyone knew. Madeleine forwarded an email Harlow sent her begging to get out of the lease to a bunch of her friends. Everyone was accusing Harlow of being a narc and a wet blanket. It was super mean girl behavior."

I chewed over this. "That sucks, but it seems like a weak motive to kill three people, just because Harlow was unhappy living with them."

Rylee ducked her head. "Don't tell anyone, but Harlow was about to lose her scholarship. She'd been failing her tests because she was barely getting enough sleep and super stressed all the time. Stacie and Larissa were, like, letting people have sex in Harlow's room during parties. And they kept breaking her furniture. This guy rode her bike at one of their tailgates and broke it, so Harlow had to walk to class. She was going to have to withdraw and go to *community college*."

I tried not to bristle at the way Rylee pronounced "community college." What Lightly had said just a few days ago, at our family meeting, came back: *An extinction event. The end of a way of life. That's a powerful trigger.*

Rylee leaned over, resting her arms on the table. "Don't you think it's weird that Lizzie loved Harlow, and Harlow was the only one who survived? And everyone knew Harlow hated living with Stacie, Madeleine, and Larissa, and wanted to get out of the lease, and now she's free? And the school is letting Harlow stay? I mean, after what she's been through and the attention she's gotten, there's no way they'll yank her scholarship. She'll come back next semester and everything will have worked out."

"That is weird," I agreed. "So why haven't you told the police?"

Rylee looked at me like I was crazy. "And what? If I'm wrong, then I'm a laughingstock. And if I'm right, then I get Harlow in trouble and make Lizzie come after me? No, thank you. She's terrifying. You saw what she did to those track girls, and who even knows what they did to piss her off? I'm just saying." She patted my arm. "I would think twice about rushing KD."

AFTER RYLEE LEFT, I SAT on a bench outside the coffee shop, soaking in the rare late-afternoon sunshine. It had been weeks since I left Florida, and except for a few text messages reassuring her that I was okay, I'd had no contact with my mother. It was time to call.

She answered on the first ring. "Jane. Are you okay?"

"I'm fine." NIU students in sweats and backpacks ambled past me. "How are you?"

"Lonely."

I guess we were done being mad at each other. Guilt pricked at me. "I'm sorry, Mom. I promise I left for a good reason."

She took a deep breath. "No—I'm sorry. I don't mean to make you feel bad. You're an adult. You're allowed to go wherever you choose."

"Wow. Okay."

She gave a pained chuckle. "I've started seeing a grief counselor. Do I sound like it?"

"You do, actually."

"Hey." Her voice lifted. "You'll never guess what I found while I was clearing out the attic."

"My Pokémon cards?"

"Well, yes. But—I found your dad's old letters. The ones he sent while he was out at sea. He sent you some, too, even though you were a baby. I used to read them to you."

I nearly flinched at the sharp emotions. To see my dad's handwriting, hear the echo of his voice. Even picturing the letters summoned an acute mix of pain and longing. "That's great."

"I'm reading through them now." She laughed. "I actually took time off work to read through them in chronological order. Is that crazy? I'm setting aside the ones for you."

I shook my head, closing my eyes against the sunshine. "No, I don't think that's crazy." I pictured the two of us on opposite sides of the country, in our pajamas, faces bent over the minutiae of my father's life. Mine lit by the glow of a computer screen, hers tracing down worn paper, but our expressions the same. Hungry, hungry.

"Mom. I wanted to ask you something." I nearly backed out—she was happy right now, and I was going to throw a wrench in it. But I had to know. "Did Dad ever tell you that he was molested as a kid?"

There was the shocked silence I'd expected and then, "No. Where are you getting that? Did he tell you?"

"One of his childhood friends told me. On Facebook. I was asking for stories about Dad, old memories, and I guess he wanted to get it off his chest. He said Dad told him when they were twelve that he and his brothers used to be touched by an uncle." It felt so gross to say it out loud.

"This is something a stranger on Facebook told you?"

"Not a stranger. One of Dad's friends. They grew up together, went to the same high school."

"He never told me that," my mom insisted. "And we told each other everything. No," she decided. "I don't believe it."

I don't know why I believed Darrel Woodruffe over my mother, but I did. "Do you think—you know how he refused medication for his blood pressure, and he wasn't doing anything to curb his weight..." I turned away from the students walking down the promenade and lowered my voice. "Do you think Dad was agreeing to die, on some level? Like he either wanted it, or he didn't care enough to fight?" It felt like a betrayal to even suggest it—but the potential of *his* betrayal, his willing abandonment of us, was greater. I had to know. "Do you ever feel like you didn't know Dad as well as you thought?"

She was silent on the other end. I listened to the swish of pant legs, students calling to each other. Finally, she said, "It hurts to think like that, Jane."

"I know." It wasn't a no.

"I don't think I can handle this right now," she said.

"That's fine. I'm sorry." Fair enough. I'd gotten used to dealing in grim realities. I'd forgotten not everyone had the stomach for it.

We hung up and I wandered campus, taking the long route. I was passing the dining hall, with its long wall of windows looking toward NIU's football stadium, when familiar faces caught my eye. I moved closer to the glass and peered. Goku and Citizen sat opposite a dark-haired man whose back was to me. They had cafeteria trays loaded with food.

This must be Odell Rhodes. I'd googled him, of course, after our last family meeting, and found a headshot of a bony, dead-eyed man on the Criminology department's website. I pictured it: that back stalking away, escaping through the sliding-glass doors. Was this the back Harlow White spotted leaving her house?

Citizen's eyes slid over the man's shoulders. I started to turn away, but it was too late: his smiled widened and he waved.

Next to him, Goku leaned over. When he spotted me, panic squeezed his face. And then, the thing I'd been dreading: the man twisted in his seat to look. His eyes found mine.

Lightning arced through me—I was caught. That face: even from far away, being looked at by a man who might've hurt women, relished in it, felt like a violation.

Citizen's waves grew faster, urging me inside. He wanted me to sit in front of Odell Rhodes. It was the last thing I wanted, but with their eyes on me, I didn't know what else to do. I made my way inside.

70

—

ODELL LOOKED EXACTLY LIKE HE did in his picture. If anything, the strange hollowness in his eyes was more pronounced. If our eyes are the windows to our souls, his had no light on. He was thin in a way that suggested he'd once weighed much more and had lost the weight too fast. His skin hung uneasily. His chin was protruding, his brow wide and low, framed by thick eyebrows. His gaze skittered around as I walked up, as if he was hesitant to meet my eyes.

"Veronica," Citizen called, pulling out a chair. "Fancy seeing you here."

"Hey, guys." I eased into the chair, panicking a little when I realized I couldn't remember what fake names Citizen and Goku were using in their ploy as NIU grad students. I nodded at Odell in a perfunctory way. "Hi."

"This is our friend Odell from the Criminology department," Citizen said smoothly. Goku was having trouble schooling his face—he couldn't hide his displeasure at seeing me. "He's a first-year grad student like us. And Odell, this is Veronica. She's an undergrad, but don't hold it against her." Citizen cocked his head. "We were just complaining about your peers having no common sense."

Odell watched our exchange carefully, so, heart pounding, I raised my hands. "I'll be the first to admit most undergrads are idiots."

Citizen laughed loudly, which cued Goku to laugh too, a little too late. I realized then that he was afraid.

Odell cracked a smile. "I don't know which is worse: undergrads or the professors. They're both entitled as shit."

The comment was sharper than I'd expected from a man with such a vacant expression. Odell had more going on in his head than his dead eyes gave away.

Citizen leaned in like he was sharing a secret. "I had this undergrad tell me after midterms—I kid you not—that I needed to change her grade from a C to an A minus because otherwise she wouldn't get into business school." He looked around in outrage. "As if that's my problem?"

"Oh yeah," I said, deciding that acting along would be the best way to settle my nerves. "There was this one time—"

"The girls are the worst," Odell blurted. "They think they're so much smarter than they are. They're like that in my program, too." He looked at Goku and Citizen. "Are they like that in yours?"

Odell was acting like I didn't exist—wasn't sitting right there, hadn't just been talking. But Citizen didn't miss a beat. "In the mathematics department? We barely have any women."

"Only one," Goku added, glancing at Odell and then quickly looking away.

"That must be nice," Odell said. "So much less crap to deal with."

"True." Citizen ripped open a bag of pretzels. "Though the one we do have talks a lot."

Odell leaned over the table. I tried not to flinch. "They're always trying to debate everything I say. They expect me to back down, but I never do. And the professors are always on their side. It's like you're not even allowed to argue with women anymore. It's PC bullshit."

"How did the three of you meet?" I asked, hoping to change the subject. Citizen flicked me an annoyed look. "Grad student mixer," he said quickly. Then something seemed to occur to him. "Hey Veronica, you're planning to rush next fall, aren't you?"

Odell's eyes swung to me. My heart nearly beat out of my chest. Why would Citizen say that? "I don't know. Maybe."

"We should probably get go—" Goku started to say, but Citizen interrupted.

"Your favorite one is KD, right?"

I felt pinned by Odell's eyes. I could feel them moving over me, assessing. I'd gone from unworthy of his attention to newly interesting, a target. My throat seized. "I don't know—"

"What do you think of the sororities here?" Citizen asked Odell. "Should she bother?"

He didn't miss a beat. Apparently, Odell had an opinion about everything. "I don't know. Are you a mindless drone?" His words were cutting, but his expression was eerily calm. "A vapid person who prefers meaningless conversations about alcohol and labels over substantive interactions with intelligent people?"

If sorority girls are so vapid, why were you messaging Madeleine Edmonds? I wanted to ask, but I bit my tongue.

"Did you know that girls in sororities are seventy-four percent more likely to be raped?" he continued. "And frat boys are three times more likely to be their assaulter."

"Yes, I knew that."

His response was whiplash. "No, you didn't."

I almost laughed. "Yes, I did. It's one of the first facts they tell you in freshman orientation." It was true. At UCF.

He pivoted. "In twenty sixteen, College of Charleston Kappa Alphas were arrested for running a multimillion-dollar drug ring across the South."

"Weed, cocaine, and Xanax, mostly," I said. "One man murdered, dozens arrested, and yet only a few ever did time." Okay, so maybe your average undergrad might not know this story, but I was a sleuth. I'd read every salacious crime story I could get my hands on.

My eyes locked with Odell's. In a flash, I saw it: those gaunt cheekbones, those dead eyes, sprayed with arterial blood as he pinned Madeleine down by her neck. His calm expression as he struck. He could do it. I could *see* him doing it.

I couldn't speak.

"See, told you." Citizen mussed my hair. "Greek life—just a bunch of criminals in disguise." Under the table, he pressed his leg against mine. Whether it was supposed to be a comfort or an apology, I didn't care. I jerked my leg away and stood forcefully enough to make my chair skitter back.

"I just realized I'm late for something," I said, ignoring the flash of concern on Goku's face. "Nice to meet you," I muttered, but I didn't wait for Odell to answer before I turned and fled.

***

The minute Citizen and Goku cracked the door on the rental house, I leapt out of the armchair. "What were you thinking?"

I'd ambushed them—they froze, halfway through shrugging off their coats. Goku's surprise quickly vanished, replaced with regret.

"What are you talking about?" Citizen asked, resuming the process of removing his jacket. "Why are you yelling?"

"You turned me into an antagonist." I was practically shouting, but I didn't care. The longer I'd sat waiting and thinking, the angrier I'd gotten. "You used me to test him."

Citizen scoffed. "You did a great job of becoming his antagonist all on your own."

"That's because he's vile. I couldn't let what he was saying go unchecked, and you knew it."

"He's definitely something, don't you think?" Citizen's expression turned eager. "Clear feelings of inadequacy and a desire to dominate to make up for it. Obvious misogyny."

"Jesus." I took a step back. "Do you hear yourself? Stop working the case for a single second. You threw me to the wolves."

They were still stuck in front of the door, but neither made a move to come inside. Goku still had one arm in his coat. "Come on, Search," Citizen said. "That's how you get a feel for people. You provoke them."

"Is that why you called me over? You saw me and thought, perfect, let's dangle Jane in front of this guy and see if he bites. You put me on his radar."

"We did," Goku said, before Citizen could protest. He pressed a hand to Citizen's chest, as if to physically check him. "She didn't volunteer to meet Odell like we did." He turned to me. "I'm sorry."

Citizen looked genuinely confused. "I thought you'd be jumping at the chance to meet him. This could be *the* guy, the person we've been after for months."

"And if it is, I don't want him to know I exist." Meeting Odell had been like meeting Greg Brownville in the Indira Babatunde case, a mistake I'd made out of sheer naivete. Both men made my instincts fire, warning me I was in the presence of danger. "What if he decides to come after the sorority-girl wannabe who mouthed off to him?"

"He won't." Citizen sounded so sure of himself. "And besides, no one's coming after you with us around."

"Newsflash," I said. "You're not in control of the universe." I whipped away from both them and ran up the stairs, only looking back to shout, "One day your ego is going to get someone *killed*."

My God, if I only knew.

71

MISTRESS HAD FINALLY GOTTEN TIRED of waiting for Bridget Howell High to email her back about their yearbook, so she decided to drive to Oregon and get the damn book herself. Citizen, perhaps still smarting from my unprecedented reprimand the day before, had taken off in his car, so Mistress was stuck paying an exorbitant fee for a long-distance taxi. Nevertheless, undeterred, she popped into my room to give me a quick kiss before leaving. I was curled in bed in my sad outfit: my dad's flannel pajamas and University of Tennessee hoodie.

"What're your plans today?" She made a quick assessment of my mood. "Sulking?"

I'd decided not to tell her or Lightly about the run-in with Odell. I'd yelled at Citizen and Goku, they'd expressed remorse—more or less—and it was over. But I couldn't hide the fact that I was still in a rotten mood.

"Probably," I agreed, and she chuckled. "My daughter used to sulk for weeks when a boy broke up with her." She backed away at my scathing look and threw up her hands. "Not saying it's about a boy. But in the absence of information, one makes assumptions..."

"Get on the road already," I said, shooing her with my foot. Mistress laughed the whole way out.

Unfortunately, in a small way, she was right. My anger at Citizen was complicated, and probably magnified by the fact that it wasn't simply my friend who'd set me up in front of a dangerous man but someone I had a crush on. Deep down, I wanted Citizen to want me, knock on my door for another kiss. Instead, he'd introduced me to a serial killer.

"Better make it a work day," I told my dad's urn, which stood on the edge of the dresser beside my bed, keeping watch. Even though I still had questions for him in the wake of Darrel Woodruffe's claim—questions it hurt to even think about—I decided I could handle only one perplexing man today, and Citizen had taken the slot.

"What do you think?" I asked, grabbing my laptop off the floor and hauling it onto my lap. "Should we humor Rylee Lopez and look into Lizzie the house mom?"

He seemed to agree. All right, then: it would be an old-fashioned research day.

It was easy to find Lizzie's full name, since each sorority house mother was listed on NIU's Panhellenic web page, along with their email address. She was Elizabeth Caitlin Bath, which sounded fairly proper, and her email was thisnursinglife@gmail.com. I plugged variations of "Elizabeth Bath," "Lizzie Bath," and "thisnursinglife" into Google, and a wealth of links popped up. Interesting—our house mom had a robust online presence.

"Does that make it more or less likely she's a murderer?" I asked my dad.

Lizzie was twenty-six years old, which was younger than I'd guessed, and a nursing student at NIU. It was no wonder she'd signed up to be the KD house mom. Quick research told me house-mom gigs paid not only a stipend but room and board. That was a pretty good deal for a grad student. I knew from Goku that Odell Rhodes lived in the shabbiest off-campus apartment complex you could imagine, spartan and painted kill-yourself gray, but it was all he could afford.

Unless she operated private Instagram and TikTok accounts for the purposes of lurking, Lizzie's only social media was Facebook, an odd choice for someone her age. Things got weirder the longer I scrolled her page. Her profile picture showed her in light-blue scrubs—normal enough—but under her affiliations she'd listed "Kappa Delta—Honorary KD." She had a massive number of Facebook friends—over two thousand, but looking through them, I saw only one other person who went to NIU. The bulk looked like bot accounts. Not a single KD from NIU was on her friend list.

The strangest part was her photo albums, which were almost exclusively pictures of the girls, labeled by event: "KD White Rose Formal," "KD Barnyard Bash," and so on. From the outside looking in, you got the impression that Lizzie had a very active social life. I scrolled through the albums, expecting to find pictures of her with the girls—maybe Rylee had dramatically overblown the level of disdain the girls felt for her— but Lizzie was nowhere. Some of the shots were intimate close-ups, girls laughing with their arms slung over each other, braced against a bar. They were the kind of pictures you had to be an insider to capture. Madeleine, Stacie, and Larissa were in a fair number of them, but Harlow was everywhere. A few of the photos were just solo shots of her, cheeks flushed from alcohol, eyes half shut, holding up peace signs.

Since I'd been so preoccupied with her potential guilt, I hadn't really stopped to appreciate how striking Harlow was. She was tall and lean, with light, glossy brown hair and wide, expressive green eyes. Across all the pictures she wore expensive-looking clothes and carried a small black Chanel bag—or, at least, a very convincing knockoff—so I forgave myself for not realizing she was a scholarship student on the brink of being dropped from the school. She seemed to be a master at fitting in—she looked every inch the polished rich girl. Was she play-acting a fantasy where she was just as wealthy as her friends, or was she actually lying to people about her circumstances? If she couldn't tell her room-mates at Queen Lace what was really at stake in keeping her grades up, that must've added so much pressure, made their dismissal of her so much worse. Maybe Harlow had gotten desperate.

I couldn't understand how Lizzie had gotten these pictures. Had she taken them herself? That didn't feel right. It wasn't until, on a hunch, I opened Larissa's Instagram page and scrolled all the way down to the pictures I remembered seeing of her at a formal event that I realized what was happening.

72

—

THE SAME SHOT OF LARISSA, Chandler, Harlow, Stacie, and Stacie's date from Larissa's Instagram grid—captioned "formal with the besties <3"—was repeated in Lizzie's Facebook album. She must've copied the girls' pictures and put them in her own albums, to give the impression the photos were hers. But why? To create an illusion that the girls were her friends? Rylee must not know she was doing this. Something told me it would've been high on her list of Lizzie's creep factors.

I returned to the photo on Larissa's Instagram and scrolled through the comments. I'd done this once before, looking for any tidbits about Chandler, but my aim was different today. And there it was, posted by a user with the handle ecb13897: "Looking gorge, ladies! Harlow, your smile is everything." I clicked on the username, but the profile was locked. I would bet anything I was looking at Elizabeth Caitlin Bath's lurker account.

The majority of Lizzie's Google hits turned out to be from Reddit, where she posted frequently under the username r/thisnursinglife. It was unnerving to discover she was a Redditor. While I'd been on r/truecrime discussing the murders, she'd been only a few subreddits over.

Mostly she participated in the subreddits r/nursing and r/studentnurse, where fellow nurses-in-training complained about being run ragged, mistreated by instructors, and desperately poor. I noticed Lizzie rarely complained herself. In fact, more often than not, she was the one swooping in to offer advice and encouragement, which earned her a lot of effusive thanks. She was quite the white knight.

I searched through her comment activity to see if she'd ever posted in r/truecrime or r/Delphinemassacres, but there was nothing. She was, however, a huge fan of *Buffy the Vampire Slayer,* commenting incessantly on r/Buffy about a slayer character named Faith Lehane. That was about as violent as her Reddit presence got: vivid descriptions of sweaty, steely Faith staking vampires through the heart.

It wasn't until I read one of her earliest comments on r/Buffy—I was up to my elbows in her comment history by then—that I saw her mention LiveJournal: "You have no idea how many of my old LiveJournal entries were devoted to Faith and Buffy, LMFAO;0)." Curious, I pulled up the site and searched for "Lizzie Bath" or "Elizabeth Bath," but got nothing. Ditto on "thisnursinglife." I leaned against my headboard and stretched, amazed at how tired you could get by traveling virtually through another person's life. Absentmindedly, I brushed the urn, right on the line Lightly had painted about being bound to the ones we love.

Lizzie had loved writing about *Buffy,* right? I tried various combinations of "Buffy," "love," and "fan," but got way too many results. I narrowed, trying "Faith" + "Buffy" and there, halfway down the second page of results, was a user whose profile said, "hi, i'm lizzie b."

Got her.

73

—

YOUNG LIZZIE HAD FIFTY-EIGHT LIVEJOURNAL entries, the earliest dated to 2012, the latest 2016, which meant she used the site exclusively during high school. "Tell me your secrets," I murmured, opening each entry in its own separate tab until my browser had turned into a virtual forest through which to search.

The later entries were all *Buffy* fan fiction, stories written from the point of view of Faith the bad-girl slayer. It was an understatement to say Lizzie seemed prone to obsession—this Faith character, the KD girls, Harlow. I found pictures of Faith online: an attractive brunette in vampy makeup, a surly expression, and tight tank tops. Interesting how different Lizzie's idol was from her.

But as I crept back in time, to the first few years of Lizzie's posting, the entries became diaristic. There were the standard teenage complaints about homework and teachers and bad test grades, but mostly she wrote about a girl named Aurora from school, chronicling what Aurora wore, who she talked to, even what she ate and where she sat in the cafeteria. Aurora was a bassist in the school band, so Lizzie wrote about picking up the flute and joining. Was Aurora a proto-Harlow? I kept returning to the way Lizzie wrote about her, trying to read whether

her interest was romantic, thinking of Rylee's derisiveness about Lizzie being "in love." I knew, as a straight girl, I wasn't the best judge, but I didn't get a romantic vibe. It was more that Lizzie seemed intensely fascinated, like Aurora and the life Lizzie imagined her leading were subjects Lizzie could get lost in.

She didn't mention anything about her home life or family until I came upon one remarkable entry from what would've been her sophomore year of high school. In it, she complained about getting into trouble "yet again" thanks to those "nosy, miserable cunts" in the admin office. It was her first vicious post. If Lizzie was getting into trouble a lot, she was definitely keeping it out of her LiveJournal. Why would she edit her own diary? I thought of Harlow and her rich-sorority-girl cosplaying. Was Lizzie living a fantasy life online? Was LiveJournal, and maybe later Reddit, a place where she could escape herself, play the person she wanted to be?

From what I could piece together, she'd gotten in trouble for "defending herself" against the worst bitch in school—Lizzie didn't say what she'd done to the girl, exactly, or what the girl had done to her. The principal had warned Lizzie's parents that she needed to start therapy or she'd be expelled. I read breathlessly as she described being forced to visit a mostly silent, stern-faced man who expected her to spill her guts while he scribbled notes. At the end of her entry, she'd typed, "and what even *is* conduct disorder? Sounds like bullshit."

It rang a distant bell. I googled and found it was a "Cluster B behavioral disorder in kids and adolescents characterized by antisocial, aggressive behavior, and disregard for others." Children with conduct disorder, I read, had difficulty behaving in socially acceptable ways; they could easily turn hostile and violent. Someone on the *PsychologyNow* forum summed it up like this: "Conduct disorder is what kids get diagnosed with instead of psychopathy. Apparently, it's too taboo to call a child a psychopath. But make no mistake—you can think of CDs as psychopaths-in-training."

My blood ran cold. I pulled up Lizzie's Facebook profile again—one of the only pictures of the real her on the internet, despite her robust presence. Was she a wolf in sheep's clothing? I scanned her image, searching for the charge of danger I'd felt in Odell's presence. Her long limbs in scrubs, her waist-length hair, her large, white, spotless sneakers.

Her sneakers. I bent closer to the screen. Lizzie was extremely tall, maybe over six feet, which meant her shoe size would be unusually large, right? We'd been searching for a killer with smaller-than-average feet, a man's size 9, but what if our Butcher was actually a larger-than-average woman?

I needed that shoe size.

I shoved my computer off my lap and ran to the closet, flinging through hangers, stopping when I got to my lone pink T-shirt.

Goku and Citizen weren't the only ones who could go hunting.

74

—

THE KAPPA DELTA HOUSE WAS eerily quiet in the middle of the afternoon, nothing like the madness of the fashion show. That was good, because it increased the odds Lizzie was in class, but also bad, because the KD house had one of those keyless locks on the front door, and it wasn't one I knew how to hack. It took nearly thirty minutes, but eventually a girl with an ice-blond bob bounced up the brick entryway to the door, then stopped at the sight of me.

I smiled and waved my folder. "Hi! I'm just here to drop off something for Lizzie Bath. She didn't give me the code."

The girl gave me a skeptical side-eye but punched in the code and held the door open. "She's not supposed to."

"Right." I scrambled to my feet. "That makes sense." Inside my folder was my application to rush, a form that was technically due to the Panhellenic office, not the KD house mom. But if there was one thing being a twenty-four-year-old woman in true crime had taught me, it was that people expected girls my age to make thoughtless mistakes. It was something you could bank on.

We faced a gorgeous spiral staircase, and the girl started pounding up it. "Uh," I called. "Where's Lizzie's room?"

"Downstairs," she called, without stopping.

"*Okay*," I mumbled under my breath, heading down the stairs. "Thanks so much for your help, Miss America."

Downstairs was, for lack of a better term, the servants' quarters. The ornate decor of the aboveground floors was replaced by small, utilitarian rooms stuffed with cleaning supplies. I knocked softly on all the doors, cracking them open when I got no response, until I got to what had to be Lizzie's room. It was empty. I thanked God and stepped inside.

I beelined to her closet. Her room was spare and tidy, a perfectly made twin bed pushed against the wall, a small bedside table empty save for a hairbrush. I paused, debating pulling hairs for a DNA sample, then reminded myself it would be useless without a warrant. DNA would have to wait.

Her closet was as organized as the rest of the room. A dozen pairs of shoes rested in a hanging shoe organizer. I scanned, looking for a pair of Vans Ward sneakers, the kind the killer wore, but found none. There was, however, an empty shoe cubby. I pulled another pair of sneakers and scanned. Size 11. My heart pounded. I shoved it back and grabbed a pair of heels—11—and then a pair of sandals. Again, 11. There was no mistaking it: Lizzie's shoe size matched the killer's frozen footprint found outside the Queen Lace house. I snapped pictures and closed the closet.

I should've left then. But maybe I was too high on adrenaline, or greedy. I paused, then turned and reopened the closet. On the floor, half obscured by Lizzie's clothes, were plastic storage bins. I bent and cracked one open. There were stacks of paper—school assignments, an old lease agreement—and spiral-bound notebooks, the kind you bring to class for notes. I pulled out one she'd drawn all over: thorny roses, hearts, and close-ups of long-lashed eyes in ballpoint pen. The pages were full of spiky, slanted handwriting. Immediately, Harlow's name caught my eye.

I scanned. The pages seemed to be full of stories. Like fan fiction, but starring real-life people.

"I didn't think you'd come," Harlow said, wrapping her hands around the bars of her cage. "I thought you were done with me."

Eliza pulled out the metal-cutters, her biceps shown off by her dirt-stained tank top. "Stand back."

Harlow did as she was told, watching as Eliza wrestled with the metal, bending and cutting until she'd created a person-sized hole. "Well, come on," said Eliza gruffly, holding out her hand.

Harlow wilted into her arms. Even in the dark basement of the mansion where she'd been held hostage, Harlow's beauty was barely diminished.

Harlow didn't release her when Eliza tried to pull back. "Eliza," she said, voice trembling. "I didn't know if I'd ever see you again." Her long-lashed green eyes stared deep into Eliza's. Her lips, so close, wobbled.

"I would never let those bitches hurt you," said Eliza. "You're safe with me."

Harlow pressed closer. "My hero," she whispered.

I flipped to the next page and found an intricate drawing of Harlow blowing a kiss.

Again—I recognized a shrine when I saw one.

Heavy footsteps creaked on the spiral staircase. "Oh, shit," I breathed, snapping a picture of the notebook and then shoving it back in the bin, closing closet doors as fast as I could. I grabbed my folder and swept out of the room. The footsteps were getting louder. Someone was definitely coming—there was no time to think. I sucked in a breath and started up the stairs.

Lizzie and I froze as we faced each other. The too-cheery expression I'd seen her wear at the fashion show was a distant memory—her bony features were stony, her expression suspicious.

"Oh my God," I said, before she could say anything. "There you are! I was looking for you to give you my rush application." I held out the folder and prayed to God my hand didn't shake.

Lizzie looked at me—really looked, searching my face. And that's when I felt it—the bone-deep understanding that I was in danger. That the person before me was capable of violence. The kind that made me lean over and throw up to witness.

"You're not supposed to be down here," she said, and even her voice was different, deeper and huskier, more suited to her height.

I blinked stupidly. "I thought we dropped these forms off with you."

"No. Who let you in?"

"Really? I'm so sorry." I didn't have to fake the emotion. "I feel so dumb." I tried to edge up the stairs, but she didn't move. "Do you know who I'm supposed to give these to?" In my panic, I kept talking. "I was at the fashion show the other day and I just fell in love with KD, so I thought I'd give it straight to you. I should've asked Rylee, though. Or—Olivia. Or River." I summoned their names like protective spirits.

Lizzie's frown deepened. "They would've told you to go to the Panhel office."

"Okay, well, I'll go there right now. So sorry, again." I held my breath and pushed past her, moving fast. She didn't try to stop me, so I kept going. It wasn't until I was at the top of the stairs that I chanced a look back to find her still rooted in place, watching. I tossed her a wave and launched myself out the door, sucking in huge lungfuls of crisp May air as I practically ran from the sorority house down the streets of Greek Row.

I made it. I probably couldn't go back, but I'd gotten my evidence and I'd made it out.

I was still power-walking across campus when my phone vibrated. I pulled it out to find a text from Mistress:

Drop whatever you're doing and meet me at White Pines Park at 4.
I found something huge.

75

—

I WAITED FOR MISTRESS ALONE in the park for thirty minutes before my heart started to sink. White Pines was a small park right beside the NIU football stadium, so there was no way I'd missed her. She hadn't responded to any of my texts, and her phone rang endlessly. Maybe her taxi had broken down? Maybe her phone was on silent or she'd lost it, and any second, she'd pull up? None of it sounded likely, but I sat on a bench and waited until the sky darkened before I forced myself to leave.

Lightly was the only one home. I found him in the kitchen, prepping dinner. "Hey, Search," he sang. "Pot roast night."

"Have you seen Mistress?" My breath was short from running.

He paused over the cutting board. "She's still in Oregon, right? Looking for that yearbook?"

"She was on her way back. She texted me that she'd found something huge and to meet her in White Pines Park, but she never showed up. And now she's not responding."

"Is her phone off?"

"No, it's ringing."

Lightly waved away my concern with a celery stalk. "She probably just fell down a rabbit hole. She gets like that. Have I ever told about the case we worked where she disappeared on me for a week? Turns out she decided to look into every single property purchase made in the county we were eyeing since 1973, just didn't bother telling me. She'll turn up." He started chopping. "Can't wait to hear what she's got."

"You don't think she's in danger?"

Lightly looked at me. "Search, Mistress is in Oregon. The killer is in Delphine. Out of all of us, she's the safest."

It hadn't even occurred to me. If Lizzie was our perp, she was on the first floor of the KD house, not in Oregon, harming Mistress. I felt my shoulders relax.

"She'll turn up, late and excited," Lightly promised. "Now, what've you been working on?"

I pulled out a stool and sat. "I think our killer is a woman named Lizzie Bath. She had a strong motive to kill the first three victims and leave Harlow untouched. In fact, I think I understand why Harlow waited to call the cops and called Jordan Beckett instead. I think deep down she suspected Lizzie was the one who killed her roommates, and she was freaking out because she knew she'd done it for her. I think that's why she hasn't said anything since the murders. She feels responsible." That is, if she hadn't outright orchestrated the killings with Lizzie herself.

Lightly dropped the knife and gave me his full attention.

"Lizzie has the means, too. As house mom, she knows where her girls live and she was *very* aware of Madeleine, Stacie, and Larissa's habits. She knew they had a party house and there was a strong chance the sliding-glass door would be unlocked on a Saturday night. She wears a women's size eleven, which is the same as a man's size nine, and Vans are unisex shoes. She got diagnosed with conduct disorder when she was in high school, and she fits so much of the female killer profile Mistress told us about. I bet if the FBI looked into her school record, they'd find a ton of disciplinary actions. And she has access to knives from the KD kitchen, which is the last place the cops would think to look."

It all came out in one long, breathless ramble. Lightly still hadn't said anything, but the look he was giving me was thoughtful, not dismissive. "She's tall and strong, and I think it's sexist to say that just because she's a woman, she couldn't stab people to death. The only thing I can't square is the second massacre." I'd tried to no avail. "I don't know what her motive is for the track girls. Unless she got a taste for killing and the second house was random."

He rubbed his chin, his gaze roaming the kitchen.

"What're you thinking?"

"Before she left for Oregon," Lightly said, his words coming slowly, like wine swilling down the side of a glass, "Mistress and I were talking about a theory. I wasn't ready to share it widely yet. I just wanted her take."

"And?"

"Walking through the kill sites with Lawrence, and looking back over the autopsy reports, little things weren't adding up between Queen Lace and Collegiate Parkway. The height of the blood splatter on the walls was different, the angles and depth of the wounds were different, even the way the killer used their Lysol wipes. In the Queen Lace house, you can see in the residue that the killer wiped the floors and doors left to right, in horizontal strokes, and in the Collegiate Parkway house it's right to left, vertical."

I sunk my chin into my hands. "Why change the way you clean?"

There was that glint in his eyes Lightly got when he was on to something. "Exactly. Mistress and I were talking through the theory that the killings were done by two different people."

I tried to wrap my head around it. "But...why?"

"I don't know. A copycat? Someone taking advantage of the opportunity, the chance to blame the original killer?"

It dawned on me slowly. "Maybe I don't need to look for Lizzie's motive for the track girls. Maybe she was Killer A, but not Killer B."

The front door flew open. I gasped, nearly slipping off the barstool. Lightly swung around the island and rushed into the foyer.

"Dear God," he cried at the sight of Citizen and Goku in the doorway, their chests heaving. "What happened? What's wrong?"

I knew, even then, in that pregnant half second before they spoke, that whatever came next would put our names in the history books. The weight of history unfolding was thick in the air.

"We did it." Goku thrust his phone into the air. "We got him."

Citizen's eyes blazed. His hands were shaking. "Odell Rhodes confessed to the killings, and we recorded it. We've got the man on tape, Lightly. We caught the Butcher."

PART THREE

———

Now I See It—

This Connection

of Everyone with Broken Hearts

76

—

WE PROCESSED THROUGH THE DELPHINE Police Department behind Chief Reingold like a Roman emperor returning from a foreign war. Officers turned to stare as we passed in the halls, naked curiosity on their faces. Either word had traveled fast from the front desk that some FBI consultants—formerly amateur sleuths—had broken the Butcher case wide open, or the sight of me, Lightly, Goku, and Citizen promenading behind the chief was strange enough to warrant the attention.

Chief Reingold brought us into a conference room. A second later, Lawrence Hale rushed in, tie askew. "Lightly." His eyes zeroed in on his friend. "Is it true?"

Lightly nodded at Citizen and Goku. "They say they've got the confession."

Police officers filed in until it was standing room only around the conference table. Chief Reingold shut the door and looked over his officers. In person, the chief cut a more imposing figure—his eyes were steelier, and there was a grit to him. Gone was the Kris Claus impression. I wondered at the tragic way some people translated on TV. "Mr. Bishop and Mr. Goddins are FBI consultants commissioned by Agent Hale"—he nodded at Hale—"to assist with the case."

All eyes in the room fell on Citizen and Goku, who folded into seats at the table. Goku's gaze dropped nervously, but Citizen held his head high. I didn't need to wonder what he was thinking. He'd beaten every single person in the room—in the world—to the killer.

If any of the officers suspected that the chief's heroes were the same two men behind the hack that had devastated their department only months ago, they didn't say.

"They're going to play a recording of Odell Rhodes, twenty-eight, first-year graduate student at NIU," said the chief, redirecting the officers' attention. "Mr. Rhodes is not previously known to us. Officer Williams is running his record to see if he has any priors, but it's unlikely, given the DNA from Collegiate Parkway had only a single CODIS hit. Mr. Bishop and Mr. Goddins obtained Mr. Rhodes's confession by posing as friends and confidants. They recorded the conversation in adherence to the state's one-party consent law." He nodded at Citizen, and Citizen pressed play.

"Oh, man." Citizen's voice rang out loudly in the room. "There's this girl in my stats class, Melody—stupid name, right? I wish I could shut her up. I literally fantasize about it. Dream about it."

"How would you do it?" asked a cold, inflection-less voice. Odell.

"Oh, I'd choke her out for sure," Citizen said, no hesitation. "Squeeze her throat until her face turned blue and her eyes popped. She'd shut up then."

Half of the officers glanced at Citizen, but he didn't flinch.

"Takes too long to strangle someone," Odell said, ever the know-it-all. "Longer than you think. Even the small ones, the girls."

"Excuse me." I slid out of my chair and squeezed through the officers to where Lawrence Hale stood, his posture stiff, hands in his trouser pockets. His eyes were on Goku's cell phone, his expression rapt.

"Agent Hale?" I whispered.

His gaze flicked to me.

"Can I speak to you in private?"

He looked back at Goku's phone, but before he could protest, I added, "Please? It's about the case."

To my surprise, I felt Lightly come up behind me. When I threw him a questioning look, he only nodded. "I've got you."

Lightly's presence must've tipped the scales. Hale did an about-face and led us out of the room, shutting the door quietly. Then he folded his arms over his chest and looked at me expectantly.

I took a deep breath. My instincts had steered me well thus far. "I know Citizen and Goku—uh, Peter and Brian—have a confession, but Agent Hale, I don't think Odell Rhodes is the only killer." I glanced back at Lightly, praying he'd back me up.

"We've been working on a theory," he said, in his deep baritone. "That there are two killers. The original and a copycat."

Hale frowned, showing deep grooves in his skin. The man had frowned a lot in his life. "But why? Isn't Rhodes on that phone"—he pointed at the conference room—"confessing to all the murders?"

"I don't know how to explain his confession," I said. "But I do know that there's another suspect, Lizzie Bath—"

"A *woman*?" The agent's frown deepened.

"The Kappa Delta sorority house mom. I believe she had means and motive to kill Madeleine, Stacie, and Larissa. And a reason to leave Harlow alone. I'm not the only one who suspects her. Her own KD undergrads do, too." A slight exaggeration.

"The theory would go," Lightly said, picking up, "that for whatever reason—glory, attention, opportunity—Odell Rhodes seized the chance to commit his own killings and point the blame at the first killer. He did the second house. Shuri, Katya, and Greta."

Lawrence covered his face with his hands and made a low moaning noise. "You're killing me here, Lightly." He removed his hands. That's when I noticed Agent Hale had deep, dark circles under his eyes. "First you show up without any warning and drop a killer on my doorstep—"

"I didn't know the boys were going so far on their own," Lightly interrupted. "I didn't think they'd press for a confession."

"And now you're telling me your man's only half right and there's another killer out there? Some sorority woman?"

"And Mistress is missing," I added. "She won't answer my calls, and I'm worried."

"Tammy Jo Frazier," Lightly translated. "Mistress is her handle."

"The older woman," Hale said, nodding as he remembered. "Murder-solving grandma. How long's she been gone?"

I checked my phone. "Three hours."

Agent Hale actually started laughing. As he faced the two of us, alone in the hallway, his shoulders shook with mirth.

I looked at Lightly, confused. He cleared his throat warningly. "Lawrence, given the nature of what the five of us have been doing for you and the Bureau, I think different parameters apply. I know standard is to wait twenty-four hours, but Tammy Jo was chasing down an important lead and asked Jane to meet her at White Pines Park. She said she had big news, then never showed. It's highly unusual."

Hale schooled his expression. "She's never gone radio silent before?"

Lightly gave me the briefest glance. "Never. Like I said, it's highly unusual."

He was lying for me. My heart lifted.

Hale sighed. "All right, old friend. I understand that sometimes the normal rules don't apply." The two men held each other's gaze for a beat, communicating a complicated message.

"I appreciate it" is all Lightly said.

"Let me hear the tail end of this confession." Agent Hale reached for the door. "And then I'll track down your girl Tammy Jo."

We walked back in to find the majority of officers pressed into the perimeter of the conference room, giving Citizen and Goku a wide berth. Goku's normally pale cheeks flamed red.

"Oh, *man.*" On the recording, Citizen laughed, presumably at something Odell had shared. "That's insane. Please tell me these guys fuck the girls afterward."

Okay, then. The conversation had progressed since we'd left.

"No, that's the thing." Odell's voice had finally lost its coldness. Now it was heated, eager, his words coming out rushed. "They don't need to fuck them. The killing itself, man, that knife going in and out, you know, that meaty tug, the iron smell in the air, the way they look at you, the sound of the scream. You've never felt so much power. You're God as long as you can get it to last. That's better than getting off. Or a different kind. That's how they describe it."

There was a greedy intake of breath, then a pause. I could almost *feel* Citizen gearing up to ask his next question.

"You ever done it yourself?" His tone was perfect—half lustful, half awed, as if Odell would be a king if he said yes.

"I, uh…" There was movement on the recording, recorded as a burst of static. Maybe Odell was shifting, looking away. "Maybe."

"Oh yeah?" Finally, Goku's voice entered, though it was higher-pitched than normal. "When?"

Even I thought he sounded like a narc. Citizen swooped in. "I bet it felt incredible. Man, you know what probably felt so good? Taking out those college girls. You know the ones who got stabbed? They're saying whoever did it was an expert. Like, pro-level, the kind of serial killer we haven't seen since Bundy or Rader. Got all the cops scratching their redneck, GED asses."

There was laughter on the tape, but stony silence in the conference room.

"Whoever did *those* girls is a fucking hero."

A single beat of tantalizing silence, and then Odell said slyly, "That might've been me."

"No way." Citizen was playing worshipful. I didn't blame him—I'd witnessed Odell's ego. "You figured out how to slip in those back doors and get 'em while no one was watching? How to clean up so no one could catch you?"

"He's leading the guy," one of the officers complained, but he got shushed.

"It was easy," Odell said, warming to the subject. "They think they're so safe they don't even lock their doors. They don't see you coming."

"How'd you do it?" Citizen asked, breathless. I didn't think it was an act. He was sprinting toward the finish line and he knew it. "What was it like?"

"Best feeling you can imagine." I could hear it in Odell's voice, the way he reveled in holding Citizen's attention. The control the crimes had afforded him; the power recounting them gave, a return to that heady sensation. "That first moment when you touch them and see them realize what's happening." His voice turned feverish. "When they go all rigid and you stick it in and you can actually *feel* them scream in your fingertips. I swear, there's nothing like it."

77

—

LESS THAN AN HOUR LATER I fled the police station and broke into Mistress's bedroom. As reassuring as Lawrence Hale had been, the FBI weren't going to move fast enough. She was out there somewhere, and no one except me seemed particularly worried. Maybe if Citizen and Goku hadn't swung in holding the grand prize, she would've gotten more attention. But I saw the way the officers in the conference room frothed at the mouth as Odell guided Citizen through the murders, or Citizen guided Odell, or whatever complicated dance had unfolded between them. I saw the light go on in Hale's eyes, the bright promise of a hunt. Every ounce of law enforcement attention in a hundred-mile radius would be marshaled to capture the Barbie Butcher before news of his confession leaked and he got tipped off they were coming. The FBI was racing against the clock on the biggest case in the country. Mistress and I were on our own.

Citizen and Goku weren't getting out of the police station anytime soon. The cops needed to go over details of their relationship to Odell again and again, gathering fodder for their warrant. Lightly wanted to watch how they were treated, so I took an Uber by myself back to our house, hoping I'd find Mistress back from a harebrained adventure, flabbergasted to hear Citizen and Goku's news. But the house was empty.

I staggered into my room and fell into bed, then grabbed my dad's urn, hugging the smooth wood against my chest. I lay there for a while, cradling him, transferring the warmth of my skin into the pine until it almost felt alive. My thoughts roamed, imagining all the places Mistress could be, retreading how unnerved I was by Odell's confession. Even though I knew it was the best possible outcome, there was something about the recording and the way we'd walked through the police station like gods that had been disorienting. Maybe I'd just become too convinced of Lizzie Bath's guilt, or maybe I was jealous Citizen and Goku had beaten me to the finish line. What was I supposed to do now?

I looked down at the urn and the obvious answer hit me: my job was to step in where law enforcement was missing. If the DPD and FBI wouldn't rally to find Mistress, I could look for her myself.

Newly energized, I leapt out of bed, replaced my father, and rushed to her room. I would sweep it for clues, then track her steps—all the way to Bridget Howell High if I needed to. I seized the doorknob, expecting it to give easily.

It was locked.

I frowned. None of us locked our doors. Troublingly, in the case of Goku, sometimes not even when we used the bathroom. Why would Mistress want to keep us out? I examined the lock. Goku had made me watch endless YouTube videos about how to break into locked doors when he was trying to convince me that even an amateur criminal could've gotten inside Bridget's house. I knew all I needed was a card that was thinner than a credit card and the right kind of jiggling. Urgency filled me, a sense that an hourglass had turned and time was spilling.

I raced to my room and dumped out my backpack, seizing my wallet. My St. Lucie County library card should be thin enough. Standing in front of Mistress's door, I tried to remember Goku's videos. There'd been a guy with greasy hair in one, who was wearing a Sailor Moon T-shirt. I remembered him most vividly not only because of the shirt but because he'd just jammed a card into the space between the knob and the door, then wiggled the knob back and forth and pushed the door at the same time, and it had opened. Almost frighteningly easy.

I tried it and heard something clicking, but Mistress's door didn't open. The man in the video had said to alter the way you twisted the doorknob, so I rotated my wrist left and right and shoved my shoulder into the door—and then stumbled right into Mistress's room.

It was as neat as the glimpses I'd gotten of her house back in Des Moines. Her bed was made, a red-and-blue quilt neatly folded at the foot, and her closet doors stood open, revealing an assortment of sweaters. The only exception was the small, round table she was using as a makeshift desk. She'd dragged it across the room to the plaid armchair in the corner, and it was covered in messy papers and a spiral-bound notebook labeled No. 48. Over the months, I'd seen her scribble in those notebooks countless times. They were where she kept her thoughts, each of them numbered chronologically. I sat in her armchair and opened it. A sense of calm filled me. Research was where I shined.

The majority of the notes outlined a story about the Delphine murders I was already familiar with: the first massacre, then the second, the surprising DNA match to Bridget Howell's case, the anonymous caller's tip about their strange classmate who may have had something to do with Bridget's missing dog. Mistress kept a running log of phone calls, people she'd reached out to trying to track down Bridget's yearbook. It showed she'd called the high school no fewer than ten times and had yet to receive a callback, so no wonder she was frustrated. She'd tried soliciting a copy of the yearbook on various Facebook alumni groups and across the true-crime forums. She'd done her legwork, I'd give her that.

I flipped to the next page and found a loosely sketched timeline:

September 6th, 2012—Bridget Howell murdered in Carraway, OR. Random or motivated?

2012 through 2024—Killer moves to Delphine, ID or nearby city?

March 2nd, 2024—First massacre—Queen Lace Avenue

March 16th, 2024—Chandler Gray beaten and put in ICU

March 17th, 2024—Chief Reingold blames true-crime community, targets MLSG&C

March 17th-21st, 2024—Media feeding frenzy; G&C get brunt of anger

March 21st, 2024—G&C release confidential Queen Lace file, humiliate DPD

March 21st, 2024—L leaves out of anger over leak

March 30th, 2024—Second massacre—Collegiate Parkway

March 31st, 2024—L swiftly rejoins MSG&C

April 5th, 2024—MLSG&C discover DNA evidence at Collegiate Parkway that links to Bridget; made FBI consultants

April 16–17th, 2024—MLSG&C relocate investigation to Delphine. M retired, L boss, S unemployed, G working remotely, C???

Hadn't Citizen said he was taking leave from the navy? We'd been in Delphine for three weeks. I tried to recall my father taking three weeks off while he was in the military but couldn't. Instead, I remembered how difficult it had been for us to take a vacation, what a relief when he'd put in his twenty years and started working on the civilian side, where time off was more relaxed.

Still frowning, I looked at the last thing Mistress had scribbled, down at the very bottom: *Peter's Signal background—why???* It was circled three times.

Why was Mistress wasting time thinking about Signal? I looked at the door to her room, hanging limply open, a circular hole where the doorknob should've been. In for a penny, in for a pound, I guess. Surely I still had time before the cops released Citizen and Goku.

Citizen's bedroom was on the second floor across from Goku's, whose door was open to reveal piles of clothes strewn over his floor, change and receipts on his desk, and two massive laptops on his bed, one encrypted for work and one open for sleuthing. In stark contrast to Goku's mess, Citizen's room was neater than Mistress's. Nothing hung in his closet—he hadn't even bothered to take his clothes out of his suitcase. His laptop hummed quietly on his bed, which was made with military precision.

Something rather shameful about me is that I liked knowing people's passwords. Not to do anything devious—just because knowledge is useful. I'd always been a quiet observer, the kind of person who didn't look away when someone typed their PIN into their phone. I knew everyone's passwords except for Goku's, and that was only because he used those computer-generated strings of random numbers and letters that had proven impossible for me to remember. But Citizen's password, as I'd observed in the first few days we'd lived together, was Betty1064. It was a reference I didn't understand, but I didn't need to. His laptop glowed to life.

I glanced out his open door at the staircase. The house was quiet, but that could change at any moment. I needed to be fast—and, unlike in Mistress's room, leave no trace.

Though it was probably too much to ask, there was no folder titled "Signal Backgrounds," so I was forced to manually search Citizen's files.

He had thousands of pictures saved. I wasn't prepared for them.

"Jesus." I flinched away from a gruesome close-up of woman's mutilated body sprawled across a dirty tile floor. The notation at the bottom identified the image as a crime scene photo from a four-year-old homicide case. I quickly closed the picture and chose another at random. A bloody paring knife with a yellow evidence tag, labeled "Maricopa County."

I dragged the mouse down the virtual waterfall of images. Citizen had worked on a staggering number of cases over the years, and it looked like he'd saved photos from most of the crime scenes. While that struck me as strange, people living in glass houses shouldn't throw stones. Who knew what a forensic examination of my own computer would yield?

I realized I could launch a temporary Signal meeting to gain access to Citizen's settings. I thanked God Signal's privacy settings meant it didn't keep a record of meetings and started the meeting—just Searcher24, talking to herself. I toggled to Backgrounds pulling up the images saved in the app. There was only one photo, and it was a sight that had become deeply familiar over the past nine months: Citizen's kitchen. The photo was taken from the exact angle I always saw it, looking out from his kitchen table, where he rested his laptop. On the left was his off-white, retro fridge, on the right his small stove, and the door to his stoop stood in the center, hung with a short yellow curtain.

It was so normal it was strange. Why would Citizen have this photo, first of all, and why was it saved as a video chat background? I was just starting to nose around in his other settings when I heard the front door wrench open.

They were home. Twenty seconds until I was caught snooping.

I closed Citizen's Signal, my hands shaking so much it took me two tries to x out. As I raced to close the image files, I heard the heart-wrenching sound of footsteps on the stairs. They were coming up.

I shut down the computer, praying to my father. The footsteps pounded up the second flight. Finally, the screen went black and I slammed the laptop shut, dumping it exactly where I'd found it and leaping across the room, whipping around to shut Citizen's door as quietly as possible.

Behind me, a throat cleared.

Fuck.

I turned slowly. I needed an excuse, and fast.

"There a reason you're snooping in Citizen's room?"

I opened my eyes at the baritone. I hadn't even realized I'd squeezed them shut. "*Lightly.* Thank God."

He raised an eyebrow. "Should I assume you've dragged my room, or is this a focused raid?"

Should I trust Lightly with what I'd found, or would my betrayal of Citizen violate Lightly's moral code and turn him against me? I scanned his fatherly face, took a deep breath—and spilled. "I broke down Mistress's door to search her room and found a question about Citizen's Signal background, so I searched his computer and found a whole lot of disgusting crime photos, but, even worse, I found a picture of his kitchen."

Lightly blinked. The look on his face suggested he was scrambling for purchase amid my onslaught. He finally settled on "His...kitchen?"

"A picture of his kitchen from the exact same perspective we see every time we log into Signal. You know—" I waved. "With the fridge here and the stove there. He had it saved as a background."

Lightly, God bless him, was already two steps ahead. "Why would Citizen want to make us think he was in his kitchen when he wasn't?"

I shook my head. "I don't know. But Mistress wondered, too."

For a long, tense moment, Lightly stared into the middle distance. I could see the wheels of his mind turning, trying to slot pieces into place.

"The boys are going to be at the station overnight. I came back to tell you the FBI's moving in on Odell first thing tomorrow morning. They got a judge to issue an emergency warrant for his arrest. They're going to nab him at his apartment at the crack of dawn."

"Wow," I murmured. "So fast."

Lightly's voice was dry. "I'm surprised they're not kicking down his door right now. But Lawrence wants to make sure they come correct. And listen." He gave me a look that nearly bore a hole in me. "The boys agreed to be interviewed by the media once the news leaks. Which they're expecting it to pretty fast, since the journos have their eyes trained on the department, waiting for movement."

"They want Citizen and Goku to talk to *journalists*?"*

Lightly snorted. "They told good ol' Chief Reingold they'd hype up the DPD. Be their civilian spokespeople before the DPD and FBI are able to issue official statements. They're going to be the chief's cheer-leaders, talking about how fast they responded to the evidence."

I shook my head. "From dissidents to champions in sixty seconds flat."

Lightly's expression was steely. "But, dear Searcher, it buys us time."

---

* I only learned this after reading Natalie's book, but hours before the raid, the Delphine Police Department tipped off the victims' families that an announcement was forthcoming. Madeleine's, Stacie's, and Larissa's families decided to be together when the news broke, so the Edmonds and Weeks were at the Flowerses' house watching when Citizen and Goku appeared on TV, announcing they'd found their daughters' killer. Laura Flowers wept. Mr. Edmonds opened a bottle of whiskey and walked out the door, disappearing for the night. And Natalie, in her own words, entered her sister's bedroom for the first time since she died.

78

—

"WE INTERRUPT THIS PREVIOUSLY SCHEDULED broadcast with breaking news," announced the NPR reporter, his voice thick with urgency.

Lightly and I traded looks. We'd been flying down the highway in our rental car in silence, waiting, and this was what we'd been waiting for. Lightly cranked the volume.

"Reports out of Delphine, Idaho, say authorities have arrested a suspect in connection with the Barbie Butcher serial killings," said the reporter. "The Delphine Police Department and Federal Bureau of Investigation, in an interagency operation, apprehended twenty-eight-year-old Odell Rhodes early this morning. Mr. Rhodes is a first-year graduate student in Northern Idaho University's criminology department. He was found in his apartment, just five miles from the site of the first massacre and six from the second."

"They got him," I whispered. From the driver's seat, Lightly remained stone-faced, eyes on the road.

"While neither the DPD or the FBI has released an official statement, unofficial sources say Mr. Rhodes was taken into custody following a lengthy confession, recorded by two FBI consultants posing as his friends."

I picked up my phone and pulled up the Network. "The forum's already going nuts," I told Lightly. "People are posting that they had Odell Rhodes on their radar and just hadn't said anything yet."

He rolled his eyes.

"I'm here outside Delphine Police Headquarters with Peter Bishop," said the NPR reporter, "one of two FBI consultants whose recording and testimony helped police identify Odell Rhodes. Mr. Bishop, what can you tell us about this arrest and your involvement?"

"And you thought the Network was going nuts before," said Lightly. "Just wait. One of their own on the news. I bet they forget all about that time they tried to take Citizen down."

"I can't say much, I'm afraid." Citizen's voice was regretful. He was as good at playing the white knight as the scumbag. "Since it's an ongoing case. But I can confirm that we have an audio recording, taken yesterday, in which Mr. Rhodes confessed to the murders of all six university women."

I was scrambling to read the Network's posts about Odell, but post after post said the same thing. It didn't make sense…

Lightly caught my frown. "What's wrong?"

I kept scrolling, looking for anything different. "No one can find anything on Odell except his student page on the university website and his Instagram. But they're saying the account's less than a year old."

"That's what you found, too?" Lightly asked. "When you looked him up?"

"I mean, I didn't exactly search his social media."

Lightly gave me an incredulous look.

"That was supposed to be Citizen and Goku's job! I had another suspect to look up." Feeling guilty despite my protests, I kept scrolling. "Everyone's saying he doesn't exist on the internet or in any records."

"Could he have wiped himself? If he's so good at disappearing from a crime scene, maybe he's capable of doing it on the internet."

I shook my head, not buying it, and then a new thread caught my eye. It was titled "Owen Rhodes—This You?" I clicked.

"Holy shit." I held up the phone so Lightly could see it. "Look at this high school yearbook photo someone found."

"See, there he is," Lightly said. "Odell Rhodes. They found him."

"This is a man named Owen Rhodes." I yanked my phone back and scanned the post. "A woman's saying she grew up with him in Pittsburgh, where he was born and raised. They went to high school together."

Lightly frowned. "No stint in Oregon?"

"Doesn't look like it. The woman says Owen was her brother's best friend for a year in middle school and the two of them used to get bullied. Then Owen turned into a troublemaker. Apparently, he got expelled from high school and had to get his GED later. There were rumors he'd either gotten deep into heroin or been diagnosed with a psychiatric disorder, but she's fuzzy on which."

Citizen's voice boomed through the car. "While of course the courts will litigate Odell Rhodes's guilt, I can share that—as someone who got to know Rhodes over the course of the past few weeks—my opinion is that he's a highly controlled predator with a compulsion to harm women. The entire Pacific Northwest is lucky the Delphine police and the FBI have acted so quickly and decisively to apprehend him."

I put down my phone and looked at my friend. "What's going on, Lightly?"

He turned his head to look out the window at the trees whipping by. "I don't know. But I think we've gotten something horribly wrong."

———

It was early afternoon by the time we got to Bridget Howell High, and campus was buzzing with students who looked impossibly young,

375

staggering under bulky backpacks half their size. Lightly and I beelined to the front office, ignoring the half-curious, half-suspicious stares of kids and hall monitors alike.

A young woman in a hoodie and yoga pants, her dark hair pulled into a high ponytail, sat behind the reception desk.

Lightly frowned at her. I could sense his confusion. She looked about twelve. "Are you...the office manager?"

"Uh-huh," she said, barely turning her head to look at us, her eyes locked on her desktop screen. "What can I do for you?"

"We're here to access your yearbook archive," I said, "if that's okay."

Her head whipped from her screen. "You're the second people in two days to come looking for a yearbook."

Lightly and I exchanged glances. At least we knew Mistress had made it here.

"It's for a project with the Federal Bureau of Investigation," Lightly said, digging out his letter of verification with the Department of Justice seal. The receptionist's eyes widened. "Wow, okay. The other lady didn't say anything about the *FBI.*" She let out a squeal. "This is exciting—like a real-life podcast! Let me print you some visitor badges."

As she ran to the printer, I leaned in to Lightly. "Went straight for the big guns, huh?"

He shook his head, his gaze on the receptionist's ponytail. "I am getting too old for this world."

———

The moment we walked up to the librarian's circulation desk and asked to see the yearbooks, she gasped and flew several steps back. "What is this, some sort of internet prank?"

"Ma'am," Lightly said cautiously, "may I ask what's the matter?"

"You're here to steal my yearbooks!" Unlike the woman in the front office, the high school librarian was a wizened older woman with a bushy halo of salt-and-pepper curls. "You tell your friend I expect my yearbook back immediately, and undamaged. That means no folding the pages!"

I chose to ignore the librarian's raised finger. "The last woman who was here—"

"Mrs. Frazier," the librarian said hotly. "She acted so friendly! Telling me she was a retired librarian and everything. Only to set me up."

Well, well, well, Mistress.

"I can assure you we're not here to steal any of your books." Lightly's voice was velvet. "We just want to take a look at the 2013 edition."

Her eyes narrowed. "How interesting. That's the same book your friend stole."

Lightly and I looked at each other. Sighing, he reached into his pocket and pulled out the FBI letter. "May we see your 2012?"

79

—

NOT EVEN THE FULL-THROATED ENDORSEMENT of the Department of Justice convinced the Bridget Howell High librarian to take her eyes off us. She led us to her yearbook "archive," which was really just a metal cabinet in a back office with the yearbooks stacked, all the way from the school's first year in 1973. We sat side by side at a study table, flipping open the 2012 volume to the Juniors section. The librarian dragged over a chair, metal legs screeching on the floor, and perched nearby.

"H," I murmured, turning pages to search for Bridget. There she was: her girl-next-door prettiness and bashful smile captured for eternity in the small square. "Sixteen," I whispered.

Lightly cleared his throat. "So we track back to the A's and start snapping pictures, and you'll text them to Susan Ramsey to see if she remembers the creep?"

"Yep," I said, flipping to the R's and pointing out Susan, a small, dark-haired girl with a pixie cut and braces. "That's the plan."

"And what do we do if the creep only moved to Carraway Bridget's senior year? What if he's in the missing yearbook?"

I could sense the librarian leaning closer and lowered my voice. "I don't think he did—Bridget's dog went missing her junior year, so I think he's got to be in here if they suspected him."

"Okey dokey," Lightly said, back to the start of the Junior section. "Let's start with Adam Abernathy."

I took careful pictures of each page as we poured through the A's and into the B's. "Carl Beelzebub," I said, shaking my head. "That's rough."

I moved the camera to the next page and snapped.

And froze.

"What?" Lightly asked quickly.

My phone clattered to the table. I didn't have control over my hands anymore.

"Peter," I whispered, eyes glued to the small square.

Lightly followed my gaze, and I knew he hit it when he said, "Jesus and God Almighty."

A young Peter Bishop—our Citizen Night—smiled at us from the yearbook, his blue eyes cherubic, his buzz fresh-cut.

"What's he doing there?" I whispered.

Lightly couldn't take his eyes off the page. "He graduated from a military academy in Montana. I looked him up when we were putting the group together. I found his records."

Tears were beginning to sting my eyes. "Could he have transferred schools his senior year?"

His senior year. The year Bridget died.

"He must've," Lightly murmured. "But why wouldn't he say anything about living in Carraway? Knowing Bridget?"

I don't know if Lightly meant those to be real questions.

We stared at our friend, lost in shock, until the librarian cleared her throat and shifted on her rickety chair.

I seized my phone. "We have more pictures to take. A lot more pages of boys."

Lightly said nothing.

"Lightly?"

Slowly, his eyes lifted. "Text Susan the photo, Searcher."

"But there's the rest of the alphabet—"

His hazel-flecked eyes were so sad. "Text her the picture of Peter."

I did. Susan answered in less than five minutes.

SUSAN RAMSEY: Peter Bishop!! Yes, that's the creep I was talking about. But I already told Tammy Jo.

JANE SHARP: I apologize, but what exactly did you tell Tammy Jo?

SUSAN RAMSEY: I remembered Peter was one of the navy base kids. It was kind of a hike back and forth from the high school to the base, so he used to hang around the school after hours, kind of kill time. I got the impression he didn't want to race home. Sometimes he'd be around when Bridget and I played with her dog Gatsby in her backyard, which backed up to the school. We talked to him a few times, let him play with Gatsby, but we didn't really like him. We were kids, so maybe we were just being mean, but we thought there was something off about him. And then Gatsby went missing, and Bridget searched everywhere for months. One day, I can't remember why, but Bridget got this idea that Peter had taken Gatsby and killed him. She was convinced of it. I think she was going to tell her parents. I told all of this to the cops but they basically implied it was kid stuff and I was wasting their time.

Lightly dropped heavily into his chair.

Citizen had gone to high school with Bridget. He was the creep she thought hurt her dog. He hadn't breathed a word.

Something bad was happening, I felt like I couldn't breathe, like I couldn't expand my lungs enough to take in air. I clutched my ribs.

"Hey, there." Lightly was at my side, rubbing my arm in a fatherly way. "It's okay, Searcher. It's going to be okay."

"I can't breathe right." I shook my head. "I don't know what to do."

"In and out, slow and steady," he coached. "Remember what you always say? We're scientists. We practice dispassion and logic. What would George and Janeway the scientists do? If this were any other case?"

I took my first full breath. "They would retrace the investigation. See where things went wrong."

Lightly nodded, giving my arm a squeeze. "Let's go find Bridget's old detective."

ON OUR SECOND TRIP TO the Carraway Police Department, we were immediately granted an audience with Chief Jim Thomson. Despite Lightly's previous grumbling about the chief's ill-timed fishing vacation, the man who sat across the desk from us didn't look like the type who took much time off. He was on the smaller side, with lines in his face so deep they looked carved. His red-lined blue eyes were shrewd, examining us as he stood to shake our hands.

"So you're my Bridget Howell people." He leaned back in his chair and folded his arms. His voice was raked over, like he'd spent a lifetime smoking cigars. "I was sorry to have missed your last visit."

"It's been hard to get a hold of you," Lightly said. He smiled, but his eyes were probing. "I must've sent you a dozen emails with no response."

Chief Thomson frowned. "What do you mean? I emailed you back every time. Frankly, I thought you must be a little off your rocker. Kept saying you were awaiting my response."

Lightly and I looked at each other. "Mistress wasn't getting any emails back from the high school, either," I said. Could Citizen have done something to block the emails from coming through on the house's network? A horrible thought dropped like a stone into my stomach: Could Goku?

Lightly turned back to the chief. "We're here now, and we have a question for you. You may not recall off the top of your head, but—"

"I remember every detail," the chief interrupted. "Bridget was the biggest case of my career. One of a few homicides here. I won't let it go as long as I live. That's why I taught myself how to read those scientific journals. Our killer probably thought he was safe, that the DNA under Bridget's fingernails was too corroded. But I kept an eye out, looking for advances I could apply to the case."

"Do you remember getting a tip to look at a high school student named Peter Bishop?" I asked. "Bridget's friend Susan Ramsey would've been the one to tell you."

"Yes, I remember Peter." To our surprise, the chief leaned over his desk. "He was one of the first suspects I looked into."

"But there was no record of him in Bridget's file," I said.

Thomson frowned. "Of course there is. Susan Ramsey's statement is right there in the Community Statements folder. Every tip we got from a community member, and a follow-up of how we looked into them. I pride myself on running a tight ship. Your group had access to that file the last time you visited."

"That was Citizen's folder," I said, remembering. "He asked to review that one in particular. He said there was nothing of note."

"He lied," Lightly said. "Walked into the beating heart of the case like he had nothing to fear and calmly redirected us."

The stones kept piling up inside, making me feel heavy.

"I'm not sure who this Citizen is," said Chief Thomson. "But you should know we cleared Peter Bishop. He had an alibi."

Lightly and I both leaned in at the same time. "He did?" I asked.

"He was in a JROTC meeting during the time frame the medical examiner said Bridget was killed. That's Junior Reserve Officers Training. All our students interested in military service join. We tend to get a lot of them, what with the naval base close by. Peter was an active member. He couldn't have killed Bridget."

This was exactly what I wanted—proof that my friend was innocent, that the last twenty-four hours of mounting dread could be wiped away. So why did I feel so reluctant?

It seemed Lightly felt the same. "You can see the high school from the Howells' old house. Are you sure it wasn't possible for Peter to slip out of his meeting and run the short distance without anyone noticing?"

"Look," said the chief with a sigh. "I promise, you're retreading ground I've walked a million times. I never thought a stranger killed Bridget. I always figured it was someone close. And something about that kid never sat right with me. He was good at telling you what you wanted to hear. But when he thought no one was looking, he turned...well, I don't know the right word for it. I've always called it cold. Shark-like, you know? But his alibi was airtight. His JROTC instructor was a retired army captain who ran the PE program at the school. Swore up and down he and Peter were in that meeting for two hours. No way he could've done it."

Unbidden, the acidic thought appeared: *You kissed that man. You wanted more.* My stomach turned. I was going to be sick.

Lightly stood and offered his hand to Chief Thomson. "Thank you for answering our questions. This has been a big help."

The chief smiled ruefully. "You're going to talk to the JROTC instructor, aren't you? Check up on my facts."

"Well," said Lightly pleasantly, "we just might."

As I forced myself to stand and shake the chief's hand, he said, "His name's Cooter Bracken. Lives over on Mallory Street, near the railroad. And if you hurry, you might just catch him 'fore he passes out of this world."

——

It was dark by the time we walked out of the police station. I sucked in deep lungfuls of fresh air, scented spicy and clean by the pine trees.

"I bet if we checked the evidence log, we'd find Citizen didn't even sign his name," Lightly said, his steps hurried. "The boy's been playing us from the get, and we didn't notice. Didn't even think to look."

I took another deep breath, stomach still roiling over the recurring sensory memory of Citizen's lips, his hands on the sides of my face. The hands that could've strangled Bridget.

Lightly eyed me. "Why don't we call it a night? We can't go knocking on a man's door at this hour anyway, and we could use the rest. Hell, we could use the processing time. I saw a Comfort Inn on the way over. We could get ourselves some rooms, grab some toothbrushes and toothpaste from the lobby store."

I was opening my mouth to admit that, humiliatingly, I couldn't afford a night in a hotel. I'd burned through my savings. But Lightly cut in. "My treat, and I'll hear no two words about it. Let's go get some sleep, Search."

That night, as I lay curled on the thin, stiff mattress at the Comfort Inn, my swirling shame and regret over being interested in Citizen conjured thoughts of my father. What I'd done with Citizen and what had possibly happened to my dad weren't the same—not by a long shot—but I couldn't help wonder if he'd known this nauseating feeling of violation, betrayal by someone you trusted. The sinking belief that no amount of logic could make go away that somehow you were at fault. That maybe they'd lied, they'd done awful things, but the guilt still lay with you. So when I finally cried, I cried for the wounded boy and the forty-five-year-old man dying alone in his bed, every time my father had been hurt and I hadn't been there to protect him.

385

81

COOTER BRACKEN LIVED IN THE run-down part of Carraway, where lawns were overgrown and rusted iron grates secured the windows. It was a cooler morning, the sun weak, heavy dew on the grass. Apparently, Citizen and Goku had wound down their whirlwind of police and media interviews, because they'd texted Lightly and me first thing this morning, asking where we were and whether we'd seen them on TV. Lightly cautioned that we should act like everything was normal until we figured out what to do, so we'd written back that we'd gone off to Oregon in search of Mistress but weren't finding much. Lots of dead ends.

Speaking of. Lightly and I walked up to Cooter's small cottage and knocked on the door.

The man who eventually answered was older than I'd pictured. He opened his door and squinted at us through the torn screen, leaning heavily on a cane. His nose was bulbous and red, his face puffy and marked with broken blood vessels.

"Mr. Bracken?" We'd decided I'd take the lead on this one, on account of my youthful, nonthreatening appearance. We were here to dig into some sore spots, after all.

Cooter's eyes were a rheumy gray-green through the screen. "Yes? May I help you?"

I gestured to Lightly. "My colleague Mr. Lightly and I are consultants with the Federal Bureau of Investigations. We were hoping to ask you a few questions about an unsolved case—"

"The Howell girl," he said. With a grunt of exertion, he turned on his cane and started hobbling away into his home. Lightly and I glanced at each other.

"I knew you'd be on my doorstep one day," Cooter said, his back to us. "You might as well come in."

———

The three of us sat around the shabby living room, Lightly and I rather gingerly in a love seat that looked like it was on its last leg, Cooter in a rocking chair. "My ex took all the good furniture in our divorce," Cooter said, patting his rocking chair. "And she deserved it, for the hell I put her through."

Gentle sunlight passed through the windows, illuminating dust motes in the air. I rested my forearms on my knees. "Mr. Bracken—"

"Cooter," he insisted. "Army nickname."

"Okay—Cooter. DNA evidence connects the Howell case to a recent spate of murders in Delphine, Idaho."

"Have you heard about the Delphine killings?" Lightly asked it gently. To me, Cooter was off-putting. But Lightly seemed to feel sorry for him. "They're calling it the work of a serial killer named the Barbie Butcher. He's slain a number of young women."

To my surprise, Cooter leaned back and closed his eyes. "The FBI— you all—you think whoever killed the Howell girl is killing more girls now? He didn't stop?"

"Yes." Lightly was focused on Cooter's face, trying to read him. "We have strong reason to believe it's the same person."

Cooter rocked back, eyes still closed. "Of all the bad things I've done in my life, this may be turn out to be the worst."

"We know Chief Thomson interviewed you twelve years ago about one of your students, a young man named Peter Bishop."

"He was in JROTC with you," I added. "You told the police he was with you during the two-hour window Bridget was killed. You were Peter's alibi."

A heavy silence fell over the room. I guess I hadn't been tactful. The implicit accusation hung in the air.

Suddenly Cooter was seized by a violent, phlegmy cough that shook his whole body, turning his face bright red.

"A glass of water—quick," Lightly said, and I dashed into the messy kitchen, opened cabinets until I found a glass, and filled it at the tap.

Cooter chugged the water gratefully, wiping his mouth. "If it's not the cirrhosis that gets me, it's going to be the emphysema."

"I'm sorry, Mr. Bracken." Lightly's gaze roamed the photographs hung around the living room—men with their arms slung around each other, dressed in army fatigues. "And thank you for your service."

Cooter seemed to slump at the words. "You want to know if I lied about Peter," he said in a low, raw voice. He raised his head. "I did. I lied to Jim and that poor Howell couple. I lied to my wife, my old friends from the army. Back then, I lied to everyone."

Any icy sensation stole through me, half shock, half dread. Cooter was actually recanting. "But why?"

His rheumy eyes dropped. "I was in a dark place in those days. My whole life, really. I can barely remember a time before I had a problem with the drink."

"You struggled with substance abuse issues?" Lightly clarified. "Alcoholism?"

He nodded. "I was at my lowest around the time the Howell girl was killed. I couldn't even get through a day at work without sneaking to my car for a drink. Used to keep a handle of vodka in the trunk." He pressed his hands together. They were shaking. "I've since found God. God and AA. But back then, I was a lost soul. I used to leave the kids to their own devices while I went and got my nip."

"Is that what happened the day Bridget was killed?" I asked. "You left the JROTC meeting?"

Cooter had a faraway look. "He was my best student, Peter. Always the most dedicated. He'd step up and lead the kids whenever I went out. I used to feel sorry for him, you know, on account of how cruel his daddy was." His voice turned into a croak. "Sometimes the military attracts men like that. Mean motherfuckers, men excited to go to war and spill blood. Gives them an excuse to get paid for it. And Peter's mother was a weak woman, I sensed. She wasn't standing up to nobody."

"Cooter," I pressed, "did you leave Peter that day?"

"Yes," he choked. "I barely spent five minutes with the kids before I went out to my car. And I was so ashamed and afraid of getting caught that I lied to everyone when they came to me. I would've lost my job. My marriage was hanging by a thread. I thought I'd lose my wife if it came out, though it turns out there was no stopping that."

I reeled back against the love seat. Silence descended on the room.

Lightly finally broke it. "Mr. Bracken, why come clean now?"

As if in answer, Cooter started hacking. He stopped himself by pounding on his chest. "I didn't think the lie would hurt nobody, I swear. I didn't think it was possible Peter killed that girl. But if there are more bodies, and you think it's him..." He cleared his throat painfully. "Well, I gotta get right with the Lord before I go. And my time is running out."

My phone chimed with a text. Embarrassed to have interrupted Cooter, I almost put it away before I saw the name. "Lightly." I grabbed his arm.

SUSAN RAMSEY: Has Tammy Jo confronted Peter yet? I'm on pins and needles.

Lightly gave me a horrified look.
"Something the matter?" Cooter asked.

JANE SHARP: What do you mean, confronted him?
SUSAN RAMSEY: She said she was in touch with Peter. She knew where he was and could talk to him. She was going to confront him about Bridget and her dog.

"Oh my God," I whispered. "Mistress went to Citizen with the yearbook." A terrible thought seized me. "Lightly, do you think he's capable—"

Lightly shot to his feet, causing Cooter and me to jump back. "We have to get back to Idaho. Now."

82

—

THE SECOND WE STRAPPED INTO the rental car, we turned on NPR. I was refreshing CNN and *CrimeFlash* on my phone and obsessively checking the Network, where there were hints that something was brewing back in Delphine, some news about to break wide open. I prayed it wasn't another victim—a woman in her sixties this time. After ten tense minutes listening to a mind-numbing report on education cuts, the NPR reporter said the magic words: "We have news coming out of Delphine, Idaho in the ongoing saga of the Barbie Butcher case."

Lightly and I straightened against our seats.

"In a shocking development following the arrest of twenty-eight-year-old Odell Rhodes in connection with the Delphine massacres, a lawyer for Mr. Rhodes announced his client has an indisputable alibi for the night of the second slayings at 1756 Collegiate Parkway. Mr. Rhodes's lawyer revealed his client's legal name is actually Owen Rhodes, not Odell, and that he only began to use Odell after his move to Idaho for graduate school."

"Oh my God," I said. "The girl from the Network was right."

"More importantly," continued the NPR reporter in his dulcet tone, the calmness of his voice betraying the incendiary news, "Mr. Rhodes's lawyer provided the DPD, FBI, and national media, including NPR, with records showing his client was in police custody the night of the Collegiate Parkway slayings. According to intake records provided by the Wellington, Washington Police Department, Owen Rhodes was taken into custody at 11:47 p.m. on the night of Saturday, March second, on charges of attempted rape."

"Jesus," Lightly whispered. "A rapist."

"While Mr. Rhodes will face trial for the assault, battery, and attempted rape of a nineteen-year-old woman in Wellington, his lawyer is calling this definitive proof that his client could not have carried out the Delphine murders and has requested the DPD release Mr. Rhodes immediately."

"They got it wrong," I murmured. "Odell's a predator. Just not a killer."

"But how did they get it wrong?" Lightly glanced at me. "How did they mess up that badly? His *name*?"

"Maybe Citizen and Goku were desperate for a fall guy, and Odell was their best shot." But I winced to myself. Saying anything accusatory about them still felt wrong.

"Whatever's happening," Lightly said, "do you think Goku's in on it?"

"I don't know," I said, and I hated that it was the truth.

"While neither the DPD nor FBI has released a statement responding to the lawyer's claims," the reporter continued, "experts watching the case speculate that the agencies may have missed Mr. Rhodes's criminal record due to the inaccurate reporting of his legal name. A response is expected soon, and we'll keep listeners updated." The reporter's voice transitioned into a prerecorded plea for charitable giving.

I put my head between my knees. Between the radio babble, the car's reckless speed, whipping down the highway, and a mess of emotions, I felt nauseous.

"Scientist Sharp," Lightly said, his voice formal, "what are you thinking?"

I turned to face him, my cheek squashed against my knees, and took a deep breath. He was play-acting for me, and I could've hugged him. "I'm remembering it was a Sunday morning when news of the second massacre came out. I was supposed to work that day, but I didn't. And the four of us were on a Signal chat, talking about the murders, when you sent a request to be let in."

Lightly nodded. "I was ready to wipe my hands of sleuthing altogether. I really was. After what went down between Citizen and Goku and the DPD, and the things Chief Reingold said about us being vampires, exploiting tragedy. It got into my head. Made me wonder if the good I thought I was doing was really just my guilt over Juliana talking. But then the news of the second massacre hit. Those poor girls, and one of them a Black woman. I saw Juliana in Shuri Washington and couldn't walk away."

"We weren't talking much that week," I said, bringing myself back. "We were depressed you weren't there. It felt like the group was falling apart, like it was the beginning of the end. That was hard for me, because..." I took another deep breath. "I'd come to need you guys."

"But I came back. We didn't splinter."

That's right. Lightly had come back, and in a twisted way, we had the second massacre to thank. If it hadn't been for the fresh killings, the little family we'd created, the one I'd always sensed meant more to me and Citizen than the others—Mistress, Lightly, and Goku all had their real-life families to provide the companionship Citizen and I only got from them—well, without the second massacre, it would've been over.

I studied Lightly's kind profile. Citizen had been the one to cause the rift in the first place. He'd disappointed Lightly, the man who felt like a surrogate father, even if neither Citizen nor I would admit it out loud. In return, Lightly was going to leave. For both Citizen and me, it would've been the second time a father abandoned us.

"What?" Lightly asked, glancing at me warily from the driver's seat.

"Is it possible..." I forced myself to speak. "That Citizen could have driven from Washington to Idaho, committed the murders at Collegiate Parkway, and then driven back? And concealed where he was on our video chat with the background photo of his kitchen?"

Lightly rubbed his jaw. "It's only an eight-hour drive from where he lives in Washington to Delphine. If the four of us believed he was at home at the time of the killings, and we'd vouch that we'd seen him in his home, that would give him a solid alibi. Signal doesn't track your location. That's the whole reason we use it. It's kind of perfect, from an exculpatory point of view."

We were discussing the ways our friend could've committed an act of unthinkable violence as if it were any other case. The surrealness was dizzying.

"And the most damning evidence," Lightly said. "That eyelash DNA you found proves the same person was at both the Collegiate Parkway murders and Bridget Howell's. If we think Citizen killed Bridget..."

"Then it has to be him at Collegiate Parkway," I finished. The car hurtled on, hitting every pothole. "If Citizen is a—a..." I couldn't bring myself to say it. "Do you think he hurt Mistress, even though she's his friend?"

"That's what I'm worried about," Lightly said. "If he really did those things—if he killed Bridget when he was seventeen to keep her from telling anyone about his violent compulsions, and he killed those college girls to get me to come back..." Lightly paused. "And probably to prove he could get away with it, too, because you know how big his ego is. If he did all that, then he's capable of killing in cold blood to get what he wants. And Mistress, if she confronted him—well, she'd be the biggest threat of all."

Suddenly, to my shock, a sound emerged from Lightly the likes of which I'd never heard. It was a wail of anguish—a cry of deepest pain. The car swerved, and we bounced onto the shoulder, skidding to a stop.

"Lightly!" I shouted.

"I'm sorry, Jane." Lightly twisted the wheel and screeched back onto the highway. "I'm so sorry."

I stared at him. Tears rolled down his face. His shoulders shook. At first, I was as frozen as I'd been by my mother's display of grief. But I thought of how Lightly would've comforted me—what my father, if he'd been here, would've done—and I reached out, gripping his shoulder. I squeezed.

"It's going to be okay," I promised.

"If he killed those girls because of me," he choked. "If Shuri and Greta and Katya lost their lives as part of some game, to lure me back…" His hands clutched the steering wheel. "If he targeted a Black girl because he knew she'd remind me of Juliana, and I wouldn't be able to turn away—all their deaths are on my hands."

"No, they're not, Lightly. Don't say that."

"I've failed so many people in my life."

"No." All I could do was grip his arm tighter. "It's okay. It's not your fault." We had three hours until we arrived in Idaho. For three hours, I could be Lightly's caregiver, his comforter. I could give back to him what he'd given to me.

I'd never gotten to do that with my own father. Never got to protect him or tell him I saw his heart, and his love for me, and would do anything to take care of him. But I was there in that car with Lightly, present in his hour of need.

Sometimes, life hands you moments of unexpected grace.

83

—

WE ARRIVED AT THE DELPHINE Police Headquarters to a roiling battleground. Those famous photographs of Delphine that rolled across every network, the pictures that topped the *New York Times* and *Washington Post* articles, those graphic images of protestors rioting—this is where they came from. Even Natalie Flowers chose a still of the riots to grace the cover of *Angels of Death*: that infamous moment when dusk was descending and a group of protestors lit the department's trash cans on fire and it looked like city would burn by nightfall.

The headquarters normally resembled a park—a large brick building flanked on four sides by trim green grass, brightly painted bike racks, and wide sidewalks. But protestors flooded the lawn, spilling over the sidewalks into the streets. They were divided into dueling factions: on the left, chanting and banging on drums, young protestors and protestors of color waved signs that read "DPD Discriminates," "BPD is Not a Crime," and "Free Owen Rhodes." Opposing them on the right were older protestors, many wearing American-flag-themed baseball caps and rifle silhouettes on their hoodies, yelling under signs that read "Justice for the Delphine Six," "Rapist + Murderer," and "Odell Deserves Death." Swarming around them were reporters with TV cameras trailing. It was mayhem in small-town America.

Lightly screeched to the curb and shoved the car into park. He'd gathered himself by then, but the skin around his eyes remained puffy, the whites of his eyes shot with red. He took a deep breath and squared his shoulders. "Come on, then. Let's see if we can part this Red Sea."

We plunged into the battleground. Lightly led, aiming for the front doors of the police station, but the crowd was too thick to make progress.

"False confessions are *real*," shouted a woman holding a "Free Owen" sign. She was so close that I jumped and nearly tripped into another protestor. "It's police abuse! Exploitation of the mentally ill!"

Lightly pushed around a group of men shouting at each other about valuing the life of a rapist over six innocent girls. One man whipped off his ball cap, and Lightly quickly veered away. Everywhere we went, people shoved us, blocking our path. It was insanity. Only the urgency of what we had to tell the cops kept me trying.

"Excuse me," I called to a young woman, whose friend waved a "BPD is Not a Crime" sign. "Are you saying Owen Rhodes has borderline personality disorder?"

She gave me a quick scan and must've decided I wasn't the enemy, nodding and shouting over the chaos: "The DPD released the information a few hours ago. Like it's some sort of crime! People with borderline aren't automatically violent—that's discrimination *and* fearmongering!" The last part she shouted in my face.

"All right, I got it," I said, backing away.

"Come on, Search," Lightly yelled. "I see a path."

"You can't let rapists walk free," a white-haired woman shouted at me. "Let this monster out, and he'll rape and kill again!"

Lightly yanked me past her, and we found ourselves facing the glass front doors. Armed officers stood on the other side, barricading the entrance. They waved at us to go away.

"Shoot," Lightly said and scrambled in his coat, pulling out our well-worn letter from the FBI. He smoothed it and pressed it against the glass.

Someone stumbled into me from behind, almost knocking me over. The officer reading the letter from behind the glass finally gave a curt nod, then turned and barked something to the officers behind him.

"Get ready," Lightly warned.

The glass doors surged open and officers poured out, waving at us. Lightly and I leapt inside. I could hear the newly animated shouts of the protestors, feel them pushing me, trying to get inside. Luckily, the officers sealed the door behind us before anyone did anything stupid. Then they turned their glares and guns on us.

"We're here to see FBI Agent Lawrence Hale," Lightly panted. "We have emergency information on the Butcher case."

———

This time, there was no emperor's walk down the halls, nor a welcoming conference table with an eager audience of cops. Lightly and I were dumped in an interrogation room, where we waited at a cold metal table in back-breaking chairs for nearly forty-five minutes. It was dark and icy; I sat with my arms wrapped over my chest, teeth chattering.

"I'm starting to think they don't like us," I managed to say over the shivering.

Lightly scanned the gray walls with a rueful look. "A lot has changed since the last time we were here. I can't imagine the DPD or FBI are very happy."

Finally, the door opened and Agent Hale swept inside, followed hot on his heels by Chief Reingold, who stabbed an accusatory finger at us. "You played us!"

Lightly looked at me as if to say *Told you.*

"Garret," snapped Agent Hale. "Calm down."

"We didn't have anything to do with Odell—Owen," I protested. "He was Goku and Citizen's suspect."

Hale sighed and pulled out a chair on the other side of the table. The chief remained standing behind him, arms crossed. "I need you to level with me, George." Hale's voice was weary. "Because the last time you and your sleuths turned up, we acted on your information and everything went to hell in a handbasket."

"Lawrence, I'm sorry Owen Rhodes turned out to be a dead end. But you and I both know it was your responsibility to vet the information."

The two old friends stared at each other from across the table. I shifted and rubbed my arms.

"That's rich," Chief Reingold scoffed. "Truly rich."

Lightly glanced at him. "Where are Brian and Peter now?"

"You don't know?"

Hale leaned back and folded his arms. "We haven't been able to make contact with Brian Goddins or Peter Bishop since Owen Rhodes's lawyer announced his alibi."

My mouth dropped. "They disappeared? Did you check our rental house?"

The chief glared at me.

"George," Hale repeated. "Given the unfortunate events of the last forty-eight hours, my superior officer is flying in from the District. He'll be here any minute, so I don't have much time. They said you have intelligence."

The chief snorted. I was beginning to think the public wasn't wrong in their distaste.

Lightly glanced at me, and I nodded. He straightened. "We do. But before we tell you, we want to strike a deal."

"You've got to be kidding," crowed the chief. He spun on his heel. "Can you believe these guys?"

Hale kept his cool, merely raising an eyebrow. "What kind of deal?"

Lightly gestured at me. "Jane told you that our friend Tammy Jo Frazier has gone missing. It's now been well past twenty-four hours. And we have reason to believe she confronted the actual Barbie Butcher and may be in life-threatening danger. You promised to look into it, but I haven't seen any help materialize from the Bureau."

Hale gave a small laugh. "I've been a little busy cleaning up the Owen Rhodes fiasco, George. The one your boys handed to me."

"Be that as it may," Lightly said, "our condition for telling you the true identity of the Butcher is that the FBI make searching for Tammy Jo an immediate priority."

"You can't leverage the identity of the Butcher," Chief Reingold thundered. "We'll charge you with conspiracy."

Lightly and I looked at each other again. Then he turned back to the chief and repeated, "Be that as it may."

While Chief Reingold cursed, Agent Hale coolly surveyed us. "All right, George," he said finally. "Jane. You have a deal." He picked up his phone, keeping his eyes on us. When the person on the other end picked up, he said, "I need a unit to track a missing person, name Tammy Jo Frazier, age—"

"Sixty-five," Lightly said.

"Sixty-five. Last seen—"

"In an Uber on her way to Carraway, Oregon."

"You catch that?" Hale asked. "Good. This is top priority. Check in circa twenty-hundred." Then hung up. "Okay. Your turn."

"This better be good," the Chief muttered, and dropped into the last chair.

"Thank you, Lawrence." Lightly nodded at me. "We're going to start at the beginning, so you can judge the evidence for yourself. Jane is the one who drove this bus, so she's going to tell it."

I unfolded my arms. "It started with the woman I told you about. The sorority house mom, Elizabeth Bath."

Over the course of the next hour and a half, Lightly and I laid out everything for Chief Reingold and Agent Hale: my online research into Lizzie, my illicit search of her room in the KD house ("You're lucky you didn't take any evidence," the Chief grumbled, "else you'd catch a charge"). Lightly's mounting suspicion that the Queen Lace and Collegiate Parkway murders were committed by two separate people, potentially Lizzie and Owen ("Absolute bullshit," protested the chief), and then the huge shake-up in the case: Mistress's disappearance. The crumbs of her suspicions that had led us to the high school, then the Carraway police station, and finally to the retired JROTC teacher Cooter Bracken. And all the evidence, piling up against our will, that pointed to none other than our friend Peter Bishop.

The chief exploded out of his chair the moment we said Peter's name. "You're fucking kidding me," he yelled. "That's it, right? This is some elaborate joke? Did Fox News put you up to this?"

Agent Hale faced the chief. "Garrett, for the millionth time, I know tensions are high and you haven't slept, but I need you to settle down." He turned to us. "Let me get this straight: you're telling me that one of the men *you* brought into my orbit, that *you* vouched for, that *you* helped convince me to make a consultant, is a serial killer. And the second one may be his accomplice."

Lightly's expression was grave. "I take full responsibility. I'm deeply sorry, Lawrence."

"No, you don't," I snapped. "If Citizen is the killer—"

"*If?*" boomed the chief. "Now you're saying *if?*"

"Then it's not anyone's responsibility but his own," I continued. "And Goku's, if he helped." I was afraid to think too hard about that or to remember Goku's fierce loyalty to Citizen.

"No." Agent Hale said the word with such firmness. "We're all to blame. The FBI's background check on Peter Bishop didn't catch anything other than some mildly concerning internet history. And maybe I didn't look deeper because I was moving fast and trusted George. This is on all of us."

The four of us studied each other—the chief, red-faced and furious; Lightly, his expression self-recriminating; Agent Hale, exhausted. "What now?" I asked.

"We cannot tell the public we've had the killer under our nose for months," burst Chief Reingold. "Or that we allowed him into this department. And the FBI. It'll be worse than Rader or the Zodiac Killer combined. The journos will eat us alive."

I gaped at him. "What are you going to do—*lie*?"

"We can move quietly. We don't even know where Bishop is anymore—for all we know, he's fled the state. He could be anyone's problem—"

"*Goddammit,* Chief!" The interrogation room fell silent. We all stared in shock at Lightly, whose face radiated anger. "Grow a spine and admit you fucked up. Take your whooping like a man."

For a long time, the chief remained quiet, staring at Lightly. Finally, he said, "Thirty-seven years I've been on the force. And this is how it's going to end." He seized the door and stormed out, letting it bang against the doorframe with a loud crack that echoed between the three of us.

Lightly looked at Agent Hale. To my surprise, Hale cracked a smile. "'Take your whooping like a man,' huh?" He shook his head. "See, this is why I don't disrespect my elders."

Lightly shifted. "What's your plan, Lawrence?"

Agent Hale straightened his wrinkled suit—the same suit, I realized, we'd seen him in two days ago—and leaned over, resting his fingers on the table. "Here's what's going to happen. This time, we're thoroughly vetting your information before making any moves. I'll have my people dig into the evidence and investigate Bishop. We'll get an emergency warrant to collect his DNA, compare it against the Collegiate Parkway sample."

"Thank—" Lightly started, but Hale interrupted. "In the meantime, Mr. Bishop and Mr. Goddins will be listed as wanted men, potentially armed and highly dangerous. We'll put out an APB alerting law enforcement to be on the lookout."

"Goku will hear it," I said. "He tracks police communications."

Agent Hale nodded. "Noted. I'm going to release you now, but I need you to remember: if there's anyone in this world Peter and Brian now have cause to want dead, it's the two of you. Play it safe."

84
—

WE DIDN'T KNOW WHAT WE'D find back at the Airbnb. Lightly unlocked the door and flipped on the lights. We both held our breath and listened hard. But it was silent, not even the whir of the air conditioner. Slowly, we made our way from room to room, flinging open closet doors and checking under beds, even pulling down the ladder to the attic. Finally, we were satisfied. Wherever Goku and Citizen were, they weren't lying in wait for us here.

After we washed up, Lightly dragged a pile of blankets and a pillow into my room and settled himself on the floor. He wouldn't hear of swapping places. We'd raided the kitchen and brought the knife block and loose steak knives with us, piling half beside Lightly, half on my bedside table. Finally, we locked the door and dragged my small dresser in front of it. If Citizen and Goku came for us in the night, we'd at least be more prepared than the poor Delphine girls.

But the next morning, gentle sunlight woke us. I rolled over to face Lightly, whose eyes were still closed on the floor. "I guess they weren't stupid enough to come."

"I guess not," he murmured.

The clicking of a lock and scrape of a door came from downstairs. Lightly and I both sat straight up. "Oh, fuck," I whispered.

"Get your knives," he said, sweeping his own butcher knife out of the knife block before creeping to the door.

I leapt out of bed and seized two steak knives, one for each hand.

The staircase creaked. "Hello?" shouted a voice. "Lightly? Searcher? You there?"

"Goku," I hissed, but Lightly turned and held his finger to his lips.

"Guys?" There was knocking below us, then more pounding up the stairs. Goku was coming to the third floor. Was Citizen behind him? I tried to count the footsteps.

My bedroom door shook as he banged on it. "Searcher, are you in here? Something's going on I don't understand."

Lightly and I looked at each other. It could be a trap.

"Goku, are you alone?" Lightly boomed.

The knocking stopped. "Lightly? Is that you? Is Searcher with you?"

Lightly shook his head at me. "Is Citizen with you?" he called.

"No, I'm alone. I don't know where he is."

"Are you telling the truth?" I yelled. "You really don't know?"

"He left me," Goku shouted from behind the door. "I don't know what's happening. Everything's falling apart, you guys. It wasn't Odell. The cops are looking for us, and I don't know what to do."

"Do you know what Citizen did?" Lightly kept the butcher knife pointed at the door.

"What do you mean?" Goku had stopped shouting, so it was harder to hear. I crept closer to the door.

"To Bridget?" I said. "Do you really not know?"

Goku's voice turned shrill, pleading. "Someone tell me what the fuck is going on—"

A crash came from downstairs, then so many voices shouting it became cacophony. I screamed, and Lightly clapped a hand over my mouth.

"What the fuck?" Goku yelled as the noise traveled up the stairs. That's when I heard it: "Brian Goddins and Peter Bishop, get on your knees!"

"It's the Feds," Lightly whispered. The door to my room boomed, shaking on its hinges, like a body had been thrown into it. I could hear Goku's screams among the shouts to get on his knees.

"Lightly—" I started to yell, but there was no time—with a mighty quake the door to my room cracked in half, a battering ram smashed through it.

"Drop the knives!" Lightly shouted, but they came through too fast, men in bulletproof vests emblazoned with the letters FBI.

"They're armed!" the first agent yelled, and we were swarmed, our hands struck with batons so our knives clattered to the floor.

"Stop!" I yelled. "We're innocent! Find Agent Hale!"

They seized us, wrenching our arms behind our backs and snapping handcuffs over our wrists, then pushed us forward so hard they nearly lifted me off the ground. My arms twisted in their sockets and I screamed in pain, begging them to find Hale, but they only shoved us down the stairs, through the living room, and out the door.

The front lawn was a war zone. Unmarked cop cars flooded the street, red-and-blue lights swirling. Black-clad FBI agents with raised guns ran past us into the house. I couldn't hear what they were shouting over the catastrophic whir of the helicopter above, kicking up gale-force winds that blew my hair back. The agent with a vice grip on my arms thrust me forward.

"You're hurting me!" I yelled, twisting to face him, but he screamed at me to face forward.

"Get on your knees," he shouted, shoving me into the wet grass, the cold dew staining the knees of my father's flannel pants.

"I didn't do anything," I yelled. Hot tears rolled down my face. Bursts of light and snapping at the perimeter alerted me to the line of reporters being pushed back by the Feds. They lifted cameras anyway, flashing at me, capturing my tears and the chaos of the raid.

"I don't care if you shoved the knife in yourself or you were just his accomplice," snarled the agent, giving me a rough shake. "You're going to spend the rest of your life in prison for what you did to those girls."

I tilted my face to the sky, searching for the clouds above the helicopter, where I was sure my father looked down. "I'm sorry, Dad." I pushed the words out between my sobs. "I'm so sorry."

Twenty feet away, Lightly landed hard on his knees in the grass, gripped by his own set of FBI agents. He was staring in horror at something in the distance. I followed his gaze and saw Goku thrashing in the arms of four agents against an unmarked SUV. "I didn't do anything!" he screamed. "Get your hands off me!"

He was going to get himself killed.

"It's over, Brian," Lightly yelled. "You need to tell them everything."

The sound of Lightly's voice made Goku turn. When he spotted us, he nearly sank to his knees, the fight in him dying. "Why are they here? What's happening, Lightly?"

I gathered as much breath as I could and shouted, "Where's Mistress?"

"I don't know!" he yelled. The agents opened the door to the SUV and began wrestling Goku inside. "I swear!" The door shut and he disappeared inside.

"Up," my agent barked and didn't wait before pulling me up by my handcuffs, wrenching my wrists. "See that car?" He pointed over my shoulder at another unmarked vehicle. "You're going there. No trouble, and no talking to reporters, you understand?"

"I got something!" came a shout from behind, startling us all enough that when I turned, my agent didn't stop me.

A DPD officer ran from the porch, waving a piece of paper.

"What is it?" I asked, but the agent holding me shoved me forward.

"Shut up and get in the car."

"Tell me what it is!"

He pushed me so hard I fell over on the leather seat, nearly landing in the lap of the seated agent waiting for me. She said nothing, inscrutable behind a pair of dark sunglasses, but got me seated and secured my seat belt.

From behind the mirrored windows, I watched FBI agents circle the DPD officer and examine the piece of paper. They all turned to face someone striding across the lawn. It was Lawrence Hale, trailed by a distinguished-looking older white man in a bulletproof vest. It must be Hale's superior officer, the one who'd flown in from DC. Hale scanned the piece of paper and barked a question. The agents looked around until one of them pointed at my car, then the car behind me. Hale said something sharp and marched in my direction.

My heart soared. I tasted something coppery and wiped my lip on my shoulder, smearing blood on my T-shirt.

Hale wrenched the door open and stuck his head inside. "Get her out of those handcuffs. Jane Sharp is an informant."

"Thank you." I was embarrassed to feel tears crawling down my face.

"What do you know about this message?" Hale asked as the other agent departed in search of keys to unlock me. "We think it might've come from Peter."

He held up the sheet of printer paper. On it was a simple message, scrawled in Citizen's distinctive neat handwriting: *She's at 1892 Border Lane. I just needed time.*

There was something about the address I recognized. I closed my eyes and concentrated until it hit me. Border Lane was where Stacie Flowers's family lived. It was where they had their big lodge and sprawling horse ranch, where I'd gone for that ill-fated dinner. "It's Mistress," I said, struggling against the cuffs. "He's telling us where she is. And I know that place—it's close to the Flowerses' house."

I could've leapt. The note had to mean she was alive, right? But Agent Hale picked up his phone and spoke sharply. "I need federal SWAT and forensic teams to 1892 Border Lane. Prepare for possible engagement with an armed perp and a homicide scene."

"Homicide?" My voice faltered as the female FBI agent tugged at me and unlocked my cuffs.

Agent Hale hung up. "We don't know what we're walking into. We could be looking at a third massacre. Think about that before you decide whether you're coming with us."

A third massacre. You and I both know, with the benefit of hindsight, that it was bound to happen. There was too much unfinished business, too much rage, justice unmet. But at that moment, bruised and bleeding in the back of a federal vehicle, I couldn't fathom it.

"So." Hale cocked his head. "What will it be?"

85

—

THE ADDRESS IN THE NOTE wasn't close to the Flowerses' house—it was the Flowerses' house. I'll never forget the terror on that family's face when an army of federal agents and a helicopter raced down their rural road and descended on their ranch. Stacie's father ran out the front door as agents in bulletproof vests, pistols drawn, poured out of black cars. He tried to shield his wife and daughter, but Mrs. Flowers and Natalie pushed out behind him.

Mrs. Flowers broke away and ran toward Agent Hale, a wild animal look on her face. "What happened to Stacie?"

Grief threatened to choke me as I climbed out. She was so traumatized that her daughter was already dead, and she still thought the agents had come to tell her something horrible had happened.

"No, ma'am," said Agent Hale, sweeping an arm to indicate the arsenal of firepower behind him. "I'm sorry to disturb you, but we have reason to believe Stacie's killer is either on your property or has placed victims here."

"Jesus," Mr. Flowers said, paling. "Why here?"

That was when I did lose control. It was my fault. Citizen must've been keeping an eye on me, following me to dinner somehow, or he'd looked into the Flowerses' ranch after I told him about my visit. He must've seen how big their property was, all the room for hiding.

"Hey." Lightly came up beside me. "It's okay, Searcher." He patted my shoulder with a cut-up hand, courtesy of the FBI.

All three members of the Flowers family turned to me. Mrs. Flowers frowned. "Veronica? What are you doing here?"

"Mrs. Flowers, that's Jane Sharp, a consultant for the FBI. She's been working on your daughter's case."

Both Mrs. and Mr. Flowers went rigid with shock, but Natalie—I have never seen a look more hateful than the one she gave me in that moment. I'd lied and taken advantage of her family's grief. I knew then that she would loathe me forever.

Agent Hale snapped their attention back. "Are there any parts of your property you haven't visited in a while? Any you can imagine someone being hidden? I know you have twenty acres." We'd been briefed on the property by FBI analysts as we raced over. "Maybe something far enough away where you wouldn't hear screaming?"

Mrs. Flowers blanched. "We haven't used any of the property since Stacie passed. It's all gone to seed."

"It's a big ranch." Mr. Flowers raked his hand over his face. "We have the horse stables, the firepit, the shed out by the fishing pond—"

"The grain silo," Natalie interrupted. It wasn't a suggestion. She said it with conviction. "If you were going to hide someone on our property, that's where you'd do it. It's the farthest spot from the house, and you can get to it from the road at the back of the property. Perfect for sneaking in unnoticed. No windows. Thick walls."

"Thank you," said Agent Hale. "Mr. Flowers, I need you to direct us. The rest of the family remains in the house."

He turned to the agents and shouted, "We have a location!" Then he looked at me and Lightly and lowered his voice. "Brace yourselves."

———

They turned off the sirens as the cars slid silently down the road. According to Mr. Flowers, the grain silo was left over from the previous owner, who'd run the ranch as a working wheat farm. When we cut close enough to see the weathered building above the treetops, Agent Hale's voice barked through the radio to halt. The SWAT team crept out of their cars, Lightly and I bringing up the rear, bound into heavy, uncomfortable Kevlar vests. It was surreal, but I told myself I'd process the out-of-body feeling later. Now was about Mistress.

The silence was shattered by shouting from the agents at the door. The swift boom of a battering ram nearly took it off its hinges. The black-clad agents flooded inside, weapons raised. But as they filed in, I heard no gunfire, no hint of Citizen screaming. An agent yelled, "Secure!" and Lightly and I pushed our way inside, scanning the large, circular, aluminum-sided space.

There was a small figure curled in a ball on the ground.

My heart crashed.

"Tammy Jo!" Lightly cried. We pushed through the agents, dropping to our knees beside her prone body.

"Mistress." She lay on her side. I shook her shoulders. She was wearing the outfit I remembered from the day she'd left for Oregon, a black sweatshirt that said "Free Mom Hugs," and jeans that revealed the zip tie binding her frail ankles. There was an empty jug of water and a pile of Nature Grain wrappers by her side. She reeked of urine.

"Tammy Jo, wake up," Lightly insisted, rolling her on her back. Her hands were bound in front of her with a zip tie, too.

"Medical to the back!" a SWAT agent shouted.

"Greg?" Mistress's voice was thin and reedy. Her small eyes squinted open, missing her eyeglasses. She sounded young and confused as her gaze shifted to me. "Kristen?"

She was alive. I pressed my face into her dirty sweatshirt. "Thank God."

"Tammy Jo, it's George," Lightly said. "George and Jane. Are you okay? Did he hurt you?"

"Thirsty," she croaked, and that's when the medical team shoved Lightly and me out of the way and snapped through the plastic binding Mistress. They took her vitals and checked her body with quick, flitting hands, looking for broken bones and lacerations.

"Severely dehydrated," one of the examiners said, and the other rooted in his bag and pulled out a bottle of water. "Take it slow," he instructed Mistress, who ignored him and guzzled the water with shaking hands. The places where the zip tie had cut into her wrist were raw and bloody.

"It was Peter" came her ragged voice. The water seemed to have sharpened her. Her eyes searched over the shoulders of the medics to find me and Lightly. "He killed Bridget."

"We know," Lightly said. "We traced your footsteps when you went missing."

She squeezed her eyes shut. "I found him in the yearbook. I was going to confront him at the park with Jane, in a public place, but he beat her there, and somehow he knew—"

"Mrs. Frazier." Agent Hale knelt beside the medics. "Where is Peter Bishop now?"

She shook her head, her small eyes filling with tears, naked without her glasses. "I don't know. He brought me here. He swore he wouldn't hurt me, said he just needed time." She coughed and brought the bottle to her lips. "He said he'd been so careful all these years, keeping track of the case. They didn't even have usable DNA until four months ago."

"He thought he'd gotten away with it," I whispered.

"He said he needed to turn in Odell Rhodes, and then he'd disappear," Mistress stuttered.

"Did he transport you in his car?" Agent Hale asked. "Is he armed?"

She made a choking sound. "I don't know. He's just a...Yes, he's in his car. I don't think he's armed, but that doesn't make him less dangerous."

I knew what she meant. Citizen's brain was the danger.

Hale barked into his phone: "Bishop is on the run in his Suburban, reported not armed, last known location 1892 Border Lane." He gestured to the medics. "Let's get her to a hospital."

As they bent to lift Mistress to her feet, my eyes filled with tears. I'd come so close to losing someone I loved again. "I'm so glad you're okay."

"Tammy Jo." Lightly's voice was urgent. "You know Citizen didn't just kill Bridget, right?"

Mistress started crying in earnest as the medics helped her across the silo. "He was my son. I can't...I think the shock is the worst part."

"I know," Lightly said. "Trust me."

Mistress turned and seized my arm. "It came back for me, Jane. All these years later."

"What did?"

Her voice wavered. "Kidnapped by a killer."

I stopped in my tracks, kicking up dust. The fate she'd dodged at twenty—being kidnapped by a serial killer—had lain in wait for her for forty-five years. The bizarre cruelty of it, as if it had been her fate. The medics escorted her forward, but I was rooted. "I'm so sorry."

Mistress turned over her shoulder, her eyes unfocused, widening, as if she were seeing something in the distance that surprised her. I wondered if she had a concussion the medics had missed. "No," she said. "It's a relief. I paid the debt. Now I'm free."

OVERNIGHT, PETER BISHOP WENT FROM an FBI consultant, decorated naval officer, and famous internet sleuth to the most wanted man in America. At least, that's what Agent Hale told us. The FBI took our phones for monitoring, shepherding Lightly and me to a safe house outside their Larabie County field office. We'd been too tired after the raid and Mistress's rescue to do anything but call our loved ones on an agent's phone before crashing. Lightly had spoken to Junie in hushed whispers for close to an hour, but I'd gotten my mom's voice-mail. I wondered what she'd think when she heard I was in the custody of the FBI, being shielded from a serial killer who had reasons to want me dead. Maybe *I told you so.* Or maybe she'd see me being apprehended on national news before she even got the message.

That was my last thought before I fell into an uneasy sleep.

The next morning Lightly and I were grumbling over the safe house's Keurig machine—"Can't even spring for real coffee for people putting their lives on the line?" Lightly grunted, and I'd agreed—when the front door opened and Mistress entered using a cane, wearing fresh clothes, and flanked by two federal agents and three middle-aged people who buzzed around her. I recognized them immediately from photos:

Mistress's son, Greg, his husband, Mateo, and her daughter, Kristen. All three of them must've jumped on flights the moment they got her call.

"Did you miss me?" Mistress sang as she hobbled into the kitchen, ignoring a protesting Greg, who insisted she was moving too fast.

"More than you know," I said. Lightly and I folded her into a three-way hug. I squeezed her, then pulled back. "Oh, God, sorry—does that hurt?"

"Pssh." She waved a bandaged hand. Both of her wrists were wrapped with gauze, as were her ankles. "Minor ligature wounds is all. Nothing we haven't seen a thousand times."

"And severe dehydration, and bruising all over your body," Greg added. "The doctors said she was lucky she'd been kidnapped and abandoned during the spring. If it had been during the Idaho winter, she would've been a goner." He frowned. "I think he was trying to make a joke."

Mateo kissed his husband's cheek while Mistress surveyed the house with a critical eye. "Hmm," she tsked. "Not as nice as our rental. But I guess we're only here to pack up and get on our way."

The six of us made our official introductions and were sitting around the living room with steaming mugs of subpar coffee, listening to Mistress recount her kidnapping ("It gets more dramatic every time she tells it," Kristen said), when the lock slid noisily in the front door. We froze, eyes glued to the entrance.

The door slowly pushed open. One of the agents who'd escorted Mistress and her family peered in, then waved at whoever was behind him to follow.

Goku took a hesitant step into the house. When he saw us, he stopped so suddenly that someone walked into him and bounced away.

The FBI had released him. Which meant they'd questioned him and didn't find him guilty.

The four of us stared at each other. No one had brought Goku new clothes. He still wore the same torn and dirty jeans and *Dragon Ball Z* shirt from the raid. His bottom lip was swollen, and a purple bruise bloomed around his left eye.

The people behind him finally shoved past into the house. Goku's parents, Sharon and Joseph, looked every inch the hippie California schoolteachers he'd described. His mother started to say something, then read the standoff and fell quiet.

"I didn't know." Goku's anguished voice finally broke silence. His dark eyes were glassy. The FBI agents tucked a row of suitcases inside the house and shut the door. "I swear to you. I had no idea what he was really doing. Who he really—" He choked, unable to finish.

"You two were so close," I said quietly, gripping my mug. "You never guessed?"

Mistress and Lightly watched him.

"No." Goku looked me in the eyes. "I know that must make me unbelievably stupid—at the very least, the worst detective in America—but I never once suspected. I thought it was Odell the whole time. I was terrified of him."

His eyes slid to Mistress, sitting on the couch with her wrists and ankles wrapped, and the tears that had turned his eyes glassy spilled over. "I can't believe he hurt you." His mother turned away sharply at the sight of her son's genuine pain, and that was the moment I believed him.

It seemed Mistress did too, because she leaned hard on her cane, ignoring Greg's protests, and rose from the couch, making her way slowly to Goku. "It's okay," she said quietly. "I know who you are." When she opened her arms, Goku clutched her to his broad chest.

Lightly and I staggered up, too, adding our hugs once Mistress released him. "I'm so sorry, Search," Goku breathed into my hair. "I feel like such an idiot."

"We all do," I promised. "The Network's never going to let us live it down." His laugh at my bad joke rumbled through him.

When we'd finished hugging, we did another round of introductions. Goku asked Lightly where Junie was.

"Probably at O'Hare, waiting on my flight," he joked. "I told her to stay put, but who knows? The woman doesn't take well to instructions."

I looked at all of them: Goku's parents, Mistress's kids, Junie, who was waiting in Chicago. Sharp pain splintered my chest. My dad would've come. He would've crossed to the ends of the earth for me. I felt the loss of him all over, a near-crippling blow.

Goku's dad rocked awkwardly on his heels. "So...anyone hear the latest in the case?"

87

—

WE WRANGLED AN FBI AGENT into finding us the TV remote, then arranged ourselves around the living room, waiting for the news.

"Turn it to Nina Grace," I said impatiently, and Goku obliged, flipping to *CrimeFlash*. An all-caps chyron under Nina's perfectly coiffed hair and red power suit screamed, "SERIAL KILLER IDENTITY REVEALED IN SHOCKING TWIST."

"If you're just tuning in to what has to be the most unbelievable, serpentine, stranger-than-fiction case I've ever witnessed," Nina drawled, "let me fill you in. In a bombshell development out of Idaho, the FBI and Delphine police have announced their lead suspect in the slayings of six Northern Idaho University students is twenty-nine-year-old naval officer Peter Bishop." A picture of Citizen looking beautiful and serious in his navy dress whites appeared on-screen. A wicked grin curled Nina's mouth, making her look positively Grinch-like. "If you're wondering why that name seems so familiar, it's because Peter Bishop is not only a well-known internet personality—you might remember him from a recent *Newsline* episode on true crime—but an FBI consultant. There's more—Bishop is also the man who turned in a recording of graduate student Owen Rhodes confessing to the murders, a confession that was later proven to be false and influenced by Bishop's leading questions."

Goku winced.

"I mean, Deacon, where do we even start?" The screen shifted, and three faces stared back at us, two guest experts flanking Nina in the middle.

The man on her left adjusted round, professorial glasses. "They're calling him the 'Web Sleuth Killer' now, aren't they?"

"Apparently the 'Barbie Butcher' is so last month," Nina quipped, and he made a show of laughing.

"What I want to know is how a person goes from being lauded by *Newsline* for solving cases to being torn apart by Chief Reingold as an example of what's wrong with true crime in America to working with the FBI. *What is* the story there?"

"And to have the very person who accused Rhodes turn out to be a suspect himself," broke in the dark-haired woman to Nina's right, her red lipstick so bright it rivaled Nina's suit. "You almost have to wonder—is no one doing their homework at the DPD or FBI?"

Nina widened her eyes. "Get this, Mackenzie. Not only is Bishop accused of the Delphine slayings, but our sources say he's also the prime suspect in the 2012 murder of a seventeen-year-old girl named Bridget Howell, who sleuths connected to the Delphine slayings last month."

"The woman who broke that news on the *Murder Junkies* podcast," Deacon said. "How is she connected to Peter Bishop?"

My throat tightened. Any second, they'd say my name.

"We don't know yet," Nina said. All I heard was *reprieve*. "Folks, you can't make this up. The Delphine Police Department was being steered by a serial killer. When in modern history have you seen something like this? It puts everything BTK did with the Kansas PD to shame."

"It's even worse than the Zodiac Killer, who taunted police with ciphers for years," Mackenzie said. "According to sources, Chief Reingold is expected to offer his resignation by end of week. Frankly, I think that's giving him too much time."

"Ouch," I murmured.

Goku shook his head. "The man was a goner the minute he cried on TV."[*]

"Let's not forget the FBI," Nina interjected. "They let this man inside their organization. This is a humiliating day for the Department of Justice. I don't want to imagine the conversations taking place behind closed doors."

"I wouldn't be surprised if Lawrence was let go, too," Lightly said.

"Maybe he can join your security firm." Mistress's voice was arch. "If you're willing to throw him a bone."

He blinked at her in surprise.

"I never forgave him for leaving you hanging after Juliana," she said, and his expression softened.

"And what's the latest on Owen Rhodes?" Nina barked from the screen.

"This lady is very unpleasant," Goku's mother observed.

Deacon glanced down at the papers in his hands. "Mr. Rhodes has been released after Washington police verified his alibi, but he's still awaiting trial in the sexual assault case. In the meantime, he's been expelled by Northern Idaho University."

"Do you think that's fair?" Mackenzie cut in. "He's being punished before being found guilty in a court of law."

"Rhodes's case is certainly causing controversy," Nina said.

---

[*] For the record, I don't think Chief Reingold was a bad cop. Some people simply aren't capable of rising to their moment in history. The fact that he died of a heart attack four months after resigning is something that will always haunt me.

"Protestors have surrounded the Delphine police station for the third day straight."

Something finally clicked. "Wait a second. Are they saying Citizen committed all of the murders? We told the police there were two killers. What happens when they find evidence that Citizen was at home in Washington when the Queen Lace murders happened? They're going to be humiliated all over again."

Everyone glanced at each other, avoiding my eyes.

"Well," Goku said cautiously, "are we sure he didn't commit all the murders?"

Jesus, this again. "Lightly said the heights of the two killers were different according to the blood splatter and angle of the wounds. Right, Lightly?"

He nodded. "That is how it appeared."

"And Citizen had no motive to kill Madeleine, Stacie, and Larissa," I said.

Mistress looked uneasy. "Serial killers don't need motives. Other than their compulsion to kill."

"What—*really*?" I was flabbergasted. "You guys, Lizzie Bath committed the first murders."

Lightly's voice was gentle. "The truth is, Search, we don't know for sure."

I sat still as a statue, rigid with betrayal.

"Police are awaiting confirmation that Mr. Bishop's DNA matches the samples collected in the Collegiate Parkway and Howell cases." Nina Grace's face had gone back to filling the whole screen.

"They found his hairs in the bathroom at our rental," Lightly said, directing the statement at me. I could tell he wanted to pull me back into the conversation, but I said nothing.

"A nationwide manhunt for Mr. Bishop is now underway." Nina

announced it with relish. "He was last spotted in Colorado, where just hours earlier, he eluded police in a car chase."

All nine of us straightened. This was new.

"Residents of Colorado and neighboring states are being asked to keep a lookout for Mr. Bishop and to alert police if he's spotted. Please be warned Mr. Bishop is highly dangerous and should not be engaged. Let's pray this hunt has a satisfying ending."

CrimeFlash cut to a commercial for the AARP. Silence reigned until Goku said, in a faraway voice, "He's really out there. A criminal being chased by the police."

"Not just a criminal," Mistress said. "A murderer. A kidnapper."

Her sons squeezed her shoulders.

Goku shook his head. "I honestly thought he was my best friend."

"Some of us have known him for almost seven years," Lightly said. "But the truth is, we never knew him. He was hiding. Psychopaths are good at that."

"Sort of," I murmured, and they all looked at me. I'd spent every private moment since Lightly and I discovered the yearbook thinking about it. "We all knew how much he loved control and wanted to win. It was borderline pathological. He would do anything to come out on top. He always needed to prove he was smartest and fastest. If we'd stopped to think about it, we would've seen his ego issues."

"He was obsessed with serial killers," Goku added. "I figured it was a professional curiosity, not a... personal journey."

"His parents," Mistress said quietly. "He used to hint that his dad bullied and tortured him, and his mom covered over it. There was a real darkness there, but he'd change the subject if I pressed. He had abrupt mood swings. A sense of grandiosity, sometimes bordering on delusion."

Lightly whistled. "Well, damn. I guess he wasn't hiding. We just didn't want to see it."

Goku's father cleared his throat. "I know I'm not, uh, officially a part of this, but I have to ask—this case is closed, right? With Peter on the run? I know there are still some lingering questions, but are the four of you done?"

Mistress, Lightly, Goku, and I looked at each other from the four corners of the living room. I could see each of them weighing.

Two quick raps sounded at the door, followed by yet another twist of the lock. Our contemplative expressions turned confused. "We're all here," Mistress hissed. "Who could it—"

The door swung open so forcefully it cracked into the wall. Lizzie Bath stepped inside, her dark eyes sweeping the scene. The same two FBI agents who'd couriered everyone else hurried in behind her. Lizzie was dressed as normally as I'd ever seen her, in a pair of jeans and a plain black T-shirt, her impossibly long hair hanging flat over her shoulders. On her feet were the pair of sneakers I'd photographed for evidence.

88

—

LIZZIE TOOK STOCK OF EVERY person in the living room, one by one, until her eyes finally landed on me. Her gaze was penetrating. It hinted at a darkness behind the curtain. It was her eyes that had always convinced me.

Icy fear worked over my body, freezing inch by inch.

"What is she doing here?" Goku asked.

"The FBI received an encrypted communication from Mr. Bishop claiming he was not responsible for the deaths at Queen Lace Avenue," said the bald agent, who seemed the friendlier one. "He accused Ms. Bath of the murders and appears to harbor a vendetta against her that we feel warrants keeping her here until we're certain Mr. Bishop's attention has shifted elsewhere."

Lizzie was still staring at me with those otherworldly eyes. "Why, hello, Veronica. Fancy seeing you here. Did you know that someone told a serial killer he could blame his work on me?" She smiled, cold and calculating. Now that I'd dropped my mask, she was free to drop hers. I looked at her face and knew—*knew,* with every ounce of intuitive power I possessed, that she'd killed those girls, and understood I knew, and I was in danger.

Mistress staggered across the room, clutching her cane, and stood directly in front of me, facing Lizzie. Lightly cleared his throat and pushed himself off the couch, taking his place beside her. I could no longer see Lizzie's face. Goku joined them, forming a three-person wall. Their families looked at us strangely, but I knew what they were saying: They were my people. I may have lost my father, my mother thousands of miles away, but they would have my back.

89

ONE MONTH LATER, THE LETTER found me at my parents'
house in Florida. I'd just returned from my first shift at Dunkin' Donuts,
where I was working to save money for my second senior year at UCF.
I'd checked the mailbox on a whim and found a few thin bills and a
package addressed to a peculiar name, inscribed in familiar handwriting.
When I shook it over my desk, two sheets of firmly creased paper and
a pre-addressed envelope fell out.

Dear Veronica,

*Don't bother tracing this letter. By the time you get it, I'll be in the
wind. And don't bother trying to track the address on the envelope
either. You should know by now that I'm too smart to be caught. No
one has evaded the law like me. Even the Zodiac Killer, who sent
more than twenty letters to the cops without being identified, had to
live concealed. The cops know who I am, the media shouts about me
24/7, and yet no one can catch me.*

*Which brings me to a small request: can you please tell reporters
to stop calling me the Web Sleuth Killer? It's so pedestrian. Call me*

the Uncatchable Killer, the Ghost Annihilator, the Peerless Predator. Something more dignified. You know better than anyone how much a good image matters. (Isn't that right, Miss Savant?)

Here's the true reason I'm writing. I swear on Heathers and my love for Goku, Lightly, and Mistress—I swear on my dead mother Betty Bishop's grave—that I did not kill Madeleine Edmonds, Larissa Weeks, or Stacie Flowers. I did not commit the Queen Lace murders. All other killings, I will exercise my constitutional right to plead the Fifth. But not Queen Lace. That cold-blooded killer is still out there.

I'm not surprised they're trying to pin it all on me. The DPD and even the FBI are full of hacks. From the beginning, all they've done is bungle these cases. The new Delphine chief that replaced Reingold is even dumber than he was. And the FBI was stupid to cut Hale, who was at least halfway decent. They're desperate to close the Delphine massacres and call it a win. They don't want to look closer at the messy truth, and that's where I come in. The perfect patsy.

I know in your heart you believe me. I remember how convinced you were that Elizabeth Bath committed the Queen Lace murders. Well, guess what? I've had a lot of time to go back over our arguments and I believe you. I was wrong and you were right. Lizzie had motive, means, and even though at first I didn't think a woman could've been strong enough to stab those girls with such force, I've revised my thinking. Also, the killer's been so quiet. Not even a little tempted to take credit. It really feels like something a woman would do, someone with a smaller ego.

Which means our mission isn't over. I vowed to be the one to solve this case, and I'm still determined to figure out the truth of what happened. And when I do, everyone in the country will—well, even if they don't welcome me back with open arms, they'll at least *know how smart I am, how capable. My dad used to say I wasn't worth the shit on the bottom of his shoes. Every day, he told me that. I'm sure he's still muttering it as he burns in hell. Do you know what corrosion it causes the soul, hearing you're not good enough from the dad you can't help but love? But he was wrong, Veronica. And once I show the world, no one will be able to deny me.*

This is where you come in. I know you have photos from Lizzie's bedroom and other important evidence. And I know you've put the pieces together. I need you to send me your work. Write it down and put it in this attached envelope. Or, if you don't feel comfortable with a paper trail, create an encrypted website. Goku can show you how. And then write the website address and send that back.

I know you might be hesitant to help me because of the things I've allegedly done. First of all, I truly regret the incident with Mistress. I was happy when I hacked the hospital records and saw she only suffered minor wounds. On the other matters, I'll say this: I would bet my life that whoever killed Bridget Howell did it on accident. I bet she was going to tell people what her killer had done to her dog, which was just a little rough play gone wrong. He was a lonely person, I would guess, and just wanted a little affection. A little time with a nice dog, because his parents wouldn't let him have one, and then things got away from him. He didn't deserve to have his life ruined over it.

I bet that's how it went with Bridget, too: Some rough persuasion tactics taken a little too far. And the second set of Idaho murders, whoever committed them, well, I would guess that person felt he had to do it to save his friends when their group was on the brink of dissolving. I would bet those friends were the only real family he'd ever had, and he would've done anything to keep them together. He was like that Flannery O'Connor story, but in reverse: only a bad man when you shoved a gun to his head.

Look, Veronica. The reason I asked you to join our group nearly a year ago is because I could see you burned for answers as much as I did. You named yourself perfectly: you are a searcher. And the world is better for your refusal to let go. Your dad is better for it. I know how you feel, by the way. I could always sense how badly you wanted to wrest your dad back from death, and it made me remember my own complicated feelings when my dad died. I know the fact that your dad is ultimately an unknowable mystery is going to haunt you for the rest of your life. But you will channel that pain because you're a fighter. You won't go gentle into that good night. You will RAGE.

That's why I know you'll help me. Because there's a part of you that will never rest until you get answers. You need the truth about who really killed those girls out there. And Lizzie Bath needs to be stopped. She's a clear and present danger. If I can find you anywhere in the world, so can she. She's smart, methodical, excellent at taking out threats. Any moment, she could be coming to silence you. Do you really want to live in fear?

Help me solve this final case in your father's honor. Imagine giving him that kind of legacy.

Your JD

P.S. I never lied about my feelings for you. In a strange way, every step you and the others took in the investigation—finding the eyelash DNA, discovering the hackable lock, tracking Susan Ramsey and the yearbook photo—made me love you more. It was as if you were the only people in the world capable of seeing me. Yes, when I discovered you'd betrayed me to the cops, my first thought was—Dammit, Veronica. We could've toasted marshmallows together. (Get it?) But I forgive you. And we can still roast 'em. Don't let me down.

I dropped the sheets of paper onto my desk, devastated that there wasn't a single thing he'd written I didn't believe.

What do you do when you're alone in the dark, with enemies closing in on every side? When your back is to the wall and there are no rescue ships—even worse, when you've realized there are no rules whatsoever, no promises or waiting heaven, just you and the things you hold dear against the bleakness of death?

I sat thinking in my Dunkin' apron until dusk descended in cool blue shadows over the palm trees and birds-of-paradise. Then I picked up a pen, wrote a single line on the back of Citizen's letter, and folded it up, placing it in his envelope.

Two days later, after I dropped the envelope in the mailbox, my mother and I flew to Italy.

90

IF YOU'D TOLD ME THAT my journey to crack the case of my father would end halfway across the world, I wouldn't have believed you. But after everything I'd learned in the past ten months, I knew Italy was the right place to go.

The Tyrrhenian Sea off the Amalfi Coast was even more beautiful than the pictures in my father's scrapbook, which showed him at twenty-one, lithe and dark-haired, grinning on a navy ship, the water sparkling over his shoulder. There was a quality to the water—a deep, rich blueness, utterly unlike the clear turquoise ocean in Florida. This water, like the ruins of Pompeii covered in ash on the shore, seemed impossibly ancient. It was the same water that had haunted me since my father died, the water I'd lost him to countless times in my dreams. Somehow, even though I'd been only four when we left Italy, my subconscious had held onto it.

If you trace your finger over a map of the country, you'll see Naples, that big, bustling, dirty port city, is only down the road from the rarefied air of Serrano and Positano, all the crowded gem-towns of the Amalfi Coast. The land is more mountainous even than Idaho, the cliffs steeper and more rugged, simmering and volcanic. And the cities curl around the water, and the water gives way to the world, the Bay of Naples flowing into the Tyrrhenian Sea, then the Mediterranean, then the Atlantic. It was a path my father charted many times.

I was pretty sure it was the most beautiful place on earth.

My mother and I went back to their first apartment in Licola, with the small garden, and discovered the larger one they'd moved to when I was born had been torn down. We found some of their old favorite restaurants, folding gooey Neapolitan pizza into our mouths and licking dripping pistachio gelato, his favorite flavor. We went to the park where they first met, but since it was part of the naval base, we couldn't get in. So we stood at the gates and peeked through the bars, my mom pointing and narrating.

Finally, there was only one thing left to do. After coming to know my father better since his death, I believed the version of him who left Tennessee at eighteen—the brave adventurer, the man who'd fallen in love with the red-haired New Yorker, the tender heart who became my father—was his ideal form, the self he pictured in his mind, even as the years aged him.

That's why I chose Italy.

We rented a small boat to take us into the Tyrrhenian Sea at sunset. My mother's hair was tied back against the wind with a glamorous silk handkerchief, but mine was loose and whipped like a flag. Our captain was young, barely more than a kid, which made me nervous. What we wanted to do was technically illegal. But as the sun started to sink, turning the waves and mountains a riot of warm colors, and I clutched my father's urn, he turned and left us to our business.

Even after all the evil I've seen, I still love humanity for its small mercies.

I dipped a hand into the urn, clutched a handful of ashes. And as we sliced through the water, I returned my dad to a place where he'd been happy.

Why did he refuse the blood pressure pills; why did he have to die? It had been nearly a year since I'd launched my investigation, and I'd collected these answers: My father had to die because the plaque building in his arteries had finally grown too thick and his blood couldn't pass. Because oxygen stopped flowing to his brain. Because despite all of his promises, he never lost the weight. Because he snuck Wendy's and McDonald's on his drives home from work. Because he needed something that was his, a pleasure unremarked upon by his wife or any of the people who did things like wince when he walked toward them on an airplane. Because growing up, his family liked to eat, poor as they were, and there being so few inexpensive pleasures. Because growing up, his family had rarely taken him to the doctor, poor as they were, and he'd never learned respect for medicine. Because he had never given his own mortality much thought, and believed those pills were unnecessary. Because he secretly believed, like many of us, that he might never die. Because he was so scared of dying that it was paralyzing, and accepting a prescription made the prospect too real. Because he didn't love my mother and me enough to do everything in his power to stay. Because he loved my mother and me so much he was too busy taking care of us to take care of himself. Because he was hurt as a boy and found comfort in food. Because he was hurt as a boy and it festered all his life, and he was ready to let go of the pain. Because he was hurt as a boy but triumphed over it and thought nothing could take him down. Because he was human and started dying the minute he was born. Because it was always going to happen, and it was always going to hurt.

It's not that there were no answers or that they were missing—I saw that now. It was that there were so many, a haystack so wide and deep it was impossible for any sleuth, no matter how brilliant, to swim through and pin down that one shining needle. In my year of living in the secret house of death, of growing close to the dead, watching their faces and voices transmitted all over the world, I'd realized death didn't translate into nothingness but a multiplicity beyond my comprehension.

Who was my father? Not one person, but many. The little boy in Tennessee, the sailor in Italy, the proud man at my high school graduation, the scribe on the deck of the *Voyager*. In his death he'd become so vast he could no longer be pinned to a single time and place. Not a black hole of absence but a vortex of possibilities.

I watched my mother scoop her hand into the urn and return the ashes of her husband to the place where she'd first loved him. When it was empty and he was in the sea, I rubbed the line Lightly had painted on the side. *It's what we will never know about the ones we love that binds us to them.* I'd finally accepted that mystery is at the heart of love. That it's our deep yearning to know the ones we love in ways that are ultimately impossible—we will never get close enough, never have long enough—that keep us bound to them, forever chasing. We are all of us searchers, I think. To love is to reach your hand across a distance that you'll never fully breach.

Here's the distance I needed to make peace with: My father had existed here on earth. He made me, gave me his dark hair and Roman nose, his laugh and love of magic. He gave me his heart. My name. Loving him was part of what I was put on earth to do. And then he left.

I trailed my fingers in the cold water. Daniel Sharp was alive. Jane Sharp was alive. For twenty-four years they loved each other. And that would have to be enough.

Citizen wrote that I was remarkable for never letting go. But I went to Italy and left my father's ashes there. I laid the investigation to rest. I let the questions go.

91

—

I KNOW. SPEAKING OF BEING satisfied. You want to hear about the third and final Delphine massacre. The most bewildering one, the one that stumped everybody, set the true-crime forums ablaze. The one I like to call my massacre, though only privately.*

It happened the day after my plane touched down in Orlando, as if he was awaiting my return. I'd just come home from a Dunkin' shift—no rest for the minimum wage—when the local CBS station interrupted a rerun of *The Office* with the news. I turned up the volume and steeled myself.

"Disturbing news out of Idaho," said the same newscaster who'd introduced me to Indira Babatunde. "Peter Bishop, otherwise known as the Web Sleuth Killer, is dead. The FBI reports he was killed in a brutal showdown at a safe house that left two others dead as well: twenty-six-year-old nursing student Elizabeth Bath and sixty-one-year-old federal agent Perry Gates."

I clutched the remote so tightly I could've cracked it.

"Authorities say Bishop entered the house while Agent Gates was

---

* As you can probably tell, I'm writing this chapter against the counsel of my lawyers.

occupied in the restroom, a breach of duty the Department of Justice is calling 'unfortunate.' He then pursued Ms. Bath. The FBI was holding Ms. Bath in the safe house out of fear she would become a target for Mr. Bishop's violence. While details are still emerging, sources say Ms. Bath and Mr. Bishop attacked one another. When Agent Gates tried to intervene, it was surprisingly Ms. Bath who delivered his fatal stab wounds. Authorities have yet to comment on how they believe that happened, but in the end, while Bishop succeeded in murdering Ms. Bath, he sustained lethal wounds that led him to bleed out. All three bodies were discovered when FBI agents rushed to the scene, responding to Agent Gates's distress call."

They were dead. A dark miracle.

"Anticipating a public firestorm over this final chapter in what has been one of the year's most highly discussed stories," the anchor continued, "the FBI is urging the public not to engage in speculation and to await further details. We'll have more on this story at eight."

I turned off the TV and pulled up the Network for the first time since leaving Idaho. As I expected, it was everywhere.

> **SeattleHawks:** RIP **@CitizenNight**. You were an asshole murderer, but you were *our* asshole murderer.
>
> **Margarita5:** I've said it before and I'll say it again: LISTEN TO WOMEN. I told you **@CitizenNight** was bad news but no one wanted to hear it when he was the golden boy.
>
> **HiltoftheSword:** Can we unpack this bonkers story? The FBI clearly doesn't want us to examine it, which is a red flag. We know Citizen— SORRY, PETER (weird)—wanted this Elizabeth Bath woman dead, because otherwise the FBI wouldn't have been guarding her in a safe house. But WHY did he want her dead? Either she had some damning evidence on him, or—here's my theory—Peter had a

vendetta against the Kappa Delta sorority, and he was taking them out one by one.

Minacaren: No offense, Hilt, but that doesn't add up. How do the track girls fit in? Bridget Howell?

Carolrichards68: Here's my Q: why did Elizabeth Bath stab the fed? Do you think it was an accident, like he got caught in the crossfire? Or do you think he was secretly in cahoots with Peter and that's why he was conveniently "in the bathroom" when Peter attacked?

YoungYung: Can you imagine what the rest of the Newsline 5 must be thinking? Their best buddy turned out to be the very guy they were chasing. I'd love if Newsline did one of those VH1-style "Where Are They Now" episodes on them.

SeattleHawks: LOL. **@GeorgeLightly**'s headline: "I'm the Guinness World Record holder for highest number of police scandals in a single lifetime." **@LordGoku**: "I was a killer's bitch for years and all I got was this lousy T-shirt." **@SleuthMistress**: "Currently posting Craigslist ads for new young criminals to hitch my wagon to." **@Searcher24**: "I had the shortest period of relevance of any 'true-crime celebrity' in history."

Minacaren: Y'all are going to hell. He kidnapped Mistress, remember? She suffered.

TheTruthIsOutThere: Is no one going to talk about the possibility that Peter Bishop knew something damning about *Elizabeth Bath*? Come on, now. There's no way a man that beautiful is a serial killer. Who else thinks Peter is innocent?

I tossed my phone. Good to know some things never changed.

92

—

IT'S BEEN A YEAR NOW, and the speculation has only grown, the conspiracies turning more fever-pitched. Pictures of the crime scene leaked, showing Citizen's body splayed face down on the kitchen floor, his T-shirt torn so you could see that snake tattoo of his awash in blood, mouth open and fangs out, on the verge of eating him up, just like the many-headed hydra of the forums. It struck me, seeing that. Made me feel like I had unfinished business.*

That's part of why I've decided to set the record straight. I know in my soul Elizabeth Bath killed Madeleine, Stacie, and Larissa. I also know the DPD and FBI were never going to charge her. They needed a single killer, and they needed it to be Citizen. Anything else was too messy, pointed too obviously at their shortcomings. And female killers are a different kind of animal. Slipperier, harder to catch. I saw Lizzie for who she was, but they couldn't see her even when she was standing right in front of them. She never would've seen justice.

---

* Citizen, you asked in your letter if I understood your *Heathers* reference. Here's my answer, which doubles as my goodbye: "Now that you're dead, what are you going to do with your life?"

I read between the lines of Citizen's letter. He was asking me to choose a side, choose what kind of person I wanted to be. And I realized: the person I most want to be is my father's daughter. Dan's girl, through and through. And I knew what Daniel Sharp's Janeway would do, because he'd written it for me.

Lizzie was an existential threat. Citizen was an existential threat. Either one of them could've found me or Lightly, Mistress or Goku. Any minute, they could've come for us, the only four people who knew the truth. Any minute, they could've started killing again. Serial killers are repeat offenders by nature—it's in the name. They were too dangerous to live.

That's why I wrote the address of the Idaho safe house where the FBI had taken us, and where they still held Lizzie, on the back of Citizen's letter. I knew he'd understand what it was, and nothing would stop him from going. I pointed those two predators at each other, the only two people capable of taking the other out, their wits and psychoses perfectly matched. Two wolves, clashing in the night. Ridding the world of each other for the good of the universe.

Yes, I know sharing the location of an FBI safe house is illegal. I know I face prosecution by confessing.

So why tell you? Because Stacie's sister, Natalie, wrote her awful book, getting everything wrong, and everyone believes her. She's emerged as a knight in a story she was only tangentially involved in. And she's painted Lightly, Mistress, Goku, and me as monsters on par with Citizen, a dark taint none of us deserve. For a year, Nina Grace and the talking heads on TV have reported every detail backwards, and no one has corrected them. There's mass delusion. If I didn't do something, history would be mangled, the truth lost forever, the real heroes vilified or nameless, the true villains paraded like victims.

The stakes are too high for that. These are people's lives and legacies we're talking about. I need you to know that I got justice for the Delphine girls and Bridget, once and for all. That despite their shortcomings, Lightly, Mistress, and Goku were good people with good intentions. And that it was my father who solved the problem in the end. His name should be recorded in the history books, not mine.

We've finally come to it: what I want most of all. Love me or hate me, I don't care. As long as you remember Daniel Sharp: a remarkable man who was this story's true beginning and its end. You see, I would do anything—publish a confession, risk public wrath, serve time in jail—to give my father the recognition he deserves. I've forked over every damning detail you asked for, and some you didn't. Won't you give me this in return?

Remember him, record him in the annals, and let us both rest in peace.

READING GROUP GUIDE

1. Question

2. Question

3. Question

A CONVERSATION WITH THE AUTHOR

Question

Answer

Question

Answer

ACKNOWLEDGMENTS

TK

ABOUT THE AUTHOR

Photo © Luis Noble

Ashley Winstead writes about power, ambition, complicity, and love in the modern age. In addition, she's a painter and former academic. She received her BA in English, creative writing, and art history from Vanderbilt University and her PhD in English from Southern Methodist University, where she studied twenty-first-century fiction, philosophy of language, and the politics of narrative forms. Her academic essays have been published in *Studies in the Novel* and *Science Fiction Studies*. She currently lives in Houston, Texas, with her husband and two cats. Find out more at ashleywinstead.com.

MIDNIGHT IS THE DARKEST HOUR

What do you fear most in the dark? The Low Man...or yourself?

For fans of *Verity* and *A Flicker in the Dark*, *Midnight Is the Darkest Hour* is a twisted tale of murder, obsessive love, and the beastly urges that lie dormant within us all...even the God-fearing folk of Bottom Springs, Louisiana. In her small hometown, librarian Ruth Cornier has always felt like an outsider, even as her beloved father rains fire-and-brimstone warnings from the pulpit at Holy Fire Baptist. Unfortunately for Ruth, the only things the townspeople fear more than the God and the Devil are the myths that haunt the area, like the story of the Low Man, a vampiric figure said to steal into sinners' bedrooms and kill them on moonless nights. When a skull is found deep in the swamp next to mysterious carved symbols, Bottom Springs is thrown into uproar—and Ruth realizes only she and Everett, an old friend with a dark past, have the power to comb the town's secret underbelly in search of true evil.

A dark and powerful novel like fans have come to expect from Ashley Winstead, *Midnight Is the Darkest Hour* is an examination of the ways we've come to expect love, religion, and stories to save us, the lengths we have to go to in order to take back power, and the monstrous work of being a girl in this world.

"Absolutely sensational—I couldn't put it down."
—Clare Mackintosh, *New York Times* bestselling author

IN MY DREAMS I HOLD A KNIFE

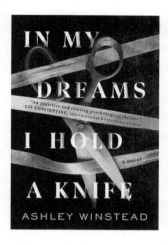

Six friends. One college reunion. One unsolved murder.

Ten years after graduation, Jessica Miller has planned her triumphant return to her southern, elite Duquette University, down to the envious whispers that are sure to follow in her wake. Everyone is going to see the girl she wants them to see—confident, beautiful, indifferent. Not the girl she was when she left campus, back when Heather Shelby's murder fractured everything, including the tight bond linking the six friends she'd been closest to since freshman year.

But not everyone is ready to move on. Not everyone left Duquette ten years ago, and not everyone can let Heather's murder go unsolved. Someone is determined to trap the real killer, to make the guilty pay. When the six friends are reunited, they will be forced to confront what happened that night—and the years' worth of secrets each of them would do anything to keep hidden.

Told in racing dual timelines, with a dark campus setting and a darker look at friendship, love, obsession, and ambition, *In My Dreams I Hold a Knife* is an addictive, propulsive read you won't be able to put down.

"Highly recommended."
—*New York Journal of Books*

THE LAST HOUSEWIFE

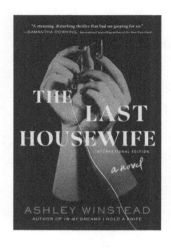

One woman, determined to destroy a powerful cult—no matter the cost.

While in college in upstate New York, Shay Evans and her best friends met a captivating man who seduced them with a web of lies about the way the world works, bringing them under his thrall. By senior year, Shay and her friend Laurel were the only ones who managed to escape. Now, eight years later, Shay's built a new life in a tony Texas suburb. But when she hears the horrifying news of Laurel's death—delivered, of all ways, by her favorite true-crime podcast crusader—she begins to suspect that the past she thought she buried is still very much alive, and the predators more dangerous than ever.

Recruiting the help of the podcast host, Shay goes back to the place she vowed never to return to in search of answers. As she follows the threads of her friend's life, she's pulled into a dark, seductive world, where wealth and privilege shield brutal philosophies that feel all too familiar. When Shay's obsession with uncovering the truth becomes so consuming she can no longer separate her desire for justice from darker desires newly reawakened, she must confront the depths of her own complicity and conditioning. But in a world built for men to rule it—both inside the cult and outside of it—is justice even possible, and if so, how far will Shay go to get it?

"Deliciously unputdownable."
—*Washington Post*

FOR MORE ASHLEY WINSTEAD, VISIT: SOURCEBOOKS.COM

Printed in the USA
CPSIA information can be obtained
at www.ICGtesting.com
JSHW021230180824
68300JS00003B/3